Praise fo

"Pamela Callow's
reminded me of the best of Robin Cook:
lightning paced, innovative, topical…and most of all,
frightening. Part medical mystery, part bloody thriller,
here is a debut that had me flipping pages
until the wee hours of the morning."
—James Rollins, *New York Times* bestselling author
of *The Doomsday Key*

"*Damaged* is a taut, edge-of-the-seat thriller
with strong characters and a driving plot that's
inspired by emerging health technologies that may
end up being, well, very bad for certain people's
health. Pamela Callow is Halifax's answer
to both John Grisham and Tess Gerritsen."
—Linwood Barclay, bestselling author of
No Time for Goodbye

"A compelling page-turner by a strong new voice
in fiction. Pamela Callow is a rising star."
—Rick Mofina, bestselling author of *Six Seconds*

"Extremely well plotted, Callow's debut novel is a
hybrid of a police procedural and medical thriller.
Heroine Kate Lange is a standout character, and
readers will certainly look forward to reading her
further adventures."
—RT Book Reviews

"*Damaged* is a chilling and darkly compelling tale
that will grip you from the very first page. Pam Callow
delivers a complex and spine-tingling thriller.
She is definitely an author to watch."
—Julianne MacLean, *USA TODAY* bestselling author

Also by Pamela Callow

DAMAGED

Look for Pamela Callow's next novel
TATTOOED
available August 2011

INDEFENSIBLE

PAMELA CALLOW

MIRA®

Recycling programs
for this product may
not exist in your area.

ISBN-13: 978-0-7783-2922-0

INDEFENSIBLE

Copyright © 2011 by Pamela Callow.

www.MIRABooks.com

Printed in U.S.A.

For those who have taught me along the way:

My father, Martyn Callow,
who made me figure out the answers for myself;
My junior high school English teacher,
who fanned the spark;
And the late Bill Martinson,
a trusted mentor and treasured friend.

_1_

The siren song of the end-of-workday bustle on Halifax's historic waterfront did not reach law firm McGrath Barrett. Ensconced in the top two floors of one of the city's landmark office towers, McGrath Barrett cocooned its staff from the hubbub of the everyday world with plush carpeting, heavily paneled cubicles and glassed-in offices. Perfect working conditions for honing concentration and maximizing billable hours.

In theory.

Late afternoon summer sunshine beat through Kate Lange's office window and landed squarely on her back. Even with air-conditioning, the relentless heat dampened her skin. She slid her office chair sideways. Didn't matter. The sun just poured through the glass lining the far wall, issuing the one siren song that McGrath Barrett could not deflect. It urged her to abandon the personal injuries tome on her desk with its impossibly small print.

She rubbed her temple. Just two more cases to review.

Get it over with, Kate. Just like you got through that brutal discovery today. It had finished an hour ago. Her head still throbbed from it, but she needed to check a couple of cases before she could end her workweek in good conscience.

And then—a run in the park followed by a night on the town. Hunching over the book, she scowled at the text, mouthing the words. Anything to make them penetrate the late-day haze surrounding her brain.

Ten minutes later, she flipped closed the research book and pushed her chair away from the desk.

Done. It was Friday. It was past 5:00 p.m. It was *sunny.* As if that weren't enough to please the residents of Halifax, it was the start of the Natal Day long weekend, Halifax's civic holiday. Three days off. In the middle of summer. She was crazy to be sitting at her desk. And from the hush outside her office, it sounded suspiciously as if she was the only lawyer still lingering.

The phone rang while she was shoving files into her briefcase. She stifled a groan. It had better not be a client. With a quick glance at the pure blue sky beyond her window, she snatched the phone off the cradle.

"Hey there."

Kate's shoulders relaxed at the sound of Natalie Pitts' throaty voice. "Hi, Nat." She balanced the phone in the crook of her neck and began stacking the reports she would take home with her.

"What're you up to tonight?" Natalie Pitts had been Kate's best friend and roomie during her university years. She had moved away after she finished her degree in journalism, only returning in May with high ambitions and a broken heart.

Kate eyed the pile of case reports she'd assembled. It was disappointingly thick. *That's what happens when you don't get your work done, Kate.* Well, at least she didn't have to lug home that massive personal injuries book. "I'm heading down to the Economy Shoe Shop later tonight with the gang from work—you know, Joanne and some of the other associates." After Kate saved McGrath Barrett's ass in May, she had suddenly been on everyone's speed dial. And, Kate had to admit, they were a decent bunch of people, despite the professional elbowing. All of the junior associates were younger than she, still on the singles scene. Kate and Joanne were the only associates in their thirties who were partnerless. The ones with kids hurried home on Friday nights, glad to put the workweek behind them. "Do you want to come?"

"Can't tonight. I've got to work tomorrow." Nat had miraculously landed a job as a reporter for the *Halifax Post,* no mean feat in the internet-plagued newspaper business. "Do you want to go out for supper before you meet your friends?"

Kate hadn't seen Nat since last week. But Alaska, her Siberian husky, had been waiting all day. Even though her dog walker, Finn Scott, took him for walks, she still felt guilty if she didn't come home right after work. "Do you want to come over for a bite, instead? My kitchen is under drop sheets, but we can eat on the deck."

"Sure. You can give me the tour. I'll bring takeout. See you in an hour."

"Can you make it for seven? I've got some errands to do and I'd love to go for a run." Kate smiled. "I was able to do the full route on Wednesday."

"Hallelujah! So the leg didn't bother you too much?" Kate's quadriceps had received a nasty stab wound from a scalpel in May—one of several injuries she'd sustained in her battle to the death with the Body Butcher, the city's first serial killer.

"Not too much." Kate shrugged. "Anyway, I can't baby it any longer."

"You mean, you won't baby it any longer."

"See you at seven." Kate hung up before Nat could chide her further. Her leg *had* hurt after the run, but Kate wasn't going to admit it. It was worth the trade-off. Running was what kept her on an even keel. The rhythmic motion, the synchronization of her heart and lungs with her pumping legs, the fresh air.

There was one other benefit she hoped to gain by resuming her hour-long run: sleep. She hadn't had a full night's sleep since she survived Craig Peters' attack. Dr. Kazowski, the therapist who had begun counseling Kate after the trauma she had gone through, thought that if Kate returned to some of her usual routines, especially ones that helped relieve stress, the nightmares might stop. Or at least decrease in frequency.

It was the only nudge Kate needed. And today the weather was giving her its blessing.

She hurried into the foyer, the pile of case reports haphazardly stacked in her arms, a sheen of sweat on her forehead and a smile of anticipation on her lips. In an hour, she'd be running with Alaska in Point Pleasant Park. She could almost feel the sea breeze on the back of her neck.

The quiet rush of a newly installed water feature was the only sound in the reception area. It provided a stunning foil to the equally new art installation that hung kitty-corner from the elevators, and served as a perfect backdrop to the new, postmodern furnishings.

Kate jabbed the elevator button. A trickle of sweat slid down her spine. The air-conditioning had been turned off for the weekend while she was on the phone with Nat. Warm air had already begun to settle in the reception area.

The lack of human sound prickled the hairs on the back of Kate's neck. Ever since her experience in Keane's Funeral Home, silent places were ominous.

To distract herself, she studied the redecorated lobby. After the hits the former Lyons McGrath Barrett had taken to its standing a few months ago, the firm was working hard to restore its sterling reputation. It needed to recover some of the clients that had fled in the wake of the TransTissue scandal. Managing partner Randall Barrett—*the* Barrett in McGrath Barrett—had hired a public relations company to relaunch the firm under its new name. In an effort to distance itself from the scandal that now tarnished its prestige, McGrath Barrett had redecorated the foyer and launched a new ad campaign.

The campaign zeroed in on the firm's best asset: Kate Lange—the woman Randall Barrett had almost fired just months before. The irony was delicious. Kate had become the firm's new poster girl, her Mona Lisa smile featured above the slogan *Integrity. Excellence. Caring.* The joke in the firm was that Kate cared so much about her clients that she'd kill for them.

Rumor had it that Randall Barrett had chosen the new furnishings in the lobby and Kate had to admit he had a good eye. She wondered what her hundred-year-old house would look like with a postmodern theme. Probably pretty nice.

Too bad she couldn't afford pieces like that. She glanced at her watch. If the darn elevator ever arrived, and the traffic wasn't too heavy, she could stop at the hardware store and get the paint for the kitchen trim before she went for her run.

She shifted the load of files in her arms, rubbing the straining muscles of her right forearm.

The elevator chimed. Kate's nerves jolted. She gritted her teeth. Her reaction to startling noises was driving her crazy. Dr. Kazowski told her it would go away in time, but so far there was no sign of it being in a hurry to leave. She yanked the strap of her briefcase back up to her shoulder, unsettling the pile of reports in the process, and hurried into the elevator.

"Hi, Kate." Randall Barrett stood in a dim corner of the elevator. He gave her a friendly but distant nod, the typical interaction of a senior partner with a junior associate.

"Hi." Kate hugged the reports to her chest, darting a sideways glance at him.

It was the first time she'd seen him in weeks. The first time she'd been alone with him since she'd returned to work in early June.

Randall's face was tense, preoccupied. He did not exude his usual vitality. In fact, he looked exhausted.

Kate stared straight ahead, unwilling to let him see how much his presence got under her skin. Did he sense her tension? she wondered. *Whatever you do, don't babble, Kate.*

At the fourteenth floor, he broke the silence. "Any plans for the weekend?" His tone was courteous. That was all.

She shifted against the wall. "Not too much. Just painting my house." She nodded toward her overflowing arms. "I'm working on the Great Life case. It's taking a lot of time."

That should make him happy. Lots of billable hours.

He nodded almost absentmindedly. "Good."

The silence grew as the elevator descended. Kate studied the numbers above the door. Eleven, ten. She heard Randall's breathing. The elevator was stuffy. She became aware of the faint scent of his sweat. Something she'd never smelled before. She darted another glance at him. He was oblivious to her.

She turned her face away. For the past three months, she'd wondered if she'd just imagined his interest in her. Then she'd tell herself, no, she hadn't dreamed his visit to her hospital room. And she knew there'd been a tenderness to his gaze the day she returned to work after recovering from her injuries.

But it had all changed. Almost overnight, he had become distant. Had seemed to avoid her. Definitely letting her know by his cool greeting and remote smile that whatever moments had been exchanged between them during the TransTissue file were not going to be repeated.

Maybe he'd been faking it. Maybe he'd just been using her to help shore up McGrath Barrett's rocky reputation after the TransTissue scandal.

He stared at the elevator doors, his shoulders tense,

his expression brooding. A man with the weight of the world on his shoulders. She wondered what he did in his spare time. Did he play sports? Read books?

Go on dates?

The fact that she knew so little about him was another indication that she should just leave well enough alone. Whatever drew her to him could not be founded on anything that promised a permanent residence for her battle-weary heart.

The elevator stopped at P1, chiming Randall's departure. He moved toward the doors. "Have a good month, Kate."

Month?

He must have read the surprise in her face because he added, "I'm beginning my vacation."

"Really?" He didn't have the air of a man about to take a holiday.

He arched a brow. "Really."

The doors slid open.

"Are you going anywhere?"

"I'm going sailing." He stepped out of the elevator. "With my son."

With a brusque nod, he disappeared into the shadowed concrete corridor of the parkade.

Kate watched the elevator doors close. Not even a goodbye.

She exhaled, staring at her dull reflection in the mirrored doors. Fine.

The elevator stopped at her parking level. She strode into the parkade, her step quick and purposeful. But it didn't matter. Her heart pounded. She could park on a different level, close to the elevator, always by an overhead light—but no matter the tricks she employed to fool her mind, her body always remembered the terror of being chased by a man intent on killing her.

She looked around. The parkade was empty.

That was almost worse.

She hurried to her car and unlocked the door, dumping her files on the backseat, then slid into the driver's seat. Only when the doors were locked and the engine was started did her heart slow down.

She eased her way out of the parkade. The brilliant July sunshine almost blinded her as she drove through the gate. It was surreal, after the dank interior she'd just exited. She rolled down her window. A warm breeze lifted the hair around her face.

This was why Nova Scotians slogged it through the winter. Because there was no better place to be in the summer if the sun was shining.

She felt her fingers relax on the steering wheel. She'd get the paint, enjoy her run, have supper with Nat and go for a few drinks.

No one would stop her from enjoying the sunshine.

2

Elise Vanderzell stuffed a potato chip into her mouth. Damn, it tasted good. That's what she loved about road trips: the junk food. She knew she shouldn't indulge, shouldn't let her kids indulge, but this was their summer vacation.

And after the hellishness of the months leading up to it, they deserved to enjoy every salt-slicked, grease-laden bite.

She eased the car into the long line of rush hour traffic on Robie Street, glancing in her rearview mirror. Her son, Nick, lounged against the backseat. It was funny how you can see someone all the time and never notice anything different, but then throw a casual look at them one day and realize that the world had shifted.

It took Elise a moment to register what was different. Then it hit her: Nick seemed comfortable in his own skin. His body was filling out, no longer a tangle of gangly limbs connected to gargantuan feet. But it was more than that.

Relaxed. Nick looked relaxed. Sated by his meatball sub, relieved by his mother's acquiescence to his plans for summer camp next week, Nick watched Halifax unfold past them with a look of near contentment.

Hope stuck a cautious toe into her heart.

Ahead, the traffic halted at the Willow Tree intersection. Elise stepped on the brake. It had been years since she'd been here, but she still remembered the Commons, stretching out in verdant green to their left. People played with dogs on the broad stretch of grass, runners doing laps around its perimeter.

Summer, Nova Scotia style.

She rolled down her window and breathed in. She'd forgotten how clean the air was here. No smog. Just fog. The silly rhyme made her smile.

Something loosened in her chest, the tightness that had been holding her together the past few months finally letting go.

She breathed in again deeply, feeling her lungs expand, anticipation giving her blood a little zing. The month spread out before her: no schedules, no routines, no demands. Just her, her cottage, her books for the first two weeks while the kids visited their father, and then hanging out with her kids for the last two. By the time they arrived at the cottage, she would be fully recovered and recharged, ready to enjoy them. She was looking forward to it. Even though the three of them lived together 24/7 in Toronto, the actual time she spent with her kids felt more like twenty-four seconds.

She reached over the gear shift and patted Lucy's knee. "This is going to be fun, Luce."

Her daughter grinned. At twelve, Lucy was a looker.

Thick, wavy blond hair. Eyes that changed like the sea. A wide, smiling mouth. Her face was still childishly round, but Elise knew her daughter would eventually sport the same broad cheekbones as she. "I can't wait for riding camp."

"You think that cute instructor will be back?" Elise teased.

"Mu-um." Lucy rolled her eyes. "I don't care." But there was a faint tinge to her cheeks. Her daughter was growing up. Nicely, Elise was proud to realize. She was mature, caring—despite what she claimed. Elise couldn't wait to see the woman Lucy would become.

"So when do we go to your cottage, Mum?" Lucy asked.

"In a few weeks. After you visit your dad." Elise tried to keep her voice casual, but Nick shifted behind her. The conversation was nearing territory that neither she nor Nick had any desire to visit.

"Is it right on the beach?" Lucy asked.

Elise's shoulders relaxed at the reprieve her daughter gave her. "Yup. And I just read that the beach is renowned for its sand dollars."

"Cool." Lucy smiled. "I can add some to my shell collection."

Elise squeezed her knee. "There's body surfing, too. And I thought we could plan a whale-watching excursion."

"Did you know we saw a whale go by Grandma Penny's house once?" Elise's ex-mother-in-law lived in Prospect, a seaside community forty minutes outside of Halifax. "It was a finback whale."

"No, it wasn't," Nick said from behind her. "It was a right whale."

"Oh, yeah, you're *right*." Lucy smirked. "Get it?"

Nick reached forward and ruffled Lucy's hair. "No one could miss it." Nick's tone was dripping with older-brother condescension, but it was also warm with affection. Elise's breath released. Nick wasn't completely cutting himself off from his family—or at least, not from Lucy.

"Are we almost there?" Lucy asked, making a show of smoothing her mussed-up hair but unable to hide her pleasure from Nick's unexpected gesture.

Elise couldn't remember the last time Nick had initiated contact with either of them. She hoped being away from Toronto would give her a chance with him. A chance to understand why Nick had done the things he did this year. A chance to change things for the better. Her heart lifted and she realized she was experiencing something she'd believed was out of her reach: happiness. "We're about ten minutes from Cathy's house," she said to Lucy.

Cathy Feldman, Elise's old law school roommate, was now a professor at the law school. Cathy had not hesitated to offer her house when she heard Elise was coming to Halifax for the month. Elise's only regret was that her friend wouldn't be there—Cathy was on sabbatical in New Zealand.

"So when do we see Dad?" Lucy asked.

Elise kept her eyes fixed on the line of traffic queued ahead of her. "I'm not sure. I'm going to call your father tonight to let him know Nick won't be going sailing with him." She threw Lucy a warning look: *don't say anything.* "I'll ask your father to take you to riding camp so I can get Nick to his camp." She glanced in the rearview mirror. Nick stared out the window, a mutinous look in his eyes, his jaw tense. He knew that phone call would not be pleasant, no matter Elise's attempts to sound unconcerned, and he was already girding himself for battle.

"Let's go out for supper tonight," Elise said. "We could go down to the waterfront. Get ourselves some real Nova Scotian lobster."

"Cool!" Lucy grinned.

No answer from the back.

"What do you think, Nicky? Up for a crustacean feast?"

"Whatever." A chip bag rustled in the backseat.

Don't get angry, Elise. He's probably just as nervous as you about breaking the news to his father.

"Do you think Dad will get mad, Mum? About Nick's camp?" Lucy asked, her voice low. The silence in the backseat seemed to breathe with her.

"Don't worry. I can handle it." That was a blatant lie—she'd never been able to manage her emotions around her children's father, but she didn't want to derail her kids' excitement about their vacation before it had even begun.

"It's just that the last time we saw him…" Lucy blinked at Elise. Unshed tears glimmered behind the worry in her eyes. "I don't want you guys to fight again."

Guilt grabbed at Elise's heart, twisting it into an even tighter knot. As usual, her daughter seemed to read her better than Elise read herself. Her child was her mirror image, except with one vital difference: Lucy was sunny where Elise was not. Funny how Lucy's infancy threw Elise into a depression so deep she barely clawed her way out of it and now her presence was the only thing that kept Elise from falling into it again.

And what had she done for this daughter who loved her with all her heart?

Not enough.

She was going to put the past few months behind her. Behind all of them. This was a chance to start over. She had made sure there would be no lasting reminders of what had transpired between her and her ex-husband in June. There was only one step left—

A car laid on the horn. She jumped.

Geez, Halifax drivers have gotten mean.

"Mum, it's a green light." Lucy glanced at her with a familiar look of concern.

Elise hit the gas so hard that the SUV lurched forward. "Luce, read me the directions again," she said, her tone reverting into we-are-starting-a-fun-vacation mode. She wished she didn't have to force it. A few minutes before, she'd been excited. *Just get the damn phone call over with and then celebrate by going out to supper tonight.*

She could do this. She knew she could. Her therapist had coached her over the phone this morning on how to handle this. But anxiety nibbled at her. She reached for another potato chip. The bag was empty.

Lucy read the scrap of paper. "It says to go down Robie until you reach the lights at Inglis Street, then turn left. Go straight on Inglis until you reach Young Avenue, then turn left onto Point Pleasant Drive."

Ten minutes later they reached University Avenue. On impulse, Elise turned right.

"Mum, that's the wrong way," Lucy cried. From the back, Elise could sense Nick's sudden alertness, but he said nothing.

"I know," she said. "It's just a slight detour. I want to see my alma mater." She drove down University Avenue, the long boulevard framed with trees, hospitals on either side and a fire station on the corner. Elise slowed when they neared the law school. It had been years since she'd been a student there, almost twenty, but they had been the most formative of her life.

She'd come to Hollis University Law School at the tender age of twenty-two, untested and unsure of her own strengths. It was hard to remember herself back then. So keen, her mind stretching and expanding to meet the challenge of abstruse legal arguments. She had found her confidence here in Halifax, found some of her closest friends and found a profession.

Surely she could find herself here again.

She wondered if all her classmates had screwed up their lives as much as she had. No. Not all of them. Not Cathy. She was just as solid as ever. Just like the building she drove by. Why had Elise wanted to see her law school? Was she hoping that it would remind her of what she had accomplished?

She was a successful tax lawyer at a prestigious Bay Street firm in Toronto. Acquaintances often asked her—with a note of incredulity in their voice—how she liked being a tax lawyer. Elise knew it sounded dull and arcane, but she loved her work. She loved the elaborate structures, the legal fictions, the satisfaction of rendering concrete an entity that was abstract. Of giving form to something intangible.

On paper, she looked pretty good. But paper was two-dimensional. Easily crumpled. Easily discarded.

Not like her mistakes.

She hooked the next left so abruptly that Lucy shot her a startled look. Within minutes, they were driving down Young Avenue. Elise took her time driving down the pretty street. It allowed her to admire the stately architecture—and to postpone the phone call she knew she'd have to make once they turned the corner and pulled into Cathy's driveway.

"This is nice," Lucy breathed, staring out the window. "Is this where we're staying?"

"We're around the corner. Right opposite Point Pleasant Park." The park was situated on the tip of the Halifax Peninsula. On the east side, to their left, lay the Halifax Harbour. Halifax's vibrant waterfront skirted the harbor, anchored with office towers and hotels on the far end and container piers at the other. On the park's west side, the long finger of saltwater known as the Northwest Arm edged some of the most sought-after real estate in the city. Her ex-husband lived in one of those neighborhoods, about a ten-minute walk to the west of Cathy's house.

Elise drove toward a large stone archway with a wrought-iron gate that declared the end of Young Avenue and its intersection with Point Pleasant Drive. Beyond the stone archway, Elise could see the park. One hundred and eighty-five acres of pine trees, old forts and walking trails. Tomorrow morning Elise would get up early and walk the trails. Long dormant anticipation uncurled. She could just imagine the cool mystery of the early morning, the long expanse of quiet ocean disappearing into the horizon, the soft crush of pine-needle-strewn paths underfoot.

"It's not far from Dad's house, is it?" Lucy asked.

Elise searched for Nick's face in the rearview mirror. All she got was his profile. The closer they were to their destination, the more remote he became.

Hang on, Nicky. Just one phone call and you're home free.

"No, it's not."

Elise slowed at the stop sign by the intersection. Lucy shrieked with delight. "Nick, look at the fountain!"

Elise laughed. A large fountain marked a footpath into Point Pleasant Park. It frothed in the sunshine, a two-foot-high mound of bubbles. Someone had put shampoo in the water.

"Mum, can we jump in?" Lucy asked. She reached for her seat belt.

"In a minute." Elise turned left. "Cathy's house is just down the hill. After we dump our bags, you guys can check out the fountain." *While I call your father.* It would give her some privacy. She didn't want the kids to hear this conversation.

Cathy's house was located in a recessed lot on Point Pleasant Drive, facing the park. It had been built on an incline that dropped off steeply in the back. Hedges outlined the side and rear boundaries of the property, much taller than when Elise had last seen them.

Cathy probably let them grow to block the sight of the container pier.

Elise pulled into the driveway. Dark green exterior.

Check. White shutters. *Check*. Large wraparound porch. *Check*. All with the slightly shabby look of an academic who was too preoccupied with cerebral matters to pay attention to peeling paint. Probably hadn't made her too popular in this neighborhood.

Late afternoon sun beat down on the car. Elise turned off the engine, suddenly desperate to get some fresh air.

She flung open the door and stood. Too quickly. Black spots swarmed in front of her eyes. She leaned against the door and breathed in deeply. The air carried a tangy breeze. The spots slowly dissipated.

"Mum, are you okay?" Lucy asked.

"Yes, I'm fine. I just need to catch my breath." She was glad she'd have a few weeks to recuperate. She'd go to a bookstore tomorrow and stock up on books, newspapers, magazines. She could hardly wait.

She just needed to get that damn phone call over with.

Then she could start her holiday.

3

Kate was at the intersection between Young Avenue and the park when an SUV with dark-tinted windows and Ontario plates turned into a driveway across the road. Kate hadn't really been paying attention, but she found herself slowing to a half jog, studying the woman who'd gotten out of the car.

Afterward, she wondered what it was about the woman that caught her attention. She was stunningly attractive—wavy blond hair that curved in layers to her shoulders, broad cheekbones and long legs. The type of woman most women would look at again. Either with admiration or, more likely, envy.

But it wasn't her looks that caught Kate's eye. It was the way the woman staggered against her car.

Was she going to pass out?

She looked as if she needed help. And Kate wasn't sure if there was anyone to help her. Her license plates indicated she was from out of town. Something about the woman's disheveled state screamed road trip.

Kate tugged at Alaska's leash. "Come on." She stepped off the curb, heading toward the SUV, then stopped as the passenger door of the car swung open and a preteen version of the blond woman sprang out.

"Mum, are you okay?" Kate heard her ask.

The blond woman straightened, pushing a hand through her mane of hair. She lifted her face to the breeze. "Yes, I'm fine," she said. "I just need to catch my breath."

She did look better. Kate stepped back onto the sidewalk, bending down to tighten her shoelace, keeping an eye on the scene across the street.

The air seemed to revive the woman, because she leaned into her car and pulled out her purse. She's not going to pass out, Kate thought. She stood, ready to move on, but Alaska slowed to sniff a tree.

"Oh, look, Mum, there's a husky!" the girl exclaimed, and rushed down the driveway toward Kate. Her mother shot an alarmed look at the large dog.

"Luce, make sure you check with the owner first!"

The girl threw a disgusted look at her mother. "I know, I was going to." She crossed the road, stopping in front of Kate, her blue eyes a shade darker than Alaska's. "Can I pat your dog?"

"Sure," Kate said. "His name is Alaska."

The girl let Alaska sniff her hand, then ran her palm over his neck. "He's so soft," she breathed.

"Yeah, his fur is nice, isn't it?" Kate said. Alaska allowed the girl to pat him for a minute, then shifted away from her, pulling his leash.

The girl stood back. "Thanks." She crossed the road, then gave a little wave over her shoulder.

"Have a nice night," Kate said. She broke into a jog, running down the hill toward the harbor, the shadowy pine trees to her right. She wondered if her quad muscle had cooled down too much and if she should stop to stretch it.

Regular physio had helped with the muscle strength in her quad, but she was still working on reconditioning the leg.

Eager not to lose momentum, Kate focused on her stride, the swing of her arms, her breathing. The irony of her final words to the girl and her mother only hit her the next morning, when she ran past the house again.

They had not had a nice night.

4

Elise gave the jogger a cool nod and turned away. She did not want others to see her weakness. They could never resist taking advantage of it.

She slung her purse over her shoulder and leaned into the car to grab her water bottle. A dark blue BMW coupe pulled up behind them.

Her body froze, knowing who it was before her brain acknowledged the man in the unfamiliar car.

Her ex-husband.

She did not want to face him tonight. She'd wanted to break the news of Nick's refusal to go sailing with him over the phone. It was safer.

There was too much pent-up hurt and grief in her to have this conversation face-to-face.

"Daddy!" Lucy called.

He waved to her, a smile warming the tension on his face. "Sweetheart."

Lucy threw herself into her father's arms. Elise took

a deep breath, her fingers tightening around the water bottle.

Damn him for reawakening feelings she thought were gone—or at least numbed by time. She'd thought her relationship with Jamie had finally closed the door on Randall. But her feelings for her lover had never been the same as the ones she'd had for her ex-husband. No matter how hard she had tried to excise Randall from her heart, she couldn't.

Damn him for making her do something she never thought she'd ever have to do.

She glanced in the rearview mirror and despised herself for doing so. God. Her skin was pale, a clammy sheen on her nose. She scrambled quickly for her compact, dusting the powder over her nose, around her eyes, and then hurriedly skimmed lip gloss over bloodless lips. She stuffed a breath mint in her mouth. Then she put on her sunglasses. At least it hid her eyes from him.

She backed out of the car, aware of how wrinkled and travel stained she looked. Had she even washed her hair this morning?

She couldn't remember. Because her brain was being bombarded with memories of the last time she'd seen her ex-husband. Of feeling him inside her. Of the look on his face when he left.

A cold sweat dampened her armpits. *Deal with it, Elise.*

But she wasn't sure if she could. Anxiety, her comrade in despair, was making her breathing uneven.

She pulled her purse strap higher on her shoulder and stepped away from the protection of her hulking car. Nick was still in the backseat. His iPhone was audible even through the heavy metal of the door. She was sure he had turned it up so he could tune his father out.

Lucy smiled excitedly at her father. He smiled back, his face more open than Elise could remember. They were picture perfect together. A small part of her heart broke at the sight.

She turned and opened the trunk, hauling out her suitcases. She locked the cases' extendable handles and began pulling them up the walkway.

Randall strode toward her. "Let me help."

"No, it's fine," she said tightly. *You owe me nothing. You made that clear enough.*

She yanked the bags over the uneven walkway. The concrete was cracked. Small spurts of grass caught the wheels of her case. She tugged at the suitcases impatiently.

Randall grabbed two more bags out of the trunk and followed her up the walkway. She felt his eyes on her. She prayed, *please don't let the sweat on my back show through my shirt.*

She lugged the suitcases up the porch steps and glanced over her shoulder, irritated. What the hell was Nick doing? She'd give him a good talking-to later. Not in front of his dad.

Just as she reached the top step, the second suitcase caught its wheel, pulling her off balance. She teetered on the edge of the step. Randall dropped the bags he was carrying, leaping up the stairs.

Knowing he was about to catch her made her determined not to fall. She righted herself, yanking the suitcase behind her.

"Damn," Randall muttered. "I'm sorry, Elise."

She glanced over her shoulder. In his haste to break her fall, Randall had dropped her overnight bag. And, she realized to her chagrin, she must have forgotten to zip it all the way closed this morning.

Now her panties, sanitary pads, two lacy bras, ibuprofen and a host of things she did not want anyone to see graced the weed-pocked grass. She hurried down the porch stairs—grateful that at least her dirty laundry was in a different suitcase—and knelt on the ground.

Randall, aware of her embarrassment, grabbed the suitcases she'd abandoned on the porch and pulled open the screen door. "The key is in the mailbox," Elise said, angling her body so she could covertly stuff the most embarrassing items into her bag. He raised his brows at this example of blithe home ownership and unlocked the door.

He disappeared into the house. Lucy, her arms full of pillows, stuffed animals, her iPod and portable DVD player, backed out of the SUV. When she saw her mother kneeling on the ground, she dropped everything on the lawn and rushed over to help.

Elise gave her daughter a wan smile. "Thanks, honey." She'd already finished repacking the bag, but she was gratified that her daughter had tried to help her. Unlike her son. What was wrong with that boy? But she knew what was wrong. She just didn't know how to fix it.

Randall came out of the house and strode down the porch steps. His eyes traveled over her. Lingering in places she wished they wouldn't. All her humiliation and anger rushed back. She crossed her arms. "The arrangement was that I would call you after we arrived."

He shrugged. His brawny shoulders moved smoothly under his pale blue golf shirt.

She could not deal with his physicality right now. The memory was too raw. It had not lessened one iota since she'd last seen him two months ago in Toronto.

"I was impatient to see the kids." Randall squeezed Lucy's shoulders.

Lucy gave him a quick smile, but Elise could see uneasiness in her eyes. Her daughter was caught between the two of them. The story of her young life.

Well, Elise was sorry about it. She was sorry about most of her life. But she refused to let Randall think that he could suddenly claim the right to show up on her doorstep whenever he pleased just because he wanted "to see the kids." If he'd wanted to do that, he should have stayed in Toronto. "You need to call first, Randall," she said coolly. "That's the deal."

Lucy threw her mother a pained look. *Don't do this*, her eyes begged. *I want to see him.*

He shrugged again, but his mouth was tight. He was fighting for control. *Good.* He had no idea what it was like to always feel as if your ex got the best of you. "Where's Nick?" he asked, his gaze turning to the tinted rear window of her SUV. "Why isn't he helping?"

Her irritation rose. As usual, he thought he could just pick up where he left off months before, and not listen to a word she said. She felt like a fly buzzing around his golden head. "I told you, you need to call first, Randall." She pulled her pride around her. Shielding the tattered remains of her dignity. "It's in the agreement."

"I know what's in the bloody agreement." His gaze

sharpened. "But if you want more money, I want more access."

Elise crossed her arms. "What, do you think they're for sale?"

Lucy pulled away from her father. She recognized that the first stone had just been thrown.

Randall shoved his fists into his pockets. "Of course not. You are deliberately misconstruing what I said."

"Oh, really?" She didn't think so. She didn't think she misconstrued him eight weeks ago when he pulled her into his arms in her Toronto kitchen and kissed her in a way that left no doubt about what he wanted.

And yet, she *had* misconstrued him. Why else the look on his face when he left her?

She had been a pity fuck.

There was no misconstruing that.

5

"**Y**ou and I both know that the last agreement was unfair, Elise," her ex-husband said. Calmly. Too calmly.

No. What was unfair was how you abandoned us and came here.

"It was more than fair," she said. A flush prickled her chest and arms. She didn't remember Halifax being so hot in the summer.

"Then why are you asking for more money?" Randall shot back.

She inhaled sharply. The bastard. He had trapped her neatly, expert cross-examiner that he was.

"You always need the last word, don't you, Randall?" She stared at him. He raised a brow. "You are such a prick!" she cried, her stomach threatening to heave. She spun on her heel.

You did this to me.

"Mum," Lucy said, putting her hand on Elise's arm. "Calm down."

Calm down? She gazed at her daughter's anxious

face. How many times during their marriage had Randall told her the same thing? Making her feel childish, as if she were to blame for their problems.

Lucy had no idea. *No idea* what she was going through right now. She jerked her arm away from her daughter. She could not calm down. And she hated herself for it. She hated that her emotions could smash through the taut barricade of her reason as if it were constructed of rice paper.

"Lucy," Randall said softly. "Go inside."

Lucy glanced at him, then Elise, her gaze helpless. "Go inside, Lucy," Elise said. "Please." Her fingers trembled.

Lucy hurried up the walkway. Elise heard the door latch squeak open, the screen door bang shut behind her.

Randall turned around and looked at Elise. His face, finally, showed his anger.

Elise welcomed it. They had spoken only twice after his life-altering visit in June. The first phone call was just a few weeks later and Elise had gripped the phone, holding her breath. Having the rules change so suddenly had left her own feelings about him in chaos.

She'd spent years regretting the end of her marriage. Then she'd met Jamie Gainsford eighteen months ago. She was one of his clients. Eight months ago she became his lover. And except for one moment of doubt, she'd thought she'd finally found love again.

But Randall's visit in June had made her reexamine her feelings for Jamie. Made her question what they were founded on. Was she just another needy patient who was experiencing transference for her hunky therapist?

No. Jamie felt the same way about her. They had a connection. There was no denying it. That was why they both took the risks they did. He'd never been involved with a client before; it violated his personal and professional ethics. She knew that if their relationship were discovered, Jamie would be kicked out of the College of Psychologists of Ontario.

It was a difficult, stressful situation. They couldn't help their feelings for one another. Yet the Ontario college stipulated that a therapist could only enter into a relationship with a former patient after the treatment had been terminated for two years.

Two years was like two centuries.

Or so Elise had thought. Until that evening in early June when Randall had confronted her in her kitchen.

Would she go back to him if he asked?

Yes.

But he hadn't asked. He'd just taken what he wanted. And when he called her two weeks later, it was his children he had wanted, not her.

He had invited the kids to spend the month of August with him. She had refused on their behalf, citing the various demands on their schedules. She had also instigated a new demand for increased child support.

But then her world had turned upside down. And suddenly Halifax in August seemed as good a place as any to lick her wounds. She'd called him back, the second and final time they'd spoken before today. He was wary. They'd had a brief conversation, agreed on the dates, then exchanged terse emails.

"Don't speak to me like that in front of the children," Randall said.

"I'll speak any way I like."

"Not to me."

"Then leave," she said, gratified that she'd turned the tables on him.

"Not until I see Nick." His face was drawn, his eyes grim. She was pleased to see she had that effect on him. "Where is he?"

"Where do you think?" She jerked her chin toward the car. "Did you think I left him in Toronto?"

"No."

"He wanted me to."

Randall shrugged. "He'll enjoy the trip. I've got it all planned out."

"Maybe that's the problem," she said. "Maybe he doesn't want you planning everything for him."

"It would be a change for him to have a parent do that." He crossed his arms. "Instead of a nanny."

She jerked back. "How dare you." Her voice shook. "I have a career, too. Why should I give it up just because you know full well that you would not make time to look after Nick?"

Randall's eyes flickered toward the SUV, but there was no sign of life within. Nick was plugged into his own world and it didn't include his father. "That's old history, Elise."

"Not to him." Her ex-husband just didn't get it. After their divorce was finalized, Nick had begged to live with his father. Since she had no moral ground to stand on, Elise had reluctantly let him go.

As she feared, it had been a disaster. Randall didn't understand Nick's issue with school. Learning had been easy for Randall; doing schoolwork a simple task. For

Nick, it was torture. Plain and simple. What Randall
took for procrastination and laziness was in reality a
paralyzing fear of failure. After a year and a half of
tears, arguments and visits to his teachers, Randall sent
twelve-year-old Nick back to live with Elise.

That was three years ago. Nick had never gotten
over it.

Randall walked around Elise to the SUV. He stopped
at the window on the passenger's side and rapped his
fingers lightly on the glass.

There was no sign Nick heard him.

Randall hesitated, then peered into the window.
His mouth tightened. He grabbed the door handle and
yanked it.

But his son had already locked the door.

Elise watched the two of them, disgust at her husband
outweighing dismay at her son's behavior. She hurried
over to the car. "You can't force him."

"Nick," he yelled through the glass. "Open the
door!"

His son turned his back to him. Part of Elise cheered
him on.

Randall slapped his hand on the window. "Open the
door right now!"

"Randall, this isn't the way to deal with it," she
said.

"Oh, really?" He turned to look at her, his eyes on
fire. "I expect him to account for himself. It's time for
him to be a man, Elise. I am willing to forgive him for
what he did with my bank account. But he can't be a
coward and sit in the car."

Elise glanced at Nick. If her son had heard his father,

he gave no indication. He sat with his earbuds plugged firmly in his ears, staring into nothingness.

"Where are your keys?" Randall asked.

She hesitated.

"Where are your keys?" He held out his hand.

Elise shook her head. "I'm not giving them to you."

Suddenly, Nick's door swung open and he stepped out, planting himself between Randall and Elise. His blond hair was longer than Randall's and he had the tall, lanky frame of adolescence, but it was clear he was his father's son.

"Stop it, Dad."

Randall opened his mouth, then closed it. He raked his fingers through his hair. "Nick. We need to talk."

A flush burned along Nick's jaw. "I already said I was sorry."

Randall sized him up. "I know. We need to talk about the trip."

"I'm not going."

"I told you that this was part of the deal. You can pay back what you owe me by crewing on the boat."

Nick grabbed his duffel bag out of the backseat of the car. He shoved his hand in a side pocket and pulled out a stack of bills. "Here's your money."

Randall unfolded the wad and briskly counted the amount. Six hundred and thirty-five dollars. "Where did you get this?" His tone was casual, but the tension in his face revealed his anger.

Nick's chin rose. "I earned it."

"How?"

"I worked at the golf club."

Randall's gaze whipped back to Elise. She nodded.

"Did your mother give you any of this?" Randall demanded.

Nick crossed his arms. "I earned it myself."

"Is that true, Elise?" Randall's eyes drilled into hers.

She forced her gaze to remain steady. "Yes."

"Why won't you believe me?" Nick asked. But they all knew why.

He'd lied before.

A lawn mower ripped to life. Nick hoisted his bag on his shoulder and spun on his heel. "Have a good trip, Dad." He headed up the walkway to the house.

"Nick, come on," Randall said. His eyes, so piercing just moments before, were dull with hurt.

Nick clomped up the porch stairs.

"Nick, you promised," Randall called after him.

That stopped Nick. He turned. Anger and hurt vibrated from his eyes. "I changed my mind." He looked at Elise for help. "I'm going to camp instead."

Randall's eyes narrowed. He turned to Elise. "When did you arrange this?"

"On our way here."

Randall gave Nick a hard look. Nick shifted his bag on his shoulder. "Why didn't you call me?"

"Because I knew you wouldn't listen to me, Dad."

"We made a deal," Randall repeated.

"You mean *you* made a deal." Nick grabbed the handle to the screen door and pulled it open. It squeaked rustily. "Anyway, I paid you back." He stepped through the doorway.

"Nick, wait!" Randall said. Nick slammed the door shut behind him.

Elise watched this drama playing out, wishing she had half the guts of her son.

Randall spun around and glared at Elise. "Congratulations. You've achieved what you set out to do."

She tried not to shrivel under the heat of his anger. "What do you mean by that?"

"You've turned him against me." There was stark pain under the accusation.

"Why are you always blaming me?" He was the one who moved to a different province. How did he expect to have a relationship with his kids?

"Because you're the one who divided this family," he said.

She flinched, unprepared for that attack. These arguments had been laid to rest years ago, but clearly the sex had raised them from the dead. She lifted her chin. "Only because you stopped being a part of it."

"Don't blame me for your infidelity, Elise. It was you who ruined our marriage. Remember that." He stalked away to his car.

"Don't worry. You'll never let me forget," she called after him. He ignored her. Just as he always did. They'd start having an argument and he'd turn on his heel and walk out.

Not this time. He would not get the last word this time.

The trauma of the past two months was too fresh in her mind. He'd opened a door she'd thought had been sealed shut. She'd glimpsed a future—had allowed herself to hope. And then found out in a phone call that she'd been foolish. Naive. Unwanted. The loss had been huge. The procedure worse than she imagined.

He was not going to get the final word.

She hurried after him. He was unlocking his door. She grabbed his arm. "I may have ruined our marriage, but you've had your revenge."

He threw her an angry look and climbed into the immaculate, shining tribute to his manhood.

She rushed around to the driver's side and pounded on the window.

He rolled it down. Anger, impatience, irritation—that one really got her—flashed across his face. "I heard you."

That's what he thought. He always claimed he heard what she said, but he didn't. He didn't hear the pain, the need, the hurt. Or he chose to ignore it.

Anger surged inside her. "If you heard me, then why don't you answer me!"

"Because I don't want to talk about it. What happened in Toronto was a big mistake. But it's over. You have to move on, Elise."

"How easy for you to say." Her voice trembled with rage. "How fucking easy for you to sit there in your new car—it is new, isn't it, darling, and yet you claim you can't afford more child support—and tell me that it's over. You've moved on. Be a big girl, Elise, and suck it up."

He stared at her. She knew he was waiting for her to vent her rage, move away from the car in a sobbing heap, and he'd roar down the street like a bat out of hell. Same old, same old.

Her hands gripped the edge of the lowered window. Her fingertips dug into fine leather, her palms pressed against hot chrome. "Let me tell you exactly what I had to suck up, Randall. Or should I say, suck out." She took a deep breath, swallowed. "Your baby." She'd meant to end it on a bitter, angry note, but it came out pathetically weak.

She wiped the back of her hand across her mouth. Randall stared at her. Then he closed his eyes and leaned his head against the headrest. "Jesus," he murmured. His eyes opened again and she saw his shock, his anger. "Why didn't you tell me?"

"I couldn't." She straightened and turned away, not wanting him to see the tears that sprang into her eyes. The pain of his abandonment had never eased. It seemed half her life had been spent getting over his desertion of her—first emotional, then physical, and finally both.

He got out of the car, his body rigid behind her. "I deserved to know."

He'd fucked her, knocked her up, left her—and then insisted he *deserved* to know.

She couldn't answer. Anger swelled her throat.

He added, "Is that why you asked for additional child support?"

Jesus. She spun around. The words jerked out of her throat. "No! The money was for Nick and Lucy."

His eyes flickered over her abdomen. She was grateful her arms were hugging her waist. He said softly, "But you said it was mine." He paused. "Wasn't it?"

She lurched back. *Bastard.* Even now, he couldn't let her forget her infidelity. That much was still the same. Only, everything was infinitely worse.

He had no idea what she'd gone through. What she was still going through. "I had an abortion." She flung the words at him. Slammed them at his face. Wished she could slap him with the words, beat him with them, make him feel what she felt. "Thanks to you."

He recoiled. "What do you mean by that? I would have paid child support."

"And made me beg for it every step of the way. You'd probably insist on a paternity test, right?"

The look in his eyes answered her question.

"You fucking bastard! You have no idea what I've gone through!" She drew in a deep, sobbing breath and despised herself for revealing, once again, her weakness in front of her ex. "I will never forgive you for this."

Tears streamed down her face. She knew her nose was running uncontrollably. She was a fucking sniveling mess. She ran up the walkway and yanked open the screen door, the complaints of the rusty hinge almost drowned by the squealing of rubber as her ex-husband took off down the road.

6

The doorbell rang just as Kate finished toweling her hair. Her shower had been refreshing, cleansing her mind of work—and of how her day had ended. She hurried to the front door, a smile already on her lips.

Nat stood on the porch, her arms crammed with take-out bags from their favorite Indian restaurant.

"Mmm." Kate held open the door. "Come on in."

"With pleasure," Nat said with a grin. She marched into the kitchen, ignoring the drop sheets, put the bags on the counter and poured herself a large glass of diet soda. Kate followed her, marveling, as usual, at her friend's insouciance. From the top of Nat's bleached-blond pixie head to her broad yet tiny feet (my little sledgehammers, Nat called them), her friend just breezed through people's defenses and claimed her place. *It's from growing up on a farm,* Nat had once told Kate. *You have to take control of the animals or you'll spend your day walking in manure.*

"Very nice." Nat gave a low whistle at the newly

painted walls, raising her glass in a toast. "Hard to believe this was once the house of gloom and doom."

The yellowy-wheat—or wheaty-yellow—paint gleamed on the once-dingy walls, rendering them clean and fresh. Kate sipped her wine, a pleasant glow in her stomach. She relaxed against the counter. "I know. I can't believe it myself."

"Is your hunky handyman helping you?"

"Nat…" Kate grinned. "He's just a friend."

Nat quirked a brow. "You sure?"

Kate nodded. "He's like…" She grappled for a description of her feelings for Finn. "He's like my little brother."

Nat contemplated Kate over her soda. Kate knew that look. She braced herself.

"Does he feel that way, too? You're pretty oblivious to how men look at you. I, crack reporter that I am, have a nose for this."

"I think he hangs around because of the house, Nat. And Alaska."

Nat gave her another dubious look.

"Seriously. He's never made a move. And he's had ample opportunity. He practically lives here." And that was exactly the way Kate liked it. Finn was great company, totally undemanding and invaluable around the house. He took the chill off her Victorian home, not just by fixing it up but by being there. Another warm body to fill the rooms.

"Here." Kate handed Nat a plate. "Help yourself." They dished up the take-out food, the aroma of fragrant samosas, butter chicken and *roghan josh* curry filling her kitchen. Alaska moved to the counter and raised his muzzle in the air. His nostrils quivered.

"Let's go outside." Kate had proudly set up two Adirondack chairs to face her garden. The bed was still a bit straggly—and hadn't benefited from the holes Alaska had dug in it—but Muriel and Enid Richardson, her elderly neighbors whom she now thought of as aunts, had pointed out the weeds versus the plants. In a flurry of beginner's enthusiasm, Kate had planted a huge variety of perennials too close together. But there were some lovely established shrubs that made up for the haphazardness of the bed. Right now, the daylilies were in bloom, their deep orange blossoms a stunning contrast against the weathered wooden fence behind it.

The garden didn't look half bad.

Alaska settled down contentedly between the two of them, knowing that Nat would "accidentally" drop some food his way.

"So, got any men lined up for the weekend?" Nat asked, stuffing a heaping forkful of butter chicken and rice into her mouth.

Randall Barrett's unsmiling face popped into her head. Kate gave herself a mental shake. But Randall was like a burr, sticking to the tender flesh of her heart. The more she tried to rip him out, the more pieces got left behind. Better to just ignore it. She forced a smile. "Nada. How about you?"

"Not yet. But I've got my eye on this homicide detective. I ran into him last week. He's come off a bad relationship and told me he could use a fun girl like me...."

Kate lowered her fork to her plate. "That's not funny."

Nat had changed when she was in Ottawa. Kate wasn't sure whether it was a by-product of Nat's career choice or a defense mechanism resulting from her disastrous relationship with Bryce, but Nat was more caustic than Kate remembered.

"Sorry," Nat said unapologetically. "But I did run into Your Ex. He was checking out a crime scene."

"Yes, I saw your report in the paper." Kate's broken engagement with homicide detective Ethan Drake was one subject she couldn't discuss. Especially with the way Nat was now. She stifled a pang of sadness. She missed the closeness she'd experienced with her friend.

But we've all changed.

"So don't you want to know what Ethan had to say?"

No. Yes.

No, Kate, you've moved on. "Not particularly."

Nat said through a mouthful of curry, "Touchy, aren't we?"

Kate shrugged. "It hasn't been that long."

They'd only truly ended things in May. And although Kate knew it was the right thing for both of them, part of her was still in mourning. She'd had six months of hope with Ethan. It had fallen apart in a very messy, very nasty way last New Year's Eve.

Then Kate had barely survived the attack, only to discover a new danger. She'd had a hard enough time getting her head around being targeted by a serial killer. To learn that Craig Peters had been infected with Creutzfeldt-Jakob disease had been the icing on the cake.

There was a remote chance—a very remote chance,

she was assured by her doctors—that she could be infected with the fatal illness. The type of CJD they believed Craig Peters had contracted was not believed to be transmitted through blood infection. But no one knew for sure. There were no tests for it. It wouldn't be until Kate exhibited symptoms such as ataxia, where her body would move jerkily, or dementia that alarm bells would ring for her doctors. And only a postmortem brain biopsy could confirm diagnosis.

She tried not to think about it, telling herself she had more chance of being hit by a bus than developing CJD, but it lurked in her mind. Usually only coming out at night.

Nat stood, shaking bits of rice and naan onto the deck. Alaska moved into position. "I've gotta run." She padded into the kitchen and grabbed her satchel. "I need my beauty sleep." She grimaced. "Actually, I need to do my laundry before tomorrow's shift."

"Why do you keep getting weekend shifts?"

Nat shrugged. "I'm earning my stripes. Anyway, I'm not complaining. In fact, I bought my own police scanner for when the newsroom's closed. The best crime happens on weekends." Her friend gave her a saucy grin. "You oughta know."

Kate had been attacked on a Friday night, as Nat was well aware.

Kate raised her wineglass in a silent toast. "Touché." She liked the fact that Nat joked about her almost becoming the Body Butcher's final victim. So many people avoided talking about it—or worse, tried pumping her for details. Nat's teasing made her feel almost normal.

Almost. There was still a void. A deep, dark blackness that had fear acidulating its edges.

Nat stopped at the front door. "You sure you don't want to know what Your Ex said to me?"

Kate closed her eyes. "Nat. Stop it. Please. I doubt he'd say much to a crime reporter."

"Thanks a lot. I'm better than you think at weaseling out classified information."

"Uh-huh."

"Kate. Seriously. Don't you want to know?"

"Jesus. What kind of friend are you?"

"A good one."

Kate studied her. Nat's cocky demeanor had softened. "All right."

"He told me to say hello."

"What?" Kate stared at her. "How did he know that we were friends?"

"I told him."

"Why did you do that?"

"Because I didn't want him to think I was biased. Which I am, but at least I'm honest about it." She winked and strode through the door. "Pray for some murder and mayhem this weekend. I want to make the front page on Sunday."

Kate closed the door behind her friend. The house seemed deflated, as if all its life force had fled on the nonexistent heels of Nat's flip-flops.

She wandered back outside again. Restlessness battled with fatigue. She did not want to think about her ex-fiancé. But Nat had practically thrown him in her face.

She wondered what Ethan's reaction had been when

Nat told him she was friends with Kate. Probably the same as hers. Dismay. Discomfort.

Pain.

Yes, she was over Ethan. No, she did not have any regrets. At least, not about ending their engagement. She did regret the manner in which it ended. New Year's Eve was ruined for her now, that was for sure.

She also regretted causing Ethan more pain when he visited her in the hospital.

She wondered what, if anything, Ethan regretted.

Two houses over, in the student flats, a Natal Day party was just getting warmed up. She sighed. It would be a noisy evening.

When the phone rang, she started, her wine sloshing over the rim of the glass onto her fingers. Would that nervous reaction ever go away?

"Hey, Kate, we're just leaving the Lower Deck," her friend Joanne shouted over the background noise of the waterfront pub. Kate could hear a Gaelic band repeating a rousing chorus with the raucous support of its audience. "We've added a few more to our numbers and are heading up to the Economy Shoe Shop. Are you ready to come?"

A hoot of laughter echoed across her lawn. What was there for her to do tonight?

Just the case reports.

That was too pathetic for words. "Sure." She tried to inject some enthusiasm into her voice. "I'll be there in twenty minutes." She put down the phone. She wasn't going to sit at home and wallow. Not anymore.

She'd had a taste of her mortality. She was seizing

life with both hands. Carpe diem and all that crap. And maybe she'd wear away through sheer exhaustion the imprint that Craig Peters had made on her soul.

7

Elise sat on the edge of the bed and stared through the patio doors. Pink and mauve tinged the sky behind the hedges, promising a stunning sunset. The day was ending on one final, glorious note.

Not for her, though.

After the blowout to end all blowouts with Randall, no one had been in the mood for a crustacean feast. They'd postpone it until tomorrow, Elise had told the kids with a forced brightness, when they all felt less tired from the trip. Lucy had nodded, her eyes mute with reproach and pain. Nick said nothing.

They ordered take-out pizza, ate it in the briefest of minutes, then embarked on an unenthusiastic walk-through of the main floor of the house. One peek down the basement stairs and the kids realized, with some disappointment, that the basement was in its original unfinished state. Even from the top of the basement stairs, the must was noticeable. A teen retreat was not to be found anywhere in the house.

Bedrooms were assigned, bags carried up the stairs, then Lucy asked if she could check out the shampoo-filled fountain. Nick sullenly agreed to accompany her.

Elise escaped into the master bedroom. She desperately needed to make a phone call.

This is the last time, she told herself. She'd called Jamie during the trip, unsure of how to manage Nick's refusal to go sailing with Randall. It had been the first time she'd spoken to him in several weeks. Ever since her abortion, she'd been trying to wean herself from Jamie, from the therapy.

He, of course, sensed it, understood it. *It's grief, Elise. And guilt. It's natural, it's to be expected. Just remember I'll be waiting for you.*

But she wasn't sure she'd come back. The sex with Randall—and its aftermath—had shaken her. She saw now that her feelings for her ex-husband were deep and unending, an underground river twisting through the cavern of her heart.

Was she capable of truly loving another man knowing that this river had a seemingly infinite source?

She'd wanted to ask Jamie, as her therapist, how to cope with her feelings for Randall. But she couldn't. She was scared she'd hurt her lover's feelings.

And when she discovered she was pregnant three weeks after Randall's visit, she was glad she hadn't said anything. It was Jamie, not Randall, who was there for her. He was the one who had listened to her fears: Would she have an unhealthy baby because she was now in her forties? How could she cope with being a single parent with two teenagers and a baby? And, the fear that terrified her the most: Would she develop another debilitating case of postpartum depression? It had been bad with Nick. It had been even worse with Lucy. She couldn't take it again.

They both agreed the wisest, safest course was to terminate the pregnancy.

She still believed it had been the right decision. But she hadn't appreciated what she would feel afterward.

Guilt, grief, pain, sorrow. All compounded with hormones that went into overdrive.

That was two weeks ago.

This trip was her chance to get back on her feet. Figure out if she had a future with Jamie. But if she did, she didn't want to sneak around anymore. She'd tried that once before and it had been the most destructive thing she'd ever done.

She wanted to be better than that.

But it was so hard to be the woman she wanted to be when she was with Randall. He'd left her with so much baggage that when he showed up unannounced today she hadn't had time to prepare herself. He had caught her off guard.

And he had reduced her to a woman that she despised. She hated that he could do that to her. She hated that she let him.

The worst thing was that until the kids were adults, she would always have some communication with him. Like this weekend. They still hadn't made arrangements about Lucy going to riding camp. Randall would have to drive her there, since Elise had to take Nick to his camp, which was two hours out of the city.

How could they get past today? How could they get past June? Or the abortion?

She needed to talk to Jamie.

She pressed her cell phone to her cheek, closing her eyes as his number rang. On the second ring, Jamie answered. "Elise." His voice was soft, gentle in her ear.

"Hi." The word practically exhaled out of her mouth in relief.

"How are you? Are you in Halifax yet?"

She swallowed. "Yes. We arrived a few hours ago."

"Everything okay?" As usual, he picked up on the tone of her voice.

"No," she whispered. "No, it's not."

She told him the whole sordid story.

"The kids have witnessed enough conflict," he replied. "You and Randall need to behave like caring parents, instead of attacking each other in front of them. Show Randall you can take control of this situation— call him first."

It seemed like exactly the right thing to do when Jamie laid it all out. Elise felt empowered, a rare emotion when dealing with her ex-husband.

"How are you feeling, anyway?" Jamie's voice dropped, became more intimate.

"I've been better." Elise tried to laugh but she couldn't.

"Listen, I know you're trying to avoid sleeping pills— and I think that's a good call. But maybe you should take one tonight. You haven't been sleeping well. You're still recovering from your procedure."

"Oh, Jamie, I don't think so." Elise rubbed her temple with her hand. "I don't want to rely on pills to sleep."

"I understand. I'm not suggesting you take them every night. But you told me you've barely slept the past few days. It might be worth thinking about. I'm worried about you." His tone changed. "Regardless, I think you'd feel a lot better if you called Randall tonight. Get it over with. That might help you sleep."

"You're right." She exhaled a breath she hadn't realized she was holding.

"And remember, Elise, you can call me any time. I'm here for you."

"Thank you. I'll call you tomorrow and let you know how I make out."

"You do that. You know where I am. Love you." His last words startled her. He didn't usually say stuff like that on the phone. Guilt squeezed her heart. She knew she should say she loved him, too. But she didn't know what she felt.

"Talk to you tomorrow," she said.

Then, before her courage could fail her, she called Randall. He listened to her spiel with barely controlled impatience. Her carefully planned words fell flat.

Finally, he said, "Is that it?"

"We need to talk about this," she said. She fought hard to keep her voice from trembling. "Can you come over?"

He hung up.

She sprang to her feet and walked onto the balcony. It was long and narrow, running the back length of the house. A decorative wrought-iron rail provided an airy contrast to the stone terracing of the garden spread out below.

Twilight crept over the rock-studded edges of the

walls below her. The terracing looked quite stunning at this time of day, full of deepening shadows that pooled, dark and mysterious, from the rock walls.

Why had she listened to Jamie?

She'd humiliated herself.

The wrought iron under her fingers had been warmed by the sun, roughened by the elements. It was exactly how she'd hoped she'd feel by the end of her vacation: her inner strength renewed, her body buffed by the sun and salt air.

Goddamn him.

A profound sense of aloneness settled around her.

Cathy had done a lovely job terracing the garden, she thought. Tears slid down her face.

Kate riffled through her closet. One item caught her eye, standing out from all the suits and running clothes, the price tag still attached to the neckline. It was a flirty little summer dress in an outrageous shade of cherry red, bought one rainy Saturday afternoon when Nat had dragged Kate to her favorite shopping haunts in Halifax. She slipped it on. It felt cool, chic. Hip, even.

She put on sandals, lipstick. The color on her lips was vibrant, but it mocked the dark shadows under her eyes. She dabbed on concealer, a new but necessary accessory since May, and gave herself a critical once-over. Her eyes still looked tired. She added a streak of gold eye shadow, feeling ridiculously glam, but liking the way it caught the amber lights in her eyes.

But more than her eyes glinted in the light. She peered at a few strands of hair. No. She wasn't going gray yet. The sun had merely given her brown hair a few honey-gold highlights. All in all, she would do. She grabbed a thin cardigan, and hurried down the stairs.

Eighteen minutes later, a cab dropped her off at the end of Argyle Street. She strolled toward the Economy Shoe Shop. People spilled out of chic bars and even chicer restaurants, relaxing on the patios that were created for Halifax's brief yet glorious summer. She breathed in the fresh, warm air. Part of her wanted to linger, to enjoy the brief caress of summer. The other part was eager to immerse herself in the chatter and laughter of her friends. And crowd out the flashbacks that would pounce on her when she left her mind unguarded.

She pulled her cardigan around her shoulders and hurried past the final patio that jutted into the sidewalk. A lone figure caught her eye. He was sitting with his back to the street, his hands clasped around a whiskey glass, but Kate recognized the thick shoulders. The blond hair. The rugged jawline that was unusually rigid as he stared into the amber liquid.

What was Randall Barrett doing on the first night of his vacation staring into a glass of booze?

She hesitated. Should she say hello?

Hell, no.

8

Friday, 8:43 p.m.

Kate glanced at her watch, hurrying past Randall's hunched form. She hoped he wouldn't see her, but if he did, she planned to make sure he didn't realize *she* had seen *him*. She headed into the Economy Shoe Shop. It was already full to the gills. She worked her way into its labyrinthine interior, scanning the crowd for Joanne's blond head. She was immediately absorbed into the throng.

"Kate, over here!" Joanne waved from the far corner, holding court at a large table. Kate slipped through the crowd and lowered herself into the only empty chair.

Her colleagues were well into a night of liquor and merriment. She looked around, hoping to catch a waitress' eye. She longed for a drink. Especially after seeing her boss.

"Kate, you know Paul Roberts from Fougere Thomas," Joanne said. "And of course you know Curtis Carey. You two are on the same case, right?"

Same case, opposite sides. And Kate had the sinking

feeling she was on the wrong side. Kate had been assigned to work with Nina Woods, McGrath Barrett's newest rainmaker, on a defense for Great Life Insurance Company. Great Life was one of the clients Nina had brought with great acclaim to McGrath Barrett two months ago.

The matter was straightforward: plaintiff Mike Naugler was suing Great Life for injuries sustained from an accident. Kate was sure Nina Woods could handle this file with her eyes closed. But Nina wanted McGrath Barrett's celebrity associate on Team Woods.

Kate supposed she should be flattered. Nina Woods was a star by anyone's definition, the type of lawyer who sprinkled major billable hours in her path to the lucky hungry associates she brought along with her.

Kate forced a smile at the man who'd irritated the hell out of her this afternoon. "We saw each other today, in fact."

Curtis grinned. It surprised Kate. She was expecting an arrogant, kind of smirky grin, but it was genuine if not liquored up. "Poor old Nina. Never thought the ice queen could turn so green." His grin grew larger. "Nice rhyme, eh?"

Kate couldn't help but grin in return. Nina reminded Kate of the white queen on a chessboard, with her bright silver hair and her commanding face. Seeing Nina Woods be human had been disconcertingly refreshing.

When Nina had arrived that morning for the discovery hearing—where one side questioned the other about their evidence and testimony—Kate had just been absorbing the fact that she recognized the plaintiff. Mike Naugler was a patient at the same physio clinic she'd attended to rehabilitate her arm and leg after the Body Butcher's attack. On more than one occasion, Kate had been in the bed next to his, separated only by a curtain. She'd heard all about his accident, his pain, his attempts to rehabilitate. Mike Naugler's injuries affected his ability to function, his ability to work, his interactions with his children.

Nina grilled the man relentlessly. Sweat had steeped dark patches into the cotton/polyester blend of Mike Naugler's Mark's Work Wearhouse shirt.

When they'd returned to the boardroom in the afternoon, a faint odor of perspiration mixed with desperation, anger and garlic from his lawyer's donair lunch permeated the room. Kate had taken copious notes, in contrast to Mike Naugler's counsel. Curtis Carey had retrieved the newspaper from inside his briefcase and perused it with an air of cocky indifference while Nina battered his client. Kate was sure that Curtis had prepared his client for this strategy but it had taken its toll on Mike Naugler.

At 2:48 p.m., Nina had paused. Taken a sip of water. Swallowed. Taken another sip of water. A light sheen of sweat had gleamed on her forehead. She had bent her head to Kate's and whispered, "I think I'm going to vomit." Her face had paled dramatically in the past five minutes.

Nina had waved at the discovery reporter to stop the recording. She pressed her hand against her stomach. "I'm afraid I won't be able to continue," she had said to Curtis Carey. "I must have eaten something that was off."

She turned to her client. "There are only a few

questions remaining. Kate will take over." With that, she had grabbed her notepad and rushed out of the room.

Curtis Carey had then unfolded the comics section. The fact that he'd read the world news when Nina was questioning his client, but had switched to the comics when Kate was conducting the discovery, irritated the hell out of her.

Between the hostile plaintiff, the insolent lawyer and the stack of research sitting on her desk when she returned to her office, it had been a hell of a way to end the workweek. Another glass of wine could not have happened soon enough. But she hadn't planned on enjoying it in the company of the first man who'd gotten under her skin today. She pushed the second man out of her thoughts. She hadn't expected to see him on her way here.

Curtis' eyes flickered over Kate's sundress. She had removed her cardigan when she entered the Shoe and now she regretted her flirty choice. His collar was unbuttoned and his tie probably stuffed in his briefcase, but everyone at the table still wore their work clothes.

The waitress appeared with Kate's wine. Curtis waved a twenty dollar bill, and she took it just as Kate protested.

He shook his head. "I owe you one. I was a bit of a prick this afternoon."

She raised a brow. "How was Dilbert?"

"Not as good as Peanuts."

That surprised a laugh out of her. She sipped her wine. "I've always had a fondness for Pigpen."

"I'm a Snoopy guy all the way." He raised his glass. "So, am I forgiven?" He asked the question with the mischievous grin of a little boy. A dimple creased one of his cheeks, giving him a lopsided—but endearing—smile. *Too endearing,* Kate told herself. *I bet he's used this since kindergarten to get himself out of trouble.*

Kate arched a brow. "This time only. I won't be so lenient again."

His eyes met hers. A slow flush warmed her chest. She sipped her wine, raising the glass to her lips so quickly that the rim hit her teeth. When had he become so cute?

Maybe when she met him at the discovery this morning and he hadn't exhibited the usual fascinated curiosity for the woman who'd slain the Body Butcher single-handedly. Most new acquaintances would eye her suit and blouse as if they expected her to rip it off and reveal her spandex superwoman outfit underneath. Or they would back away ever so slightly, as if the thought of getting too close to a woman who had violently killed was too risky. Not Curtis. He treated her just like anyone else. Add the dimple to the package, and he was looking pretty damn good.

"What does Kate do on her time off?" His voice was low, meant just for her. She darted a glance at the other associates. Joanne was saying, "I heard that Nina told Randall that if he didn't…" Then Joanne's voice lowered. The other associates leaned in closer. Any other time, Kate would want to know about Nina Woods and her power plays, but not this moment. Not when Curtis Carey's gray eyes were fixed on hers. Waiting for her answer. She smiled. "I take my dog running."

"Yeah?" There was no mistaking the appreciative

gleam in his gaze as he skimmed the bare shoulders, revealed by her sundress. "I run, too."

She let her own eyes wander. Lanky, well-muscled under that crisp blue shirt, she bet. He could probably keep up with her.

Just like Ethan had. And where had that led her?

To heartbreak.

She drained her wineglass. Curtis wasn't Ethan. She had to remember that.

"I usually go for a run on Saturday morning," Curtis said, his eyes intent on hers. "Do you want to join me?"

That startled a nervous laugh out of her. "But we're on opposing sides…"

"I won't pump you for information." He placed two fingers against his heart. "Scout's honor."

When he put it like that, she felt ridiculous objecting in the first place. And besides, he seemed like a nice guy.

Not like those losers who called her in the weeks after she killed Craig Peters. They'd asked her out on dates, either to be associated with her fifteen minutes of fame, or—this had made her sick—to convince her to reenact in the bedroom what she'd done to Craig Peters. She'd had to delist her phone number.

She shivered.

"You cold?"

She had the feeling if she said yes, he'd be offering to warm her up. She pulled her cardigan around her shoulders.

"Nope. Fine." She smiled brightly. "I usually run at Point Pleasant around 9:00 a.m."

His dimple creased even deeper. Kate felt a heat in her belly.

It had been too long since she'd had a man hold her close. She looked at Curtis' hands, one clasped around his beer glass, the other splayed casually on top of the table.

He had nice hands. Strong fingers.

She reached for her wineglass, then realized it was empty and raised her hand for the waitress. Another glass of wine was just what the doctor ordered, before she parched her thirst in a wholly inappropriate way.

She might find Curtis Carey hot, sexy and totally devourable—this minute—but that didn't mean she should jump into bed with him.

Right?

How would they feel on Tuesday morning? In the boardroom, questioning the medical expert hired by Great Life?

That could be very messy.

Or it could be one hell of a way to spend the weekend.

Her wine arrived. Curtis raised his glass in a toast. His gaze held hers.

Desire flared in a hot rush.

She looked away.

She knew what his eyes were telling her. What they were inviting her to do.

Alaska was waiting for her at home. So was an empty bed.

A scary bed.

A bed that let her exhausted body rest on it and then

tangled her in its sheets, holding her captive while Craig Peters slipped into her mind.

She drained her glass.

Curtis watched her.

She stood. "I'm heading home," she announced to the group.

"Already?" Joanne asked. Her eyes darted between Kate and Curtis.

"I'm going running tomorrow." With a faint smile, Kate walked away.

9

Elise knocked on Lucy's door, hoping her eyes didn't look too reddened. She could hear her daughter's iPod playing on speakers from inside her room.

"Come in," Lucy called.

Elise turned the old brass door handle and walked in. The bedside light was the only illumination in the room. Its muted glow cast Lucy's hair into molten gold. Lucy sat cross-legged on a white pine sleigh bed, dressed for sleep in a loose T-shirt emblazoned with her basketball team's logo and a pair of penguin-patterned pajama bottoms.

Her daughter was so beautiful.

All of Elise's protective instincts surged in her.

Lucy looked up from her journal entry, a frown of concentration still blurring her brows. "Hi, Mum." Her blue eyes searched her mother's face. "Are you feeling better?"

"Yes," Elise lied. "I'm sorry it was such a hard way to start our vacation."

Lucy shrugged, but Elise knew her fight with Randall had deeply upset her daughter. A wave of fatigue hit her. She was exhausted by Randall's anger. She was disappointed that Jamie's advice had blown up in her face. She'd always thought he could cut through the suppurating flesh of an issue and get to the bone. But tonight his advice had only succeeded in making her feel worse.

She'd go to bed and get a good night's sleep. Then tomorrow morning she'd wake up early and make the kids a big pancake breakfast. They'd forget tonight ever happened and start their vacation properly this time.

She rested her hand on her daughter's shoulder. "Let's do something fun tomorrow, Luce. We could go down to the waterfront and take a boat cruise or something. And I owe you two that lobster dinner."

Lucy's face lit up. "Yeah. Sweet!"

Elise grinned at her. "Now it's time for bed. You need to put away your memoirs."

Lucy placed the ribbon marker precisely between the pages, which Elise noted were crammed with her loopy, generous handwriting.

"No peeking," Lucy chided, stuffing the journal under her pillow.

"Of course not." Elise meant it. "I would never pry. That's your private stuff, honey."

Lucy slid her lean limbs under the sheets. Elise marveled at the perfect symmetry of her daughter's body. She was stretching out, her body morphing into a young woman's. Once again, Elise's protective instincts rose, honed recently to quivering alertness. Lucy was still a child despite her changing body. She was just becoming aware of her effect on boys.

She reached over, turning off Lucy's iPod and her bedside light. "Have you taken out your contacts?"

"Yes."

"Brushed your teeth?"

"Ye-e-s!" Lucy said with the righteous indignation of a child who had remembered this time.

Elise bent over and kissed Lucy's cheek. Her skin was so smooth. "Sleep well, darling."

"I love you, Mum," Lucy murmured.

Those words gave Elise more comfort than anything. She just needed to keep it that way. She walked through the darkness to the door. "Love you, too. See you in the morning."

"Uh-huh," Lucy said, already drifting into sleep. Her daughter had an uncanny ability to fall asleep at the drop of a hat that Elise envied.

She padded across the hall. Nick's room was in darkness, but she knew he'd be lounging on his bed, surfing his laptop. She hesitated outside his door. The urge to talk to him about his behavior with Randall was almost overwhelming. He couldn't provoke his father like that.

But he'd be quick to throw it all back in her face. And she knew her actions had been just as deplorable.

She put her hand on the brass doorknob. It was cool under her fingers. It seemed to her that Nick was holding his breath on the other side of the room.

What would she say to him?

Nothing that he hadn't heard a million times.

She could just picture his face when she opened the

door. The deliberately blank eyes. The sullen, unsmiling face. The reluctance to greet her.

Fatigue washed through her. She did not have the energy for yet another fight this evening.

There was time enough tomorrow. When the sun was up and their stomachs were full of her special blueberry buttermilk pancakes, the events of today could be discussed with calmness. Maybe she'd even joke about it with Nick to take the sting away.

Her fingers slid from the doorknob and she walked slowly to her own room.

She shed her clothes and threw on a light cotton nightgown in white with pale blue trim. Her breasts swayed heavily under the gown as she carried her overnight bag into the bathroom.

It took only minutes to get ready for bed. Most of her eye makeup had come off as a result of her weeping. She stared at herself in the bathroom mirror. Her blond hair, always wavy and full, was tangled around her face. Her eyes, puffy. Her skin, drawn.

This was not the way she wanted to live her life.

She took out her contacts, tossing them in the garbage, and caught her reflection in the mirror again.

Her face was satisfyingly blurred.

10

Friday, 10:35 p.m.

The light breeze stirred the tendrils by Kate's ears, tickling her neck. She stood on the curb outside the Shoe, waiting to flag a cab. It wasn't cold, but she shivered. Every nerve was on edge, her body suffused with the heat of her reaction to Curtis. Now, away from him, the breeze played with her nerve endings.

A cab cruised down the street. She raised her hand, then lowered it. The cab's light was off. She exhaled in frustration. All the taxis were full by the time they reached her; she'd need to go back to the corner where she'd been dropped off.

She walked down the sidewalk, eager to get home and see Alaska. At least she had one male who was always happy to see her, always waiting for her.

"Let me see you home," Curtis said, placing a hand on her arm. She jumped. And cursed herself.

"Sorry, did I startle you?"

Kate shook her head, flashing him a quick smile. "No. I'm fine." But she shivered again.

He slid his hand up to her elbow. His grip was sure, his palm warm. She allowed her body to lean toward his. Her skin buzzed. Kind of like her head. She'd drunk a lot of wine tonight. Too much. "Feel better?"

"Yes." The word breathed between her lips.

He didn't say anything else, but his fingers danced down to her wrist, caressing the delicate skin that was screaming in a very indelicate way under his touch.

Curtis waved at an empty taxi. He held the door open for her, letting her slide in, then eased his long frame right next to hers. His arm stretched along the back of the seat. Kate gave her address to the cabbie.

They drove in silence, but Kate's body was talking to her the whole while.

Please. Please let me do this.

Please let me forget.

The cab pulled into her driveway. Curtis paid the driver, and followed Kate up her darkened walkway.

Her breath paused in her throat.

The next move was up to her.

Her body screamed, *do it.*

Her mind said, *you're a fool.*

Did she dare?

Curtis stopped on the porch. Waiting.

She turned. "I had a lot of fun."

He smiled. The dimple. Oh, the dimple.

"Me, too." His fingers brushed a wisp of hair from her face. The gesture reminded her of Randall and her heart froze.

She raised her chin. Not anymore, Randall Barrett. Not after the way you've avoided me. Not after the way you walked out of that elevator.

She swayed toward Curtis. His hand cupped her cheek. Her eyes drifted shut and she waited for sensation to fill all the empty spaces. All the spaces Ethan had stormed out of, all the spaces Craig Peters had torn open, all the spaces her own loneliness had left destitute for too long.

It had been too long.

Much, much too long.

Her lips parted, ready for the taste of this man who now pulled her tighter against him.

His lips found hers. They were warm, searching, hungry.

Her hand crept up his neck, savoring the hard columns of muscle and tendon. His stubble was soft and yet bristly at the same time.

He was man.

Boy, he was man.

And right now, all she wanted was a man to fill her up from the inside out and make her forget.

What was so wrong with that?

She ran her hands over his shoulders. Muscle, taut with need, tensed at her caress. She enjoyed her power over Curtis. She smoothed her palms down his chest. His skin burned through the cotton of his shirt, his heart thudding under her hand.

He buried his face in her neck. "May I come in?" he breathed. His teeth caught her earlobe. "I promise I won't snore." His heart pounded, strong, urgent. Alive under her hand.

There was nothing she wanted more than to feel his body in hers. To feel his rhythm in her blood. To have him take over her body and leave no room for anyone else.

She would not think about Tuesday morning.

She would live the moment.

And goddamn it, she would enjoy it.

She took his hand and curved it around her hips while she fumbled open her purse. Her fingers shook, then clasped the cool metal of her key.

Alaska padded to the door. He eyed Curtis, sniffing the proffered hand. Curtis gave him a scratch on the ears.

The normalcy of the gesture snapped Kate out of her passion-induced fog. She took a step away, heart thudding, mind veering between desire and fear.

Curtis grasped her hips. "Kate, don't change your mind now." How did he know what she was thinking? She stared into his eyes. Gray, like the fog that swept over the water. But clear. Strange. Randall Barrett's eyes were so sharp you'd think you could see straight through them, but they deflected any attempts to see beneath the brilliant surface.

Curtis' mouth swept the curve of her jaw. "It'll be good. I promise." He caught her lips with his and kissed her.

Desire burned deep in her. But it wasn't the promise of what she would enjoy that made her kiss him back. It was the knowledge of what she wouldn't have to endure—another night of facing her bed. Alone.

She caught his lower lip in her teeth, running her hands over his chest. He groaned. Her fingers tugged his shirt loose from his waistband. With a swiftness that left her gasping, he scooped her up in his arms.

"Lead the way, my lady," he whispered. It could have been a corny line, but it wasn't. Kate wrapped her arms around his neck and let him carry her upstairs. He held her tight against his body, each step jostling her breast against his chest.

When they reached her bedroom, he lowered her onto the bed. Shadows hung from the corners. Kate closed her eyes. She would not think of the room. She would not think of the doors. She would not think of the secret staircase with the exit right next to her bedroom.

She inched her dress with great deliberation up her legs. Curtis' eyes raked her body. When the hem reached her upper thighs, he leaned down and ran his hand over her leg.

"You are so hot." He grasped the strap of her dress and tugged it over her shoulder.

Kate watched him, mesmerized by the intensity of his eyes as they swept over the swell of cleavage he had just exposed.

A loud, insistent scratching on her bedroom door made Curtis groan. "Your dog has impeccable timing."

"Alaska, go away!" She caressed Curtis' arm. "Sorry, he always sleeps with me."

"He's obviously a very intelligent dog."

Alaska scratched again. "No, Alaska," Kate called.

They waited, like two guilty teenagers caught in the act, only relaxing when they heard Alaska pad back downstairs. It was funny, but Kate also felt a bit sad. Alaska had been the only male sleeping with her since she ended things with Ethan.

"Now, where were we?" Curtis smiled down at her. She exhaled slowly.

Alaska would just have to get used to sleeping in his crate. She couldn't become a nun to please her dog.

She tossed her dress on the floor.

Curtis' eyes traced every swell, every curve, every dip of her body, taking in the lacy bra. The sliver of panties. He planted his arms on either side of her. She gave him a playful push. "Not so fast. Your turn."

He smiled. A slow smile that teased the dimple in his cheek. His shirt was unbuttoned and thrown on the floor in a matter of seconds, revealing a torso that could grace *Men's Health*.

Kate stared. He was so strong. So muscular. She knew exactly how much pressure she would need to drive a scalpel between the muscle and bone of his chest.

The memory had slipped into her mind on stealth feet and sliced through her desire. She had killed a man. Roughly the same age, roughly the same build as the man before her. She swallowed.

Curtis disposed of his pants just as quickly and lay down next to her in his boxers. The fine fabric did nothing to disguise his arousal.

His fingers traced the lace edging her bra. "So pretty. I knew there was a sexy woman under that suit," he murmured. His hand curved over the swell of her breast. Kate tried to relax.

But his hands, so close to her exposed throat, reminded her of someone else's hands. Gripping her throat with a ferocity that was fueled by madness and bloodlust.

She flattened her palms on Curtis' back, focusing on the heat of his skin, the smooth hardness of muscles rippling under her touch. His mouth found hers.

She tensed. He buried his face in her neck. His breath was moist on her skin. "What's wrong?"

"Nothing." She pulled his face up to hers. Her lips grazed his jaw. "Keep going."

"Your wish is my command." He grinned and lowered his head to her chest, his stubble softly scratching. His mouth traced a path down her abdomen, down to the warmth between her thighs.

Kate closed her eyes and tried to focus on the pleasure he was giving her. But despite his skill and obvious desire to please her, her mind refused to engage in what her body urged her to do.

Not for the first time in her life, she faked it. In fact, she'd pretty well faked it all through university. Ethan had been the first to dig deep enough through her barriers to reveal the pleasures of passion. And look where that got her...

Now, as she lay under Curtis, she wondered if she'd ever experience it again. She closed her eyes and let Curtis satisfy his own need. He'd certainly earned it. Within minutes, he rolled off her, sated and gasping for breath.

"That was amazing," he murmured. He pulled Kate into the crook of his arm. His skin was slightly damp, with a not unpleasant tang.

Kate listened to his heartbeat under her ear. She was a fraud in more ways than one. She'd just pretended to enjoy sex. And with a man she barely knew.

How in the world had her love life come to this?

She stared at the darkness beyond Curtis' shoulder. She knew how.

Craig Peters had boxed her into a corner of shadows

and fear. She'd won the battle in May when she killed him. But he was winning the war on her mind. After months of nightmares pounding at her reserves, she was ready to do pretty well anything to keep Craig Peters out of her bedroom.

And really, she could do worse. Curtis was an attractive man and a considerate lover.

His breathing slowed. Soft snores filled her ear.

She lay in the dark, her hand spread on his chest. She'd achieved what she set out to do—she had a warm body to keep her safe tonight.

But although her flesh was hot against his, the warmth did not go any deeper.

She couldn't wait for morning to come.

She couldn't wait to say goodbye to her lover.

Her shoulder became cramped. She eased herself out of bed and tiptoed to the bathroom. When she returned, she hesitated by her bed.

A headache had formed in her right temple. It throbbed a beat of recrimination. Man, she was so screwed up. She wanted to be happy. She wanted to enjoy all the good things that were coming her way.

Curtis Carey had been wrapped up in a very nice package. And had had an unexpectedly soft center.

And she was unable to enjoy it.

Familiar footsteps padded down the hall. Alaska nosed her knee. She wished she could just curl up on the bed with him and send Curtis home.

How perverse could she be?

A loud shout of laughter followed by excited yelling jarred the silence. A whiff of marijuana drifted in through her window. The student flat two doors over.

Kate glanced at the neon dial of her alarm clock. It was 11:58. She prayed the party would head downtown to the bars.

Her mind jumped ahead to Tuesday morning, when she would be facing Curtis Carey and his client at a second discovery hearing.

How could she sit there and pretend nothing had happened? He had stroked her body, felt her desire. Would he exchange secret smiles with her? Would she be seduced by his dimple and regret it yet again? She had an awful feeling Curtis would demand more than she was willing to give.

Music throbbed through her walls.

Curtis snored softly. Alaska jumped onto the bed, sniffing the alien human that sprawled amongst her sheets. He gave her a look that clearly suggested she'd made a big mistake.

It was no use. She would not be able to sleep tonight.

Another hoot of laughter mocked her.

Giving Alaska a dirty look, she stalked to the bathroom and yanked open the medicine cabinet.

There was an assortment of pills, offered like party favors when she was discharged from the hospital in April. Some of the medications had been prescribed for pain, some prescribed to manage the infection of her leg wound. And one bottle had been prescribed for the final trauma that had not healed itself.

That had, in fact, worsened as the months went on.

She grabbed the bottle, twisted open the cap, and swallowed the little blue pill before she could second-guess herself.

The doctor had told her it was okay to use the sleeping pills occasionally.

And if this wasn't an occasion to put her mind to sleep, she didn't know what was.

She returned to her bed, her body an inch from the edge, every nerve vibrating, every muscle on alert, waiting for sleep to dull the pictures in her head.

11

Friday, 11:59 p.m.

As the clock neared midnight, Elise buried her face in her pillow.

The sleeping pill was calling her now. She cursed Jamie for tempting her. *Just for tonight*, Elise thought. *If I could get just one good night's sleep, I'd be able to handle everything tomorrow.*

Just tonight.

She'd really been trying to stop taking them. The last sleepwalking episode had freaked her out. But then Randall came in June and it tipped her over the edge. The anxiety from the pregnancy, the stress from the abortion, the trauma afterward—her body refused to give her rest.

And the past two nights had been worse than usual. She'd lain awake in roadside hotels, worrying about Nick, stressing about Randall's reaction to Nick's decision not to go on the trip, and dreading the moment she'd see her ex-husband face-to-face again.

It had been as bad as she feared.

No, it had been worse.

The scorn, the contempt, the pure anger that had been directed at her.

She needed sleep to deal with this. And the way her brain was wound up right now, she doubted she'd get any tonight.

She threw back the covers and strode into the bathroom, swallowing a pill before she could change her mind.

It wouldn't take long for it to work. She lay down on the mattress. The pillow cushioned her head. Which was already feeling calmer. Lighter. Nicely blurring all the unpleasantness that lurked behind her eyes.

She'd made the right decision.

She exhaled softly, curling her palm into her cheek.

Tomorrow would be a better day, she thought.

Sleep claimed her.

An hour later, so would death.

12

Saturday, 1:15 a.m.

The night was black. Cold and wintry. Yet a chill dampness in the air foretold spring.

She shivered and slid another foot forward, testing the ice.

It was thick. Black as the night that surrounded her. And mushy on the surface. That's what scared her.

Spring was coming. Warmer water ran under the ice, eroding it from the inside out. She knew that, but she couldn't make anyone understand.

They told her to keep going.

She looked around, panicked.

She couldn't see the edges of the lake. From every direction, black ice stretched into the darkness.

The group she'd followed was barely visible. The others were all ahead of her. She was the last one.

No one waited for her.

"It's not safe!" she called into the night. "Come back!"

No one replied.

She needed to catch up.

She did not want to be left alone.

She put another foot forward. Her boot sank into the mush.

She peered down at it. Was it cracking?

She looked ahead to the others, about to call one more time. But her voice stopped in her throat.

Moonlight shone on a long pool of black water. It stretched in the distance. She craned her head. Was it just a layer of water skimming the ice?

Or was it open water?

She threw a desperate look behind her.

Blackness stretched into infinity. No shoreline visible. She could no longer sense the thick trees that had been an ominous, dark presence at her back. When had they disappeared?

She needed to retrace her steps.

But to where? It had all gone.

There was just her and the dark and the ice.

And under it, cold, black water.

It hunkered under her feet, still, expectant.

Panic erupted in a torrent of cold chills.

Stop shaking. Stand still.

She hugged her arms.

A low, primeval groan vibrated through the soles of her boots, echoing across the lake.

The ice heaved behind her.

She threw a panicked glance over her shoulder.

Something moved.

It was under the ice. Coming toward her.

A dark form in the water sliding right up against the underbelly of the ice.

She stared at it in horror.

It couldn't be—

A long crack split the ice straight between her feet.

A hand shot through the crack, chips of ice flying off blue fingers, and locked around her ankle before she could move.

It yanked her over.

She fell, crashing through the ice.

Cold.

The water was so cold.

It shocked the air out of her lungs.

She flung her arms out, trying to push herself up to the surface.

A hand clamped on her shoulder. It pushed her down.

She struggled, kicking as hard as she could to propel herself upward. Her lips, then her nose cleared the surface of the water.

She gulped in air.

A hand grabbed her hair. It yanked her head back viciously. Pulling her, pulling her. Pulling her under.

No!

She arched her back, trying to escape. But the hands were too strong.

She closed her eyes. The water rushed over her. Smoothing the surface of the lake over her head as if she'd never been there.

Her lungs burned. But her flesh was cold. So cold it hurt.

She kicked, flailing her arms, trying to reach air again.

The hands grabbed her neck.

They squeezed.

Throttling one last bubble of air from her throat.

She opened her eyes.

And stared straight into the eyes of Craig Peters.

"No!" Kate bolted upright. Her fingers fought to free themselves of the sheets tangled around them. She clawed at her throat.

"Kate! Kate!"

A man's voice invaded her consciousness.

She leaped from the bed.

"Kate, it's okay," the man said, reaching toward her. His voice was soothing. She backed away from the naked man with the powerful arms. Then she realized it was Curtis. The man she'd slept with only hours before. "Kate, you had a bad dream. Are you okay?" He tried to pull her against his chest but she stepped back. She stared at him.

"Kate, say something."

Her mind struggled to break free of the terror submerging it.

"Kate, please." Curtis ran a hand through his hair. "Say something. You're freaking me out."

Alaska lurched to his feet and nosed her leg.

"I'm okay." Her whole body was covered in goose bumps. She rubbed her hands over her arms. "I'm fine."

He reached for her again. She flung out her hand. "Don't. Please."

His arm fell. "Sorry."

Silence covered them.

Kate longed to wrap herself in the sheet, but Curtis stood between her and the bed.

He seemed to sense her awkwardness, because he grabbed the throw off the foot of the bed and drew it around her shoulders. He pulled on his boxers, then reached for his pants.

"No." Her voice was startling in the stillness of the room. "Don't go, Curtis. Please." She forced herself to touch his arm. "I don't want to be alone."

His eyes met hers. "I don't blame you." He led her back to the bed. After she settled herself down on one side, he lay down next to her. But he didn't touch her. Instead, he said very softly, "Do you want to talk about it?"

Part of her longed to share the terror, but she knew it wasn't something that could be described. It could only be felt.

"No. But thank you."

She closed her eyes. She listened to Curtis' even breathing. Eventually, he fell back asleep.

Daylight was only a few hours away.

13

Detective Ethan Drake pulled in front of the house on Point Pleasant Drive and took a quick swig of his herbal tea. He grimaced. What he really wanted was coffee. Preferably coffee that had been sitting on a burner for far too long. Black, thick, bitter coffee.

But the ulcer he'd developed over the winter made him pay—in spades—every time he gave in to his craving.

He stuck the mug back in his cup holder, grabbed his notebook and hurried over to the sergeant waiting for him at the end of the driveway.

"Ident here yet?" he asked Sergeant Sue MacLeod by way of greeting.

She glanced over his shoulder. "They're just pulling in."

He turned and saw the van slow down in front of the house.

"Where's the victim?"

"She's around back. Looks like she fell off a balcony."

"Fell, tossed or jumped?"

Sue shook her head. "Hard to say. She's got two kids. The son, who is about fifteen, says he heard something but didn't see what happened."

"What about the other kid?"

"She's twelve. She was asleep, she says. She only woke up when she heard someone running down the stairs." The sergeant shrugged. "But I just have a feeling about this. Thought you should come and do a prelim, anyway."

He nodded. Sue MacLeod was a good cop. She'd covered a lot of scenes. She wouldn't have called him in at two in the morning unless she thought it was worth it.

Two Forensic Identification Services detectives approached them. They were dressed in uniform—not bunny suits—and carried their cameras in one hand, evidence markers in another. Their cargo pockets bulged with swabs, magna powder to dust for fingerprints, fingerprint lifters and clear tape for collecting fiber and hair samples.

Ethan nodded to the Ident guys. "We'll do a prelim to start with. See if we come up with anything that requires us to hold the scene."

Sue headed to the backyard. "She's around here."

"Name?" Ethan asked, falling into step beside her.

"Elise Vanderzell. She's visiting from Toronto, according to her children."

"Anyone else home?"

"No. The kids were on their own when I got here.

They're staying in this house while the owner is in New Zealand."

"What about the husband? Is he in Toronto?"

"No. He lives here. But no one has been able to reach him."

"Is he away?"

The sergeant shook her head. "Apparently the victim and her kids traveled from Toronto to see him. They arrived around 5:30 p.m. He showed up just after that but left."

"So she arrives this afternoon and is dead by tonight…" Ethan murmured. "Not a great way to start a vacation."

Sue gave him a warning look. "The kids are still with their mother."

They rounded the corner and stopped, scanning the scene. The fire department had set up lights so the grounds were well lit.

Two Emergency Health Services technicians were putting away their equipment. Fire personnel were carrying ladders back to the truck. One of the FIS guys peeled away from the group and began placing markers for photographing.

In the middle of all this uniformed bustle sat two kids. Blankets draped their shoulders. A patrol officer crouched awkwardly with them on the grass. Neither of them paid attention to him. Both kids just hugged their knees. Both stared at their mother. She lay by the top of a concrete stairwell that led to a basement door. Ethan bit back a sigh. It was obvious that where she had been placed wasn't where she had fallen. Her body was straight, although her gown was rumpled around her knees. A large pool of blood was adjacent to her body but not under her head, yet the signs of massive head injury were obvious even from a distance.

The other Ident guy knelt by the victim. Ethan followed him, planting himself between the victim and the kids.

"It's time for the kids to go inside," Ethan said to the uniformed constable.

The girl stood obediently, but the boy just raised sullen eyes. "I'm not leaving her."

"What's your name?" Ethan asked, his tone gentle.

"Nick."

"Nick," he said, "this isn't something you need to see."

The young man's jaw clenched. "I'm not leaving her."

His sister threw him an alarmed look.

Ethan gave a subtle nod to the constable. The constable leaned down and grasped Nick's arm. "I'm sorry, but this is police protocol. We are conducting an investigation. We need to examine her." Nick's eyes dropped. What kid would want to see their dead mother being examined for trace evidence?

The constable tugged gently on Nick's arm. "Let's go, Nick." The teen stood, his stance suggesting defiance but his eyes expressing defeat. He pulled his arm from the constable's grasp and looked at his sister. "Come on, Luce."

Ethan watched the brother and sister leave. Their bodies leaned toward one another, but whenever the sister got too close the brother shifted away.

They needed to get a child worker in first thing tomorrow to interview these kids.

The Ident guy was taking photos of the victim's body, starting at midrange, then moving in for close-ups.

"Can I have a quick look at her?" Ethan asked the FIS technician. He wanted to get a feel for the victim before examining the crime scene. The detective nodded, lowering his camera. Ethan knelt carefully by Elise Vanderzell.

Did she know she was about to die when she arrived this afternoon? he wondered as he studied her empty eyes.

That was the million-dollar question. They'd have to check for signs of suicide—a note, prescription drugs, depressed behavior. Other signs, like putting out garbage when it wasn't garbage day or excessive cleaning, were unlikely, as she had only just arrived.

A dark, glistening mask of blood on one side of her face had the effect of highlighting her pure bone structure. She was a beautiful woman, Ethan realized. And in the prime of her life, judging from the toned limbs revealed by her spaghetti-strap nightgown.

No markings on her neck. Just a smooth column that fanned out into tanned shoulders and swelling breasts. He scanned her nightgown inch by inch. The FIS detective would use a Lumalight to look for hidden stains— semen, in particular—but the only thing that was visible to Ethan's gaze was a tear in the fabric near the hip of her nightgown. Had it caught on the edge of the balcony when she fell? Or was it a sign of a struggle?

There was a massive bruise on one shin and one of her toenails was broken. He studied her arms. She wore no jewelry. Was that a faint bruise on the wrist? It was hard to tell. Again, he would need the pathologist to determine the injuries and date them.

Her fingers bore no marks of struggle.

He stood. All in all, a fairly nondescript body in terms of evidence. What he observed could easily be explained away if she had hit the balcony or a wall as she fell.

He studied the balcony. It acted as a fire escape, as well, with a set of wooden stairs running diagonally across each floor of the house. Decorative wrought-iron plant hooks had been mounted on the posts at each staging. Those could certainly do some damage to the fine skin of a scalp. FIS would have to examine them to see if any trace could be found and analyze the blood spatter dotting the fire escape to see when and how the trauma had occurred.

Sue MacLeod hurried toward him, her broad, hunched form sending gnomelike shadows across the deep yard. Ethan turned and surveyed the property. His heart sank. An extremely tall hedge enclosed the terraced garden. "Shit," he muttered to Sue. "No one would be able to see anything through those trees."

"Or the hedges," Sue added. The yard was extremely private, to the delight, Ethan was sure, of its owner.

"Could you see any houses from up there?" Ethan jerked his head toward the balcony that hung over them.

"Not too many."

"Get patrol to start canvassing any houses that could possibly have a view."

Sue nodded. "Will do. But don't hold your breath."

He grimaced. He doubted they were going to come up with any witnesses, given the shield of foliage. "Let's see what the bedroom tells us."

Bedrooms, in his experience, held many secrets.

And, remembering the beautiful, damaged face of the victim, he bet that Elise Vanderzell's was no exception.

14

Several patrol cars blocked the driveway, lights flashing. Every other second, the lights flickered over a red Volkswagen Beetle, spotlighting the haphazard parking job done by its owner.

A distraught family member.

From the gray hair and the familiar embrace she gave the victim's daughter—who sobbed brokenly into the older woman's shoulder—Ethan guessed the owner of the red Beetle was the girl's grandmother. He was glad to see the kids had a family member to comfort them. Even better, she might know the whereabouts of the victim's husband.

Sue headed to one of the patrol cars to get the canvass organized. Ethan walked toward the girl and the older woman. They stood near the last patrol car. Ethan glanced in the backseat and saw the son, Nick, slumped with his head in his hands.

The older lady lifted her head, throwing a concerned glance at Nick as Ethan approached, but did not relinquish her hold on the girl.

"I'm Detective Ethan Drake."

"Penelope Barrett," she said, her eyes assessing him. "Their grandmother." She hugged the girl a little tighter.

"I came as fast as I could," the grandmother added, more for the girl's benefit than for his, Ethan guessed. "I left home as soon as Lucy called me. But it's a forty-minute drive from Prospect. Where I live."

She did look as if she'd run from her bed, her short gray hair swirling around her head, a pair of bifocals in a striking blue shoved crookedly on her nose. They seemed too vibrant for the grief shadowing her deep-set eyes. There was something very familiar about her face—she was still attractive, the benefit of good bones—and yet Ethan knew he hadn't met her before. It would be hard to forget someone like her. She was a tall, lanky woman, and her loose sweater and slightly askew wrinkled skirt hung from her spare frame. On her feet were green rubber boots—the type that had a permanent shelf at Canadian Tire—covered with splashes of paint. The colors were too vibrant and eclectic to be house paint. She was an artist, Ethan bet.

Lucy wiped her nose with the back of her hand and gazed at Ethan with an expression so bereft that he had to look away.

"Can I take them home now?" Penelope Barrett asked softly. "They're exhausted."

"Mrs. Barrett—" *Mrs. Barrett.*

No. It couldn't be.

He felt as if he'd been punched.

He cursed his gut for denying him his coffee. He'd have picked this up right away if his brain weren't so sluggish.

Her eyes narrowed. He was sending off signals to her that he needed to control. He forced his face to relax. "Mrs. Barrett," he began again. "You are the children's paternal grandmother?"

"That is correct." The whole artsy getup she had going on could not disguise the steeliness in her eyes. This woman was no flake.

"What is your son's name?"

Lucy stiffened. Ethan glanced at Nick. The teen hadn't moved an inch, but Ethan sensed he was listening intently.

Penelope Barrett's gaze was level. "Randall Barrett."

Je-sus.

Ethan strove to keep his voice neutral. "Do you know his whereabouts this evening? We haven't been able to locate him."

Lucy threw a panicked glance at her grandmother, then at her brother. Had there been a flicker in Nick's eyes?

Penelope Barrett straightened, keeping a comforting arm around her granddaughter. "I do not know where he is."

Ethan's gaze shifted to Lucy. "Do you know where your dad is, Lucy?"

She shook her head. "I kept calling him but he didn't answer his cell phone." Her lip trembled. "What if something happened to him, too?"

"I'm sure he's fine, Lucy. But we need to track

him down. He needs to know what's happened." She flinched. He turned to the young man slumped in the car. "How about you, Nick? Do you know where your father is?"

Nick stared at Ethan for a minute. "No," he said finally.

"But you did see him earlier today?"

"Yes, he came by earlier." Lucy jumped into the silence, her gaze earnest. The muscles around Nick's eyes relaxed. His sister had spared him from answering.

Ethan turned to Lucy and Penelope. "I'd like to have a few minutes with Nick. Could you go wait by your car, please."

"Is that okay, Nick?" Penelope asked.

Ethan's mouth tightened. Most people would just do as they were asked, too traumatized by events to question authority. "Yeah." Nick crossed his arms. His body language clearly signaled that Ethan could talk to him until he was blue in the face but he wasn't getting anything from him.

Ethan slid next to Nick in the backseat of the patrol car. "Nick, I realize you've gone through a very traumatic experience."

Nick's breathing quickened.

"Tomorrow we'd like to spend some time finding out exactly what you witnessed. But for now, I'm just trying to track down your dad."

Nick's shoulders relaxed a fraction. "I told you. I don't know where he is."

"But you saw him earlier, right?"

"Yeah."

"When?"

"After we arrived."

Ethan knew that Randall Barrett and his ex had split in a very messy way several years ago. Yet, she'd brought their kids to Halifax to see him. Had they reconciled?

"Did your mum invite him over?" Ethan gave Nick an encouraging smile. "After all, they hadn't seen each other for a while, right?"

"They're divorced. My mother hates him." Nick spat out the words. But the anger in his eyes extinguished as soon as he realized he'd spoken about his mother in the present tense.

"So why did you come to Halifax?"

"My sister wanted to visit my dad."

"What about you?"

Nick's lips pressed together. He wasn't going to answer in words, but the look on his face spoke volumes. So Randall had alienated his son. Ethan wasn't surprised. The guy was a prick.

Ethan arched a brow. "You say that your mother hated your dad." He decided to fish a little. "How did she react when she saw him?"

A very faint sheen of perspiration marked the boy's upper lip. "She got mad at him."

"Why?"

Nick blew out air heavily between his lips. "Because he got mad at me. He wanted me to go sailing with him."

"On his boat?"

"Yacht," Nick corrected. "My dad owns a yacht."

"And he wanted you to go sailing on it."

"There was no way I was going to spend a week alone with him."

Ethan couldn't blame him. "So did you tell him that?"

"Yes."

"And how did he react?"

"He got angry."

Did Nick realize how this was sounding? Ethan wondered. "What did he do?"

"He yelled at me and my mum."

"She was trying to defend your decision?"

Nick looked away. "Yeah," he said softly.

"Did he get violent? You know, hit you or your mum?"

Nick tensed. "No."

"So what happened?"

"He got in his fancy new car and left."

"Was that the last you saw of him?"

Nick stared straight ahead, his expression wooden again. "Yeah."

Ethan opened the door to the patrol car. The night air rushed in, cool and holding the breath of fog.

"Do you think your dad could be on his yacht right now?"

Nick shrugged. "Maybe."

"Don't worry, we'll find him."

Nick shrugged. "Don't bother on my account."

Ethan stepped out of the car. "We'll talk to your grandmother about coming to the station tomorrow. We need to take a more detailed statement."

"But I already told you and some other officer everything I know."

"A good night's sleep might help you remember

things. We need to piece together what happened to your mum."

Ethan left the door open and walked over to Penelope Barrett's red Beetle. Lucy and her grandmother leaned against the hood of the car. Lucy clutched a blanket around her shoulders. As Ethan got closer he could see she was trembling. "Mrs. Barrett, we are going to send patrol over to your son's house, his office and his yacht."

"His yacht! Of course, I should have thought of that." Relief warmed Penelope Barrett's voice. "He keeps it at the Armdale Yacht Club. It's white. It's called *Ex Parte*."

"Can you think of any other places he might be? Does he have a cottage? Or a friend he visits regularly?"

Ethan used the euphemism for Lucy's sake. Her grandmother didn't miss the nuance. "No. He doesn't have either a cottage or a place he goes to regularly." Penelope Barrett smoothed Lucy's hair, which Ethan realized looked just like her dead mother's. She gave Ethan a warning glance. "I need to get Lucy and her brother home. They're in shock."

"Just give the patrol officer at the end of the driveway your address and a number to reach you tomorrow. We'll need to get their statements at the police station."

Lucy closed her eyes as if the thought was too much for her. Penelope Barrett nodded brusquely. "I understand."

Nat drove slowly down Point Pleasant Drive. It was easy to find the house in question: several patrol cars sat in the driveway.

She raised her brows at the sight of the FIS van. A murder? When she'd heard the original call over her new scanner, patrol had said a woman appeared to have fallen off a balcony on the north side of the house. The watch commander hadn't given any more details.

She'd grabbed her satchel. A woman had died. Fallen to her death. And in an area of the city known for its wealth, not for its crime. That would be attention-grabbing. Everyone loved to read how the wealthy had fallen—literally.

Sounded like a story worth checking out.

Nat parked her car across from the house and gave a low whistle. The house wasn't one of Halifax's Victorian grande dames, but it was still impressive. She glanced at her iPhone directory. The house was owned by Catherine Feldman, associate professor at Hollis University Law School. The law school's website announced that she was currently a visiting professor at the University of Auckland law faculty in New Zealand. She must have hired someone to take care of the place, because the lawn had been recently mowed—although not weeded—and the garden looked as if it was getting regular watering.

Who had fallen off the balcony? A caretaker? A family member?

There was a small cluster of onlookers, a couple in bathrobes, a few others in T-shirts and shorts. Looked like neighbors, attracted by the police cars and FIS detectives combing the property. *Perfect.* Hopefully someone had been interviewed by the police and could give her the lowdown. She had loved weekends when she covered the crime beat in Ottawa, but Halifax was proving to be much more fertile ground than the staid nation's capital. *Take that, Bryce.*

She grabbed her notepad and hopped out of her car. There was surely someone in that crowd with a story to tell. As she neared the group, she realized they were all watching a scene unfold twenty feet away. A silver-haired woman was ushering two kids into a red Beetle. The hairs on the back of Nat's neck tingled. This was the victim's family, she was sure of it. She whipped her camera out of her satchel, taking a picture of the three head-on before they realized what was happening.

The grandmother hurried the kids into the car, glaring at Nat as she sped away.

"Bad luck," a man murmured, nodding his head toward the crime scene tape. He edged closer to Nat. "She'd only just arrived, I think."

With that opener, Nat got her story.

As she left the scene of Elise Vanderzell's death, she should have felt satisfied with her night's work. But she didn't.

The look on those kids' faces had been so desolate. Some days she hated her job.

15

Ethan stood in the doorway of the master suite in which Elise Vanderzell had not even had one full night's sleep. It had originally been a large bedroom in the center of the house that had been doubled by removing the wall from the east-facing bedroom. A walk-in closet sprawled over one wall. Half of the back wall boasted a sliding patio door that opened onto a narrow balcony.

The balcony from which Elise Vanderzell fell.

An FIS technician photographed the bedside table. There was nothing remarkable about it. The clock radio, lamp and travel magazines had the air of a still life. But there was no dust on them. Ethan guessed that the room had been recently cleaned in anticipation of Elise's stay.

Even the matching cherrywood king-size four-poster bed with pale blue and cream bedding appeared barely inhabited. The duvet had been pulled back on one side, revealing only slightly rumpled sheets. The pillow cradled the faint imprint of a lone head. The other side of the massive bed was neatly made. It would appear that Elise Vanderzell had slept alone tonight.

Had she been so alone, so desolate that she threw herself over the balcony?

A large framed picture of a beach dotted with shells hung over the bed. The master suite had been decorated by a romantic, it seemed. Ethan wondered how much trace evidence they'd have to eliminate because someone else normally occupied the room.

He looked down at the floor. Hardwood. Wouldn't give much in the way of footwear impressions, but it was a perfect trap for blood spatters. A large pale blue Persian rug lay on the floor by the bed.

"Get any impressions from the rug?" Ethan asked the FIS technician.

The technician shook his head. "Nope."

"Have you taped any of the floor yet?" FIS technicians use clear tape to pick up fibers and hairs from the floor.

The technician shook his head.

"I'll be careful." Fortunately, the bathroom door was ajar, so he slid sideways through the doorway, stopping on the threshold. The blue-and-cream theme had been extended to the matching bath, with gold faucets and gold-speckled tile adding a touch of luxury. Nautilus-themed hand towels hung from a gold towel bar. The carefully decorated interior was in striking contrast to the indifferently shabby exterior.

But Ethan wasn't here to admire the decorating job. What he was looking for sat on the gold-flecked vanity, right next to the shell-shaped sink.

A bottle of pills.

He snapped on latex gloves and picked up the bottle.

The label confirmed his suspicions. Prescription sleeping pills. But his eyebrows rose at the brand. *Delteze.*

There'd been a lot of press about those pills. Originally touted as one of the best treatments for insomnia, reports surfaced of strange side effects: people driving their cars at night, binge eating and sleepwalking—with no memory of it.

He shook the pills onto his palm and began counting. The prescription was a month old. If Elise Vanderzell had followed the prescribed dose, there should be thirty pills missing, max.

There were exactly fourteen pills unaccounted for.

Had she taken them all and OD'd?

Or had she taken one pill and sleepwalked to her death?

"We've found the husband," Sue announced in the doorway. "Or should I say, ex-husband."

Ethan spun around. He'd been standing on the balcony outside the master suite, surveying the surrounding buildings. He couldn't see much through the foliage. He'd hoped that there might have been late-night party-goers taking advantage of the long weekend who might have witnessed something—but he doubted anyone could see through the hedges or trees. Still, you never knew.

"Where was he?" Ethan retraced his steps through the bedroom. He'd seen enough. There was no obvious sign of struggle. Nothing to suggest Elise Vanderzell had met a violent death. It was now up to the FIS technicians to reveal what could be concealed to the naked eye.

Sue's mouth twisted. "You're gonna love this one. The harbor patrol found him."

"The harbor patrol? He was out on his yacht?"

"Yup. He was heading down the Arm when they flagged him down. Drunk as a skunk."

"Where was Barrett going?" Ethan asked.

"He says he was going on the trip he was supposed to take with his son." Sue arched a brow.

"Why couldn't anyone reach him on the phone?"

The sergeant shrugged. "He says he'd turned his phones off. Wanted some time for reflection."

Ethan frowned. The guy was an act-first-and-ask-forgiveness-later type of guy. And Ethan knew from personal experience that he rarely did the latter.

"Is he down at the station?"

Sue shook her head. "He asked to be taken to his kids."

Fair enough. Randall wasn't charged with anything—yet.

What the hell had happened between Barrett and his ex-wife? The woman had only arrived and now was dead.

Ethan knew that this situation presented him with two options. He'd either end up pitying Barrett. Which he was loath to do.

Or charging him with murder.

16

Saturday, 5:44 a.m.

A cab drove Randall Barrett down the hill that led to the small fishing community of Prospect. The forty-minute drive had been interminable. He longed to be alone. But he was still riding out the alcohol he'd consumed last night. He didn't dare risk driving—especially since the police were now on his case. The cabbie had been eager to chat, but after a few monosyllabic responses from his withdrawn passenger, he gave up.

Now, Prospect Bay lay below them, fierce and beautiful. The early morning tide lapped the dark rocks that made this bay's shoals notorious for shipwrecks. If there were ever a place that could make a man feel humble, Prospect was it. Houses perched on stony edges, anchored there with God knew what. Private fishing wharves poked out from the shore, swaybacked and stilted. From a distance they resembled weathered gray fingers, testing the water. Never quite belonging. Because this bay could not be tamed.

The signs of the community's lifeblood casually

dotted the yards of the village houses: fishing traps, buoys, dories with their bleached hulls facing the sun, a few rusty anchors. But it was a totally different sign warning drivers to reduce their speed that made Randall's cabdriver bark with laughter. "Look over there." He pointed to a reddish-brown shack with a white wooden sign nailed to the wall. "It says, *SLOW—Don't Be a Bonehead*."

Randall managed a grunt. His head ached in a way he couldn't imagine. But he'd never imagined his heart could hurt like this, either.

"Take the next right," he said.

"Whoa." The cabbie braked sharply. The road to Penelope's house was a rutted track. A sign warned them there was no turning. The cabbie threw a glance over his shoulder. "I don't want to back down. I've got neck problems."

"Just stop here." Randall pulled out his wallet and shoved a fifty dollar bill at the driver. He climbed out of the car, the fresh tang of air hitting his nose. Until now, he hadn't realized how stale everything smelled. How stale *he* smelled.

The track was wide enough for a single car. Someone had added a folk art flare near the bottom: on his left, a trio of propane gas tanks painted to resemble pigs smiled at him under a cheeky Piggy's Cove sign—a play on the international tourist attraction Peggy's Cove, just fifteen minutes away. It only served to remind him what little right he had to smile anymore.

Five minutes later, he'd climbed to the top of the track. His chest strained, the alcohol he'd drunk hours earlier threatening to expel. He swallowed. His mother's house sat on the right, the final dwelling before the broad heather tract that reached the ancient granite cliffs overlooking the bay.

Randall cleared his throat and opened the gate that extended to Penelope's front door. It was unlocked, as usual. Even if it had been her habit to lock it, he suspected she would have left it open, knowing he would come here looking for his children.

He dropped his jacket on a chair. The house was silent. It was the silence of wakefulness, not slumber.

He was so tired he could barely think. Yet his mind raced mercilessly. Twelve hours ago he had left his office, thinking he would be setting sail this morning with his son, hoping to mend a rift that was growing by the day.

But he'd had no idea that the rift was, in fact, an abyss. So deep and so wide that a sailing trip would never to able to breach it.

How could he have been so oblivious?

The force of his son's resentment had been as strong as a blow. He'd been unprepared for it.

He'd been even more unprepared for Elise. Everything about her had shaken him. Her haunted, exhausted eyes. The extra curves to her body. The defensive hunch she adopted when she saw him. Like an animal that had been shown no kindness and only expected the worst.

But then she'd gone on the attack and his disappointment, his pain at his son's hostile rejection of him—and, he could finally admit, his shame at how he'd treated Elise—flared an anger that had been suppressed for years, he realized now. Being made a cuckold by his beautiful wife. Being the subject of gossip and innuendo. Being blamed for his son's problems. The list went on.

He doubted she'd planned to blurt out her pregnancy to him. Certainly not in public. But she'd been driven to the point of no return.

Had he driven her to that?

I'll never forgive you for this. Those were the last words she'd said to him face-to-face. And one of the last things he could remember until the harbor patrol found him early this morning.

His teeth ground against each other.

Her blood was on his hands.

"You're up," his mother said. She stood in the doorway to the living room, clothed for the day. Just as he was. Except his clothes were put on yesterday.

"Couldn't sleep." He didn't want to talk to his mother. To anyone, for that matter. He couldn't.

His guilt was overwhelming.

"Neither could I." She'd changed her clothes into more businesslike attire, a holdover from her days managing a bank, a reminder of what the day would bring: the interviews at the police station.

She stepped toward him. He stiffened. He did not want her to come too close. She would smell his guilt.

"Why did you go out on your boat last night?" Her voice was low, as if asking the question too loudly would give it an inquisitorial edge.

He shrugged. He didn't want to tell her he had no frigging idea. The double scotches he'd consumed after his fight with Elise had wiped out that part of the evening. So he said what he guessed his intoxicated brain had been thinking: "I decided to leave early. Nick and I were supposed to go this morning, remember?"

"He told me that he decided not to go."

"That's right. He decided to go to a camp instead."

Penelope placed her hand on his arm. Her fingers were cool, steady.

He wanted to throw them off, but he couldn't do that to her. He stared at a point in the horizon that had the faintest lightening of blue. The juncture where sea and sky met.

When the harbor patrol stopped him, he'd been sailing toward that juncture. If they hadn't intercepted him, he could have lasted for days out on the ocean. He'd stocked *Ex Parte* thinking that a teenage boy would be on board.

No matter what Elise said, he still believed she'd played a role in Nick's decision to not go sailing with him. It was the kind of revenge she liked to exact on him.

And given what she'd blamed him for, she probably thought it was completely justified.

How could she not have told him?

How could she just throw that bombshell at him in the driveway of a stranger's house?

He'd gone home, then to a bar downtown, drinking until the sight of all those people enjoying themselves turned the booze in his stomach.

The next thing he saw were red-and-blue lights, flashing and bobbing next to him. A siren blaring, then his name shouted through a bullhorn. It was the police. They were on a boat.

He'd slowed down his yacht, afraid he would vomit.

Two police officers boarded his boat, smelling the alcohol that wafted off him. They'd informed him that Elise was dead and that they would like him to come to the station for questioning. He'd realized that they weren't going to bother arresting him for a DUI—there was much more at stake than to worry about a charge like that. But he was sure it would be duly noted.

And used against him if necessary.

It was interesting what light could do to a crack.

Nick stared at the ceiling. The crack ran almost the length of his bed. The moon illuminated it. He'd been staring at the crack for a long time. Hours, in fact. He'd been dozing lightly, his anger dissipating into an exhaustion that weighed his limbs but couldn't fully silence his mind.

The creak of his grandmother's hundred-year-old front door jolted his body awake. Then he heard the murmur of his grandmother's voice and his father's, and his anger surged from its uneasy rest.

The crack looked like a fuse. He was at the skinny end. His father was at the other end where some of the ceiling had crumbled. It looked as if it had been smashed with something.

He visualized his father on that smashed ceiling. His face smashed. His body smashed. His life smashed.

Just as his father had smashed his mother's head with a club only five hours before.

17

Saturday, 7:15 a.m.

In Kate's half doze, the ringing phone morphed into an elevator chime. She bolted up in bed, her heart frantically trying to flee.

The phone rang again. Her head throbbed. *God almighty.* She could not drink ever again. Soft snoring reminded her she was not alone. She threw a quick glance at Curtis, then squinted at the caller ID.

She didn't recognize the number.

Daylight picked its way daintily through her blinds, illuminating corners with a false cheeriness that had seemed ominous and dangerous only hours ago.

Curtis opened an eye, gave her a questioning smile. *Who's calling you at this hour in the morning?* his one open eye asked.

She raised her eyebrows and snatched the receiver. "Hello?" Her voice, she was pleased to note, had not croaked despite her parched throat and aching head.

There was a hesitation. "Kate?"

At the sound of Randall Barrett's voice, Kate's headache intensified a hundredfold.

Why in the world was the managing partner calling her at seven on a Saturday morning?

And wait. Wasn't he supposed to be on a sailing trip with his son?

Curtis had opened his other eye and now his gaze was fixed on her face. A flush rose in her chest.

Why, after all these months of silence, was Randall Barrett calling her early on a Saturday morning when she was naked with a strange man in her bed? She shook her head at the gods of the universe. She could not lie next to Curtis while talking to Randall. It just seemed… wrong.

She threw her legs over the side of the bed. Everything wobbled, then shifted into place. Alaska nosed her hand. "Is everything okay?" she asked Randall in a low voice.

Another pause. "Why do you say that?"

As cagey as always. Her tone sharpened. "It's a bit unusual for you to call me at seven in the morning."

Randall cleared his throat. Something *was* going on. "I need to ask a favor."

She had to admit to being annoyingly flattered that he would turn to her for a favor, but she was also surprised. Why not a friend? Or another partner? "Of course."

"My dog, Charlie, is in her crate at home. My mother was supposed to go over this morning to take care of her while my son and I went on our sailing trip, but—" His voice choked off. *What the hell?*

"Are you okay?" she asked, her voice low.

Curtis sat up and edged along the bed toward her. As

if he had a right to be part of what was clearly becoming an intimate exchange. His presence was so suffocating that she forced herself to not hunch her shoulders away from him.

Randall cleared his throat. "My wife—I mean, my ex-wife—died last night."

Kate's breath caught. "I'm so sorry, Randall. What happened? Was she in a car accident?"

"No. She fell. Off a balcony. My kids found her."

Kate closed her eyes. "Oh, God."

"It's been a tough night for them. And it will be an even tougher day. The police want us to give statements." His tone became brisk. "Could you go feed Charlie for me? She's very friendly. I don't think she'll give you any trouble."

"Of course."

"I have a spare key in my office. It's in my left desk drawer."

"I'll go right now."

After telling Kate how to disarm his alarm system, Randall hung up.

Kate put down the phone, her mind whirling.

"Bad news?" Curtis asked.

"Yes." At his inquiring look, she added, "My boss' ex-wife died last night."

He stared at her. "You mean Randall Barrett's ex-wife?"

"Yes."

"Jesus. That's terrible."

"Yes." She stood, yanking the crumpled throw around her. "I need to go get his dog."

"His dog?" The shock in his gray gaze had been replaced with…what?

She didn't have time to worry about it. "Yes. He left the dog alone last night. He was supposed to go on a sailing trip today, so he thought his mother would be picking the dog up this morning, but it turns out they all have to go to the police station to give statements."

She walked toward the shower, but Curtis' next question stopped her cold.

"The police station? Why, was she murdered?"

"No. I mean, I don't know." She glanced at him over her shoulder. "All I know is that his dog is waiting for me."

Her tone would have given a much less intelligent man than Curtis the hint that it was time to put on his clothes and go.

Curtis' jaw tightened. Kate felt a pang of remorse. She'd hurt his feelings.

But she hadn't liked that look of salacious curiosity in his gaze when he questioned her about Randall's ex-wife.

"Thanks for everything," Curtis said. The way he said it could have easily meant "thanks for nothing."

"Curtis…" Kate exhaled. "I'm sorry. About last night. I want you to know how much I appreciated you staying with me."

He pulled on his pants. "Glad to be of service."

Ouch. She hurried over to him, put her hand on his arm. "Please don't be angry with me."

"I'm not." But his eyes told the truth. Curtis had sensed that Randall's phone call had put everything they had shared clean out of her mind. Not something easily swallowed by an alpha male like Curtis. He gave her a tight smile. The dimple refused to appear. "See you Tuesday."

"See you Tuesday," Kate echoed. He left, just as Kate wanted. She resisted the urge to run after him.

She'd treated him badly.

But she didn't know what she could have done differently.

The scalding water she stood under when she took her shower was a small attempt at self-flagellation, but she shouldn't have bothered. Her mind, as always, delivered a much more potent dose of self-punishment than her body could ever produce.

As she went through the motions of removing all traces of her evening with Curtis, her mind taunted her.

Had Randall's ex-wife come to Halifax to reconcile?

Was that why Randall had been so aloof since Kate had returned to work in June?

She scrubbed the conditioner out of her hair with more vigor than was required. Only here, in the privacy of her burning hot shower, would she admit that she was hurt.

There had been something between her and Randall after the TransTissue debacle, she knew that.

What she hadn't known was why he was keeping his distance.

She had assumed it was because of the inappropriateness of their attraction. She was grateful for his restraint, she'd told herself as days passed—and then weeks—and there had been little or no contact between them.

But if she was honest with herself, it hurt.

Man, she was screwed. How could she feel jealous of his ex-wife when she'd died in the prime of her life and left two grieving children?

And, without any doubt, a grieving ex-husband?

She turned the water onto the cold setting and stood there until her body was numb.

Only then did she feel she could face the day.

18

Alaska's tail went up as soon as Kate opened the car door. He hopped out, sniffing the grass edging Randall's driveway. "Come on, boy," Kate said, tugging his leash. She hurried up the walkway to Randall's house, looping Alaska's leash around a column by the front porch. Alaska watched her, his ears pricked. *What about our walk?* his eyes asked.

"Don't worry, you'll get it." Kate rubbed his ears, then slipped Randall's house key from her pocket. "We're not too far from the park."

Randall lived in the deep south end, an exclusive and expensive area of Halifax, close to Point Pleasant Park. But if his neighborhood didn't surprise her, the house did. She was expecting something modern and severely stylish in its aesthetic. It was modern, but not severe. The glass-and-wood exterior sported unpainted shingles weathered to a silver-gray. Lush green foliage, orange and yellow daylilies and a Chinese dogwood flanked the stone path to the front porch. The main door was glass. When Kate peered into it, she could see all the way through the house to the back garden.

She unlocked the door, noting how easy it was to turn in comparison to her old, uneven lock, and disarmed the security system with the code Randall had given her.

A dog whined. She hurried into the kitchen. Charlie was in her crate, her ears erect at the stranger. She barked. Kate smiled at the dog, murmuring encouraging words as she bent down and unlocked the Lab's crate. The dog stepped out hesitantly. Kate held out her hand, letting Charlie sniff her. She knew she'd have Alaska's scent on her, which would intrigue the dog. She pulled out a biscuit from her pocket, blessing the Lab for being so trusting, and watched her enjoy the treat. Then Charlie gamboled out into the back garden.

It was definitely a garden. No, it was more than that. It was a respite, a work of art. A sanctuary.

Kate had not intended to follow the dog outside, but when she glimpsed the landscaping, she couldn't resist exploring. A path curved under a large arbor covered in grapevines. She marveled at the mature hostas, lilies, roses, echinacea and bee balm. A faint scent of lavender grew stronger as she neared the stone patio. Comfortable-looking garden furniture sat in a patch of early morning sun. Kate imagined Randall lounging there on a Sunday morning, reading his paper with Charlie at his feet.

She pushed the image away. It seemed too intimate. And intrusive, given what was happening in Randall's life right now. She looked around for Charlie. The dog squatted in a patch behind the stone wall and then trotted toward her.

Kate was impressed. She never knew when Alaska would obey her commands. Maybe Labs were just born obedient, she thought.

"Time for brekkie," she told the dog. Charlie ran back into Randall's spacious kitchen, Kate hurrying behind her. The kitchen was everything she wanted and could never afford: a large stone-topped island, bleached wooden cabinets that had room to spare.

On the walls hung a series of paintings in deep blues, grays and white. They were stunning—abstract and yet with enough form to discern that the paintings represented the ocean in its infinite moods. Kate peered at the signature. *P. Barrett.* Someone in Randall's family was talented.

Charlie stood by her food bowl. For the life of her, Kate couldn't remember if Randall had told her where to find the dog's food. So she opened the stainless steel fridge, scanning the shelves. It only took her seconds to realize that all the perishables had been cleared out in anticipation of Randall's sailing trip. Just condiments remained. Her mouth quirked at the jar of caviar, the specialty relishes, the Thai fish sauce, the designer barbecue marinades. An oversize bottle of ketchup—almost empty—clownishly towered next to a half-opened bottle of wine with a label that Kate didn't recognize but guessed was very expensive.

It looked like an upscale version of her own fridge.

Feeling like a snoop, she opened all the cupboards, secretly fascinated by her glimpses of Randall's simple white china, his cut-glass crystal wineglasses that she guessed were individually hand-blown by Nova Scotia Crystal and the gleaming bottles of single-malt scotch.

After investigating the pantry with no luck, she found Charlie's kibble in a custom-built pull-out drawer next to the dog's bowl.

Hello, Kate. Welcome to the modern kitchen.

Carrying Charlie's water bowl to the sink for a fill-up, Kate saw the first item out of place in Randall's immaculate kitchen: a crystal glass holding the remnants of an amber liquid sat by the drain. She sniffed the glass. Scotch.

She put it back and filled up Charlie's water bowl.

The phone rang, startling her so much that the water sloshed over her hand. "Damn!" she muttered, wiping her hand on her shorts. She searched the kitchen for the phone, discovering it on the wall by a cleverly inset computer desk. The phone rang again, insistent.

She hesitated. Should she answer it?

What if Randall was calling her?

She hurried over to the phone. "Hello?"

"Randall Barrett, please."

Kate's heart sank. She had an awful feeling she knew that voice. She just hoped the woman on the other end wouldn't recognize hers.

"He's not here. May I take a message?" Kate fumbled on the desk for a Post-it note and pen.

"It's Nina Woods. With whom am I speaking, please?"

Kate almost groaned. She didn't want to admit to Nina she was here, in the managing partner's home, early on a Saturday morning. After he began vacation. It seemed way over the line.

"Uh…" She cleared her throat. "Nina, it's Kate. Kate Lange. How are you feeling?"

Kate could tell that she'd shocked the partner. Nina's voice was even brusquer than usual. "Better. What are you doing there?"

"Randall asked me to look after his dog." So far, the truth. She hoped Nina was buying it.

There was a pause. McGrath Barrett's newest partner was mulling over the mendacity of the statement. "How did the rest of the discovery go on Friday?"

"Fine. It wrapped up quickly."

"Good. I want you to do Tuesday's discovery. I've got some matters to handle."

Kate's headache returned full force. She swallowed. "You aren't going to be there?"

"That's right." Kate closed her eyes. *Just her and Curtis Carey going head to head.* The thought made her sick. "Tom Werther thought you did a fine job." There was a note of grudging respect in Nina's voice. "And besides, you won't be doing the questioning."

"Sounds good." Kate knew she should be pleased Nina trusted her enough to handle the discovery with one of Nina's carefully cultivated clients, but she didn't.

Nina paused. "I'm calling because I heard about Randall's ex-wife. Where is he, by the way?"

"He's at the police station. Giving a statement."

"I see. Tell him to call me as soon as he comes home." The phone clicked in Kate's ear.

"O-kay," Kate said, grimacing to the dog.

But the Lab wasn't there.

Kate spun around. Charlie was not in the kitchen.

She checked the patio door. It was closed. The dog couldn't have gotten outside.

Where was she?

She heard the faint jingle of dog tags.

Sounded as if they were coming from upstairs.

She began climbing the curving wood-and-metal stairwell leading to the upper level. It seemed to float between the two floors. Behind it, a multistoried window ran the full length of the house, showcasing a stunning view of the terraced garden.

"Charlie." Although the stairs felt solid under her feet, she couldn't escape the feeling that she was about to take flight. She wouldn't want to walk down these stairs in the dark.

The tags jingled again.

The dog was definitely upstairs.

She glanced in each room as she hurried down the hallway. Two bedrooms, one decorated in royal blue and very masculine, the other in pale greens and soft blues, sat untouched, but ready for visitors. She guessed they were for Randall's kids. Opposite them was a full bath with seaglass-colored tile, and an office, in burnt orange and cherrywood, lined with books, navigational charts and ancient maps.

A thump at the end of the hall announced Charlie's whereabouts.

Darn. The dog was in Randall's bedroom. It was one thing to look around his kitchen, it was another thing entirely to check out where he slept. Or made love to other women.

A flush warmed her chest as she walked into his bedroom. She hoped she wouldn't see his underwear on his tallboy. But then wondered if he wore boxers or briefs.

Get a grip, Kate. You need more ibuprofen.

As she guessed, the dog was lying on the bed. A low, king-size platform bed, finished in ebony wood, it was spare. Manly. Incredibly comfortable looking. Creamy-white linens in Egyptian cotton, with a thread count that had to be written in exponents, looked crisp against a simple yet elegant headboard of ebony wood. In contrast, the deep rich nap of the chocolate duvet begged to be snuggled under. Kate eyed it, envious of the bliss it seemed to invite. She hadn't gotten much, if any, sleep last night.

Charlie lay curled by Randall's pillow. Her head rested on her paws.

"Come, Charlie."

The dog lifted her head, one eye lazily surveying her.

"Here, girl."

Charlie wagged her tail. *Join me,* she seemed to be saying. *You know you want to.*

Kate gave the dog a wry smile. "You don't realize what you're asking." She deliberately turned her back to the bed. It was too unsettling. Too tempting. She wasn't Goldilocks.

She scanned the room, waiting for her breathing to slow down. Near invisible blinds hung from the back windows. They were open, and sun streamed early morning warmth onto the cream walls.

She turned—and gasped at the sight of a woman standing in the corner, eyes glinting at her.

It was her reflection in the mirror. "You are really going cuckoo, Kate," she muttered. But she couldn't resist glancing back at herself. The scar on her thigh looked as bad at a distance as it did up close, so she quickly moved her gaze upward. Her face was drawn, not what one would hope after spending a night with a guy like Curtis. The only glow she could claim was the nervous sweat she'd broken into when she walked into this room. *Nice.* Just the way she wanted to look in Randall's bedroom. At least her butt looked good.

Fortunately, Randall would never know she was in here unless—

She spun around, eyes searching the corners of the ceiling. Please don't have security cameras in here, she prayed.

She exhaled in relief. Randall's room did not have cameras—and as rational thought overrode her guilty conscience, she realized how weird it would be to have security cameras in your bedroom, although Randall's room did have a lot of high-tech entertainment equipment. A massive built-in wall unit housed the requisite large-screen plasma TV. Under it sat a sophisticated stereo system. She was sure the whole room was wired for sound, high speed and whatever else divorced managing partners of boutique law firms liked to play with when they drowsed in their king-size platform beds.

She waited for a beautifully modulated woman's voice to speak from some hidden computer and ask her for a drink order. Like in *Star Trek.*

She shook her head. *Alaska is waiting for his walk.*

She turned to Randall's dog. "Right," she said, her voice brisk, striding toward the bed. "Time to go, Charlie."

The dog breathed a deep, shuddering inhale of pleasure, rubbing her nose against Randall's pillow. Kate wondered if Randall's sheets smelled like him.

Time to go, Kate.

The dog wagged her tail again. *Come on*, she seemed to be saying, *why fight it?*

The phone rang. Kate jumped, her usual startle reaction compounded by her guilty conscience. She felt as if she'd been caught red-handed. Standing in Randall's bedroom. Wondering about his underwear, his sheets.

Her cheeks flushed.

The phone rang again. Could it be Randall?

And where, in his technologically advanced bedroom, was his phone? It rang again. Close to Kate.

She lifted the pile of magazines that were stacked haphazardly on the side table. They revealed a crystal tumbler sitting in a ring of liquid, but no phone.

Then she saw the cradle for the phone, hidden under a guidebook titled *Exploring Nova Scotia's Waterways.*

But no phone receiver.

The phone stopped ringing.

Damn, it must have gone to voice mail.

Charlie stretched and Kate saw the phone receiver, lying half under a pillow, as if it had been thrown there.

What if Randall had been trying to reach her? She picked up the phone. Maybe he had left a message on voice mail.

Seven missed calls, the call display informed her.

Should she check his messages?

No. She couldn't violate his privacy like that.

Glad to see you have some standards, Kate, after snooping through his kitchen and checking out his bedroom.

Seven missed calls.

But what if he *had* called her? She could just check the caller list. If one of the callers was Randall, she'd listen to that message.

She skipped through the phone numbers. The first one had a Toronto area code. The second one was a different number with a Toronto area code. The same person then called two more times. The rest of the numbers were local calls. But none of them were Randall's cell phone number.

So he had not tried to reach her. But it looked as if his family had been trying to reach *him*.

Kate returned the phone to the cradle. She picked up the crystal tumbler, leaning over to wipe the ring left by the scotch with the edge of her T-shirt.

Her gaze fell on a double photo frame housing pictures of Randall with a boy and a younger girl. They were in the cockpit of a boat. Blue water shimmered behind them. Judging by the kids' ages, the photos were taken when Randall still lived in Toronto. The daughter was stunning, wide blue eyes, thick blond hair, beautiful bone structure. She looked oddly familiar. The son definitely had his father's genes. But not his confidence. His shoulders were tense, his eyes wary.

Randall was tanned in the photo, his daughter leaning against his shoulder. But his eyes appeared strained.

Kate wondered if the person who took the photos was the fourth member of that seemingly happy family: the faceless and now dead Elise. Her infidelity had been lovingly described in the Halifax gossip rag when Randall moved here. It was perfect tabloid fodder: the unfaithful wife who betrayed her charismatic husband.

Had Elise been a good mother even if she hadn't been a good wife?

Was she blond like her husband? Or a dark, striking beauty? There was no doubt in her mind that a man like Randall would have a wife who was as attractive as he.

"Come on, Charlie. It's time for a walk." Something in Kate's tone of voice must have conveyed she meant business, because the dog jumped to the floor.

Kate found the leash hanging on a hook by the side entrance and put it on the dog's collar, leading her to where she'd tied Alaska out front. The husky greeted them both with a low whine. Here was the moment of truth: Would the two dogs get along enough that she could run them together?

After a generous amount of sniffing, they seemed to accept one another. She shoved several poop bags into the waistband of her running shorts and began warming up her thigh.

But Charlie was excited with all the strangeness and pulled on her leash. Kate was impatient, too, impatient to forget her glimpses into her managing partner's private life, impatient to forget her memories of last night.

Ten minutes later, she jogged down Point Pleasant Drive to the park.

And slowed.

A large, dark green home was encased in crime scene tape. Several FIS vans were parked on the street beside it. A patrol officer stood in the driveway.

Almost in the same place as the blond woman Kate had waved to yesterday.

And even though Kate's gut reaction wasn't confirmed

until the evening news aired, she knew that the woman whose death police now investigated was the same woman she'd seen stumbling out of her car.

A stunning blond in the prime of her life. Who had appeared ill. And embarrassed by her weakness.

But had still kept a careful eye on her daughter.

And from Randall's phone call this morning, she could only conclude that this dead woman was none other than his ex-wife.

19

"**Y**ou're starting now, Dr. Guthro?" Ethan hadn't expected the medical examiner to be so prompt. He thought Vanderzell was second in the autopsy cue. He glanced at his watch. "I've got interviews to do with her children this morning. And her ex this afternoon." He looked around the bullpen. Lamond was going through some files, getting ready for a trial next week. Even though this wasn't a murder investigation—yet—Ethan was sure Lamond would benefit from the extra seasoning an autopsy would provide.

"Just a sec, Doctor. I'll see if I can get Detective Lamond." He put a hand over the mouthpiece. "Hey, Lamond, can you do the Vanderzell autopsy?"

Lamond glanced up from his paperwork. "Since when did this become a homicide?"

"It isn't. Not yet. But I think we should have an MCU detective there."

Lamond nodded reluctantly. Ethan knew he was remembering the last autopsy he attended. Lisa Mac-

Adam's. He'd left in a hurry. Ethan was glad to see his partner's penchant for junk food had decreased as a result of viewing the victim's stomach contents. "Detective Lamond is on his way," he said to the medical examiner. "Thanks, Doctor." He hung up the phone.

Lamond grabbed his jacket. "So why'd you ask me?" he grumbled. "I had a great day planned." He pointed to his thick file. His even taller coffee. "You need to start drinking coffee again, man. It'd do you good."

Ethan gave him the finger. "See this? This victim has all ten of these. You'll get to see an autopsy where the M.E. finds trace under the nails."

"Gee, thanks," Lamond said. "So why can't you go, anyway?"

"I have to do the interviews of her kids."

"On your own?" Lamond suddenly looked interested.

"No. With Tabby."

"Ooh, man, I knew you were screwing with me. You take the autopsy, I'll take Tabby." The bullpen erupted in snickers.

"In your dreams," Tabitha Christos said, striding into the bullpen, her black curly hair pulled up in a loose topknot, her tailored blouse and jeans doing nothing to hide her curves. She looked like a Greek version of Sophia Loren, Ethan thought. His grandmother would probably declare him disloyal to his Italian heritage, but Tabitha Christos had that effect on people. And, he said silently to his *nonna,* she *was* sweet like honey.

She gave Lamond a good-natured wink and passed Ethan an extra-large gourmet coffee.

Lamond turned an interesting shade of pink and

drained his cup. He nodded toward Ethan's coffee. "Since you've quit, you could at least give me your coffee."

"In your dreams," he repeated Tabby's retort with an arch look at Lamond and took a sip from the cup. The coffee hit his tongue with such intense flavor that he at once blessed and cursed Tabby for tempting him. He'd have to remember this moment when his stomach gave him grief in an hour.

"You'll be sorry, Drake," Lamond said. He turned to Tabitha. "Just wait till he starts holding his tummy. He's like a big baby."

She watched them with the patient and amused look of a woman who has seen men grandstand for her attentions all her life.

Ethan's body, starved for caffeine, was already buzzing with the jolt. He added one more dig for good measure. "Don't stop for more coffee on the way, Lamond. You don't want to make a mess on your nice shoes."

Lamond slung his jacket over his arm. The sun beat in through the windows. His face lost its teasing expression. "I'll call if the M.E. comes up with anything."

"Remember what Ferguson said. There've also been a couple of break-ins in that neighborhood over the past few weeks—just the usual stuff, electronics, jewelry, money. No one has ever been home."

"You think someone broke into the house and was surprised to find it occupied?" Tabby asked.

Ethan shrugged. "I doubt it. There was no forced entry, nothing was stolen. But the door could have been left unlocked by accident. Elise and her kids were new to the house. And if a thief went into her bedroom and was surprised…"

"But there were no signs of struggle, were there?" Tabby had already read his rough notes of the crime scene.

Ethan took a gulp of his coffee. "I know, I know. But I just don't want to assume the killer is Barrett. Yet."

Lamond threw his coffee cup in the garbage. "Hopefully the M.E. will find some trace under her nails."

Ethan picked up his files. "Keep me posted."

Lamond nodded and walked out of the bullpen.

And so their workday began. Again.

Ethan tapped Tabby on the arm. They'd worked together on and off for the past few years but he hadn't seen her for months. And man, she was a sight for sore eyes. He wondered if she was still dating that lawyer. "Let's do a quick conference before we begin."

They headed into the interview room. Like all the interview rooms in the station, it was small, with off-white concrete-block walls. A panel of soundproofing on the wall by the table and a ceiling-mounted video camera made no bones about the fact the conversation would be recorded. And like all the interview rooms, the walls were scratched with graffiti from suspects who had used a belt buckle or a key to carve their disdain.

"Already have my questions drafted." Tabby held up a slim portfolio. He'd called her a few hours ago, briefing her over the phone. "So who's on first? The fifteen-year-old or the twelve-year-old?"

"I'd like to do the girl first. Get her version and then compare it to her brother's."

"You think he's hiding something?"

Ethan thought back to last night. "Yeah. I do." He took a sip of his coffee. "You handle him, Tabby. He shut down on me last night." He added with a sly grin, "Plus, I think you might get more out of him than me."

She arched a winged brow. "I know you're referring to my expert interviewing skills, Detective." With an M.A. in child psychology and years working for Child Protection, she wasn't kidding. Nor was he. He bet Nick was just like any other fifteen-year-old boy. A woman like Tabby could fuel a teenage boy's imagination for many a love-starved night.

His cell rang. It was Nadine from the front desk. "The Barretts are here."

"I'll be right down." He glanced at Tabby. "It's showtime."

He left her studying her notes and went downstairs to the foyer. Three generations of Barretts were waiting for him: grandma bear, papa bear and two baby bears. He wondered which one would attack first.

Glancing at their faces, he'd put his money on any of them except the girl. She looked too distraught to do much but play along. But the rest...

He was glad they decided to do Lucy Barrett first. She'd give them the straightest goods. And they'd use what she said as a yardstick to measure the truth of the statements from the rest of her family.

His gaze flickered over to Randall Barrett. His expression was bland, but Barrett couldn't control the muscle that jumped by his right eye. Ethan's presence had unnerved him.

Ethan hoped it would continue to rattle him when they got him in the interview room. He was glad to see that the normally Hugo Boss–clad managing partner of McGrath Barrett was dressed in a pair of wrinkled khaki trousers, a limp pale blue golf shirt and leather Docksiders. He had a day's worth of stubble on his face. *Good.* He wanted Randall Barrett in rumpled clothes. And if they stank of his day-old sweat, all the better. He wanted him rank and uncomfortable.

He turned to Randall Barrett's mother. "Mrs. Barrett, I am Detective Drake." He held out his hand. He wasn't sure he'd have recognized her from the previous night except for the aqua-blue eyeglasses. Her short silvery hair was now stylishly coiffed around her face, a touch of lipstick and blush giving her skin the color it lacked when he first met her. Her eyes needed no enhancing— they were the piercing blue that her son had inherited.

Eight hours ago she had been in artist's garb. This morning she was dressed for battle, wearing an elegant tailored suit in a muted blue and matching low-heeled sandals. A single pearl hanging from a chain around her neck like a teardrop caught Ethan's eye.

Penelope Barrett grasped his hand and then let go. "Yes, Detective Drake. I remember you from last night." Lucy flinched. Randall moved toward Lucy to comfort her, but Penelope put her arm around the girl. Was the grandmother just offering solace—or protecting her from her father?

"I'd like to extend my sympathies to you all," Ethan began. "I realize this is a difficult time for you—" He glanced at Lucy. She looked exhausted. "—and I appreciate you coming down to the station to help us piece together what happened last night. We'll try to be as quick as possible." He pressed the button to the elevators.

The ride in the elevator was brief—only twenty seconds, in fact—as the interview rooms were up on the next floor. But in those fleeting seconds, the elevator vibrated with a nervous energy that undercut the exhaustion on the faces of Elise Vanderzell's family.

The doors slid open and Ethan led them down the corridor to the interview rooms. A tall, coppery-haired constable leaned against one of the doorways. She straightened at their approach.

"This is Constable Brown," Ethan said. "She'll be assisting today."

She stepped forward. "Hello."

"We'll begin with Lucy," Ethan said. "Nick, make yourself comfortable in here—" He opened a door to a small room with a table and two chairs. Before Nick could respond, Ethan opened the door opposite and said, "Mr. Barrett, if you could wait in here—"

"Hold on, Detective Drake," Barrett said, his jaw tightening. "I'm going with Lucy. You aren't interviewing her on her own. And my mother will wait with Nick." Barrett moved to stand next to his daughter. Lucy froze, immobilized by yet more drama, her eyes darting from her father to the homicide detective.

"Sir, we have a youth worker waiting in the interview room," Ethan said, enjoying the narrowing of Barrett's eyes at being addressed as "sir" by him. "She will speak to each of your children to ensure their rights are adhered to. If one or both of them wish to have a family member present, we will inform you."

Barrett crossed his arms.

Ethan pulled open the door to Barrett's waiting room. Constable Brown stepped closer to the doorway. "Until then, please wait in here. Mrs. Barrett can wait with Nick, if he so wishes."

"I don't want anyone with me." Nick crossed his arms. Ethan was sure he had no idea that he had copied his father's belligerent stance. "I want to be alone."

"But not during the questioning, Nick." Barrett's eyes entreated his son.

Nick refused to look at him. "I do not want my father or my grandmother present," he said to Ethan. "Period." He spun on his heel and stalked into the room Ethan had assigned him, slamming the door shut behind him.

For the space of a heartbeat, everyone stared at the plain plywood door. Then Barrett turned to Lucy. "Honey, the police are going to question you about Mum's…accident. It's strictly voluntary. You don't have to do it."

"I want to," Lucy mumbled. "They're trying to figure out what happened to her."

Ethan nodded. "That's right, Lucy. And we really appreciate you helping us."

Barrett's eyes sought his daughter's. "You can tell Detective Drake that you want me to be there with you."

Lucy stared at the door that Nick had closed on them. Tears glimmered beneath her lids. She hugged her arms. "I'm okay. They just want to know what happened."

Barrett swiped his hand through his hair. "Honey, your brother did not make a good decision. Let me come in with you. I'm a lawyer, I can—"

Ethan stepped in front of Lucy. "Sir, your daughter has made her wishes clear."

Barrett's face tightened. He looked as if he wanted to push Ethan out of the way.

Just try it, Barrett. Just try it.

"Why doesn't Grandma Penny go in with you," Barrett asked, his voice calm, the look in his eyes anything but.

Lucy nodded. "Okay."

"Let's do it, then," Ethan said. "Lucy, Mrs. Barrett, this way, please." He ushered them through the doorway, then gave one final glance over his shoulder.

Constable Brown stepped toward Barrett. He had a stunned look on his face. Both children had rejected his help. Only now, in the soulless air-conditioned doorway of a police interview room, had he glimpsed the consequences of being AWOL when his children found the bloodied and smashed body of their mother.

Ethan closed the door behind him.

They'd start with Lucy and hope she'd seen enough to give them a gauge of just how much everyone else was lying.

20

"Kate." Nat's voice was tense, excited.

Nat had gotten a scoop. Kate gripped her cell phone, putting it closer to her ear. She was heading to the park, in the warm-up phase of her run, both dogs happily trotting at her heels.

"A woman fell over a balcony a couple of hours ago. The police aren't sure what they are dealing with. But I found out who the victim was." She paused for effect. "It's Randall Barrett's ex-wife."

She knew she was about to ruin Nat's obvious pleasure in breaking this juicy piece of news to her.

"Kate. Did you hear me?"

"Yes, yes, I heard you." She slowed down to a walk, panting lightly. She couldn't have this conversation running. "Look, Randall called me today to see if I could take care of his dog."

"So he told you what happened?" Nat's voice took on the unmistakable treble of excitement.

"Not exactly."

"What do you mean by that?"

"He told me his wife—I mean, ex-wife—had fallen off the balcony. He thinks it was an accident."

"Oh, really?" Nat didn't bother to hide her skepticism. "So why was he hiding?"

"Hiding? He was hiding? Why?" She realized she'd repeated Nat's words like a drunken parody. The alcohol from last night seemed to have killed off more than its fair share of brain cells.

"Why do you think, Kate? His ex-wife is dead. And it sounds like they had one hell of a row before she wound up with her brains splattered on the concrete."

Kate's insides clenched. Nat's blunt words brought to mind a picture she did not want to imagine. Of that woman, blond hair waving in the breeze. Trying to ensure her daughter wasn't going to get hurt by a large dog. And now, dead. In a very traumatic manner.

Her mind jumped to another traumatic death. Craig Peters. Facedown in a pool of blood. She remembered lying on the ground, gasping for air after Craig Peters' hands had finally loosened their stranglehold, watching his blood creep toward her. She had willed her limbs to reoxygenate, to let her escape. But she had been too weak. So she had lain there, watching Craig Peters' blood, staring into his empty eyes.

She had done this. She had stabbed him. She had taken his life.

Had he left behind any grieving family? She had never asked, didn't want to know. But she knew that Elise Vanderzell had left behind plenty of grieving family members. Had her children seen her smashed body after she fell?

She said softly, "That wasn't necessary, Nat."

Nat exhaled. "Sorry. Sometimes my mouth runs off with me."

"I…I saw her, Nat. Yesterday."

"You're kidding me."

Kate's hand tightened on the leashes, although Charlie and Alaska were walking sedately by her side. "I think she'd just arrived. Her daughter wanted to pat Alaska."

"Whoa. What was she like? Did she know you worked for Randall? Did she say anything about him?"

"I didn't talk to her, Nat. I just happened to walk by her."

"Was Randall Barrett with her?"

"No." Kate thought of his face, at the outside patio. Closed. Angry. Bitter. With a shock, she realized his expression reminded her of Ethan at his angriest with her. "I didn't realize he was a suspect."

"Of course he's a suspect. All husbands—especially ex-husbands—are suspects."

Yeah, but do all ex-husbands refer to their former spouses as their "wives"? "Is that what the police are saying?"

"It's what they aren't saying, Kate. They are keeping things very close to their chests right now. But I did hear that Randall was arrested by the Halifax police's harbor patrol—"

"The harbor patrol!"

"Yup. He was speeding out into the harbor on his yacht. At two-thirty in the fucking morning."

"Are you sure?"

"Yes. And he was drunk," Nat added for good measure. "Your boss is in deep shit."

Kate's heart began to pound. *What the hell had happened? Why were Randall and Elise arguing?* "Has he been arrested?"

"Not yet. The Ident guys are checking out the house." Nat paused. "There's one more thing…"

Kate took a deep breath. "What?"

"Your Ex is the detective leading the case."

"But he's Homicide."

"I know. That's what's making this thing so damn interesting. Why would they call in Homicide?"

And why Ethan, of all people?

Did Nat know about the bad blood between Ethan and Randall? Kate hoped not.

Kate had slowed to a walk but her heart still pounded. "Have you spoken to Ethan?"

"Just got off the phone with him." Nat's tone was casual, as if she spoke to Ethan all the time.

"Oh." The thought her ex-fiancé having frequent chats on the phone with her newly returned college friend made her chest tighten.

"He's one of my sources, Kate." As usual, Nat picked up on Kate's unease. "He's one of Homicide's lead detectives. I've got to talk to him."

"You're right. Sorry."

Kate walked through the gates of the park's upper parking lot. It was busy, everyone wanting to take advantage of the beautiful morning. She kept the dogs on a tight leash, wary of cars.

"So what does Ethan think?" The last thing she wanted to know was what her ex-fiancé thought. But she was involved in this whether she liked it or not. Randall—and now Nat—had dragged her into it.

"He confirmed Elise Vanderzell fell off a balcony."

Elise Vanderzell. That was Randall's wife's full name.

It was a pretty, feminine name. Kate thought of the blond woman she'd seen. The name seemed perfect for her. "So is it officially a murder investigation?"

"He's not saying much." Nat sounded frustrated.

Surprise, surprise. Ethan was an experienced homicide cop. He'd be careful with the media. Even with someone as disarming as Nat.

Why did Nat think he'd give her the inside scoop?

Nat wouldn't try using her friendship with Kate to buy Ethan's confidence. Nat was edgier than she remembered, but she wasn't unethical.

And she wasn't stupid, either. She knew Kate and Ethan weren't on speaking terms, although they weren't angry with each other anymore.

They'd gotten past their private grievances. Had recognized their own mistakes and acknowledged each other's mea culpas. But in May, five months after their engagement ended, Ethan had again declared his love for Kate. And Kate had turned him away.

He'd accepted it with grace and regret.

But it didn't mean he liked it.

And it didn't mean they were friends.

It just meant they weren't enemies. Anymore.

"Kate," Nat began, "I know you probably won't tell me—"

"Then don't ask, Nat." She added, her tone softer,

"Look, you're my friend. I can't confide in you if I think it will be in tomorrow's morning edition."

"But do you realize that you are in the middle of one hell of a story?"

"I'm not in the middle of anything, Nat. Randall just called me to ask if I'd take his dog out for a pee. That's it."

"Okay, fine. Look, I gotta go."

"Just one thing." Kate left the parking lot behind her and walked into the park. The dogs stopped to sniff the stone wall marking the boundary. "What time did his ex-wife die?"

"They think she fell around one-thirty in the morning."

So Elise died several hours after Kate had seen Randall drinking on the outdoor patio.

And harbor patrol stopped him at 2:30 a.m. It only took about twenty minutes to motor down the Arm to the mouth of the harbor. So where had Randall been between 8:30 p.m., when she saw him, and 2:30 a.m., when the harbor patrol stopped him?

And why couldn't anyone reach him? She thought of all those phone calls. All those Toronto numbers. Had the calls been placed in the middle of the night?

"Look, I gotta go," Nat repeated, a sudden urgency to her voice. "Someone else is beeping in."

"Thanks for calling, Nat. I appreciate it."

Kate hurried the dogs farther along the path, away from the house where Elise Vanderzell had plunged to her death just hours earlier. Randall's home was less than a ten-minute jog away.

She wondered when Nat would connect the dots.

21

Ethan ushered a rigid Penelope Barrett and a trembling Lucy into the interview room. The girl's thick blond hair hung around her face, brushed but obviously cried on all night. Despite the warmth outside, she wore an aqua blue hoodie zipped up to her neck. Ethan's heart constricted. The kid was shaking like a leaf.

Tabby came around the table and held out her hand to the older lady. "You must be Lucy's grandmother. I'm Tabitha Christos. Everyone calls me Tabby, just like the cat." Her last comment was directed to Lucy. Tabby smiled, her warmth flowing over the cold concrete of the walls. "I'm a child worker. I'm here to ensure that Lucy's best interests are represented during her interview." She let her words sink in for a moment. Then she said, "Lucy, Detective Drake and I have some questions about what happened to your mum. It may be upsetting for you." Her eyes took in Lucy's pale face, her hunched shoulders. "Are you up to doing this?"

Lucy straightened. "I want to do it." Her eyes darted

between Tabby and Ethan. "I'm sorry I can't stop shaking."

"You don't need to apologize, hon," Tabby said, putting a reassuring arm around the girl's shoulders. She led her gently around the table and sat her down, gesturing for Penelope Barrett to take the seat on the far side of Lucy.

Ethan gave Lucy his gentlest smile, feeling like a wolf about to pounce on a lamb.

Lucy met his gaze. Then her body convulsed in a big shudder. She closed her eyes for a moment, leaning back against her chair.

"I really don't think Lucy is up to this," Penelope said, frowning. "She's been terribly traumatized. And she hasn't had any sleep."

"I understand, Mrs. Barrett," Ethan said. "We wouldn't have asked Lucy to come down if her information wasn't critical to our investigation. Lucy was at the scene. She is a key witness." He looked over at Lucy. "But if you aren't feeling well, we'll wait until you are better." The last thing Ethan wanted was for the case to be tainted with the suggestion that he bullied the girl into giving her evidence.

Lucy shook her head. "I'm okay, Grandma." Her face, though, was pale.

"Would you like some hot chocolate?" Ethan asked.

She looked faintly nauseous at the thought. "No, thank you."

Tabby turned toward her. They were almost knee to knee. "Lucy, do you know why we want to talk to you?"

"You want to know what…" Lucy blinked. "What happened last night."

Tabby gave her hand a pat. "That's right. We're trying to piece together why your mum fell." The words needed to be said. They couldn't pussyfoot around it the whole time. Tabby said them in such a straightforward, yet gentle, tone that Lucy gazed at her with relief. Even Penelope's guard dropped a notch.

Ethan studied Lucy. Her eyes were an indefinable color. They reminded him of the bottom of a tide pool—blue, gray, green. Color that shifted and redefined itself every time you blinked. Mysterious.

Odd to see that in a young girl's eyes.

He wondered what she would tell them today.

What her eyes would tell him.

Tabby began the interview with some easy questions, things that would loosen up Lucy before having to remember the circumstances surrounding her mother's death.

"So, Lucy, you just finished sixth grade."

"Yes."

"What's your favorite subject?"

"Language arts."

"Do you play any sports?"

She nodded. "Basketball in the winter. I swim and play tennis in the summer. I was going to try a horse-riding camp, too…" Her lip began to tremble.

"On your vacation?" Tabby asked.

Lucy nodded. "Next week," she managed to whisper.

"Do you have any pets?"

Another nod. "Two cats. Knitty and Purly. They're brother and sister."

"What fun names," Tabby said with a warm smile. "Let me guess—is Pearly white?"

Lucy shook her head. "Everyone thinks Purly means a pearl. But it's the other kind of purl. When we got them my mum was learning to knit. They'd get all tangled in the wool. So Mum called them Knit One and Purl Two."

"Did your mum like to knit?" Tabby ventured onto this uncertain territory with the delicacy of a feline.

That actually prompted a smile out of Lucy. "No! My mother only did it because her therapist told her she needed to do something to unwind. But she never liked it because it was so unrewarding, she said. It took too long to make anything."

Ethan jotted down *therapist—still seeing?*

"Did your mother find some other hobby?"

Lucy's brow furrowed. "No. She was always so busy. She said she'd find a hobby when we were in university…" She trailed off. Her eyes clouded with tears. "But she did do yoga sometimes," she added in a wobbly voice.

"Tell me why you all came to Halifax."

Lucy wiped her eyes with the sleeve of her hoodie. Ethan pushed a tissue box toward her.

"My dad wanted us to come."

"All of you?"

She nodded. "He wanted to go sailing with my brother while I went to riding camp. Then we were going to stay in his house."

"What about your mother?"

"Mum was going to stay at Cathy's for a few days. And then go to a cottage. It had sand dollars…" Lucy's voice trailed off just before it could turn into a sob.

"By Cathy, you mean Dr. Cathy Feldman, the law professor?"

"Yes."

"She was a friend of your mum's?"

Lucy nodded. "They met in law school."

"So after you went to riding camp, the plan was that you were going to spend some time with your dad?"

"Yeah."

"Do you see your dad very often?"

"No. That's why he wanted us to come visit this summer. Because we'd hardly seen him this spring."

"When do you normally see him?"

"Usually a weekend every month. But ever since—" Lucy threw Ethan a horrified look. Her grandmother tensed.

"Ever since what, Lucy?" Tabby asked, her voice soft. "Please tell us. It might help us sort things out."

Lucy darted a nervous glance at Ethan, then turned to Tabitha. "Uh…my brother got into a fight with my dad," she said, pulling her sleeves over her hands. "Ever since that, my dad hasn't been to Toronto."

"Had he been there at all since Christmas?"

Lucy nodded. "But when my brother got into this fight—"

"A fistfight?"

"No. My dad just got mad at my brother for something he did."

Ethan sensed, rather than heard, a slow exhalation from Penelope Barrett.

"What did he do, Lucy?"

Lucy threw a desperate glance to the door.

Bingo, Ethan thought.

"Um…he didn't mean to do it," Lucy said. She pushed her hands up opposite sleeves and hugged herself. "It was a mistake."

"Do what?"

Lucy looked over to the door again.

"You're upsetting her," Penelope Barrett said. "I think she's had enough for today."

She pushed her chair away from the table, but Ethan caught Lucy's gaze. "Lucy, you're doing a great job. I know it isn't easy to talk about things that are upsetting. But it's our job to collect any information that might help us figure out what happened to your mother. The good, the bad, the funny, the sad." His tone softened. "If you don't want to continue, you don't have to. But all we are trying to do is help your mum."

Lucy glanced at her grandmother.

"I don't see what Nick's actions in Toronto have to do with this," Penelope said.

"Mrs. Barrett, at this stage, I don't either. But that's our job—to piece together information until it forms a picture." Ethan's tone was mild, but he was damn sure Penelope Barrett knew full well that a family conflict a few months ago could have led to last night's events. He gave Lucy an encouraging smile. "Every bit of information you give me is like a piece of a puzzle. Some of it clearly forms the outline of the picture. Other bits are like those dull background pieces that seem to fit nowhere until all the pieces are assembled. That's why we want you to tell us what you know. Even the stuff that you'd rather forget. Because it could be important, Lucy. It could help us."

She bit her lip. "Okay."

A flush rose in Penelope Barrett's cheeks. She threw a look at Tabitha Christos. *Do your job. Protect Lucy's interests.* But they all knew it wasn't Lucy's interests Penelope was trying to protect. It was Nick's.

Ethan held Lucy's gaze. "What did your brother do by accident?"

Lucy hesitated.

"It's okay, Lucy," Tabby said. "We're not here to judge your brother. We just want to know what happened."

She swallowed. "He accidentally took some money from my dad's bank account."

Penelope Barrett's eyes widened.

Accident, my ass, Ethan thought. He tried not to show his skepticism.

"And what did your dad do?"

"He was really mad. He flew up to Toronto and told my brother he had to pay it back."

"When was this?"

"In June."

"Was it a lot of money?"

"Um…six hundred dollars."

Lucy's grandmother's eyes were fixed on Lucy.

"So how did your dad expect your brother to pay it back?"

"He told him he could crew for him on his boat this summer."

"So your dad was going to hire him?" Bribe him, more like it. Only way to get his kid on his "yacht."

"Yes. But Nick got a job instead. He earned all the

money back." Lucy stated this accomplishment with obvious pride, ignoring the fact that Nick had owed the money because he had "accidentally" stolen it.

"Did he give the money to your father?"

"Yes. But my dad got really mad."

All these "really mad" episodes of Randall's weren't reflecting too well on him. Penelope Barrett frowned. Ethan wondered when Lucy would figure that out. "When was this?"

Lucy finally seemed to realize what the questions were leading to and she shrunk in her hoodie. "Yesterday."

"When you arrived."

"Yes."

Alarm flashed through Penelope Barrett's eyes. But she held her tongue. Ethan suspected that she now was in information-gathering mode. It was obvious that some of Lucy's admissions about Nick were revelations to her. He could tell she wanted to know as much as they did about what had happened at Cathy Feldman's house in the hours before Elise Vanderzell's death.

"Tell us about the trip, Lucy. You drove from your home in Toronto to Halifax?"

"Yes."

"How long did that take you?"

"Two days. We stayed overnight in New Bruns-wick."

"Why didn't you fly?"

"My mum said she wanted to bring the car. It was easier to carry all our stuff and she was planning to do a lot of day trips."

"Did your mother do all the driving on the trip?"

"Yes. Nick isn't old enough to drive yet."

"Was she excited about her vacation?"

Spending it in Halifax with her angry ex-husband and thieving fifteen-year-old son? Sounded like paradise. At least the weather had been good.

"Sort of," Lucy said. "She said she needed some time to recuper—"

Tabby and Ethan exchanged a glance. Now they were getting somewhere. Tabby said, "Recuperate?"

Lucy nodded.

Tabby leaned forward. "From what?"

Pink tinged Lucy's cheeks. "She'd had some kind of thing done a few weeks ago and she'd been feeling sick ever since."

"You mean a medical procedure?"

"Yeah."

"Do you know what it was?"

Lucy shook her head. She looked down at the table. *Something that embarrassed her,* Ethan thought. He wrote: *Check with M.E. Two weeks ago: Cosmetic surgery? Breast implants?* Elise was a woman in her forties. She could have had some kind of procedure for perimenopause. He remembered his mother had gone through something like that. He added to his notes: *Or OB/GYN.*

Could the procedure have made her depressed? Or subjected her to hormones that caused mood swings?

"So you go to Cathy's house. What happened then?"

"My dad came."

"Were you happy to see him?"

"Oh, yes."

"And what happened?"

"They got in a fight."

"Who?"

"My mum and dad."

"Why?"

She looked away. "Because that's what they always do."

"Was there a reason this time?"

She shrugged, then picked at the edge of her sleeve. "My mother put Nick in a camp because he didn't want to go sailing with my dad."

"So who got angry first?"

"I don't remember."

"What did your father do?" *Hit your mother? Smack your brother? Throw your mother off the balcony in the middle of the night?*

"He got in his car."

"And?"

"My mother stopped him. They had another argument."

"What about?"

Lucy shook her head, tears trembling on her lashes. "I don't know," she whispered. She swiped the sleeve of her hoodie across her cheek again.

"Okay, Lucy, tell us what happened after your dad left."

"We were supposed to go out for dinner. But Mum was really upset. We ordered takeout and then she went to her room."

Tabby glanced at Ethan. "What did you do?"

"I unpacked. We went and checked out this fountain. It had bubbles in it…" Her voice trailed off.

"And then what did you do?"

Lucy shrugged. "I watched some TV. Then I went to bed and did some writing."

"Writing?"

She flushed. "I keep a journal. It's kind of stupid."

"I kept one, too, when I was your age," Tabby said. "It helped relax me."

Lucy nodded, her gaze inward looking. "Me, too." Ethan wondered if she'd let him read it.

"Did you go to sleep after that?"

"Mum came in and kissed me good-night."

"How did she seem?"

Ethan leaned forward. *Depressed? Agitated? Suicidal?*

"Okay. She told me we could go to the waterfront and take a cruise tomorrow." Her lip trembled again. She wiped her sleeve over her mouth. "Then I went to sleep."

"You're doing a great job, Lucy. I know how hard this is for you." Tabby patted Lucy's sleeve. "We just have a few more questions. It's really important you think hard about them, okay?"

Lucy straightened in her chair, bracing herself for the moment she'd been so obviously dreading since she'd walked into the room.

"When did you wake up?"

"In the middle of the night."

"What woke you?"

"I heard a noise. A—" she closed her eyes "—a thud." She shuddered. "And it sounded like some people were running. Down the stairs. I didn't know what to do. It was dark. So I turned on my light and looked into the hall. Nick's door was open. I was going to go down the hallway and then I heard Nick shouting.

"What did he say?"

"'Mum's been hurt!'" She covered her face with her hands. Penelope Barrett leaned toward her, face stricken, and rubbed her back. "'Mum's been hurt!'" She looked up at Tabby. "I ran to the stairs because Nick's voice was coming from downstairs. Then he shouted at me to call 911."

"And did you?"

"Yes."

"Where did you find the phone?"

"I didn't know where the phones were." She glanced sheepishly at Ethan, as if she thought a police detective would judge her harshly for her lack of investigative skills. "I have an iPhone. So I ran back to my bedroom and called them."

"How did you remember the address?" Tabby asked. "You'd just arrived."

"I had the address in my backpack. That's where my phone was. I was just lucky, I guess."

"No. You were very smart," Tabby said with a gentle smile. "Then what happened?"

Lucy looked down at her hands. "I ran downstairs to find Nick and Mum."

"What did you see?"

"Not much. It was dark in the house. And I had taken out my contacts." She seemed embarrassed by this admission. "I almost fell. But the front door was open so I went outside." She sighed deeply, her breath catching in her throat. "I could hear Nick's voice. But I couldn't see him. I ran down the walk but his voice got fainter. So I ran into the backyard."

"And what did you see?"

She was almost in a trance now. "I saw Nick. He was kneeling on the ground. He was holding Mummy. I ran toward them. I thought she'd passed out or something, outside. But when I got close…"

She buried her face in her hands again. Sobs shook her shoulders. Penelope put an arm around her back and stroked her hair. "Lucy, I know how hard this is for you," Tabby murmured. Lucy raised her face. Her eyes were so anguished Ethan felt tears prick the back of his lids. This kid had really loved her mother. And what a way to find her.

Lucy swallowed. "She was dead. I could tell. Her eyes…" She choked on another sob. "Her eyes were wide open."

"Did you see anyone with your brother?" Ethan asked. Despite his attempt to soften his voice, it jarred the silence in the room.

Lucy threw him a startled glance. "No."

"Was your dad there?" he asked.

Penelope Barrett's face tensed.

"No. I told you, he'd gone." Lucy pulled at her cuffs, her fingers agitated,

"Did he come back?" Tabby interjected, throwing Ethan a warning glance. He got the message and leaned back.

"No."

"Did you call him after you found your mum?" Tabby asked.

"Yes."

"And what happened?"

Ethan watched Lucy closely. So did Penelope Barrett. They all knew no one had been able to reach Randall Barrett.

"He didn't answer his phone." Lucy's voice wobbled. As if remembering how scared she'd felt when she couldn't reach her father.

"Did you have his cell phone number?"

She flashed Tabby an indignant look. "Yeah. But he didn't answer that either."

"Did you leave a message?"

"Yeah." She glanced away. "I asked him to come."

"And did he?"

"He came to Grandma Penny's house."

Penelope Barrett nodded.

"Later." Ethan's eyes searched Lucy's.

"Yes."

"Did he tell you why he didn't answer the phone?"

"He said he'd turned it off."

"Did he say why?"

"He told me he was upset and needed some time to think." Lucy threw Ethan a defiant look even though it had been Tabitha who'd asked the question. "He also said he was really sorry."

Tabby said, "I'm sure your dad feels really badly about missing your calls, Lucy."

"He does." Her eyes welled with tears again. She looked at Tabitha. "Can I go now? I feel kind of sick."

Tabby patted her back. "Of course. If I or Detective Drake have any more questions, can we talk to you again?"

Lucy nodded. Ethan stood. Penelope Barrett and

Lucy followed him out of the room, exhaustion weighing their steps. It had been a grueling interview. Ethan glanced at the clock. Eleven forty-five. And they were just getting warmed up.

22

Kate unlocked the door to Randall's house. Both dogs rushed in and headed straight to Charlie's water bowl. Alaska got first dibs. Once he finished, Charlie lapped up the rest.

Kate glanced at the clock. It was just before noon. The morning had gone quickly. She'd been lost in thought ever since Nat's phone call.

Randall had not been home when his ex-wife fell to her death. Where had he gone?

He could have been on his boat. That was where he was found, ninety minutes later.

But why hadn't anyone been able to reach him?

Her gaze returned to the phone that sat on the counter. There had been seven calls to Randall's number last night. When had they been placed?

And by whom?

And had anyone left a message?

As soon as the thought crept into Kate's mind, she

recoiled. Checking his messages would be a violation of Randall's trust in her.

And yet…

Was one of those Toronto numbers from Elise's cell phone? Had she left a message?

Part of her yearned to know what Elise might have told her ex-husband. And part of her knew that she would always regret knowing.

You don't want to know, Kate whispered to herself. *You don't want to know.*

She glanced at the clock. Randall would probably be at the station for a few more hours. And who knew what demands would be placed on him by his family. And his firm. Nina had already been calling.

If Kate put Charlie in her crate now, she might be in there all day. The Lab seemed to sense her indecision, because she turned a soulful gaze on Kate. Then she plopped herself next to Alaska.

"Okay, fine, you can come over to my house." Kate found a notepad and pen by the computer and wrote out a quick message for Randall to call her when he came home.

It seemed like a mundanely domestic thing to do. Eighteen hours ago, she'd been fuming as he left the elevator without a goodbye.

Now she was looking after his dog, roaming his bedroom and leaving Post-it notes in his kitchen.

She hurried out the door, Alaska at her heels, Charlie in tow, and locked it behind her.

She didn't want to get too comfortable.

23

Nick had been sitting in the isolation chamber, as he'd nicknamed the holding room that sat apart from the interview rooms. He had never felt so alone.

Get used to it.

The room had some kind of retro tacky table set that was probably not really retro but just really old.

Nick stared at his iPhone. There were at least five instant messages waiting for him. The number on the inbox increased the longer he stared. They were probably from Will. He was setting up a Facebook page about Nick's mother. Or Steph. She'd surprised him. He thought they were over. She'd been pretty clear about that. But she'd sent him two IMs and they were really nice.

A week ago if he'd gotten those IMs from Steph, he'd have been stoked. He would have grabbed his hockey stick and whacked pucks for hours in the net at the end of his driveway. Then he would've biked over to her house and spent the evening hanging with their friends, grateful he was back in the gang.

But it wasn't a week ago.

It was today.

He was exhausted.

Numb.

His chest and limbs felt frozen. Thick, dead flesh that had no feeling in them. He could poke himself and feel nothing.

Nothing at all.

But deep inside him, under all the deadness, was a burning, fiery core. Like an erupting volcano at the bottom of a cold, unmoving ocean. It spewed a molten anger. It snaked through his veins, pushing the blood through his body, igniting his nerves with an inextinguishable rage.

He had read about teens who preyed on other teens. About teens who killed their parents. Their siblings. Their girlfriends.

They had always seemed alien.

Inhuman.

But he realized now that they were flesh and blood. Just flesh and blood that had been putrefied from an inner rage, a poisonous jealousy or just plain evil.

He understood.

Because he was now one of them.

He turned off his iPhone and put it in his pocket.

He was on his own now.

Until the job was done.

"Nick? Could you come with me, please? We have some questions we need your help with."

Nick stared at the detective. He was a good-looking

guy. Looked as if he played sports. Maybe even hockey.
Nick's hockey coach had always told him, "Look in their
eyes. You'll know if they're playing for keeps. If they
are, let the fuckers think they're going to win. Then
show 'em how delusional they are."

This detective was playing for keeps.

So was Nick.

He gave the detective a brusque nod and got to his
feet. He was about the same height as the police officer. He sauntered by him and walked into the interview
room.

His gaze immediately fell on the woman who sat
behind a fake plywood-topped table. She came toward
him, her denim-clad hips easing around the chairs, her
full lips smiling at him. Her blouse was really fitted and
he couldn't help himself when his eyes darted down to
skim her chest. He felt his heart jump. She was gorgeous.
Like, really hot. He just imagined what the guys on his
team would sa—*they're not your team anymore*. That
thought stopped him cold.

"Nick, I'm Tabitha Christos. You can call me Tabby.
Like the cat," she added with a smile. Knit-Wit and
Purl-head suddenly popped into his head. How Purl-
head would drape himself across his neck. And Knit-Wit
would bat his hockey puck along the kitchen floor.

He'd never see them again.

He swallowed, hoping Tabitha Christos and the detective hadn't seen the tears that pricked his eyes. Tabitha
held out her hand. "I'm a youth worker."

A youth worker?

Was he already under suspicion?

That would really screw up his plans.

He took her hand, barely shaking it before dropping it as if he'd just touched a dead fish.

She led him behind the table. "Please sit down." He noted his chair was facing not only a video camera but also the detective.

He could not let them see what he was thinking. He was so tired, though. So wiped.

He slouched a little farther down in his chair. "Where's my sister?" he asked.

"She's with your grandmother. Having lunch. We ordered in some subs," Tabitha Christos said. "Would you like one?"

"No." He wasn't going to bother being polite with these guys.

"You've gone through a pretty tough time," Tabitha said.

"Yeah."

"Detective Drake and I are really sorry about your mum."

He glanced at the detective. There seemed to be some sympathy softening his gaze, but his eyes were still watchful.

Nick had to stay on his guard.

Why did he have to be so wiped?

"Could I have some coffee?" His abruptness seemed to startle Tabitha Christos. "With lots of milk and sugar. Please." The detective got to his feet and left the room.

Tabitha turned toward him. Her blouse strained against the swell of her breasts. It wasn't like she was being sleazy, Nick thought, wondering why he felt the need to defend her—she just had really full breasts.

Really full. He'd learned from Steph just how delicious
and tantalizing and painful it felt to curve his palms
over that fullness.

He dropped his eyes back down to the safety of the
table. The dark swirls that formed the plywood pattern
reminded him of chocolate. As he studied the swirls he
realized some of them were stains from coffee mugs.

"So, you just finished grade nine, Nick?" Tabitha
leaned back in her seat as if to remove her breasts from
his gaze.

He nodded, refusing to let his gaze stray. *So far, so
good.*

"Did you have a good year?"

He shrugged and looked away. He never had a good
year. But this year was the worst one so far. Then he
realized there was an upside to his plan: he wouldn't
have to go to school again. He smiled to himself.

Tabitha took it as an invitation to make conversation.
"What's your favorite subject?"

"Phys ed."

"Ah, you like sports?"

He nodded.

"I played basketball. How 'bout you?"

The detective opened the door, carrying three plain
coffee cups. Obviously police issue. The coffee would
probably suck, but Nick didn't care. He took the cup
from the detective with a mumbled thanks and sipped
it. It did suck. "Hockey."

The youth worker glanced at the detective. "Did you
play, Ethan?"

The detective took a gulp of his brew and suppressed
a shudder. "Yeah. But I was better at soccer. The ball

is bigger. Harder to miss." He took another gulp and smacked his lips. "Geez, I missed this stuff."

"No wonder you've got an ulcer," Tabitha said with a wry look.

Nick watched the exchange, sipping the disgusting coffee. It was all an act. A little joking to warm him up.

He drank some more of the coffee. He needed to be alert. Ready for the question he was sure the detective would slide in when he thought Nick was lulled into security. Wasn't that how they always did it on *Law & Order?*

"Do you play rep hockey?" Tabitha asked.

"No. I played for my school team." Until he was kicked off. That part he wasn't sharing. Even though it happened six months ago, it still hurt. Or at least the memory hurt. Because he was deadened now. Deadened to all pain.

He shut the image of his mother's staring eyes out of his mind.

"What position?"

He shifted in his chair. "Let's cut the small talk." That was a pretty good line. He could handle these guys. "I have other things to do."

"Okay, Nick," the detective said, his eyes taking on that gleam that made Nick's back stiffen. "We don't want to keep you here longer than necessary." Was that a warning in his voice? "We need to talk about a few things."

"Like?"

The atmosphere had taken on an edge. *It's face-off time, buddy.*

Tabitha threw a warning glance at the detective. Time for the cute chick to take over, Nick thought. "Nick, we're trying to figure out what happened last night."

Over my dead body.

Or should I say, my father's.

Then you can figure it out all you like.

But not before then.

He stared at the thick sludge at the bottom of his coffee cup. What did they use to make this shit? That polluted water all the Halifaxians—or whatever the fuck they call themselves—complain about?

He took a deep breath. He knew he was getting all defensive. He needed to calm down. Buy himself some time. "Can I have some more coffee?" He stared straight at the detective. *Go get it, coffee boy.*

"We ran out," the detective said. "I'm glad you like it, though. Obviously haven't lost my touch. Maybe next time you come in."

Nick was so busy figuring out if the detective was threatening him that he almost missed the look Tabitha gave the detective.

"Nick, tell us about your trip to Halifax."

"It sucked."

"Did you all drive here?"

They knew the answer to that. He stared at them.

"Your mother drove and your sister came with you, right?" Tabitha asked, her voice patient. The tone reminded him of his reading tutor. And it irritated the shit out of him.

He wasn't in school anymore.

And wouldn't be going back, either. Not after he took care of things.

He shrugged.

"Nick, if you could answer the questions, we'll all get out of here a lot faster," Tabitha said. Her brown eyes were earnest, kind.

He mumbled, "Fine." The sooner this was over with, the sooner he could finalize his plan.

"How was your mother on the drive?"

"Fine."

"But she was recuperating from something?" The specificness of the question made Nick dart a look at Ethan's notepad. Something was written on it. And underlined. Sometimes he could read upside down better than right side up, so he tried to study the words without them seeing him, but the detective inched the notepad away and covered it with his hand.

What had Lucy told them?

Now he felt like the sucker with the blindfold in blind man's bluff. He'd always hated that game. Always hated not knowing who was out there. Around him. Taunting him.

"Yeah. Some medical procedure."

"Do you know what it was?"

"No." Although he suspected what his mother had done. And he didn't want to think about it. Didn't want to know.

"So when you arrived at Dr. Feldman's house, did you unload the car, check out the new place, have a barbecue?"

Why were they asking him this shit? Lucy would have already told them. He crossed his arms. "No."

"What did you do when you arrived at the house?" Tabitha's gaze challenged him. *Come on, be a man. You can do better than this sulky shit. You* are *better than this,* her eyes seemed to tell him.

Maybe he once had been. But not anymore. Last night had changed all that.

He shrugged. "Nothing."

"Okay. What did your mother and sister do?"

He exhaled heavily. He wasn't going to lie. About this part, at least. The fewer things to trip him up, the better.

"They started unloading the car. My dad showed up."

"And?"

"He got mad at me. Like he always does."

"Why does he get mad at you, Nick?" Tabitha asked, her voice soft. Too soft. It was really pissing him off. He wasn't a kid anymore.

"Because I'm not a chip off the old blockhead."

"You look a lot like him."

"But I'm not him, okay! I'm. Not. Like. My. Father." He fought to control his temper. That would haunt him to the rest of his days. Looking in the mirror and seeing his father's face. *The bastard.*

"What's your father like?"

"He's full of shit."

The detective seemed to nod to himself. He jotted something on the notepad.

"Why don't you get along with your dad, Nick?"

Nick crossed his arms. "Because I'm not smart enough for him. I'm always making mistakes."

"You mean mistakes at school?"

"Yeah." Those were just the tip of the iceberg, but they didn't need to know about the rest. Getting caught for cheating. Getting kicked off the team. Taking money out of his father's account. They didn't need to know about that stuff.

"But he couldn't have been mad at you about school this time, Nick. School's been out for a month."

"He wanted me to go sailing with him. I didn't want to go."

"Why didn't you want to go?" There was a forced casualness to the question that put Nick on edge. What did they know?

What had his little sister told them?

She wouldn't have said anything on purpose. But she was too trusting. They could've weaseled something out of her before she knew what was what.

He held Tabitha's gaze. "I wanted to go to a camp, instead."

The detective wrote something on his notepad. *Shit.* Lucy had told them something.

"Did you tell your father that?"

"My mum did." He shifted in his chair. "He got really mad."

"What did he do?"

"He blamed it on her. They had a fight. Then he drove off."

"Did you see him again last night?"

His breath stopped in his throat. He felt his palms prick with sweat. Then he realized he had the perfect answer. "Yeah. At my grandmother's. He came to her house this morning."

He rubbed his palms lightly over his shorts. He was still in control of this.

"Okay, Nick, we need to ask you about what happened yesterday after your father left. What did you do?"

"I unpacked my stuff. Then I set up my laptop and downloaded some photos." He remembered his sullenness about not going out for supper. They'd just arrived and she'd gone to her room. *Some way to start a vacation,* he'd thought. He glanced down at his hands. "Then I was hanging out in my room. Syncing my iPhone and stuff."

"Did you go to sleep?"

"No."

"Did you talk to your mother at all that night?"

He swallowed. He had heard his mother leave her room to say good-night to Lucy. He had heard her footsteps hesitate outside his room. She wanted to talk to him. He'd sensed her need through the door. But he'd done nothing. "No."

"Was your room next to your mother's?"

"Yes."

"Did you go to sleep after that?"

"No."

"So you were awake the whole time?"

"Yes."

The detective and the babe exchanged glances. "Did you hear or see anything before your mother's fall?"

He stared at his fingers. "I heard a thump."

Ethan glanced at his notes. "From outside?"

"No. Inside her room."

"And where were you?"

"In my room. On my iPhone," he added.

"What time was this?"

He shrugged. "I don't know. It was after midnight."

"How big a thump was it? Was it like someone jumping to their feet, or someone falling off a bed?"

"I guess it was like someone bumping into something."

The detective wrote that down.

"Then what happened?"

"I thought my mother was going to the bathroom." He couldn't admit he thought his mother was coming to talk to him and he'd held his breath in the dark, praying she wouldn't. Because he'd give anything to have acted differently.

"Did you hear a toilet flush or the taps run?" the detective asked.

"No. Then I heard the sliding door open."

"How many minutes later?"

"One, maybe two." Nick shrugged. The detective's eyes narrowed. He hadn't liked the casualness of the gesture.

"You could hear it from your room? Weren't your earbuds plugged in?"

"I wasn't listening to any music then."

"Why did you think you could hear the door slide open? Was it squeaky?"

"No. It sounded like it hit the stop at the end of the runners really hard. Sort of like it bounced against something."

"Then what happened?"

Nick breathed in deeply. This was the crucial time. They were closing in for the kill.

24

"I heard my mother moan," Nick said.

"Why did she do that?" The detective's eyes did not leave Nick's face.

Sweat pricked the back of his neck. "I don't know."

"What did you do?"

"I jumped off my bed and ran to the door in my bedroom."

"The sliding door?"

"Yeah."

"What happened when you got to the deck?"

Nick looked away. "I tripped."

"You tripped?" The detective stared at him. As if he was trying to figure out if he was lying or not.

Nick met his gaze. "Yeah. There was this pot by the end of the door and I didn't see it, it was dark and I ran right into it…"

When he raised his head, he'd seen a man ten feet away. His back was to Nick. He had a stocking over his head.

Nick's hands clenched. Then he realized he'd made fists. He unlocked his fingers, smoothing them over his shorts.

"Did you fall?" Tabitha asked, her eyes sympathetic.

"Yeah."

"Did you hurt yourself?" The detective did a quick once-over of Nick's exposed skin. Checking for proof of his fall.

"Nah."

The sweat on the back of Nick's neck turned icy. He knew what the detective was after—he'd seen enough *CSI*. They were hoping he'd cut himself and left some DNA somewhere.

"Okay, Nick, I want you to pretend that your eyes are like a video camera. Tell us what the video saw after you fell on the deck."

Nick had stared, frozen with shock.

The man had his back to Nick. But he could see something white fluttering from the man's arm. It looked like a sheet. The man raised his arm. He held a small club. It was black, heavy.

He smashed his arm down. Nick heard a whimper. His heart stopped at the sound. It was his mother. What he'd thought was a white sheet was his mother's nightgown.

And the man who'd struck his mother with a club was his father. Nick recognized his shoulders. A stocking covered his father's head, but he could see his telltale blond hair crushed against his skull.

Nick swallowed. "I looked up. I heard a noise at the railing."

"What kind of noise?" the detective asked.

"Like someone climbing over the rail."

"*Climbing* over the rail?" The detective's eyes narrowed.

Nick nodded.

His father lifted his mother over the rail as though he was dumping a sack of potatoes.

"No!" Nick tried to shout but his voice had been paralyzed with horror. He lunged toward his father. Toward his mother.

"Are you sure, Nick?" Tabitha asked.

"Yeah."

"And what did the video capture?" the detective asked.

"My mother. She had her leg over the rail. About to jump."

"Jump or fall?"

"Jump."

Then his father dropped her.

He saw the white floating beyond the black wrought-iron rail. Then his mother's long smooth legs...her feet... her pale pink polished toes...

His father spun on his heel and ran through the sliding door back into his mother's bedroom.

Nick closed his eyes. *I'm sorry, Mum. It's only for a few days. Then the real truth will come out.* He exhaled heavily.

"So the video filmed your mother jumping over the rail?"

"Let's just cut the video shit, okay?" It cut too close to home. The scene replayed itself in his head endlessly. He couldn't get it to stop. And the coffee that son-of-a-bitch detective had made him roiled in his stomach, churning his anger. "I saw my mother jump over the fucking balcony." He glared at the detective. "Make sure you write that down on your fucking notepad." He jumped to his feet. "I'm done." He stalked toward the door.

The detective pushed back his chair and blocked his path. "Just a sec, Nick."

"Nick," Tabitha said. "I know how hard this is."

You have no fucking idea. Telling the cops that his mother had killed herself had almost killed *him*. But it was the only thing he could think of to get the cops off his father's trail. He needed to keep them away from his father until Nick was done with him.

I'll make you pay, Dad.

I'll make you pay for this.

"Nick, please sit down."

"I'm done," Nick said again. He wasn't going to let this guy tell him what to do.

"Nick, we are trying to solve the questions around your mother's death. We need your help." Tabitha's eyes searched his. "Can you help us, please?"

He stared at her, his brain flying. He didn't want to answer any more questions; he was scared they'd trap him. But it was obvious they weren't going to let him be.

He lowered himself to the chair. "How much longer?"

"We just need to make sure you understand what you told us."

"I know what I said."

"You told us your mother jumped over the rail."

"Yes."

"Was she awake?"

That question startled him. Weren't most people awake when they killed themselves?

Then he answered his own question. Not if they took pills...

And his mother had sleeping pills.

He hadn't thought of it, but maybe it would be even better if it seemed she was strung out on pills...but could they figure out she hadn't been?

He pressed his palms into his shorts. He didn't know what to say. Should he say she was awake? Or asleep?

He felt their eyes on him.

He knew it was important he got it right.

His heart hammered.

No. Don't psych yourself out.

It was just like writing a test. When he thought too hard about the answer it made him clumsy.

He always got the answer wrong.

They were waiting for him to crack.

"I don't know." That was safe. That was a good answer.

The detective wrote something on his pad.

"Did she moan again?"

"No." His mother *had* moaned. Whimpered.

He would never forget the sound.

She'd sounded so defenseless.

And he hadn't been able to save her.

He felt sweat bead his brow.

He glanced at the detective. The cop was watching him closely.

Too closely.

He was sure he saw Nick sweating.

"Did she see you?"

Oh, God. The question stabbed him. It was a physical pain. Through the numbness. Through the deadness of his flesh.

He had seen her eyes through the railing.

In a flash.

A split second.

Had she actually seen him?

He didn't know.

He hoped not.

Then her last thought would have been of how her son hadn't saved her.

His throat tightened. His heart pounded.

He could barely breathe.

"Nick…" Tabitha Christos' voice was a soft murmur in his ear. She was leaning over him. "Nick. Just breathe slowly. In." She breathed in. "Out." She exhaled.

He let her guide him. He needed to control his emotions.

He couldn't let himself be at the mercy of his feelings anymore.

"No," he whispered, his voice unrecognizable. "No. She didn't."

"Did she say anything? Was she mumbling or talking in her sleep?"

"I don't know. It happened so fast."

It was true. It did happen so fast. A blur of pain, rage, loss.

"So after your mother jumped over the rail," Tabitha said quietly, "what did you do?"

Nick chased his father out of his mother's bedroom.

His father ran into the hallway and leaped down the stairs. But Nick was gaining ground. He could almost grasp his shirt.

Then Lucy shouted, "Nick! Nick!" And in that split second of hesitation, his father ran through the front door.

Nick yelled over his shoulder for Lucy to call 911. He lunged through the door. His father ran into Point Pleasant Park. Nick hesitated. Should he follow him? Or look after his mother?

His mother lay on the ground. Injured. She needed his help.

"I ran outside to help her. But I was too late." He shook his head. "I was too fucking late."

Tabitha put her hand over his. "Nick, you can't blame yourself."

Oh, yeah?

Yeah. I can.

The detective said nothing. Just looked at him.

"Then the ambulance came—Lucy had woken up when she heard me running down the stairs and I got her to call them." He stood. "You guys know the rest."

Tabitha rose, as well. The detective just watched him.

"Can I go now?"

Tabitha and the detective exchanged glances. She seemed to be urging him to let Nick go. He glanced at his notes, then looked up at Nick. "We're done for today. But we may have more questions."

Nick was sure they'd have more questions.

He wasn't sure how long the suicide story would stand up.

25

Over the past hour and a half, Randall's initial shock, pain and humiliation at the rejection by his children had flattened into a heavy numbness in his chest.

Randall knew the police would start with the kids first. They had been on the scene. But he also knew that whatever his kids told them, they would try to use against him. Unless, of course, Elise's death was ruled accidental. Or suicide.

He rubbed his face. He couldn't believe she was dead.

His beautiful, fucked-up ex-wife.

Guilt and sorrow pulled his heart, one way, then the next. A tug-of-war that could not be won. Minute by minute his heart was being shredded into long, ragged strips of remorse.

Ethan pulled his cell out of his pocket. Time to check in with the twilight zone, aka the path lab. "Lamond, anything interesting so far?"

"Just the usual. They've completed the pictures, done the Lumalight—"

"That show any trace?"

"Nothing so far. She's clean as a whistle. No sex, no blood and no rock 'n' roll."

"So she wasn't a drug user?"

"No signs of needle tracks or cocaine residue."

"How about her fingernails?"

"The M.E. has done the swabs but there wasn't anything obvious."

"Any signs of struggle?"

"A few bruises and a scrape on her thigh, but that could have been from the fall."

Interesting. So if someone had killed her, she had either been completely taken by surprise or she had trusted her killer.

"Okay, here's something to get the M.E. to check out. Her daughter says that the victim had some kind of procedure done a few weeks ago that made her feel sick. I'm thinking it was either cosmetic or something relating to female problems. You know, an OB/GYN-type of thing."

"Okay, I'll pass that on."

"I'm interviewing the ex-husband next, if anything else comes up."

"Roger."

"And Lamond...? I'd skip lunch if I were you. Remember what happened the last time you looked in someone's stomach."

Ethan popped three Tums into his mouth and chewed, then stretched. He needed to be calm, relaxed, despite the adrenaline that surged through him.

He glanced over at Brown. She was giving the faxed report from the harbor patrol a final once-over. Tabby sat at the other end of the boardroom table, analyzing their notes.

"You ready?" he asked Brown, grabbing his portfolio. Ethan wouldn't be in the interview room. He would be in the room next to it, watching the video playback and listening to Randall's statement through headphones.

Brown stood, her six-one frame always eye catching, especially since it was crowned with coppery shoulder-length hair. Her freckled features were lightly tanned, bringing out the green in her hazel eyes. All in all, Liv "Copper" Brown was a striking woman. That wasn't why Ethan asked her to do the interview. He doubted Randall Barrett would be distracted by Brown's looks. He wanted Brown because her no-nonsense manner would help defuse the animosity that Randall harbored toward him.

She nodded. "Let's do it."

He walked into the small room off to the side of the main interview rooms, and sat down behind a desk with a monitor, placing his notepad next to it. He put the headphones on.

Brown walked into the interview room with Barrett. He sat down behind the table. He stared right into the camera at Ethan. Even though he was unshaven, his face drawn with exhaustion, his eyes were sharp. Focused.

Ethan leaned forward.

"Where are my kids?" Barrett demanded. His eyes drilled into Ethan's through the camera lens. *You fucker,* they screamed at him.

"Having lunch," Brown said, her voice calm. Cheerful, even. "They'll be waiting for you to finish up in here." A clear message that it was Barrett, not the police, who was keeping him from his kids.

Barrett gave a final glare into the camera, then turned his gaze to Brown. "Let's move this along."

Brown ran through the routine statements about the interview being recorded, then said, "Mr. Barrett, I'm very sorry about your wife's death. As you know, we are trying to determine what caused it."

Barrett had not missed Brown's deliberate slip of the tongue. His voice crisp, he said, "Elise was my ex-wife. We'd been divorced for three years."

"Can you tell me why she came to Halifax?"

"She was bringing my children. We were going to spend several weeks together."

"All of you?"

Barrett shifted. "No." Then he added, "Elise was going to rent a cottage on the south shore and spend the month there."

"And what were you going to do with your kids?" Brown's voice remained sympathetic throughout. Ethan knew her hazel eyes would be concerned, empathetic. Not revealing that they knew Barrett's plans had been thwarted by Nick at the outset.

"Lucy was going to a riding camp the first week. Nick and I were going on a cruise."

"On your yacht?"

"Yes."

"When were you planning to go?"

"Today."

"Did you see your family before your wife's accident?"

"Yes."

"When?"

"I stopped by after I left work yesterday."

"How did you know they had arrived?"

He shrugged. "I guessed."

"And what was your ex-wife's state of mind?"

He gave a wry look. "She wasn't overjoyed to see me, if that's what you were wondering."

Brown gave a little chuckle. "I hear ya. My ex never greets me with open arms, either."

Ethan felt himself relax. Brown was doing a good job warming up Barrett.

"So what happened?"

"I hugged my daughter, Lucy. Then Elise told me that Nick wanted to go to a camp."

"How did you feel about that?"

He shrugged. "I was disappointed. I was looking forward to spending some time with him."

"So what did you do?"

Would he admit to the arguments? Ethan almost hoped he wouldn't. But he knew Barrett was too smart to make such an obvious mistake.

Barrett's eyes met Brown's. "I spoke harshly to my son. And my ex-wife."

"What did they do?"

"Nick went into the house. I decided it was time to leave. But Elise was upset and stopped my car." He looked away. "We argued for a bit more and then she went into the house."

"So you argued the whole time about Nick's decision to go to a camp?"

Randall's mouth twisted. "You know what it's like

with ex-spouses, Detective. A little issue can be debated for a very long time."

"Did she seem more upset than usual to you, Mr. Barrett?"

"Elise was an extremely warm person. A very devoted mother. But she had problems with anxiety." He crossed his arms. "It was difficult to discuss things with her."

"So, how was she yesterday?"

He looked at a point just to the right of the camera. His gaze was inward, thoughtful.

Was it an act? Was he trying to appear that he was reflecting on Elise's condition? Would he try to make her seem unbalanced to deflect attention from him?

When he spoke, his voice was soft, and Ethan strained to hear. "She was distraught. Upset. I think the drive to Halifax might have taken a toll on her."

"Why, was she a nervous driver?"

"A little. But she also relied on sleeping pills. She wouldn't take them if she was driving for a length of time. She was worried it would affect her reflexes."

So far, everything he said was consistent with what they'd found.

"Do you think she was overtired?"

His gaze flickered. It was almost imperceptible. But it was there. "Yes."

"Do you think there was more to it than sleep deprivation?"

"I don't know."

"Did Elise ever have problems with depression?"

"She had postpartum depression. With both our kids."

"And your youngest is twelve?"

He nodded.

"Any depression since then?"

"I know she found the divorce difficult."

"Did she seek any medical treatment?"

"She saw a therapist."

"And what about now? Was she seeing one?"

"I don't know. We didn't share that kind of information with each other." He rubbed his jaw.

Brown's voice was very quiet in the room. "Do you think your ex-wife might have chosen to take her own life, Mr. Barrett?"

Barrett jerked back in his chair. "No. I mean, I don't know." He fell silent. A minute ticked by. "It's a possibility."

"But one you hadn't considered?"

"It crossed my mind, but Elise was a devoted mother." He stopped abruptly. Cleared his throat. "I hadn't thought she'd leave her children."

Brown leaned closer. "What do *you* think happened, Mr. Barrett? How did Elise fall?"

Barrett exhaled slowly. "I thought she'd taken one of those damn pills. They've made her sleepwalk before. Lucy told me."

"So you think she sleepwalked?"

"Yes. She was in an unfamiliar house. I think she just walked out the door and fell over the balcony."

"Were you there?" Brown asked very softly. "Had you gone back to smooth things over?" Her tone encouraged him to admit it.

He started. "No. I was on my yacht."

"Why were you on your yacht?"

"I like being on it."

Brown allowed a hint of disbelief in her voice. "What time did you go to your yacht?"

There. Just the slightest flicker of his eyelid.

Barrett shrugged. "I don't know. I wasn't paying attention to the time."

"Where were you before you went to your yacht?"

"I was at a bar. Having a drink."

Brown raised a brow. "How many drinks?"

Barrett shot her a look of disgust. "You've seen the harbor patrol's report. You know I had too many." Ethan studied Barrett's face. He looked like crap. Circles under his eyes, skin pale, clammy.

"How many?"

Barrett gave her a level look. "Enough."

They weren't going to get any more out of him. Brown shifted gears. "So what did you do when you got to your yacht?"

Again, a split second of hesitation. Then he said, "I took my boat out."

"According to harbor patrol, you were under motor. And moving quickly." Her tone was bland. "After you returned to shore—" no mention of the fact that harbor patrol escorted him back, Ethan noted with approval "—what did you do?"

"The harbor patrol had told me what had happened. I was worried about my kids. They told me they were at my mother's, so I took a cab to her house in Prospect." He glanced up at the camera. *He knows I'm listening,* Ethan thought. "I'm exhausted, Detective Brown. I haven't had any sleep. Are you done?"

"Yes. Thank you for all your help, Mr. Barrett."

Brown stood and held the door open for Barrett. Barrett strode to the door, his face marked by fatigue.

Ethan shut off the equipment and waited until they'd gone back into the waiting room before following. The kids were slumped in chairs. The food the police had ordered for them had been barely touched. "Your mother is just about finished, Mr. Barrett." Ethan looked at the kids. "Thank you for your help during such a difficult time."

Warren opened the door and brought in Penelope Barrett. For the first time, she looked her age.

Barrett stood and took his mother's arm. "Let's go." The kids rose, suddenly energized with the knowledge they didn't have to sit in this windowless, airless room any longer. Ethan led the way to the front entrance. Everyone was silent. Spent. Numb.

Ethan held open the main doors. Beyond them, the sky stretched out, blue and more blue, like a Walt Disney World brochure. Sugary sweet and just an illusion.

"David called me," Penelope told Randall as they walked to the car.

He glanced at his mother. David was Elise's father. "And? Are they able to come?"

She shook her head, sympathy softening her sharp blue gaze. "He's really distraught. He wants to come, but Jane just can't travel anymore. She's hooked up to oxygen now." Jane, Elise's mother, had had a debilitating stroke two years ago.

"So what are they going to do?"

"They've asked me to keep them abreast of what's happening here. I, of course, said yes. David's going to work on the funeral arrangements." Her voice had dropped to a low murmur. The kids were just behind them.

Randall nodded.

"I think the children should stay with you," his mother added. "I'll bring their suitcases over later today."

"Good." They reached Penelope's red Beetle. The kids had squished into it this morning for the drive into Halifax, although Randall had picked up his car from the yacht club early this morning. Their preference for driving with their grandmother was not lost on him.

Nick reached for the door handle on the car. "Nick," Randall said. "You're coming with me."

He had meant his words to sound casual, but even to his ears they sounded like a demand.

Nick flashed him an angry look. "I'm going with Grandma Penny."

His mother put a hand on Nick's arm. "Why don't you stay with your father. I'll come over to see you all."

Nick shook his head. "I'm not going with him." He crossed his arms.

"Nick, be reasonable, please," Penelope said in a low voice.

"I'm not staying with him!"

Penelope's face registered her dismay at Nick's vehemence. Randall just stared at his son.

He hates me.

I can feel it.

My own flesh and blood hates me.

His mother's eyes searched his. *What do we do now?*

The only way Nick would come would be to physically propel him into Randall's car. And that was ridiculous.

He moved away from his son. "You go with your grandmother." He turned to Lucy. She was watching the three of them, clearly torn. "I know Charlie's been dying to see you."

She nodded.

"I'll call you later," he told his mother. He glanced at his son, who glared in return. Randall sighed, put his arm around Lucy's shoulders and led her to his car.

He opened the sunroof, trying to cool off the interior. The temperature was hot, but a cool breeze off the ocean made it comfortable. Everything was still green because of the rain in July.

Lucy slid into the front seat and buckled her seat belt. Normally, he'd enjoy wowing her with all the gadgets on his car, but not today.

They drove to his house. Lucy stared out the window. *Was she wishing she were with her grandmother? Her brother?*

Everything he'd believed to be true had been thrown in his face. He knew his relationship with Nick was rocky, but had hoped a week together on his yacht eating steak and potato chips would bring them back together.

How wrong he'd been.

26

"Detective Drake."

Ethan straightened. Even over a cell phone connection, there was no mistaking the rich lilt of the medical examiner's voice. "Hello, Dr. Guthro."

"I have some preliminary findings that may be of interest. I'd like to show them to you. Could you come down to the lab?"

Ethan grabbed his jacket. It was perfect timing. They were done with their interviews. "I'm on my way."

Ten minutes later, he was navigating the labyrinthine basement of the Greater Halifax General Hospital, known in the city as the GH2. Lamond met him at the door to the path lab. "It's been quite a morning."

Ethan studied his face. It looked pale, but not green. Lamond was toughening up.

"Ah, Detective Drake," Dr. Guthro said, ushering him into the bloodied, metal-filled room with the expansiveness of a country gentleman at his club. "Good to see you."

Ethan smothered his amusement. "And you, Doctor." He grabbed a gown off the shelf and slipped it on. "How did you make out?"

"Mixed results." Dr. Guthro led them to the autopsy table where Elise Vanderzell lay, naked. Ethan had seen a lot of dead bodies in his time, and a lot of undignified deaths. So he was unprepared when his heart constricted at seeing her there. Was it seeing the crude marks of the autopsy marring her body? The long row of broad stitches marched up her torso, branching off into the arms of a Y on her chest. Somehow, it seemed obscene on this woman. Maybe it was because she had been so beautiful. He shook his head at his fancifulness. Even in death, the beautiful garnered instinctive sympathy.

Dr. Guthro glanced at his notes. "Did you know the decedent had had an abortion several weeks ago?"

Ethan stared at Elise Vanderzell's stomach. "We knew she'd had some kind of procedure." *Talk about adding fuel to the fire.* Suddenly, the case for homicide had legs. "Can you harvest any tissue for a DNA analysis?"

Dr. Guthro shook his head. "Not from her. The clinic that performed the procedure might have kept paraffin-embedded tissue. You'll have to ask."

And he'd need to get a DNA sample from Randall Barrett...

He almost rubbed his hands together in anticipation.

"Do you think she was deliberately killed, Doctor?"

Dr. Guthro raised a brow. "Has this become a homicide investigation?"

"Not yet. But we've got a neighborhood that had recently reported break-ins. I've also got my sights on her ex-husband."

"Could be challenging to prove based on the autopsy findings. Head injuries are tricky. It can be difficult to differentiate what caused the injury, and what ultimately caused the death."

Ethan's heart sank.

"Did you find anything at the scene to suggest a homicide?"

"Not yet." Based on the fact there were no signs of obvious struggle and the discovery that nothing had been stolen, the likelihood of Elise being killed by a random intruder seemed low. Ethan thought of what Nick had told them. And what Randall had not said.

Abortion was such a touchy subject. There could be any number of motives to kill Elise. If his ex-wife had had a lover, Randall Barrett might have killed her out of spite. Or, if Elise was pregnant with Randall Barrett's child, that raised a whole new set of dynamics that could have triggered a homicidal rage.

Yet, they couldn't rule out suicide. Elise Vanderzell could have been depressed because she'd had an abortion. Or her hormones might have triggered another case of postpartum depression.

And what about the missing sleeping pills? "Her daughter told me that they'd made plans for today. But her son told me he'd seen her jump. And her pill count didn't match." Ethan's words seemed unnaturally loud in the room. "What do you think, Doctor?"

Dr. Guthro rubbed his chin. "How many pills were missing?"

"Fourteen."

"So…it adds a complication to the equation. Did she overdose? Then how would she have jumped over the rail? We'll have to see what the lab report tells us. On the other hand, even a single sleeping pill could have made her more suicidal."

"Really?"

"If she had a history of depression, Delteze could enhance suicidal thoughts."

Ethan thought back to his interview with Barrett. "Her ex-husband said she had a history of postpartum depression."

"I'm surprised that she would have been prescribed these pills." Dr. Guthro shook his head. "Was she still depressed?"

"Her ex-husband didn't think so." Ethan flipped open his notepad. "No. Wait. He said he didn't know. But he did say that his daughter told him the pills had made his ex-wife sleepwalk before. Could she have done it last night?" Ethan studied Elise Vanderzell's face. It was bloody and staring, the features blurred by blood from the scalp that had been folded over her face during the autopsy.

"If she had a history of reacting to Delteze in such a fashion, it is possible. And her reaction would likely be exacerbated if she took more than one pill." Dr. Guthro pointed to a series of dark bruises on her rib cage. "There are more on her back. The contusions are consistent with a fall."

"So. Strange house. The pills make her sleepwalk straight out her room and over the rail?"

"It's possible."

The patio door sounded like it hit the end of the runners really hard. Sort of like bounced against something, Nick had said. "Would she be able to use a lot of force to open the door if she was asleep?"

"With drug-induced somnambulism, she could easily have done that. This is what is so disconcerting about sleeping pills—Delteze, in particular—the behaviors are more complex than usual parasomnias. For example, there have been reports of people getting out of bed, taking their car keys and driving—all while asleep."

"With their eyes open?"

"Most definitely. And they could even speak. Although it is usually gibberish."

"So when her son, Nick, says he saw her commit suicide by climbing over the rail—"

"—she could have been in the deepest stages of sleep."

"Nice," Lamond said. "Accidental suicide."

"Are there any injuries to suggest it wasn't accidental?" Ethan asked.

Dr. Guthro moved around to Elise Vanderzell's head. Her hair had been pulled over her head and to one side, revealing the bloody scalp underneath. "This is where it gets tricky." He leaned over her head, using a swab as a pointer. "See, here, in the back of her skull?" This part of the skull had been removed to conduct the examination of her brain, but the bone had been stuck back in the hole. "Her scalp had an elongated laceration. The X-ray confirmed her skull had a fairly extensive depressed fracture. This is consistent with impact on the upper region of the occipital area."

"From hitting the ground?"

"Precisely. The brain shows an acute subdural hematoma under the skull fracture. This commonly occurs when the skull fragment is pushed into the brain.

"Over here," Dr. Guthro continued, pointing the swab to above Elise Vanderzell's ear, "in the temporal area, we found a *contrecoup* contusion on the brain, which, again, is consistent with the type of fall she experienced."

Lamond glanced at Ethan. *What the hell is a* contrecoup *contusion?* his eyes asked.

"What exactly does that mean, Doctor?" Ethan asked.

Dr. Guthro's face lit up. He was a teacher at heart, and enjoyed any opportunity to expound on pathology. "*Contrecoup* injuries occur when the head is moving and is stopped by a hard or immovable object. In this case, the decedent was falling backward, headfirst. Cerebral spinal fluid would accumulate to the back of the skull due to gravity. When her skull hit the ground, the brain would normally bounce against the skull, but the CSF provides a cushion. So the brain rebounds against the opposing skull wall—in this case, her temporal area—and it suffered a contusion at that point of impact."

Lamond squinted at the victim's temple. "I don't see anything."

"The skull does not need to be fractured for the brain to suffer an injury. This type of trauma happens from the inside out."

"Ah." Lamond stepped away from the body.

"So is the fall the cause of death?"

Dr. Guthro inhaled sharply between his teeth. "Yes. She was alive when she fell."

"And you see no other injuries that could have killed her?"

"No obvious injuries. Except…" He rubbed his chin. "Do you think she was deliberately killed?"

"Not sure. We were wondering about an intruder. But the scene doesn't support that theory. On the other hand, her ex-husband had both opportunity and, we think, motive. Especially since she had an abortion."

Dr. Guthro pushed Elise Vanderzell's hair away from the area of the *contrecoup* injury. "There is some bruising on the scalp. I wondered about it, but I think it's more likely she hit something during her fall."

"Could the bruising be from a weapon or a fist?"

He shook his head. "In my experience, not likely. There normally would be lacerations or abrasions. The skin is intact. And the brain injury is completely consistent with the fracture on the other side of her skull."

"But you wouldn't rule it out?"

"I wouldn't rule it in, either. Sorry, Detective."

Dr. Guthro gave him a rueful shrug. "If you find anything of interest, let me know. I am willing to revisit this. The findings won't change. But, as you know, how you interpret them depends on what you are trying to prove."

27

Saturday, 3:01 p.m.

Light and shadow played across the front lawn of Randall's home. He sat in his car, absorbing the graceful stems of the lilies, the verdant mystery of the hostas, the elegantly curved walkway that led to his home.

The glass-and-shingle take on the classic Cape Cod had been his own design, inspired by his mother's seaside home. Designing it had been his outlet during his first year in Halifax, when he still grappled with his decision to leave Toronto. Building the house had been a declaration of his intent. A haven to lick his wounds. And a source of creative joy. Few knew of his love of architecture. Even fewer knew of his landscaping talent.

It had been everything he had wanted, he had needed.

Until today.

The beauty of his house now jarred him. As if he had no right to be there.

As if he had no right to enjoy it anymore.

He flung open the car door, turning away from the

house. Lucy sat huddled in the back. "Honey, we're h-here," he said. He'd almost said *home*. Not only did it sound like a line from Ward Cleaver, it also seemed insensitive. Lucy didn't view his house in Halifax as her home.

Not yet.

He exhaled deeply. He wanted the kids to stay with him. It wasn't even a conscious thought. It was instinct. The knowledge that this was the right thing to do. He was their father. He'd left them with Elise in Toronto because he felt that their mother had the presumptive right to the children. But now that she was gone...

His gut constricted. The issue of custody was up for grabs. He knew Elise's parents would want the kids to stay in Toronto. But Jane's stroke two years ago had left her dependent on a walker and on her husband. They could not manage two children.

Still, that didn't mean they would make things easy for him.

Lucy stared at the house, her face unreadable. "Come on, honey, let's go in," he said.

She made no move to leave the car. "When will Nick come?"

He'd love to know the answer himself. "Soon. Let's go see Charlie."

Her face brightened. "Yeah."

Randall followed her up the walk. She'd grown since he'd last seen her. Her body had changed, the limbs long and lean, like a stripling maple. But the supple strength she usually possessed had shriveled in the past few days. Had she eaten anything? He couldn't recall seeing her put a single morsel of food in her mouth.

She hiked her backpack onto her shoulder and waited for him to open the door. Her passivity unnerved him.

What do you expect? She's in shock. She's been traumatized. She's not the same girl who threw herself in your arms yesterday afternoon, with sun gilding her hair and love lighting her eyes.

Would she ever be the same again?

His throat tightened. He unlocked the door and turned off the alarm. "Let's go see Charlie." He forced a light tone into his voice.

Midafternoon sun streamed through the kitchen windows. The room was warm, the air still. Too still.

Charlie wasn't there.

As soon as the realization hit him, he saw the Post-it note stuck on his counter. *I've taken Charlie home with me,* Kate wrote. *Just call,* she'd added.

"Where's Charlie?" Lucy asked. "Is she okay?" Her voice wobbled.

"She's fine, Lucy. A junior in my firm is looking after her for me."

"Oh."

"Why don't you go upstairs and get yourself settled into your room. I'll call Kate and ask her to bring Charlie over."

"Okay." Her voice was almost expressionless. Randall tried not to let it alarm him. *Give her time. She needs time.*

She left while Randall was reaching for the phone. He didn't hear her go, her footsteps so hollow that they made no sound.

He dialed Kate's number, his fingers fumbling on

the keypad. He disconnected, then tried again. He was more tired than he realized.

Kate answered on the second ring. "Randall?"

His throat closed up when he heard her voice. He swallowed. "Yes."

"Did you get my note?" Kate asked.

"Yes."

"Charlie's doing great. You don't need to worry about her."

"I'm sure she's fine. But my daughter would like to see her..."

"Of course!" She sounded embarrassed. "I didn't realize your daughter was with you... But of course she is. I'll bring Charlie over now."

"Thanks." He disconnected the phone. He leaned back against the counter and closed his eyes.

His head throbbed. Viciously.

Images flashed behind his eyelids. Elise's face yesterday. Twisted with anger and pain. Betrayal.

Elise, the first time he saw her. In the library of their firm on Bay Street. Her head bent, her brow furrowed as she skimmed a case report.

Elise, giving birth to their first child. Exhaustion and doubt giving way to elation.

Elise, admitting to her affair, the defiance in her eyes masking pain. And need.

His heart constricted.

He stared down at the phone in his hand. She'd called him last night. He'd been in the kitchen, nursing the first of four doubles. He'd picked up this very phone. Spoken to his ex-wife.

The rest of the night was a nightmarish blur. Like a

Hieronymus Bosch painting. When all his demons, emboldened by the alcohol, attacked him at once. Exacting their vengeance.

He hurled the phone at the back window.

It smashed through the glass, tiny splinters windmilling through light and air before the shards pierced the pale petals of a rose.

Charlie was so excited at the sight of her home that she strained at her leash, pulling Kate with her.

Kate reached for the doorbell.

The sharp cracking of glass startled her. She fell back a step. Charlie let out a low whine.

She hesitated. *What the hell was going on in Randall's house?* Maybe she should come back later. But Randall's daughter wanted to see his dog. The subtext of his request had been clear: his grieving daughter needed the comfort of the family pet.

She listened for another moment. No sounds of chaos within.

Taking a deep breath, she rang the doorbell. Charlie nosed the door, readying herself to lunge as soon as the door opened.

Footsteps approached. The door swung open. Charlie leaped onto Randall with a joyous bark. He bent over to pat her, the tension in his body obvious. He straightened. "Please, come in."

"No, it's okay." His appearance shocked Kate. It wasn't the rumpled clothes, messy hair or unshaven jaw. It was his face.

No. It was his eyes. Normally they would pierce through you without revealing a thing.

Today they were so full of loathing that Kate couldn't meet his gaze.

"Please."

She forced herself to look at him. The loathing had retreated, swiftly and with no trace. But Kate knew how Machiavellian self-loathing could be. It would wait for the moment when your defenses were down, and then it would strike.

"Okay, sure, I'd love to come in."

Relief crept across his face. It was like dawn breaking. Only then revealing how dark it really had been.

He led her into the kitchen. "Would you like a drink?" He stopped at the massive granite island and pulled out a leather bar stool. "I don't have a lot in the fridge, but I could make you some tea."

"Tea would be lovely, thanks." She slid onto the stool.

It was then she saw the broken window. So that's what she heard when she stood on the front porch. "What happened to your window?" She jerked her chin at the gaping maw of glass. It looked ugly and raw against the cool serenity of the kitchen.

He was rooting around in the cupboard for some tea bags. He glanced at the window. "Oh, that." He turned back to the cupboard. "I lost my balance and fell against the glass."

"Are you hurt?" She hadn't noticed any abrasions or cuts.

"No. No, I'm fine." He placed two mugs on the counter next to the kettle. It was sleek, burnished metal. Just like all the appliances in the kitchen.

Silence fell between them.

Kate glanced around. "Where's your daughter?"

"She's up in her room." He ran a hand through his hair. "I'll let her know that Charlie is back."

He left. Kate stared at the broken window. The glass was jagged. Wicked looking. There was a distinct hole in the middle. She wondered what had been thrown through it. And by whom.

Glass glittered against the tile floor. Perfect for slicing open a dog's paw. She hopped off the bar stool and began picking up the shards, placing them carefully on her palm.

"I'll do that," Randall said from behind her. She started, her hands reflexively curling into her palm. Her skin stung.

"I think I got the worst of it." She rose to her feet. "Where's your garbage?"

He led her to a garbage unit that had been emptied in anticipation of his sailing trip. Kate shook the glass pieces off her hand. A blood-streaked piece gleamed against the pristine white plastic liner.

"You cut yourself," Randall said, frowning.

"It's nothing." She curled her fingers over her palm.

"Let me get you a Band-Aid." He turned to yet another cupboard—how did he keep track of them all? Kate wondered—and pulled out a box of Band-Aids and some antibacterial ointment. He held out his hand. "Let me see."

"It's just a scratch, Randall."

"Let me see."

She opened her hand. Blood highlighted the lines of

her palm in pale red. "You need to wash it," Randall said, turning on the faucet.

She placed her palm obediently under the cold stream of water. "Where's your daughter?"

"She's fallen asleep. I decided not to wake her."

Randall pulled a dish towel from a drawer by the sink. Unlike the many designer elements of his kitchen, it was an ordinary white tea towel with a yellow border. He took her hand and wrapped the towel around her palm, keeping pressure on the cut.

Kate could hear her breathing. His breathing. She couldn't look at him. So she stared at her hand. But his hand was covering her hand, and she found herself studying the curve of his fingers. The light hairs on the back. The ringless third finger.

She pulled her hand away. "That feels much better. Thanks." She unwrapped the towel. A smear of blood marred the white weave. She hurried over to the garbage and threw it in. "Sorry, I ruined your dish towel."

He stared at her. "That was just a drop. It would have washed out."

Probably. But she wasn't sharing her blood with anyone. Not after Craig Peters had bled all over her. She knew she was being paranoid—if she had CJD, it was unlikely it was transmissible by blood, and certainly not transmissible by touching a light bloodstain on a dish towel—but it didn't matter. The sight of her own blood panicked her now. "I'll get you a new one."

"Don't be ridiculous." The kettle had begun to boil. Randall dropped two tea bags in the pot and poured in the boiling water. Kate busied herself with applying a Band-Aid to her cut.

Charlie nosed her leg. She'd been lazing in the sun on a large doggie bed. But the sounds of Randall's tea preparations had roused her.

"Alaska and Charlie got on very well," Kate said, trying to break the silence that had descended on them yet again. She regretted her impulsive acceptance of his invitation into his home. She did not belong here, she did not want to be a witness to his grief and tragedy.

As soon as she could down her tea, she was gone.

He passed her a steaming mug. "Milk? Sugar?" He placed a carton of milk and a simple white sugar bowl in front of her. She added both, pouring in a generous amount of milk to cool down the tea. She'd be able to drink it more quickly.

They sipped their tea in silence. Kate couldn't help but reflect on how bizarre this whole situation was. Here she was, in the kitchen of the managing partner who'd avoided her since June, drinking tea with him the afternoon after his ex-wife died a tragic death, staring at the cracked edges of his broken window.

"Where were you last night?" The question bubbled out from her throat.

He stiffened. "What do you mean?"

"After your ex-wife…" She swallowed. "After her accident, no one could reach you."

"Where did you hear that?" *From Ethan?* his eyes demanded.

"From a reporter. Who contacted me."

That surprised him. "Natalie Pitts?"

"Yes."

"Why did she contact you?"

Kate exhaled. "Because we're friends."

He turned away from her and leaned over the counter. "Jesus."

"I didn't say anything, Randall."

"Then how did she know?"

"I don't know. She's a reporter. She has her sources."

He turned to her. "Kate, I need to be able to trust you."

Why?

The question was reflected in his eyes, too. "You are an associate of my firm," he added. "You can't speak to the media."

They both knew what he'd just said was bull. "Anyway, you still haven't answered my question. Where were you last night?"

He picked up his mug. "On my yacht."

"The whole time?"

He slammed his mug down on the counter. "No. I stole away for an hour to kill my wife." His expression clearly said: satisfied?

Kate noted he said "wife." Not "ex-wife." Her stomach tightened. She placed her mug on the counter. "I think I should go now."

He was so close, the fine arteries of his bloodshot eyes were visible. "No. Don't leave."

"You accuse me of speaking to the press. Then you refuse to answer my question. You say I'm the one you need to be able to trust. Did it occur to you that the onus is reversed? *You* are the one who went AWOL last night."

The silence was so palpable that Kate couldn't breathe.

A fly buzzed through the broken glass. It darted around Kate's head, then back out the window. "Goodbye." She pushed away from the counter.

"I was on my yacht." His voice was low.

"The whole time?" This was the test.

A muscle ticked beneath one corner of his eye. "No. First I got drunk."

"Where?"

"Here. Then at a bar. I drank more than I've drunk in years."

Some of the tension in Kate's shoulders eased. "How did you get to your yacht?"

He shook his head. "I think I drove. I don't remember." He wiped his mouth with the back of his hand. "I'm lucky I didn't kill someone."

Kate stared at him. "You mean you were so drunk you had a blackout."

He looked away. "Yes." Then his gaze swung back to her. "This is the first time it's ever happened, I swear it."

"Why couldn't your children reach you?"

He jerked back. "How do you know they tried to call me?"

The Toronto phone numbers on Randall's call list flashed through Kate's mind. She hoped her flush of guilt didn't show through her tan. "Your kids found her, didn't they? It stands to reason they'd try to call their father."

"Yes. It stands to reason. I failed them, Kate. I was so drunk I didn't even think about whether they could reach me." Pain, remorse, guilt. It was in his eyes, his voice. He gave a derisive laugh. "I discovered my phone was turned off this morning. I must have turned it off last night. I obviously forgot what it was like to be a parent. Elise did all the day-to-day stuff. I forgot the cardinal rule—you never turn off your phone. Ever." He crossed his arms. "I failed them."

She didn't know what to say. He *had* failed them. Gone off, gotten drunk, wallowed in whatever had upset him and not been there at the most traumatic moment of his kids' lives.

"You didn't know what would happen."

"It doesn't matter. The kids won't rationalize that part. All they know is that their dad wasn't there when their mother died."

The self-loathing had returned in his eyes. Kate wondered if her own father had been so consumed with recriminations after he pulled them under and then left them. She doubted it.

But what she did know was how it felt to be twelve years old and have your world irrevocably destroyed. And to realize that your father was not there to help you when you needed him the most.

"Dad." Lucy stood in the doorway. Her face was swollen from sleep, her hair tangled. Kate gave her a tentative smile. Would she remember Kate from when she patted Alaska yesterday? The girl's gaze swept over her. A flicker of recognition was all Kate got. Her animation, her impish smile were gone. In its stead was apathy. "Where's Charlie?"

At the sound of Lucy's voice, Charlie bounded from her bed, throwing herself against Lucy with enthusiastic kisses. Lucy sank to her knees and buried her face in Charlie's fur.

It took Kate a moment to realize that the girl's shoulders were heaving. Randall hurried over to his weeping daughter and put his hand on her shoulder. She shook it off.

"I'll see you later." Kate edged around them, wishing she'd left the first time she'd said goodbye.

Randall caught up with her as she walked through the front doorway. He gripped the door frame with bloodless fingers. "How can I make it up to her, Kate?"

It was the one question today that Kate could answer with confidence. Her own past gave her that authority. "You can never make it up to her, Randall."

His fingers tightened. It was not the answer he expected to hear. Or wanted to hear. It never was. She placed a hand on his wrist. "But you can start over. Just take it one step at a time."

She walked away, down the elegant stone walkway. For a man like Randall, the hardest part of her advice would be the last part. He lived life in the fast lane. Now he would have to slow down. And not make the assumption that taking things bit by bit would be easy.

The pitfalls for the impatient on the road to redemption were many.

Only a few succeeded.

For the sake of his daughter, Kate hoped he would be one of those few.

But at some point, the law of probabilities dictated that a man who had won so many times would inevitably lose.

Kate wondered if Randall's luck had run out.

28

"**I** don't think Elise Vanderzell killed herself," Ethan said.

Detective Sergeant Deb Ferguson did not look impressed. In fact, she looked for all the world like a scornful, big-boned milkmaid. Except she sat behind a large desk instead of a reluctant cow. Plaques awarded for outstanding police work and volunteerism dotted the wall behind her. "So you think this is a homicide investigation?"

"Yes. Right now, I'm working on two theories. The first theory is that she was killed by a random intruder. The whole area around Point Pleasant Park was being targeted for break-ins. And we know that Dr. Feldman's house had not been occupied prior to Elise Vanderzell's arrival. She might have surprised someone."

Deb nodded. "And what's your second theory?"

Ethan shifted in his chair. He knew Deb wouldn't like it. "It was Barrett. He had every opportunity to kill Elise Vanderzell."

"But neither the scene nor the autopsy have given us a damn thing."

"But Barrett also had motive, Deb."

She raised a brow.

"The autopsy revealed she'd had an abortion."

"Was the baby his?"

Now came the hard part. "The clinic says it doesn't ask who the father is. But Elise Vanderzell put down Randall Barrett's name as next of kin.

"Dr. Guthro told me that the clinic might have tissue samples. We could run the DNA—"

"It still doesn't give us motive, Ethan. Randall Barrett might have been very happy to not have a third Barrett from his *ex*-wife."

Ethan looked away. He knew the evidence was flimsy. But his gut was telling him that there was more to this than met the eye.

"I believe she was murdered, Deb."

She crossed her arms. "By Randall Barrett?"

He shrugged. "Possibly."

"Are you sure you don't have blinkers on? You two have some nasty business between you."

He stiffened at her reference to the Clarkson file. "That's not the reason. Give me some credit, Deb."

Her eyes narrowed. "What about the son? He was present at the scene."

"I know."

"He could have killed her and lied about seeing her jump."

Ethan's skin prickled. Deb had just pointed out what his mind whispered every time he zeroed in on Barrett. "I know. But I don't think he did it."

"Could he be protecting someone?"

"It wouldn't be his father. He hates him."

"What about someone else?"

"Who else would he know? He just arrived in Halifax."

"So maybe he killed his mother." The mildness of Deb's tone belied the hardness in her eyes. "But right now, there is no proof this is a homicide. FIS has come up with nothing, the M.E. isn't giving us anything. In fact, the only eyewitness we have is Vanderzell's son, and he says that she jumped."

"Come on, Deb. An innocent woman is dead. Her death is suspicious. We can't just ignore it. Think of what the media will say if some other woman ends up killed." He raised his brows. They both knew what he was referring to. The Lisa MacAdam case. The Major Crimes Unit had thought she was the first victim of a serial killer. Turned out there had been many before her. And no one in the Major Crimes Unit had made the connection.

Deb exhaled. Loudly.

"Okay. But keep Barrett under wraps for now. The shit will hit the fan if we begin filling out warrants on Randall Barrett with what we've got so far. The JP will stop answering his phone." She leaned toward Ethan. Her eyes locked onto his. "Not to mention the field day the media will have with this. Do you really want all that bad blood between you and Barrett printed in black and white on the front page of the *Post?*"

She was throwing the media card back in his face, he knew that. It still didn't stop his gut from clenching.

"We are maxed out as it is on the Robichaud file." She

twisted her mouth to the side, a sure sign she was going to tell him something he didn't want to hear. "In fact, I wanted you to be the file coordinator on Robichaud."

"Okay. Just give me a week. I've got a couple of leads. One of Elise Vanderzell's final phone calls was to a Dr. Jamie Gainsford. I think he might be her therapist. He could help us establish her state of mind. And the toxicology report hasn't come in yet."

She waved him toward the door. "You have five days. If you haven't come up with anything, you're on Robichaud."

29

Aisle number eleven was where Nick Barrett found his murder weapon.

He hadn't thought it would be so easy. So...well, normal.

This morning, his grandmother told him that she was going into town to see Lucy. It had been a perfect opportunity to take the first step of his plan. He told her he'd come with her. And that he wanted to spend the night at his father's.

Surprise, pleasure, hope—each of those emotions flickered through his grandmother's eyes. He knew she was thinking that her ex-daughter-in-law's death might have one unexpected silver lining: that her grandson might reconcile with her son.

They left his grandmother's house in Prospect after lunch. It was all Nick could do to hide his anger. His hate. He stared out the window. He loved his grandmother, but she was blinded by the golden glow of his father.

Everyone was. *Grandma Penny, you are so wrong. You are so wrong about your own son. He's evil.*

His father greeted them at the door of his house, weary hope in his gaze when he saw Nick's duffel bag. Nick had challenged him with his eyes. *Just admit you killed her, you bastard. You know I saw you. Stop fucking pretending.*

But his father just ushered them in, offering them a drink. Nick hoisted his duffel onto his shoulder and stomped upstairs. His room had been redone since he was last here: there was a new Mac in the corner, an iPod stereo system on the bureau and a guitar leaning against the wall.

It sickened him. His father was trying to buy his affection, trying to assuage his conscience by tricking out his room.

He dumped his bag on the floor and left.

He went back downstairs and asked his father if he could buy a baseball bat. His father had seemed startled, but then said, "Yes, of course. It would do us both good to get outside."

Typical of him to expect that Nick would want to play ball with him.

Nick had barely been able to swallow the putdown he longed to throw in his father's face. His father had offered to bring Lucy shopping, but she'd refused. She wanted to read a book, she said. Nick bet she was writing in her journal.

He could just imagine the entry she would make tomorrow. *"Nick killed Daddy."* She'd probably underline it down the whole page.

222 *Pamela Callow*

But Luce, he wanted to tell her, *you didn't see what he did to Mum.*

You didn't hear how she moaned. You didn't see how he lifted her right over the rail.

And then let go.

When you know the real story, you'll understand.

And you'll thank me.

They drove to the store in silence. The parking lot was busy; the sun was shining and people were buying things for their barbecues, their trip to the beach, their water sports. Nick scanned the signs hung over the aisles.

Aisle 11—Baseball and Racquet Sports. He headed straight to it. The baseball bats were lined up by price. Nick stopped, studying them, breathing hard. He wanted something with heft.

His father turned in to the aisle and walked up behind him. Nick stiffened. He tried to ignore his father as he examined the bats, the hair on the back of his neck quivering, but his father reached over and picked one with Slugger written in extravagant letters across the side, then weighed it in his palm. "How about this one?"

Nick grimaced. Typical of his father to choose something, instead of letting Nick pick it for himself. But in this case, having his father pick the bat that would kill him had a certain poetic justice.

"Let me see." Nick took it from his father, being careful not to make contact. His hands curled around the handle. He backed away, swinging the bat in a small arc. It would do. "Okay."

His father smiled. "Let's get some balls. We'll go to the field after this. I'll pitch."

Nick shook his head. "I'm tired. Maybe later."

He saw disappointment flare in his father's eyes. Nick turned and walked toward the checkout.

His father followed, grabbing a package of balls on his way.

30

Ethan sat at his desk, the file with Elise Vanderzell's crime scene photos and phone records spread out in front of him. He dialed Dr. Jamie Gainsford's phone number. He used the one from Elise's cell phone records, not the business number that was listed on the Ontario Yellow Pages website, hoping that Dr. Gainsford would answer this number on a Sunday.

"Hello?" The man's voice was calm, crisp. Slight accent. Australian, Ethan guessed.

"Dr. Jamie Gainsford?" he asked.

"Yes. Who is this?"

"Detective Ethan Drake, Halifax Major Crimes Unit." Ethan let that sink in. "I'm calling regarding Elise Vanderzell. One of your patients."

Dr. Gainsford hesitated. "She is one of my clients. Is she all right?"

"I regret to inform you that Elise Vanderzell died early yesterday morning."

"Oh, my God." Dr. Gainsford paused, cleared his

throat. "What happened? I'd only just spoken to her on Friday night."

Ethan's gaze fell on the crime scene photos. "She fell over a balcony at the house she was visiting."

"Dear God. When did that happen?"

"On Friday night."

"Good Lord. What time?"

"Just after one in the morning. What time did you speak to her?"

"She phoned me around eight. Eight-thirty. I don't know." He spoke quickly.

"Why did she call you?" Ethan hoped the doctor's shock might keep him talking.

No such luck. "Detective, she was my client. I am bound to keep those conversations confidential."

Damn. Ethan stared at the photo of bloody concrete where Elise Vanderzell had landed. "We are trying to establish her state of mind. We aren't sure if she fell, jumped or was murdered." He added, "You were the last person to speak to her before she phoned her husband. You aren't betraying a confidence by telling us what might have led to her death."

Dr. Gainsford swallowed. "I can hardly believe she's dead." He cleared his throat again. "I can't give you specifics of our sessions, but in my opinion, she wasn't suicidal. The reason she called was that she'd had an argument with her ex-husband. She wanted some advice."

Ethan's neck prickled. "What advice did you give her?"

"I advised that she call her ex-husband and tell him they needed to behave like caring parents."

Ethan scanned the phone record. Six minutes after Elise Vanderzell ended her conversation with her therapist, she phoned Randall Barrett. "Do you know what they said to each other?"

Dr. Gainsford exhaled. "No. I'm afraid I don't. I wish I did…"

You and me both, Doctor. "At present, we are still determining whether Ms. Vanderzell's death was accidental or an act of homicide. If she was killed, we will need to trace her movements and talk to people who knew her. Including you, Doctor."

"As I said before, our communications were confidential." He paused. "However, if it appears that Ms. Vanderzell was a victim of homicide, I have provided evidence in domestic homicide situations with the approval of the College of Psychologists of Ontario."

He absorbed the implications of what Elise Vanderzell's therapist was telling him: the psychologist thought if his client had been murdered, her husband could have killed her. He wouldn't push Dr. Gainsford for more information. Yet. He'd wait until they got the toxicology reports. "Thank you, Doctor." Ethan hung up.

He ran through what information he knew. Elise had called her ex-husband. But it was a brief conversation.

Then Barrett got drunk.

And she fell off the balcony.

Her therapist, one of the last people to speak to her and probably the person most privy to her mental state, did not think she was suicidal.

And yet her son said he saw her jump.

Who was right?

Had her son killed her?

Or had Barrett killed her—and Nick was protecting him?

Ethan scratched the last possibility off his list. He could not believe Nick would protect his father.

So, if the therapist was right and Elise wasn't suicidal—then why did Nick say he saw his mother jump?

He stared at that bloody patch of concrete in the photo. It had told the FIS team everything it could.

But he didn't think Elise's family had done the same. He needed to bring Nick in again. He'd ask Tabby to conduct another interview tomorrow. The kid was not playing straight with them.

Then he'd bring in Nick's father. He wasn't playing straight with them, either.

Like father, like son.

Who knew that there was so much psychology in color? Kate thought, swiping her hair off her face with the back of a paint-splattered hand. Paint cascaded down the front of her T-shirt in a trail of yellowy cream puffs.

It was disturbing to think how her mood could be manipulated by the hue surrounding her. Was she really so suggestible?

Hell, yes. And she needed a dose of bright, mood-lifting color right now. Too many things had upset her equilibrium this weekend. First the unpleasant Naugler discovery on Friday afternoon; then her chilly encounter with Randall in the elevator; then the disastrous one-night stand with Curtis; and finally, and most disturbingly, the death of Randall's ex-wife.

She still didn't know why Randall had called her.

She sensed he was asking for more from her than just looking after his dog. And she sure as hell didn't know what she was willing to give him.

For the tenth time today, she pushed the thought of him out of her mind. She slapped the paintbrush on the wall, adding more cream puffs to her shirt. Despite her lack of skill, the freshly gleaming walls of her kitchen looked pretty damn good.

Although it would look so much better with white cupboards, like Randall's.

Stop it. When you make partner, you can afford your dream kitchen. Just be grateful the paint was on sale. Now you can get new blinds.

"Almost done the closet," Finn said, backing out from the pantry with a roller, pan and two brushes in his hands. Finn Scott, dog walker extraordinaire, had adopted her house like a mangy dog in need of a good grooming. Since he'd begun walking Alaska in May, he'd put dead bolts in her bedroom, fixed her screen door, replaced the rotting boards in her back porch and replaced leaky faucets. Twice.

"It'll take a couple of days to dry in this heat," Finn said. Sweat dampened his still-pristine Green Day T-shirt to his back.

He knelt down, placing the pan on a drop sheet, and poured more paint into it. Not a drop spilled. How did he do that? It was like the guy had been born with a Mr. Fix-It gene that had an extra shot of neat added to it.

Finn picked up the roller, then balanced the paint pan on his forearm as he straightened. Kate rolled her eyes. "How do you do that?"

"It's all in the wrist." He grinned.

"I owe you a nice dinner. Big time," Kate said. "Too bad I can't cook."

Finn's eyes lit up with mischievous excitement. She should have guessed what was coming, knowing there was one thing Finn wanted from her that she had so far refused to give.

"Instead of dinner," Finn said, "let me look around that secret staircase of yours."

The blood drained from Kate's cheeks. Finn didn't know what he was asking, she knew that. Just a few months before, Kate's elderly neighbor Muriel Richardson had pried away an old bookcase in the closet and revealed a half-door to a "secret" staircase. She and her sister, Enid, had played in the staircase as children.

Every night, when Kate woke up drenched with sweat, her mind filled with Craig Peters and his bloody hands, it was the staircase next door to her bedroom that fueled her insomnia.

"Come on, Kate, you've never even looked up there."

His eyes beseeched her. On the wall behind him, the fresh paint gave the kitchen a radiance and warmth that made her nighttime fear of the staircase seem remote. Silly, even.

"We'll go together," Finn added, sensing her indecision.

Maybe going up there, seeing the plaster and feeling the wood under her feet, would dispel her aversion. After all, wasn't it fear of the unknown that made it all seem so much worse at two in the morning?

He put down his painting gear and rummaged through his toolbox for a hammer. Kate followed him into the closet. Despite the fan that spun with a low hum, the small area was stifling.

Finn had painted all the walls except the back wall. It loomed, muddy brown and gloomy, over the half-door, like an entrance to a troll's cave.

Hooking the hammer's claw into the nail heads, Finn's back muscles strained with the effort of pulling out the nails he had so thoroughly hammered only months before. With a grunt, he removed the final nail. He yanked the board off the wall and pried the small door from the wall.

"Ta-da!" He opened the door with a flourish, turning to grin at her.

Sweat, which had until now been a light dampness on Kate's skin, erupted in a stream under her arms. "You go first."

He knelt in front of the half-door and poked his head inside. "We need a flashlight." He backed up, wiping his hands on his shorts.

It took only two strides for Kate to return to the kitchen, but the contrast hit her immediately. Light. Air. Safety. She found a flashlight, pushing the switch to check it worked. But in reality, she was working up her courage.

Shake it off, Kate. Shake it off. Dr. Kazowski will be proud of you. She'll think you're making progress. That would be a change.

Kate spun on her heel and strode into the closet before her courage left her.

"Here." She shoved the flashlight into Finn's hand.

He dropped to his knees and shone the light up into the stairwell. He gave a low whistle. "Very fancy." He crawled through the doorway. Kate watched his ankles, then feet, disappear into the black hole.

Taking a deep breath, she lowered herself through the doorway. And inhaled a large dust bunny. She coughed, swiping at a cobweb by her hair, and crawled into the stairwell.

The temperature was at least ten degrees hotter than the kitchen. Sweat matted Kate's hair to the back of her neck. She straightened, conscious of the ceiling just above her head. There was maybe two inches' clearance. Finn had to keep his neck bent. He shone the light on the steps between them. "How are you doing?" he asked.

"Fine." She forced a smile on her face. It was just as dark and unpleasant as she thought it would be. She wondered at the young children who had thought this was a fun place to play. They were made of stronger stuff back then, she supposed. Or just had fewer options.

Finn stood one step above her. "Cool, isn't it?"

"Uh-huh."

He ran his fingers over the wall. "You know, I think I should paint these walls. I could install a light in here. It would really brighten it up."

And stop me from being scared. She rubbed her arms. "I'm not sure, Finn…"

"Choose the brightest, funkiest color you like and we'll transform this space."

"This isn't a home reno show, Finn."

He grinned. "Not yet. But this old house has good bones, Kate. She deserves some TLC."

"She's getting it."

Finn crossed his arms. "Come on, Kate. It's just a staircase."

Kate pushed a wisp of hair off her face. "Exactly. It's a staircase I don't use and will never use. Why waste our time on it? I've got a ton of work to do tomorrow." She grabbed his elbow. "I don't have time to take on another project for something I plan on locking up."

She dropped to her knees and crawled out of the half-door before he could say any more.

It was true. All of it. She would never use the staircase—over her dead body, which had a strangely prophetic ring. And she had that load of case reports sitting on a chair in her spare bedroom upstairs. Tomorrow was a holiday. She needed to buckle down and get work done before Tuesday's discovery.

Oh, man, and wasn't that something to look forward to. Discovery with Curtis Carey.

She definitely needed to be prepared. She didn't want to look like more of a fool than she already did.

After dinner, she'd put a bolt on the half-door that led to the secret staircase. That should end any further debates about giving her house extra TLC.

It was getting lots of TLC. Way more than she was.

31

Monday, 12:48 a.m.

Nick sat on the bed in his father's house, his iPhone plugged in his ears, dressed in a black T-shirt and black track pants. The stretchy kind, not the nylon ones that crinkled when you moved.

He hit the bat in rhythm to the music. Every time the wood smacked his palm, his fingers curved around it, feeling the cool, smooth wood. The weight of it.

Earlier this evening he'd practiced swinging it until the motion came naturally. Then he'd pounded the bat against his pillow. Again. And again until the pillow had given way at the seams. Then Nick had thrown himself onto the bed, sweat slicking the bat in his hand.

He took a shower. Ate supper in his room. His father had not protested. He seemed to want to play nice, going out of his way to please Nick, as if he was trying to prove how glad he was Nick had done an about-face and decided to stay with him. But every time Nick looked at him, all he could think was, *You know I saw you. You make me sick.*

He stood. He stretched his muscles, warming them up. He played the song on his iPhone one final time. Cranked it up even louder. The drums stirred a primeval instinct, the electric whine of the guitar screeching through his muscles. His adrenaline pumped higher.

The moment of reckoning had come. Nick whacked the bat against his palm. Those visualization techniques he'd been taught over the years were finally worth something. He pictured his father's head on its king-size pillow.

It's like a melon.

It's like a melon.

A bloody, bursting melon.

The song ended. He turned it off quickly, before the next song could begin. He didn't want anything to break the rhythm of rage coursing through his blood.

He needed to do it.

Right now. Before his brain could think.

32

Monday, 12:49 a.m.

Kate leaned her head against the screen of her bedroom window. A breeze stirred the damp hair on her neck.

She closed her eyes. Then opened them wide, not even daring to blink. Craig Peters crept behind her eyelids, skulked deep in her mind, lurked in the blood that flowed through her veins. She could not get him away from her.

Her fingers gripped the window ledge. In a few moments, when the air had sufficiently cooled her sweat-drenched body, she would close the window and lock it. The air in her room would become stifling. Again.

But she had no choice. She could not sleep with the window unlocked. Nor could she sleep with the staircase that Finn had unboarded. Because in her dream, Craig Peters had crept up those stairs.

Tears of frustration sprang behind her eyelids. She hated being held hostage to this nighttime terror. It was eating her up.

Sometimes when Kate lay awake at night, trying

to calm her racing heart after another terror-inducing dream of Craig Peters, she thought of Ethan. He'd told her once that he'd killed a man in self-defense.

She'd been sympathetic, stroking his chest, murmuring her condolences. But she'd never understood. Never truly comprehended what it was like to end another human's life. To see that person's life force drain in front of your eyes. To know that it would stain your soul for the rest of your life.

Sometimes, in the very deepest part of the night, she was tempted to call Ethan. He would know what to say to her.

But then her conscience would demand: Did he still harbor feelings for her? Or was that declaration of love in May simply miscategorized relief that she had survived the Body Butcher's final—and most brutal—attack?

She'd never know. She didn't want to know.

She wanted it to be a chapter in her life that wasn't dog-eared from return visits. She didn't run the same route in the park anymore. She avoided Ethan's favorite coffee shops.

So every time her hand crept toward the phone, toward reassurance and maybe just a hint of salvation, she would snatch it back under the sheets. She couldn't ask that of Ethan.

Then she would cry. Not because she regretted her decision to end the purgatory they'd been in since New Year's Eve, but because she knew she was completely alone. Just her and her pathetic memories.

She locked her window and returned to her bed. The bottle of sleeping pills sat beside her bedside light, the two objects lined up like sentinels against the terrors of the night. The light guarded her against her fears; the pills warded off insomnia.

Her fingers trembled—just once—as she slipped the pill between her lips, washing it down with a sip from the glass of lukewarm water on her bedside table.

<u>33</u>

Monday, 12:52 a.m.

Nick glanced to his left. Lucy's door was still closed. He'd checked an hour ago, and she'd been asleep. She was a sound sleeper, so he was positive he didn't have to worry about her.

His father's bedroom loomed at the end of the hallway, the door open. Just in case any of his grieving children needed nighttime solace.

He stopped in the doorway. Through the blood pounding in his ears, Nick heard the sound of his father's heavy breathing, punctuated by Charlie's snores.

It was dark. He couldn't make out his father's form on the bed.

But Charlie heard him. Her snoring stopped.

There was a jingle of her dog tags as she lifted her head.

Shit.

She was going to wake up his father.

He edged toward the bed. His heart began pounding crazily. He tried holding his breath, to be soundless, but he couldn't hear anything, the blood was pounding so hard in his head.

His father lay on his back, an arm flung over the pillow next to him.

Nick watched the even rise and fall of his father's chest.

The hand that was curled over the sheet.

The hand that had pushed him in a swing, that had held his own small hand until Nick was ready to let go and skate by himself.

He swallowed. He was about to make that hand lifeless. His fingers trembled. Then tightened on the bat.

Charlie watched him, still lying down. But every muscle was tensed.

Bile rose in the back of his throat. *Come on, you can do it.*

It was the same hand that had smashed a club on the side of his mother's head. The same hand that had dropped her over the balcony rail.

He killed Mum.

The bastard killed Mum.

He whacked her on the head and dumped her like a sack of potatoes.

He felt his strength returning.

It filled all his muscles, fired his blood.

He glanced at Charlie. He could see her confusion in the tilt of her head. He was her friend.

But she could sense his vibes. She knew he was threatening her owner. Her ears went back.

Shit. Was she going to attack him?

His father's hand spasmed reflexively. Nick practically jumped out of his skin. His own hands were slippery with sweat. He couldn't control his breathing anymore. He was going to wake up his father.

He had to do it.

Now.

Now.

He stared at his father's head.

It's a melon.

It's a fucking melon.

Do it, you fucking coward!

He raised the bat. It brushed the edge of his father's bed.

DO IT, YOU FUCKING COWARD!

Charlie growled low in her throat.

Nick swung the bat with all the strength of his fifteen-year-old hockey-honed body, closing his eyes.

His mother toppled over the balcony rail. Her staring gaze met his.

He heard the smash of breaking glass, the sound of an eighty-pound Labrador retriever leaping off the bed, his father reacting in a blur of sheets and blankets, as he swung again, his bat connecting with a satisfying thud.

A dog yelped in anguish.

He opened his eyes. He saw the broken bedside light hanging by a chord from the side table. Charlie lying on her side at the opposite edge of the bed. His father scrambling over to the dog while looking back at Nick in confusion.

Then anger.

Nick's jaw dropped. He'd hit the dog.

He'd hit the fucking dog.

She was panting heavily.

"Charlie!" His father picked up the dog and cradled her in his arms. He didn't seem to know what to say. He looked at Nick. At the bat.

A whimper escaped from Charlie's throat.

"What the fuck were you trying to do?" his father spat, scooping up the Lab and rushing across the room. Charlie's head hung heavily over Randall's arm.

"What the fuck did this dog ever do to you?" His father pushed past Nick, tears glistening in his eyes.

He heard his father running down the hallway, calling for Lucy. It took three tries before Lucy responded. She didn't answer with her usual sleep-drenched voice. Instead, her voice was panicky, wobbly. *That's what happens when your mother is killed by your father in the middle of the night.*

Nick's fingers slowly unclenched around the bat. It fell to the floor with a sharp crack, then rolled under the bed. He walked on the balls of his feet down the hallway, so lightly that he couldn't hear himself move.

Like death walking. Never knowing when it's going to approach and then boom! It hits you.

Or your mother.

Why the fuck hadn't it hit his father?

He'd fucked up. Big time. Big fucking time. He gripped his cheek with his hand and dug his fingers in, feeling the skin stretch against his cheekbone.

The lights had been switched on downstairs. They illuminated the stairwell. He stood in the shadow of a wall, listening.

Lucy's distress was loud and hysterical. "What happened to Charlie? Is she okay? We need to go to the vet, Daddy!"

He couldn't hear what his father said to her.

Then his sister said, "But why can't we take her? I want to go!"

His father spoke a bit more sharply.

He made a phone call. It was brief. He hung up, spoke to Lucy again. She said, "Can I go with her, too?"

His father must have said yes, because then Lucy said, "I'll go get my stuff."

He heard his sister come up the stairs. He ran as softly as he could back to his room and closed the door.

He could not face her.

He began to shiver. He could not face her.

And he hadn't even killed his father yet.

Lucy's footsteps hesitated outside his door.

But then they moved on.

She couldn't face him, either.

It was his father's fault.

He'd make him pay. His fingers clenched into fists.

He'd finish the job he'd fucked up.

He'd do it right this time.

The doorbell rang. Nick heard a woman's voice, a soft exclamation of dismay. Within seconds the car had left.

Nick heard the front door close.

Silence.

Then he heard his father's footsteps.

They were coming up the stairs.

34

Monday, 1:21 a.m.

Even at one in the morning, with no traffic, the drive
to the vet hospital seemed interminable. Kate knew she
shouldn't be driving, not after taking the sleeping pill,
but adrenaline pumped through her. She locked her gaze
on the road, willing her brain to bypass the chemicals in
her bloodstream, willing the car to get to the emergency
clinic before Charlie gave up on them.

When Randall phoned her twenty minutes ago, she'd
just fallen back asleep. Exhausted, she'd been reluctant
to pull herself out of her dreamless state and answer the
phone.

But the phone had been insistent, so she groped for
the receiver, part of her wondering who it was, but part
of her already knowing. Only a few people would call
her in the middle of the night. She wasn't sure how it
had happened, but for some reason Randall Barrett had
decided she was his go-to girl.

"Kate," he'd said, his voice so raw and tight and heavy

and angry that her sleeping-pill-induced grogginess had dissolved instantly like sugar in hot water.

"What's wrong?"

"It's Charlie." His voice choked off. He cleared his throat. "She's been hit by a baseball bat. Can you take her to the vet hospital for me?"

The way he said it, Kate knew that whatever had hurt Charlie hadn't been an accident. "Of course." She flung back the covers, forcing her leaden muscles to move, flipping on all the lights. Alaska leaped to the floor and watched her. "I'll be there in ten minutes." She'd thrown on some clothes, mixing some instant coffee with hot tap water and downing it in a gulp that almost made her retch the disgusting brew. Then she had driven to Randall's house with her heart in her bile-laced mouth.

When Randall opened the door, the look of desolation on his face was so absolute that she wanted to throw her arms around him and comfort him. But then she saw his daughter.

And his dog.

Randall carried Charlie in her crate to Kate's car. He lowered the crate gently, carefully, onto the backseat. "Hang in there, girl," he said. "Please."

He straightened and looked at Kate, a sheen of tears in his bloodshot eyes. "Take care of her for me."

He hugged Lucy, a brief, fierce hug, then pushed her into the car, closing the door. Kate pushed the gear into Drive, her foot hitting the accelerator so hard that the rubber squealed.

Charlie, in her crate on the backseat, did not react.

Don't die, Kate begged the dog in her head. *Please don't die.*

Lucy sat in the backseat, her arm draped over Charlie's crate. She murmured words of comfort to her. Occasionally, the words were choked off by her sobs.

"When are we going to get there?" Lucy asked. She wiped her nose with her sleeve.

"Just five more minutes." They were on the MacKay Bridge now, one of two bridges connecting the city to its twin, Dartmouth. Beneath them, the harbor stretched out, black and still. Kate glanced in the rearview mirror at Lucy.

The girl's face was white and scared. "Her breathing is getting heavier." They drove the rest of the way in silence. The car hit a pothole. Charlie let out a low whimper. Kate flinched. Finally, they saw the lights of the vet hospital. She hit the gas, speeding into the parking lot. Three other cars were there. She and Lucy carried each end of Charlie's crate inside, placing her gently on the floor.

The technician at the counter took one look at the injured dog and said, "Follow me." They carried her into an examining room in the back. The technician helped Kate lift Charlie out of her crate. She lay on the cold examining table, her mouth open, her chest heaving. Brokenly. Unevenly. Lucy hovered over her, stroking her head. "It's okay, Charlie," she whispered. "You're gonna be okay." But her voice lacked conviction.

In less than two minutes, the vet hurried in. Instead of the usual introductions, she went to work right away on Charlie, placing her stethoscope on the dog's chest. Kate glanced at the name written on her white lab coat. Dr. Chung.

The vet looked up at Kate, frowning. "What happened to her?"

This was the hard part. Randall had given Kate a terse explanation, which wasn't an explanation at all because it didn't explain anything. "She was hit by a baseball bat."

The vet's eyes narrowed. "Deliberately?" Her fingers began probing the Lab's abdomen. The dog tried to escape her fingers. "Please hold her head," the vet said to Kate.

Kate grasped the dog's skull, gazing straight into her glazed eyes. Dr. Chung's question still hung in the air. It didn't take a rocket scientist to guess that something very wrong had happened. She glanced at Lucy. Tears slid down her cheeks, racing one another to be the first to reveal the truth to the vet.

Dr. Chung felt the dog's lower abdomen. "Who hit her?" This time she looked at Lucy.

Lucy's eyes were huge. Stricken. "My brother," she whispered.

"How many times?" The vet's voice was brisk, but Kate could not miss the tension in her shoulders.

Lucy shook her head. A tear wobbled on her chin. "I think just once," she whispered. And then covered her face because she knew just once was too much for this broken dog.

Dr. Chung looked at Kate. "She's in bad shape. Her pelvis is fractured. That we can fix. I'm worried about her liver." She turned to the technician. "Get an IV in her. And prep her for surgery."

Kate stroked the dog's head. Charlie's eyes had

closed. Her whole body seemed limp. "Don't give up, Charlie. Please."

The vet was furiously writing in the dog's file. "The owner is Randall Barrett, correct?"

"Yes."

"You do understand I have to notify Animal Cruelty Services."

"Yes."

"She may be put up for adoption if she survives the surgery." With those final words, Dr. Chung left the room. Kate glanced at Lucy. Her face quivered. She was trying as hard as a girl who'd lost her mother and is about to lose her dog could to control her distress. Kate edged closer to her. Would she allow Kate to comfort her?

The technician waved toward the door. "Charlie needs to be taken in for X-rays now."

Kate gave the dog a final pat. Lucy kissed Charlie on the muzzle, her tears dampening the dog's nose. Kate put her arm on the girl's shoulders and gently drew her away. "We have to leave her now, Lucy."

Lucy nodded, wiping her nose with her sleeve. "I'll see you when you wake up, Charlie."

They walked into the waiting room.

"Do we wait here?" Lucy asked.

The technician at the desk shook her head. "No. We'll call you when she comes out of the O.R."

Lucy opened her mouth to protest, but the technician said, "We'll call you the minute she wakes up, promise."

Kate led Lucy to the parking lot. The night air was soft. Lucy shivered.

Kate's heart thudded against her chest, protesting the sleeping pill/caffeine combo she had ingested.

She headed onto the main highway leading to the bridge. Her vision blurred. She blinked furiously, trying to clear her vision, trying to loosen the clutches of an old terror. She'd been in a car accident before. A fatal one. A car accident where she'd been driving—and her sister hadn't survived.

She gripped the wheel with clammy hands, furious with herself for forgetting a fifteen-year-old vow to never drive under the influence, wishing she'd never taken that stupid pill. And praying she would get to Randall's house before she hurt someone.

The top stair creaked. Signifying his father's imminent arrival. It was about time. Nick had been waiting for over half an hour. Right after the woman had come to take Charlie to the vet, his father had started up the stairs. Then turned around and went back downstairs.

Nick felt awful about Charlie, but he couldn't let it stop him. He'd made a promise.

A pledge.

No, a vow.

But how could he be so stupid to leave the bat under his father's bed? He'd waited in his room in agony, wondering if he could steal into his father's master bedroom to retrieve it. After waiting what seemed like forever, he decided his father was not going to come upstairs after all and it was safe to sneak into the master bedroom. His hand was on the doorknob to his bedroom when he heard his father come up the stairs. Within a minute, his father had yanked open the door.

The hall light threw a shadow across his face. But Nick could see his father's anger in the way he stood, smell it in the scotch that wafted off him in caustic, furious waves.

Now his father knew how Nick felt.

"You coward," his father said. His lip curled. "I thought you had more courage than that."

Nick's chin rose.

His father saw the movement. His nostrils flared. "Charlie was just a defenseless animal. She loved you—"

Don't say that. Don't say that. Don't say that.

He tried to block his father's words. He did not want to hear about the fucking dog. If he allowed himself to think of her in pain, he wouldn't be able to do what he needed to do.

He pressed his hands over his ears.

His father shouted, "You attacked an innocent animal, Nick! What is wrong with you?"

There was nothing *wrong* with him. It was his father who was wrong.

Nick hadn't wanted to.

He hadn't wanted to do any of it.

It was his father who made him.

His father stared at him, challenging him.

He would not let his father win this time.

Not this time.

Rage propelled him forward.

His father staggered back under Nick's weight. He'd caught his father by surprise.

Triumph flashed through him.

He could do this. He could fucking do this.

His father crashed onto his back, his head striking the floor. Nick planted himself on his father's chest. His father stared at him, dazed.

He could win this. He could do this.

He scrambled to pin his father's arms down with his knees. He wasn't going to fuck up killing his father again.

He wrapped his hands around his father's throat.

When his palms began to press against the tendons of his father's neck, understanding finally dawned in those damn blue eyes that used to be able to pin him to the spot.

He watched his father's eyes change. Horror, disbelief. Then anger.

All the while Nick squeezed his father's throat.

All the while Nick saw his mother's body, sprawled on the concrete. Her head, turned toward him. Her face no longer the face of his mother.

His father got an arm free.

No!

Nick squeezed harder, his strength fueled by panic. His father was bulky with muscle. He couldn't let him go.

His father swung a fist at Nick's head before he could duck.

He hit Nick square on the temple. Black spots spun in front of Nick's eyes.

Those two seconds cost him his hold on his father's neck. His father yanked Nick's hands off his neck, and then, before Nick knew what was happening, flipped him over.

Shit! Fucking bastard. His father panted over

him, his fist pulled back and ready to punch Nick in the face.

Then his father lowered his arm.

And turned away.

Don't you underestimate me anymore, you bastard! Don't you dare think I won't do it!

Nick grabbed his father by the shoulder and slammed his fist into his father's face.

Randall's head snapped back.

Nick punched him again. The power of his skin and bone smashing into his father's skin and bone exhilarated him. His head buzzed.

Blood spouted through a slice in his father's cheek. *Yes.*

He wanted his father's head to bleed like his mother's. He smashed his fist into the opened skin. Blood spattered his face. His father's blood. Warmth trickled through his closed fingers.

Randall scrambled back into the hallway. "Nick, stop it."

Nick lunged forward, his fist raised. Blood ran down his wrist. With all his might, he slammed his fist into Randall's ear. His father crashed against the wall. He crumpled down.

Through the roar in his own ears, he heard Lucy shouting.

But nothing could stop him now. Nothing.

He grabbed his father's throat and began to squeeze. His father's eyelids—one almost swollen shut—fluttered. "You fucking bastard." He spat the words. Every one of them gave him strength. He was close, so close. He could feel his father losing the fight.

Lucy threw herself at him. "Nick, stop it, please, Nicky, stop!"

He closed his eyes, shutting out his sister's desperate face.

And squeezed as hard as he could.

His mother's body drifted down from the balcony, white, fluttering. Like a snowflake.

He never saw the bottle coming at his head.

35

Kate stared down at the blond, sweaty head of Randall's son. Her eyes blurred, then focused.

She'd stunned him, not killed him. He swayed. His fingers still held on to Randall's throat.

"Lucy, call the police. Now!" Her voice was shrill, unrecognizable. She raised the bottle again, her fingers trembling. Her sluggish brain was trying to comprehend the scenario: Randall lying beaten and bloodied against the wall; Nick choking his father, his face contorted with rage. "Nick, let go of your father."

Nick turned his gaze to her.

The expression in his eyes made Kate's heart shrivel: the acknowledgment of his damnation.

And worse, the resolve.

She raised the bottle over her head. "Let go, Nick!" She was panting now. Her arm shook with effort.

Nick's nostrils flared. She braced herself. He was taller than she, but she had the bottle. She could protect herself. But could she protect his sister, too? She darted a glance at Lucy. The girl pressed against the wall. Her eyes were huge with confusion. Fear. Disbelief at the sight of her brother trying to murder her father.

Nick's fingers tightened around his father's neck.

Randall was semiconscious now, his breathing ragged.

"Nick, let go!" Kate smashed the bottle down on Nick's arm. Then she threw herself on his back.

He twisted violently, trying to throw her off. She wrapped her arm around his neck and pulled. His head jerked back against her shoulder. She could smell the rank odor of boy-turned-killer.

Before she could react, he smashed his fist into the side of her head. Her head snapped sideways, her ear exploding with pain. She bit down on her jaw, tears springing to her eyes, clinging to him. She'd managed to get him off Randall. She couldn't let him go now.

Randall rolled over onto his hands and knees. He gasped for breath, struggling to stand. Blood gushed down his cheek. Kate's eyes met his and she saw his fury that his son had attacked her, his fear that Nick would hurt her. He wanted her to get away. He swayed, his head drooping.

Then Nick swung his fist again.

Kate acted on instinct. She kneed him from behind, between the legs. He yelped, dropping to his knees and rolled, cupping himself.

She snatched the bottle off the floor, raising it over Nick's head. If he moved, she would hit him again, so help her.

"Freeze! Police!" Two patrol officers stormed into the

hallway, weapons drawn. Kate started, whirling around to see one of the cops pointing his gun at her.

"Facedown. Now!"

Kate froze. *Who, me? I'm not the one you want,* her brain protested.

"Drop the bottle!" one of the cops shouted, lunging toward her. "Facedown on the ground!"

The bottle slipped from her fingers and hit the ground. It rolled by Randall's feet.

She lowered herself to the floor and stretched out, her cheek pressed against the wood. It was cool and hard under her skin. It seemed like the only thing that was real. Everything tilted. Was the sleeping pill screwing with her brain?

Maybe this was all a dream. A hallucination. That was a side effect of Delteze, she recalled.

The other cop put his foot in Nick's back and pushed him over. "Facedown! Hands behind your back!" Nick rolled onto his belly, putting his hands behind him, his face contorted with frustrated rage.

"You!" The cop turned to Randall. His eyes flickered over Randall's bloodied features, lingering on the red marks around his throat. "Get down!" Kate watched Randall ease himself onto the floor, a grunt escaping him before he was fully prostrate. Couldn't the police see that he needed medical attention?

The first cop turned to Lucy. She stood a half-step behind them, a look of horror on her face at what she had invoked with her 911 call. "Were you the girl who placed the call?"

Her head bobbed.

"You said someone was killing your father."

She darted a panicked glance at her brother. He returned the look with the bitterness of betrayal in his eyes.

The cop pointed to Randall. "Is that your father?"

Lucy nodded again.

"And that's your brother?"

"Yes," Lucy said in a whisper. Her eyes did not venture to Nick's face.

"He was trying to kill your father?"

Randall stiffened. "He wasn't try—" He began to cough. He rolled onto his side, doubling up with the spasm. After a few seconds, he cleared his throat. "It was an argument," he gasped. "That's all."

"Yeah, that's all." Nick's voice mocked Randall's pacifying tone. "That's not fucking all!" He twisted, trying to get his feet under him. The cop stepped on his back and shoved him onto the floor.

Tears ran down Nick's face. He stared straight at his father. "He killed my mother!" Nick twisted under the cop's foot. "He fucking killed my mother!"

Lucy jerked, then swayed. The cop grabbed her elbow. Kate stared at Randall. He had a look of stunned horror on his face.

"Tell us down at the station," the first cop said.

36

Monday, 6:45 a.m.

"Nat, I need you to do me a favor." Kate's voice was low. Nat glanced at the clock. It was early. It was Natal Day, she remembered. A civic holiday. She should be sleeping in. She stifled a groan.

"Sure thing."

"Can you run over and let Alaska out for me? I called Finn, but he wasn't home."

Two things caught Nat's attention: Kate wasn't home; nor was Finn. One made her curious. The other, piqued.

"What's up? Did you finally get laid?" Nat asked.

"No…"

Kate's lack of reaction to her crudeness got Nat's reporter antennae vibrating. "It's got something to do with Randall Barrett, doesn't it?"

"Yes." Another pause. "Just wait…" Nat heard a door closing. "I'm in the stairwell at the police station. I can only talk for a minute."

"Jesus. What happened?"

"This is off the record, Nat."

Nat squeezed her eyes shut. Her gut was screaming *scoop*. "Look, if it's a police matter, it'll be on their phone line, Kate."

"Not all of it," Kate said. "I can't tell you if I think it's going to be in tomorrow's paper, Nat."

You're killing me, Kate. She exhaled. "Fine. Off the record. Spill the beans."

"Randall's son tried to kill him last night."

"Je-sus." Nat squeezed her eyes even tighter. This wasn't just a scoop. This was the scoop of the century.

"I was…involved."

"You? How?"

"His son hit Randall's dog with a baseball bat. I took her to the vet hospital with his daughter. When I brought his daughter home, Nick was strangling Randall—" The words came out in a low torrent of disbelief. Nat heard a door open and close.

Then Kate spoke again, her voice forced. "So if you could give Alaska a cup of kibble and let him out to pee, I should be home soon." She hung up before Nat could say another word.

Nat stared at the phone. Then she threw it on the bed, scrambled out of the tangle of sheets and ran to the bathroom, shedding her T-shirt and pajama bottoms on her way.

First, she'd look after Kate's dog.

Then she'd head to the newsroom. See what she could unearth without using Kate as a source.

She turned on the shower. Even though the water always ran freezing cold for the first twenty-seven seconds (she'd counted), she didn't bother to wait for it to warm up.

There was a front-page scoop with her byline on it.

The thick file folder with his name written in bold letters was Nick's first clue that Detective Drake had taken things to a whole new level.

He knew, without needing to see what was written inside, what those notes would tell. And he knew, from looking at Tabitha Christos' worried face, that he was in serious shit.

They would hammer him. Just like his school principals from the many schools he'd attended, his guidance counselors, tutors and therapists. They all used different methods, but they all had the same goal: for Nick to do what they wanted.

He was always the loser.

Nothing had changed.

He had screwed up.

And now his father would get away with murder.

Nothing in life is easy, his father used to lecture him when Nick would put his head down on the kitchen table and cry futile tears over his homework. Except when you're Randall Barrett. Superstar lawyer, superstar killer.

"Nick, do you know why we asked you to come here today?" Tabitha Christos asked. She wore another blouse that hugged her breasts. Nick kept his eyes fixed on the table. He searched for the whorls and burn marks he'd spotted the last time he was here. When he found them, his shoulders relaxed.

"Yeah." *Of course he knew, he wasn't stupid.*

Tabitha's eyes told him what she had refrained from saying: we are going to pick apart your lies until you tell us the truth.

He waited for her to begin the interview, but she leaned back in her chair. No sweet talking today, Nick thought. It was the cop's turn to do the questioning. The detective's eyes drilled into his. "Nick, you committed a serious assault yesterday. Why did you attack your father?"

He raised his chin. "Because he killed my mother."

"But you told us that your mother killed herself."

Nick rubbed his palms lightly over his pants. When he realized what he was doing, he stuffed his hands in his pockets. "Could I have some coffee?" he asked, his voice hoarse. "Please?" He stared at Detective Drake. The detective made no move to get up.

"Sure." Tabitha picked up the phone and asked for coffee to be brought in.

"Nick, why do you think your father killed your mother?"

"Because I saw him do it."

The detective exchanged a look with Tabitha. A cop came in with three mugs of coffee. Nick grabbed his cup with a defiant look and gulped the coffee, the hot brew scalding his tongue, yet comforting him at the same time.

"So tell us what really happened."

Nick stared down at the table. "Everything happened that night just the way I told you. I heard my mother moan so I ran onto the deck. But I fell. Over a flowerpot."

That fucking flowerpot. His mother had died because of a fucking flowerpot.

The detective nodded slightly. "Then what happened?"

Nick's heart thudded. The caffeine jolt made it worse. "When I looked up I saw my father. He was holding my mother."

"Was she struggling?"

"No. She just lay in his arms."

"Do you think she was asleep?"

"I don't know."

"Then what happened?"

"He hit her. With a club."

"Can you describe it?"

"It was small, black. The end looked like a leather pouch."

"A blackjack?"

"Yeah."

"And then what happened?"

Nick had scrambled to his feet, his eyes trying to make sense of the black-and-white blur of motion ten feet away from him. Then his father lifted his mother in his arms.

"He threw her over the balcony."

Nick had lunged forward, trying to reach through the wrought-iron railing to grab her hand, her leg, her nightgown. Anything. But his fingers grasped empty air.

"Then what happened?" The detective's voice was low, intense. Nick looked at him, then at Tabitha Christos. Both of his interrogators appeared transfixed by his story.

"My father ran back through my mother's bedroom. I chased him. But then he ran into the park." Point Pleasant Park, conveniently located across the street for any fleeing wife murderers. "I couldn't follow him. I had to see if—" he swallowed "—if…my mother was still alive."

"Did your father see you?"

Nick's face burned. "When I fell over the flowerpot, he looked over his shoulder and saw me."

"So his back was turned to you on the balcony?"

The detective exchanged another glance with the babe. "Yeah."

"What was he wearing?"

"Black clothes. A dark stocking over his head."

The detective leaned forward. "How could you tell it was your father?"

"I know my dad. And I could see blond hair smushed under the nylon." For the first time, Nick saw a glimmer of doubt in the detective's eyes. "It was my father. I swear it."

"Did he say anything to you?"

"No."

"Your mother?"

"No." Nick gulped his coffee. His father hadn't needed to say anything. Nick just *knew*.

"Tell me exactly why you think it was your father, Nick," Tabitha said.

Nick sighed. Heavily. "The guy was built just like my dad. Same big shoulders. Same height. And he had blond hair." He stared into the detective's eyes. "Besides, who else would want to kill my mother?"

He knew he got them with that question. Tabitha Christos nodded, a thoughtful look on her face.

The detective's eyes narrowed.

And realization hit Nick. How could he have been so stupid? *Because you* are *stupid, stupid.*

Shit. They think I killed my mother. He sat on his hands.

"Why did you lie to us about seeing your mother kill herself?" the detective asked.

Nick looked to Tabitha Christos, but there was no empathy oozing from her warm brown eyes.

"Because I didn't want you to think my father killed her."

"Why not, Nick?"

"Because then you'd arrest him."

"Isn't that what you'd want if your father killed your mother?" Tabitha asked.

"Not when it's *my* father." The detective nodded his head slightly. Detective Drake got what he meant. "My father knows everyone. He's loaded. He'd get himself off in no time."

"This isn't a banana republic, Nick. Your father can't buy his way out of prison," Tabitha Christos said.

Nick shrugged. "He'll hire some top gun who will screw around with you guys until the case is kicked out of court. I know how this works."

Detective Drake's mouth tightened. Nick had scored a bull's-eye. They all knew it was true.

"So you lied to keep us from figuring out your father killed your mother," the detective said. "And then what was your big plan?"

Nick's eyes met his. "I was going to kill him. An eye for an eye."

"So that's what you were doing on Sunday night?"

"Yeah."

"But you didn't kill him."

Nick looked away, his fists curling under his thighs. He hadn't killed him. And he'd regret it for as long as he lived.

"No. The fucker."

"Nick, if we find evidence that your father killed your mother, we would need you to testify in court." Detective Drake's face was somber, but Nick saw a glimmer in his eyes. The detective was excited, he realized. "Would you be willing to do that?"

"I want my father to pay for what he's done."

The detective stood. "You realize that if you're lying again, there will be serious consequences. You've committed a serious crime, Nick. A very serious crime."

Nick didn't answer.

His grandmother met him in the waiting room. "Ready to go, Nick?" she asked, her eyes scanning his face.

"Yeah." They walked out to the parking lot. The morning fog had burned off to reveal a glorious afternoon. Several blocks over, Nick could see Citadel Hill, the massive hill in the middle of the city with the fort on top. It looked kind of cool. Couples draped themselves over towels, clad in bikinis and shorts, facing the sun. If he lived here, he'd take Steph to sunbathe with him. He thought of her smooth limbs, the freckles on her arms, the curve of her thighs. The way her skin soaked up the sun until it was so hot to the touch.

His grandmother unlocked the car. Nick threw himself into the passenger seat and rolled down the window. In Toronto, he took the subway everywhere or his bike. He hated being chauffeured around, like a kid. He'd been counting down the months until he could get his beginner's license.

His grandmother pulled the car into traffic. "When we get back to my house, why don't you take Scrubby for a walk," she said. Scrubby was her dog, a mix of border collie, beagle and German shepherd. "It's such a beautiful day."

"Is my father coming over?"

His grandmother threw him a startled look. She could not quite mask her fear at his question.

She was a smart woman, he thought.

"I'm not sure when he's coming," she said, her voice even.

He shrugged, his mind already on the next stage of his plan. He hoped his father would come before the police arrested him.

One niggling thought broke through: Would they let him get his driver's license in prison?

37

The row of crisp, black stitches ended abruptly by the far corner of Randall Barrett's right eye, a broken railroad track permanently marking his train-wrecked face.

Mottled and swollen, Randall Barrett had had the crap beaten out of him. By his own son.

Ethan wondered how that would feel. He'd seen it many times before, father pitted against son, the upstart rebelling against the old man.

But this attack was different in nature. It wasn't fueled by rebellion, but vengeance.

Of the most deadly kind.

Nick had not intended to beat up his father.

He'd meant to kill him.

That must have shaken Barrett.

So must the accusation his son had leveled against him in front of everyone.

How did it feel to have your own flesh and blood accuse you of murder?

Ethan stirred his coffee. Barrett had declined a drink of any sort, although Ethan guessed his throat must feel pretty scratchy after the stranglehold Nick had had on it.

Thanks to Nick's statement, they now had a homicide investigation. "Your son committed a serious assault." Ethan made a point of glancing at his file. The patrol officers' report sat prominently on top. Under it, he had stuffed a bunch of youth-offender files to make the folder appear nice and thick.

Barrett slouched in the hard chair, his shirt specked with blood, his arms crossed. Bruises marred his knuckles. His bloodshot eyes remained impassive in his swollen face. Ethan knew it would take some work to get a rise out of him. He took another sip of his coffee. Time to get down to business. "Looking at those marks on your neck, we could make a case for attempted murder."

"It would be hard to prove," Barrett rasped.

Ethan shrugged. He knew that Barrett would never go to court and testify that his son had tried to kill him. He had more pride than that. He bet it took all of Barrett's self-control not to yank his collar over his son's thumbprints. As for Lucy Barrett and Kate Lange, they'd only arrived at the end. Without Randall Barrett to testify, the case would be weak.

"Interesting timing, though, wouldn't you say?" Ethan took another drink of his coffee. After what had happened in the Barrett household last night—and after he had heard who had been there at two o'clock in the goddamn morning—he needed that coffee. He bit into his bagel. Maybe it would soak up some of that acid.

Barrett watched him, his arms crossed, his eyes alert.

His mouth shut.

"Sure I can't get you something?"

Barrett just looked at him.

Ethan leaned back in his chair. "Why would your son attack you two days after your ex-wife was killed?" he asked, his tone conversational.

His choice of words was not lost on Barrett. There were no more euphemisms about Elise Vanderzell falling to her death. Barrett's jaw tightened ever so slightly.

"Your son says you killed her." Ethan bit into his bagel.

Not a flicker, not a twitch. That itself was a giveaway: Barrett was trying to control his reactions.

"He says he saw you hit her head with a club. It wouldn't be a blackjack, would it?" Made of a smooth leather pouch about six inches in length, they were spring-loaded, lethal weapons. Perfect for inflicting maximum damage with little outward harm. He couldn't wait to call Dr. Guthro with this new information.

A slight flush to Barrett's bruised face was the only sign he registered Ethan's goading. How does it feel to strike a lethal blow to a woman you had made love to only months before, who had borne your children, whom you had cradled in your arms just before killing? Ethan wondered.

Barrett stared at him. The sliver of bloodied eyeball revealed by his swollen eyelid had gained an awful intensity.

"Your son says he saw you toss your ex-wife over the

balcony." Ethan made his voice soft, willing Barrett to strain closer to hear.

He was gratified to see his ploy worked. When he had Barrett nice and close, he said, "He says he wanted you to pay," uttering the words as viciously as a snake digging its fangs into an exposed vein.

Barrett jerked back.

Anger flared in his eyes. But not fast enough to hide the anguish in their depths. Barrett stood. "I have a phone call to make. To my lawyer."

He walked out the door.

Ethan watched him leave.

He'd put the ball in motion.

Now he just had to make sure it didn't get away from him.

He picked up the phone and called Redding. "We need search warrants for Barrett's house, his office, his car and his yacht." Nick Barrett's statement had given them enough cause for a JP to authorize it.

He gulped the rest of his coffee. He needed his brain to be on full alert to deal with his next interview.

Kate Lange, the woman who he had once thought would be his wife, was cooling her heels in the waiting room.

He was about to find out why she was in her boss' house at two o'clock in the goddamn morning.

38

He knew he should have asked Brown to do this one. If he'd been smart, he would have.

But Ethan never claimed to be a genius. Ergo the empty extra-large coffee cup that had released enough acid in his stomach to cauterize his entire intestinal system.

He just wished it would cauterize his nerves. Everything jumped into high gear when Kate walked into the room.

His eyes skimmed her from head to toe. She raised her chin, a slight flush putting color into her cheeks.

He watched her walk toward him. She swayed ever so slightly. Still recovering from the thigh injury? He hadn't seen her since he'd visited her in the hospital in May, although her picture had been plastered over all the media outlets for weeks.

But seeing her in the flesh…now he realized every feeling he'd hoped had been dead and buried had merely been comatose. Desire and pain swelled to life in his chest. His voice literally stuck in his throat.

He'd loved her.

He'd deeply loved her.

He loved her still.

God, no.

Not after she'd told him so definitely it was over.

Even the way she looked at him right now told him it was over. At least for her.

Put it behind you, Drake. It's over.

For you, at least.

But what about Randall Barrett?

His teeth ground together. When Barrett called him last May to tell him that Kate was in danger, he could tell from the tone of the man's voice that it was more than just fear for Kate's safety that had spurred his phone call.

Did Kate return the feeling? Had her own crisis and her firm's involvement in the TransTissue fraud drawn her closer to Randall Barrett?

Why else would she be at his house in the middle of the night?

A suspicion snaked through him. *Had Barrett's involvement with Kate compelled him to murder Elise?*

Ethan's eyes flickered over Kate, trying not to linger on the high curve of her butt in her faded, paint-splattered jeans, or the smooth swell of her breasts under her running jacket. Her choice of clothing did not suggest she'd been engaged in a night of lovemaking at her boss' house. When Ethan and Kate were together, she'd made an effort. Body-skimming knits. Lace-trimmed bras. Matching panties.

Did she wear the same lingerie for Randall Barrett? Did he take those delicate wispy nothings off with his teeth, his lips grazing the sensitive skin of her thighs? Making her moan a low, throaty animal call to mate?

Acid churned a big ball of gaseous fire in his gut.

He stood. Forced a smile. She smiled back. It was tentative. Tired.

Apprehensive.

She sat down in the proffered chair. Her eyes, clear despite the dark circles beneath them, met his.

He let the silence grow between them. He needed to get control back. He needed to erase from his memory those images that attacked him like stealth missiles, detonating pain and desire in his chest.

Focus, Drake. Focus on the facts: she had been caught assaulting a fifteen-year-old boy.

She never called you after you visited her at the hospital.

Jesus, get over it, would you?

Fact two: she had been at her boss' house in the middle of the night, just two days after Barrett's ex-wife had been murdered.

That worked. His head felt clearer. "How are you, Kate?" He managed a relaxed tone.

She gave him a wry look. "Busy." Her hair was pulled up in a loose ponytail, revealing the delicate veins behind her ears. He noticed the summer sun had lightened her hair. "How are you?"

"Good." He picked up a pen. "Things are good."

"Good." She smiled. Waiting expectantly.

He caught himself rolling the pen between his fingers. *Good grief.* He was behaving like he was a fifteen-year-old moron again. "Things aren't going so good for your boss, though."

"It's terrible about his wife." Her eyes were open, disingenuous. But he sensed it was an act.

After all, she'd said "wife." Not "ex-wife." What was going on between Randall and Kate? Randall and Elise?

"Elise Vanderzell was murdered, Kate."

Kate looked away. "So I understand."

"And Nick Barrett tried to kill his father."

Kate's eyes returned to his. There was a sadness in their depths. He knew why, he understood it now. But he couldn't let it affect him. "Tell me what happened," he said softly.

She exhaled. "I don't really know. When I got to Randall's house, Nick was choking him."

"Why were you going to your boss' house at two in the morning?"

A light flush crept up her neck.

Damn it. There was *something going on.*

"I had to bring his daughter home."

That surprised him. "You mean Lucy?"

"Yes. I had taken her to the vet hospital with me." She tucked the wisp of hair behind her ear again. "Randall's dog was sick."

"What was wrong with her?"

"She broke her pelvis."

He sensed she was being deliberately vague. "How?" His voice was curt.

Kate flashed him a look. *Aha.* He was getting under her skin. "Nick hit her with a baseball bat."

"Deliberately?"

She exhaled. "I don't know. Randall called me. I took the dog. When I came back, Nick was choking Randall."

"Then what did you do?"

Her eyes flashed a you-know-damn-well-what-I-did look. "I hit Nick with a bottle. Randall was almost unconscious by then." She glanced down at her hands. As if she couldn't believe what they'd done. Then she looked back at Ethan. They both knew her hands were capable of being so much more deadly than that. "He said that Randall had killed his mother." This was said wearily.

"I see." Ethan made a show of writing this down.

Her gaze followed the movement of his pen. "You think Randall did it, don't you?"

He looked up and met her eyes. For eyes so clear, he couldn't read the expression. Hadn't that always been the way? She always held back a piece of herself. "The evidence is stacking up."

"But why would he do it, Ethan?" she asked in a low voice. "What motive did he have? They were divorced."

Ethan's heart constricted.

He may not be able to read her eyes, but he could read between the lines.

Those stealth missiles had been tipped with poison, he discovered. Jealousy burned a straight path into the darkest part of his heart.

"Kate." He made his voice soft, caressing. The way he used to speak to her after they made love. "You ever heard of ex sex?"

39

Monday, 9:14 a.m.

Blood rushed to Kate's head.

Ex sex.

The words conjured up memories she'd been desperately holding at bay since she walked into the room and saw Ethan sitting behind the table.

Now the sensations flooded her: Ethan's skin, hot and smooth, under her hand. His tongue, whispering words of pleasure in her ear before flicking her nerves into ecstasy.

Her last lover had been Curtis, but he hadn't gotten into her heart. Not like the man staring at her across the table. The man who'd shown her how passion could be. The man who had been the most generous, thrilling lover she'd ever had.

The man who had deliberately dropped this bombshell with cruelty in his eyes.

She had no right to feel hurt. But she did.

He waited for her reaction. Which was the last thing she wanted to give him.

She leaned back and crossed her arms. "Your point?"

"Your boss' ex-wife had an abortion two weeks ago."

Her breath stopped. "And?"

"She'd been in the first trimester of her pregnancy."

Kate began to feel sick. Ethan was playing out the information for a reason. She'd wait it out. Wait for the bombshell she sensed he was about to drop.

"Randall Barrett visited his ex-wife in early June."

He'd laid out the timeline neatly. Leaving her to come to the same conclusions she could read in his eyes: that Randall Barrett had impregnated his wife and she'd had an abortion.

"Is he the father?" She forced her voice to remain cool, professional.

"If you're asking if we have tangible proof, the answer is not yet. But I'm confident a DNA sample will confirm our suspicions."

"How? Do you have tissue samples?"

"We're checking with the abortion clinic right now. They haven't gotten back to us yet."

So. What the police had right now was circumstantial evidence. The facts could be interpreted a number of ways, she knew that.

But she didn't feel reassured.

The timeline Ethan had provided fit in with her own personal interactions with Randall since the TransTissue affair: his sudden preoccupation, his deliberate aloofness toward her.

Damn. Damn. Damn.

He'd slept with Elise. And then his ex-wife had come to Halifax for the month.

Kate barely focused on the rest of Ethan's questions. Partly because her brain was unsteadily jumping from fact to fact, trying to absorb what Ethan had revealed to her, partly because the rest of his questions were routine. He'd accomplished what he'd set out to do: he'd pulled the rug out from under her.

And that really stung.

She scrambled out of the room, hoping Ethan hadn't seen how much he had hurt her.

Or how much more Randall had hurt her.

40

Monday, 2:52 p.m.

He was in deep shit.

Randall sat on the edge of the bed in his hotel suite. His suitcase sat on the other bed, untouched. When the police came to his house to serve the search warrants, he hadn't been surprised. The writing was on the wall. Drake's taunting this morning had given him a good indication of how confident the police were that they were on the right trail.

His trail.

So he'd packed a bag, leaving his home to be rifled by the police. Already the house had distanced itself from him. As if it was bracing itself for its violation. And blaming him. It had become, in the past few days, just a space with objects.

Before he left, he called the daughter of his neighbor. She agreed to water his garden.

He locked the door. He didn't look back.

Couldn't look back.

Because he had the feeling he was never going back.

It was a melodramatic thought, an emotion bred by the trauma of the past few days.

But he couldn't shake it.

He had acted recklessly. Drunkenly. Disgracefully.

He hoped that was all.

Dear God, he hoped getting drunk was the worst he'd done.

Because what Nick accused him of shook him to the core.

What if…?

He jumped to his feet. He couldn't think about it. And yet, his son believed he'd seen him killing Elise.

And he had no idea where he'd been that night.

He couldn't have done that.

Could he?

He lowered his head into his hands.

It was time to meet his lawyer.

He found himself hurrying to the hotel bar, gazing straight ahead to avoid the stares from the other guests. He looked as if he'd been hit by a truck. He wanted to shock the curiosity out of their faces, tell them that you too could look like this if your teenage son tried to commit patricide.

When he pushed open the glass doors of the bar, he forced himself to take his time. Intimate pairings of sofas sat on Persian-style rugs against one side of the room. From the farthest corner, his lawyer gave Randall a small wave.

Randall moved toward him, passing a group of tourists who had either had enough of the Natal Day celebrations or were just getting warmed up. They stared at him, unable to disguise their shock at his battered face, unable to meet his unswollen eye.

Bill Anthony shook Randall's hand vigorously. Randall was not going to let this guy see how tender his own hand was. He forced a smile. "Bill, good to see you." As if this were a regular business lunch.

One of Halifax's top—and highest-profile—criminal defense lawyers, Bill Anthony was only average height, with stubby salt-and-pepper hair and a face Randall was sure only Bill's mother loved, but he exuded the confidence of a man who knew he was the best in his profession. His eyes, sharp and bright like a ferret's, flickered over Randall, noting his stitches, swollen eye and bruised neck with a glint of amusement. "So, tell me what they have."

Randall gave him all that he knew. He tried to be objective, lawyer to lawyer, but when he described Nick's first attack, the words got stuck in his throat. Randall had assumed Nick was acting out by hitting the dog. But now he realized Nick had never intended to attack Charlie. He'd been gunning for Randall. And the dog had saved him.

He still could not comprehend it.

Bill popped a peanut in his mouth. "So your son explained the attack by telling the police he saw you throw your ex-wife over the balcony?"

Jesus. Did he have to say it like that? "Yes." Randall took a long pull on the rum and Coke he had ordered.

What had gone wrong between him and Nick? That Nick could believe he was capable of killing someone, let alone his ex-wife?

"Do you think your son killed your ex-wife?"

Randall stared into his drink. The slice of lime had turned brown, sinking to the bottom of the glass. "No. He had no reason to."

"And yet he tried to kill you."

"He wanted revenge." Randall forced himself to sound dispassionate, but his mind was protesting: *I can't believe I'm saying these words about my own son. My ex-wife. My family.*

"And where were you the night she died?"

"I don't know." His admission was soft, but rang in his ears.

Bill Anthony's eyes narrowed. "What do you mean?"

"I had too much to drink. I can't remember anything after I went to this bar downtown."

"Blackout?"

"I suppose so." He felt humiliated. He'd never in his life lost his faculties like that.

What if...?

He quashed the thought.

"What kind of condition were you in when the police found you? Were you disheveled? Bruised? Did you have any scratches you don't remember getting?" As he spoke, Bill Anthony's eyes scanned Randall's hands, face.

Randall tried not to flinch under his lawyer's gaze. "I don't think I was any more disheveled than you'd expect when you've drunk that much booze."

"Look, Randall, the police are lining up their ducks. They just need the murder weapon and they'll be after you." Bill chewed another peanut, vigorously. Thoroughly.

Randall watched Bill's jaw work. How could someone spend so much time masticating one frigging peanut?

"They may try to charge you even without the weapon." Bill reached for another peanut. Randall had to restrain himself from grabbing Bill's hand and yanking it away from the bowl. "If they think your son's testimony is strong enough." He chucked the nut into his mouth.

"So what do you think we should do?"

Randall's question halted Bill's hand in his quest for the peanut bowl. His dark eyes locked onto Randall's. "First of all, make them realize that they may have the wrong guy. Your son has a history of problems. He attacked your dog. He just tried to kill you. They shouldn't rule him out."

"There's no way I'm deflecting this onto Nick."

"How do you know he's not deflecting it onto you?" Bill scooped up a handful of nuts and jiggled them in his hand. "Either way, he's taking you down, Randall."

Randall stared at his drink. It was dark and murky. His bile rose. "I can't do that."

"Then we go with plan B."

"Which is?" Randall knew he wasn't going to like this. Maybe it was the way that Bill's eyes had narrowed. Or the way that he'd thrown all the nuts in his mouth.

"We argue that your ex-wife killed herself."

Randall stared at him. Had Elise killed herself? He didn't know. His gut told him she hadn't.

She loved those kids too much.

"We know that Elise was under the care of a psychologist, that she'd just had an abortion and that she had a history of severe postpartum depression."

Randall closed his eyes. It was sure to be all over the media. *Successful Lawyer Victim of Depression*. Then the media would provide salacious details of Elise's previous postpartum issues under the guise of shedding light on an important social issue.

"What about my son's testimony?"

"We'll show he had reason to fabricate a story. Besides, it was dark. He'd fallen."

"So your strategy is to make my ex-wife and my son look like basket cases?"

"Exactly." Bill reached for the final peanut in the bowl.

Randall was sure Bill Anthony would mete out the same vigorous mastication to his ex-wife and child. "No, thanks." He stood, then stalked out of the bar. A waitress stepped out of his path. The fear in her eyes forced him to slow down. He looked like a crazed beast, with his beaten-up, angry face.

This depersonalized box dressed in heavy brocade and fake mahogany wood wasn't helping. He felt like a caged animal. He was scared he would begin to behave like one. Real air was what he needed.

He drove his rental car down to the water by Point Pleasant Park, yearning for his own vehicle that had been seized by the police under the search warrant. The salty breeze ruffled his hair, cooling his inflamed skin. Sunlight swathed the water in ribbons.

He had planned to be far out on the ocean by now. Just him, the water and his son.

His phone rang. "Randall, I've been trying to reach you," Nina Woods said, her voice crisp, holding an edge of accusation.

"I've been held up." *So would you, if your ex-wife was killed and then your own son tried to murder you.*

"I left a message with your associate at your home." There was no mistaking her tone: What the hell was Kate Lange doing at your house?

He wanted to leave Nina Woods stewing over that, but it wasn't fair to Kate. She had to work with this woman, this rainmaker who had saved Randall's ass just a few months ago.

She'd been a coup, bringing Great Life Insurance and several other corporate entities with lucrative business to the newly branded McGrath Barrett, providing a needed income stream for the partners. It had helped eradicate some of the doubts about Randall's leadership. But Nina Woods was well aware of her value.

"We need you to come in," she said.

The fact that Nina Woods felt confident enough to make demands on the firm's managing partner told him that he was no longer in charge. And her choice of words insinuated that he was no longer part of the "we." She had turned his partners on him.

Although, he suspected, they hadn't been hard to persuade. It was telling that it was the newest partner in the firm who'd called him. The partner who had the least history with him.

"When?"

"Tomorrow—9:00 a.m."

He hung up.

The wind was picking up, the ocean no longer ribboned in silver. Instead, the wind ruffled the surface into white-tipped swells.

He raised his head and let the wind fill his ears. The

wind could tell you a lot. Whether there's a fog lurking beyond Chebucto Head, whether a warm rain was coming from the south, the wind never lied. Never betrayed you. It will give you the full force of its wrath or cool you from the midsummer heat, it will caress your cheeks or whip your hair into a tangle. But it will always play straight with you.

And the wind was telling him he'd better watch his back.

41

It was becoming a compulsion. Every few hours he would check the *Halifax Post*'s website, searching for a mention of the Barrett case—searching for another photo of Lucy Barrett.

There were several updates, but none that involved Lucy. On Monday, the *Halifax Post* reported Randall Barrett had been assaulted by his son, Nick.

He had scrolled down the article, his fingers shaking with impatience, only to find that the photo accompanying the report had been mined from a hockey tournament in which a flushed Nick, bulky in his hockey gear, grinned at the camera.

Disappointed yet again by the lack of fresh material on the website, he clicked on the archives, plowing through the links until he found the photo of Lucy taken the night her mother died. He let out his breath.

Her grief, her shock, her softly rounded vulnerability never failed to stir him.

It had been like that with Becky Murphy, too. In the beginning.

A runaway with a tough attitude smeared over her childlike features, Becky was the first girl with whom he'd been able to consummate his desires without fear of reprisal. He'd picked her up on a rural road in the heart of Nova Scotia, about one hundred miles away from his cabin. She hadn't gone willingly into the specially fitted basement, but she was easy enough to overpower. She'd been the first girl he'd ever abducted, the first girl he'd ever physically restrained. He'd been amazed at how easy it was.

It had been perfect in the beginning. Becky, unloved and unwanted, had blossomed under his care.

He'd visited her on weekends, and occasional weeknights. After each of their weekends together, he would shackle Becky to a ring in the wall, assuring her that it was a symbol of his commitment to her. He would never abandon her, he'd explained. He would always come back and unlock her.

She had never complained. And the chain had been long—she had plenty of room to move. The basement was furnished with a small refrigerator, a tiny bathroom with a bath, a TV (no cable but with a DVD player and a generous assortment of DVDs), a bed and his *coup de grâce*—a pair of lovebirds.

Becky had loved the birds. She'd never had a pet before. She had named them Hugs and Kisses. Given a chance to love something that loved her back, she'd matured and finally learned to trust.

Perhaps that had been the turning point. Or perhaps it was the fact that there was no immediate danger to what he was doing. And even though she was technically his captive, she had been so pathetically eager to see him that the whole situation was depressingly domestic.

One Friday night in May, she'd thrown herself in his arms, then placed his hand over her stomach. "You knocked me up," she'd said. Her words were crude, but a small glow of excitement had lit her eyes.

She was going to be a mother. Another little bird for her nest of captivity.

And he couldn't help but suspect that this was a ploy to get his attention. She had sensed his distance. She had been desperate for him to lavish her with the love he'd given her at the beginning. So she had tricked him. They had always used condoms that he'd left in the tiny bathroom. Had she tampered with them?

Becky Murphy had become a liability. He couldn't let her have his child. Besides, her pregnancy had been the tangible proof of what his subconscious had been telling him: Becky was no longer the prepubescent girl he'd abducted.

She had become a woman.

The next week, while she was stroking Hugs and Kisses, cooing to the birds in a high-pitched voice that set his teeth on edge, he had slipped an electrical cord around her neck.

Garroting her had been simple.

He'd killed her quickly, while she was with those she loved most in the world.

He'd buried her in a shallow grave in the basement. That was three years ago.

There had been no other girls since Becky.

Until now.

He ran his finger over Lucy's face, imagining the velvety texture of her skin, the smoothness of her mouth.

His finger left a smear of sweat on his laptop screen.

42

Monday, 6:03 p.m.

His mother greeted Randall with her usual hug, but only their arms embraced; their bodies did not touch. Penelope had never been a physically demonstrative woman, although Randall never doubted her love for her family, for her art, for her little Cape Cod perched on the edge of the ocean or for her dog, Scrubby.

He stepped back and studied his mother's face.

Lines of fatigue were etched around her eyes and mouth, deepened over the past few days by sorrow and confusion. But not suspicion. Her gaze was level. He let out a breath he hadn't realized he was holding. His mother did not think he'd killed Elise; he could see it in her eyes.

He wanted to hug her. Tight this time. He wanted her to tell him that the kids were okay, that he was okay, that life was okay.

He stepped back. "How are things?" he asked in a low voice.

"David called. About Elise's funeral." Randall's

shoulders tightened. He dreaded seeing Elise's parents, even more so now, with his face branded by Nick's accusations. Penelope hesitated. "Randall, David told me they want custody of Nick and Lucy."

His chest tightened. "I'm the legal guardian."

"They think you were responsible for Elise's death." Randall noted his mother couldn't bring herself to say he killed his ex-wife. She was trying to protect his feelings, but her choice of words made him feel worse. "They want to fight for custody."

He crossed his arms. "My children belong with me. I'm their father."

Penelope looked at him with such profound sadness that fear curled through him. "What do you think the children want to do?" she asked, her voice soft.

"Lucy will want to live with me."

"And Nick?"

He looked away. "He'll come around."

"Maybe."

He cleared his throat. "When are they planning the service?"

She bit her lip. "They were told by the police that the homicide team is still waiting for toxicology reports. Since it's a long weekend and some of the lab staff are out on summer vacation, they think it could be over a week before the police will release her body."

"That long." Though it would give him some time to sort things out here.

"Yes."

"We'd better get our flights booked. Could I ask you to do that?"

Penelope put a hand on his arm. "They don't want

you to come, Randall. They asked if I could chaperone the children on the airplane."

Rage burst through his hurt. "Goddamn them!"

There was an uncustomary sheen of tears in her eyes. "I'm sorry."

"She was my wife. My *wife*. The mother of my children. I want to mourn her, too."

"I know." Penelope's voice was husky. "I understand. But they lost their only child, Randall. To a violent death. And their own grandson thinks his father did it." She blinked. For a moment, she looked frail. Old.

He didn't know why he was arguing with her. It was Elise's parents—not his own mother, who had stood by him—who needed to hear his frustration. He cleared his throat. "How is Lucy doing today?"

Penny shook her head. "She won't come out of her room. She's barely eaten anything. I'm worried about her."

"I'll go up and see her."

But he made no move to go. There was one more member of the family he had not inquired about. "What about Nick?"

Penelope's eyes welled. "He won't come out of his room, either." She looked past him, at the ocean. The metallic-gray water heaved against the shore. "I'm scared, Randall," she said in a low voice. "He's completely changed."

"Has he threatened you?"

After Nick had attacked him, the police had taken them into custody but no charges were laid, so they were both let go.

Nick, deflated and sullen, had returned to Penelope's

house. Randall had assumed that his son's rage had only one target: him. But now he cursed his lack of judgment. How could he have left his mother with Nick? She was vulnerable. So was Lucy.

The thought snaked into his mind again: Had Nick killed his own mother?

God, how had his family turned on itself?

"I'll deal with it."

"No. Wait." Penelope grabbed Randall's arm. "I don't think you should speak to Nick. He'll just explode again." Her eyes, so like his own, so like his son's, forced him to acknowledge the truth of what she was saying. "He needs help, Randall. Professional help. I think Lucy should have some, too."

"We're fine." He tugged his arm, but she would not let go.

"No. You can't deal with this yourself, Randall. Neither can I. These kids are in shock. You need to get them some help."

He swiped a hand through his hair. What was wrong with him? He'd always been so sure of his decisions, but now he doubted himself. His kids were shell-shocked. *For God's sake, his son had tried to kill him.* And he'd just told his mother they were fine.

His mother watched him.

"Maybe we should call a psychologist." His words dragged, reluctant to face the light of day.

Penelope's hand relaxed on his arm. "I think that would be a good idea." Remorse stabbed Randall. He was putting his mother through something she did not deserve. He was making her bear the cost of his mistakes. "In fact—" She stopped abruptly.

"What?"

Penelope exhaled. "Lucy spoke to me a little about Nick. About his behavior. I think she blamed herself for what happened on Sunday night. Apparently, after Nick stole that money, Elise asked Lucy to come to a few of her therapy sessions to talk about Nick. The therapist was hoping that Lucy might know more about what was going on at school, et cetera."

"And…"

"Now Lucy's worried she missed something. Something terrible about her brother that might have prevented what happened. She feels guilty, Randall."

He couldn't speak. Lucy shouldn't have to carry this burden.

"I was just thinking," his mother said softly, her eyes searching his, "maybe we should call this therapist. His name is Dr. Gainsford. He knows the family dynamics. He met Lucy. She seemed to like him. It would be one less strange thing for her to have to deal with. We can ask him if he can recommend someone for Nick, too."

Randall closed his eyes. He'd been so blind, so wrapped up in his own fucking problems he hadn't even seen what his young daughter was going through. "Call him. I'll fly him in from Toronto if need be."

Penelope exhaled. "Thank you." Exhaustion pulled at her features. "I'll make some tea."

"I'll go see Lucy." The narrow wooden staircase, warped by age and damp, creaked under Randall's weight. Nick's door was to the right. Closed tight and probably locked on the inside.

Lucy's was on the left. It was partly open. He knocked.

"Come in."

Lucy gasped when she saw his face. He was able to control his own reaction to her appearance. Her normally peach-colored complexion was so sallow it looked almost yellow.

And her eyes…

His own eyes pricked with tears.

Her eyes were pools of loss. Despair. So deep, so still.

He swallowed, trying not to weep when Lucy wrapped her arms around her knees. Instead of wrapping her arms around him. "Daddy," she whispered. "Where were you?"

"I told you, honey, I had to go to the hotel."

"I meant the night Mummy died."

The surf crashed against the rocks, elemental, unstoppable.

He reached out a hand and stroked her hair, no longer smooth and soft, but tangled and greasy.

She pulled back against the headboard. Her eyes were full of fear. She was scared what he would say. She was scared he would tell her that he killed her mother.

"I was on my boat, Lucy." She needed to believe him. He needed to believe it, too. "I swear to you, I did not go back to the house."

"But Nick says he saw you—"

Randall shook his head. "It wasn't me. I would never do that." *Would I?*

She looked away.

His heart broke.

She doesn't believe me.

My own daughter, the child I rocked to sleep and carried on my back, does not believe me.

"Lucy, I swear to you I did not—" He couldn't say "kill." He could not use that word with his daughter. "I would never hurt your mother."

And yet, wasn't that a lie? He'd hurt Elise in a thousand different ways.

As she'd hurt him.

Oh, God.

"I tried calling you." Every child's unspoken reproach: Why weren't you there when I needed you?

"I'm sorry, Lucy. I'll never turn my phone off again." He meant it. He was now the sole parent. He edged closer to her, needing to make contact, craving the reassurance that he still had a family. "What can I do to make it up to you?"

She closed her eyes. "Nothing. I don't want anything." She curled sideways and rolled facedown into her pillow. "I just want to be left alone."

He put a hand on her shoulder. She shook it off.

"Leave me alone. Please." It was her politeness that killed him. She spoke to him as though he were a stranger.

His mother was right. His children needed help.

He hoped Elise's therapist would know what to do.

He left Lucy's room. There was nowhere to go but back downstairs.

The wood creaked under his weight.

43

Fog had moved in during the night. It settled over Halifax, warm and damp. Kate glimpsed mist sparkling on her hair as she rode the elevator up to MB's offices, then turned her face so she could not see her reflection in the mirrored wall. No need to be reminded of the deep circles and bloodshot eyes that had greeted her this morning.

Even the sleeping pill she took last night couldn't erase those. What the pharmaceutical companies really needed to do, she thought as she hurried down the corridor to her office, was create a sleeping pill that made you *look* rested, even if you didn't feel rested. Profits would soar.

Because she wanted to look good this morning. Damn good. She did not want Curtis Carey to think she'd lost one iota of sleep over him.

Even now, seventy-two hours later, her cheeks burned at how she'd treated him. She flipped open the Great Life file, flopping behind her desk, frowning furiously at the independent medical expert's report on plaintiff Mike Naugler's injuries. Thank goodness she'd already gone through it yesterday with a fine-tooth comb, because the words swam in front of her eyes. She wouldn't have much to do today, anyway. The questions would be asked by Curtis, who would be poking around the medical expert's opinion to check its watertightness.

She glanced at her clock. The old battered silver travel clock ticked toward twenty to nine. *Showtime.* She grabbed her notepad, stacking it on the thick file folders in her arms, and headed to the boardroom.

Besides the discovery reporter, she was the first to arrive. Just as she planned. She lined up her notepad and pen, spreading out her files with the multicolored tabs. Cupping a coffee mug in her hand, she stared through the window. Gray.

"Kate." Rachel, the new receptionist, stood in the doorway. "Dr. Mercer is here." Her client's medical expert pushed through the doorway. Impeccably attired, with a look of self-importance on his face, he did nothing to reduce Kate's contempt. This guy was a hired gun; a doctor who didn't actually have his own practice but instead flew all over the country giving "expert opinions" to his insurance company clients.

The receptionist added, "Tom Werther from Great Life called." She glanced down at the message in her beautifully manicured hand. "He says he became sick very suddenly and won't be able to attend the discovery."

"He must have caught Nina Woods' bug," Kate said, rising to her feet to greet her expert. "Dr. Mercer." She held out her hand. "I've reviewed your report. Nina

Woods told me she'd already briefed you with the questions we expect will be asked by the plaintiff."

"Yes, she did."

"Do you have any questions?"

"Where's the coffee?" He grinned. Kate forced herself to return his smile.

"Just over there. Help yourself."

He turned to the back of the room where refreshments and pastries were set up on a credenza.

Relax, Kate. Whatever you do, don't let Curtis see that you dislike your own client.

Rachel knocked lightly. Curtis Carey ushered in plaintiff Mike Naugler. Both of them were damp, the fog giving Curtis' hair a slightly shaggy wave. His hair had been soft and thick, Kate remembered. Just as soft as the matting of hair on his chest. She remembered the low groan he'd made when he came.

She dropped her eyes to her notepad, her cheeks burning. What the hell was she thinking? She had mentally undressed the guy and had sex with him—and he'd only just arrived.

Curtis' eyes flickered over Kate. She prayed he wasn't doing what she'd just done. She gave him a quick nod then pointedly ran her pen along a paragraph as if Dr. Mercer's words were worthy of such attention.

The plaintiff glared at the good doctor, who sank his teeth into a glistening mound of jam in the center of a pastry. A dot of jam oozed out of the corner of his mouth.

"Ms. Lange." Curtis gave Kate as brief a nod as humanly possible.

"Mr. Carey. Mr. Naugler. Good morning." She rose

to her feet, the brisk hostess to this hostile proceed-
ing. "Coffee and pastries are at the back. Please help
yourself."

Curtis walked to the coffee station without a word.
There would be no dimples today.

Homicide unit sergeant Deb Ferguson had called in
Ethan, Redding, Lamond and Warren for the first team
meeting of the day. Lamond had stopped at Tim Hortons
and bought everyone a double double.

"Did you get the toxicology report back yet?" Deb
asked.

Redding shook his head. "The lab's backed up. Between the long weekend and summer vacations, they told
me they wouldn't have anything until next Monday."

Ethan stared at Redding, dismayed. "Vanderzell's
parents keep calling."

Redding shrugged. "She's gonna be on ice for a while.
The lab told me the *earliest* would be next Monday. We
wouldn't be able to release the body until Tuesday."

"So what's the story with Nick Barrett?" Deb
asked.

"He says he saw his father hit his mother with a
blackjack—"

Lamond slapped his palm on the table.

Ethan raised a brow. "Easy on that coffee."

Lamond grinned. "That's why the M.E. didn't see
any lacerations on Vanderzell's head."

Ethan nodded. "And then he dumped her over the
balcony."

"Why didn't the kid stop him?"

"He says he tripped over a flowerpot." Ethan pulled

out a crime scene photo of a large urn. The stem of a geranium had been broken. "People have done stupider things. He could be telling the truth. It was dark. He was in a strange house."

"So he trips over the pot."

"And when he looks up, he sees his father kill his mother."

"So that's what he told you," Deb said. "Lamond, what about the break-and-enter angle?"

Lamond threw a quick glance at Ethan, then flipped open his notepad. "The neighborhood had been hit with two B and E's in the past ten days. Same M.O.— someone popped a patio door off its runners, grabbed whatever was in sight and ran off before patrol could investigate."

"How about Feldman's house? How did the intruder get in?"

Lamond blew out a breath. "There was no sign of forced entry. No fingerprints on windowsills, door frames, nothing."

Deb arched a brow. "So how do you think the intruder got in?"

This was the moment Ethan was waiting for. "We think Barrett walked in."

"You mean through the front door?"

"Yes. It was unlocked. We know Elise called him earlier. Maybe he told her to leave the door unlocked so he could slip in quietly and not wake the kids. He doesn't show. She's upset, takes a sleeping pill, forgets all about the door…"

"Got any evidence of that?"

"His prints are on the door, Deb." Ethan tried not

to let his excitement show. "I know that he was in the house earlier, but we don't have anyone else's prints but his, the house cleaner's, Elise's and her kids'."

Deb tapped a pen against her cheek. "Okay," she said slowly. "But what if it was our neighborhood thief who wore gloves? He gets a surprise when he tries to steal the jewelry in the master bedroom."

"There was no sign of struggle. Nothing had been gone through. Elise's purse was sitting on a table in the front hallway. Her wallet had one hundred and eighty dollars in cash in it."

Deb glanced at Lamond. "Whaddya think?"

Lamond straightened. "I don't think the break and enters are connected. The M.O. is totally different. The guy who killed Elise was careful. Everything seemed planned out."

Deb nodded, sipped her coffee. "So, Drake, you said that Nick Barrett told you his father turned around just after he dropped Vanderzell."

Ethan cleared his throat. Deb was warming up to their theory. "Right."

"Did his father see him?"

"Yes. He looked over his shoulder when he heard Nick trip."

"Over his shoulder?" Deb put down her coffee. "You mean he had his back to the kid?"

This was where things got a little slippery. "Yes. But the kid swears it was his dad."

"Why?"

"His build, hair color. He wore a stocking over his head, but Nick says he could see blond hair under it."

"Ethan, it was dark. How could he tell?"

"The light from the kid's bedroom reaches the balcony. I checked."

Deb shook her head. "I don't think this will stand up under cross-examination. Did he see what happened to the weapon?"

"No. He says his father ran away with it. Into the park."

And the park, of course, bordered the Atlantic Ocean. The chances of locating the weapon were slim to none.

"Nothing Nick Barrett has told us would stand up in court," Deb said.

"Come on, Deb. He was an eyewitness! That counts for something."

"Not with the bad blood between them." She pointed to the thick file folder with Nick Barrett's name on it. "Putting a kid with Nick's history on the stand is like giving a defense lawyer a license to kill. He'll be eaten alive."

"He had a learning disability."

"He also lied, cheated and stole."

"But he doesn't have a record."

"He doesn't have credibility, either." Deb's gaze narrowed. "What makes you think Nick Barrett didn't do it himself? He tried killing his father. Maybe he hated his mother, too. There's a lot of insurance money when they both kick the bucket."

Ethan shook his head. "I don't think he's motivated by money, Deb. The kid is devastated by his mother's death. He wanted vengeance. An eye for an eye." He leaned forward. "It's the only motive that makes sense. He had no reason to kill his mother."

"Except for money."

"The kid had all the money he wanted."

"Then why did he steal from his father?"

Why, indeed? "I think he hated him. He was acting out." Ethan flipped through the file. "Look, I have his employment records. He was a reliable employee. According to his sister, he used that money to pay back his father."

"So he pretended to be a good boy. To deflect suspicion."

Ethan stared at his notes, frustrated. The team played devil's advocate all the time—they had to, to figure out motives and leads. But right now, Deb's skepticism was pissing him off.

"Look, I interviewed the kid with Tabby. She thought the same thing as me. Randall Barrett did it."

Deb exhaled. "Ethan, we need more than this."

Ethan's mind raced. What more could they get? They had no weapon. They had only one eyewitness. As much as he disliked what Deb was telling him, he knew she was right. "I'll give Vanderzell's therapist another call. See if I can get more out of him."

"Good." Deb looked at the rest of the team. "Redding, I want you to conduct another canvass with Lamond, see if anyone has seen a man matching the description Nick Barrett gave. Warren, we need to mobilize a K-9 Unit and search for the weapon in the park." She grinned. "I've been known to get lucky at blackjack."

44

No matter how expensive the suit, it could not compensate for the crassness of a beaten face. There was not a single colleague in Randall's acquaintance who had shown up to work sporting the evidence of a fistfight. At least, not since university days. And those were long gone, left behind as Randall faithfully trod the road to prestige, wealth, power. Brawling was not part of that package.

And certainly being assaulted with deadly intent by one's own son was not part of it, either. Randall shot his cuffs and stepped out of the elevator into the MB lobby. He nodded to the new receptionist. She tried her best to hide her reaction to his face, but she was young. He smiled, letting her know he was not offended, and strode toward the boardroom, his eye drawn to the visual installation on the far wall. It had the power to both soothe him and stir him at the same time.

He looked away. His emotions were too close to the surface. Too raw. Like his face. He could not allow himself to be thin-skinned, not when he entered the dragons' cave.

Nina rose from her seat at the foot of the table when he strode in. "Randall." She nodded, her face somber as befitted the circumstances. "Thank you for joining us." Again, her choice of words was brilliant, he thought. Deliberately designed to keep him on the outside of this exclusive enclave.

He closed the door. His gaze traveled around the table, stopping for a full second on each partner's face. Some gazed back with sympathy, others looked down at the table, and a pitiful few glanced, tellingly, at Nina Woods. His lip curled.

The chair at the head of the table was empty. So Nina hadn't quite dared to take that over. Not yet.

He strolled over to the chair and sat down, clasping his hands loosely in front of him.

"How are you, Randall?" This question came from across the table. Tony Maybourne, one of the more senior partners of the firm, gazed at him through his wire-framed glasses. Tony and he had taken their clients golfing on many occasions. An intellectual, somewhat shy man, Tony was lousy at golf, but Randall had always enjoyed his dry sense of humor.

Randall shrugged. "As you can see, it has been a difficult weekend."

The partners began to murmur their condolences. Randall felt his body grow hot. This was not what he came in for; he knew it, they knew it.

He fixed his gaze on Nina Woods. Her face was composed in an expression of horrified sympathy, but he sensed that her gaze took in the muted circus with the air of a bored ringmaster, biding her time for the tiger to be let out of its cage.

"Shall we begin?" he asked.

Her eyes met his. They reminded him of blood diamonds, so pale, so hard. "We called you in today to conduct a partners' vote."

Silence fell over the boardroom.

He raised a brow. "Regarding?"

"Appointing an acting managing partner who will take over your duties until you are able to resume them."

"I feel completely capable of continuing as managing partner."

"I have had great difficulty reaching you," Nina said, glancing around the table. "McGrath Barrett needs a managing partner who is accessible at all times. And due to your unfortunate circumstances, you are not."

He felt his jaw go rigid. "By 'unfortunate circumstances,' are you referring to the murder of my ex-wife?"

Nina Woods stared at him. Challenging him.

Tony Maybourne gave him a placating look. "Randall, the partners feel that you cannot carry on your role as managing partner when your personal situation is consuming so much of your time. We just want you to be able to devote your attention to your family…" His voice trailed off.

Randall nodded, unwilling to skewer his old friend. He believed Tony wasn't trying to screw him. Nina, on the other hand, was clearly in this for a power grab.

In the silence that fell around the table, Nina added, "McGrath Barrett is still in a delicate stage of recovery."

Due to your mismanagement, her eyes said. "The firm cannot afford to have its leader mired in personal legal problems."

Randall's brows rose. "Which legal problems are those, Nina?"

"The murder investigation of your ex-wife."

Tony gave Nina a disgusted look. Several partners shifted. Randall both admired Nina and reviled her at the same time. How she could be so coldly assured as she spoke of his personal horror was impressive.

"Why, exactly, do you think the murder investigation constitutes a legal problem for me?"

Nina's face tightened. "Because you're one of the suspects, are you not, Randall?"

"Why would you think that?"

"I understand you spoke with Bill Anthony."

Randall bit down on his teeth. Hard. *The shit.* So much for solicitor-client privilege.

Suspicion edged his partners' faces. Thanks to the local gossip rag, everyone knew that Randall had been involved in a humiliating divorce. Thanks to this Sunday's edition of the *Post,* everyone knew that he'd argued with Elise the night she died.

He rubbed his jaw. And saw Tony Maybourne eye his hands, his gaze fixed on the garish bruises that swelled Randall's knuckles.

Tony is wondering if I did it.

Randall's face flushed. "I'm not privy to the police investigation, Nina. I can, however, assure you that if I am charged with a crime, I would step down as managing partner to fully focus on clearing my name."

"I'm calling the vote right now, Randall."

Randall looked around the table at his partners. "Is this what you want?"

"Randall, it's not that we want to replace you," Tony said. His eyes beseeched Randall. "We just want someone to take over the management of the firm until you are able to return. Nina is correct—the firm is just getting back on its feet. We can't afford another setback."

He knew Tony was right. He knew that. So why was he fighting this?

Because it's the last thing you've got, Barrett.

He pushed away from the table. "No need to vote. I'll step aside." He strode to the door, then paused. "Who, may I ask, will be filling my shoes during my absence?"

Nina smiled. "I'll be taking over."

On a permanent basis, if you can convince my partners, right, Nina?

Did they have any idea what they had just unleashed on themselves?

"You reap what you sow," he muttered, giving Nina one last look.

Just as he was closing the door behind him, he heard one of the partners murmur, "So do you, Randall."

Lucy's phone rang. The ringtone, which had been funny and quirky when she downloaded it before her trip, jangled in her ear. "Hello."

"Lucy."

His voice was not unexpected after what Grandma Penny had told her. What surprised her was how welcome his call was. A huge, shuddering sob escaped from her chest. She pressed the cell phone against her cheek and burrowed deeper into her bed. "Dr. Jamie?"

"Hello, Lucy." His normally light, crisp voice was heavy. "Your grandmother called me. Asked me if I could talk with you." He cleared his throat. "I know your mother would want me to make sure you're all right."

"It's been awful," Lucy whispered. She shook her head, staring at the ceiling.

"Do you want to talk about it?"

No. Yes. There was something about Dr. Jamie that just made her want to confide in him. "It was so horrible..." Words burst from her throat, fleeing from the battering ram of memories: Nick, running down the stairs. Her mother, lying on the ground in a glimmering pool of blood.

The look of hatred in her brother's eyes.

The phone, ringing endlessly in her ear as she tried calling her father.

He hadn't come. Not until the early hours of the next morning. And then, as he pulled her into his arms, murmuring his apologies, all she could smell was the whiskey in his skin. He'd been drunk while her mother had died.

He'd tried to make it up to her.

But she didn't think he ever could.

A sob built in the back of her throat, escaping in a weird, embarrassing hiccup.

"Lucy." Dr. Jamie's voice was quiet but steady. "It's all right."

Lucy had wanted her father to say it was all right. She'd needed him to say those words after...after... Instead, Nick had attacked him. And accused him of something so horrible she didn't want to think about it.

She missed her mother so badly. It was like a big hole where her chest had been. She wanted to bury her face in her father's shoulder, share her grief with her big brother, silently cry in Charlie's fur.

Instead, Charlie was fighting for her life. And if she survived, the vet said she'd be given to another family. One that didn't hurt her.

Her brother had transformed into a violent, scary monster that she didn't know existed. Had he always been like that and she'd never known? He'd been her best friend. Had she missed something? Could she have stopped him from turning on their family? Pain at his abandonment stabbed her.

And her father. She curled tighter into a ball. Her brother said her father was a murderer. That he had brutally taken the life of the person she loved with all her heart.

She had no one left. Except her grandparents. But it wasn't the same. They were trying. But it wasn't the same.

Tears trickled down her cheeks. "Nicky tried to kill my father," she whispered.

There was a silence. "Why?"

"He says my father killed my mother." She couldn't believe she was saying those words. Three days ago it wasn't something she could ever have imagined. Then, she was looking forward to riding camp, getting her own mare, hoping she'd clear the second jump. She'd been thinking about that jump all winter. Determined that this was the year she'd do it.

And hoping that her father would forgive her brother. And that her mother would feel better.

There'd been a lot of hope in her heart.

"Where's your father now?"

"He's at a hotel."

"And your brother?"

"He's here. At my grandmother's." But not here. Not anymore. He was just a scary pale shell of the boy she'd grown up with. A sob built in her throat. She gulped hard. She never usually ever cried. But the tears just kept coming. Like the sea pounding on the rocks. Wave after wave.

"Do you feel scared of him?"

Yes. No. She didn't want to feel scared of him.

He was her big brother.

Her protector.

He tried to kill her father with a baseball bat.

"I don't know," she whispered. The tightness in her throat eased a tiny bit. Dr. Jamie was the only person right now who demanded nothing from her. He had a way of listening that calmed her down. She remembered that feeling of peace she had after she'd visited Dr. Jamie's office in Toronto. She had been too embarrassed to tell her friends she was going, but her mother really wanted her to go. She told her that Dr. Jamie thought she might be able to help them understand what was going on with Nick. At first, she resisted. She didn't want to go behind her brother's back. But when her mother told her how worried she was about Nick— and about how he stole from Dad's bank account—she agreed. She was worried about him, too.

When she and her mother walked into Dr. Jamie's

office—which was on the main floor of an old brick house—she immediately relaxed. Sun poured in through the windows. His office was like a big den, lined with books. A collection of wooden monkeys perched on a shelf. Warm, soft sofas with bright pillows in African batik clustered around a coffee table. A zebra-skin rug lay on the floor. The space was cheerful, yet calm and peaceful. Not like her house, when every night Mummy and Nick would argue about his homework.

Her mother had seemed different in his office. More open, less anxious. And Dr. Jamie had let Herbert, his big marmalade cat, sit with them. Then they talked about her family.

"How is your brother?" Dr. Jamie asked her now.

A big sigh escaped her. Grief had taken over her body and she couldn't control it anymore. "He's really mad. He's changed." She thought of Nick's defiant eyes. He'd shut her out. He'd abandoned her. She pressed Oscar, her threadbare stuffed giraffe, harder against her chest. "It's really awful, Dr. Jamie," she whispered. "I miss my mother so much." Tears ran down her cheeks.

"I know, Lucy, I know." His voice was so soothing. She felt as if he'd wrapped her up in a warm blanket and hugged her. She wished her father would do that, but she couldn't let it happen now. Not when Nicky attacked him and accused him of things she couldn't let her mind think about and now he was in a hotel.

Did he really kill her mother?

Fear gripped her from the inside out. She pulled the quilt tighter around her. She didn't want to talk anymore. "I'm tired, Dr. Jamie."

"Of course. You rest. And remember, you can call me whenever you need to talk."

He hung up. Lucy closed her eyes. His voice had drowned out the ocean, but now the sound drummed in her ears again. Cold and unrelenting.

45

You made your bed, Kate Lange. And at the rate you're going, it's going to stay empty for a long, long time.

Curtis Carey had barely looked at her since he walked into the discovery. He settled in his client with a lumbar support and a cup of coffee, opened his file and locked his gaze on Dr. Mercer.

Here's my cue for the comics, Kate thought. But she wasn't going to engage in petty tactics. Although if she'd had a newspaper, she would have been tempted to bury her face behind it so Curtis could not see the flush in her cheeks.

"Dr. Mercer, tell me why your opinion was solicited for this file," Curtis began without preamble.

It only took ten minutes for Kate to figure out Curtis' strategy. He was systematically burying Dr. Mercer's opinion under insinuations of bias.

It was exactly what she would have done.

The sad thing was that there wasn't much she could do to deflect the dirt. Dr. Mercer was a hired gun. He had to wear it and believe that his opinion was unbiased enough to be considered reasonable by the judge.

Which, based on what Kate had seen, it wasn't. But that was a battle to be fought on another day.

The questions continued for hours. Kate drank four cups of coffee and tried to keep a calm facade. Curtis was doing a thorough job of poking holes at every recommendation by Dr. Mercer that was unfavorable to his client's claim.

Finally, Curtis closed his file folder and said, "I have no further questions at this time." He stood, stretching his back. Mike Naugler raised himself from his chair, gingerly, glaring at Dr. Mercer.

"Where's the men's room?" Mike Naugler asked.

"Just down the hall," Kate said, holding the door open for him.

Dr. Mercer packed up his briefcase but pulled out his laptop. "Can I use the boardroom for a bit? I've got some work to catch up on."

"Sure." Kate grabbed her stuff and hurried to the door, glad to be away from this man who had said nothing this morning to change her opinion of him. Curtis followed her.

She strode into the foyer. Curtis caught up to her. "He's a quack, Kate. You guys don't have a hope in hell. I'm not going to let Great Life snowball Mike."

Good was what she wanted to say. "I'll send the transcripts as soon as they are ready."

Mike Naugler headed toward them.

Curtis turned his back so that their conversation was private. "Kate, I'm sorry about what happened."

He stood only inches from her, so close that the memory of his bare skin on hers flared in her blood.

Her face turned hot. As did a few other parts. "I should be the one to apologize. I was shocked by Randall's news."

His eyes had softened, no longer a steely gray. "So was I." He hesitated. "How's he doing?"

She wouldn't reveal what she knew, no matter how much she liked Curtis. "Under the circumstances, he's holding up remarkably well."

He glanced around him, then said quickly, "Are you still interested in going for a run sometime?"

Kate shifted back on her heels. "I don't know if that's wise." She jerked her head in the direction of his client, who walked haltingly in their direction. Although it wasn't the client that was the obstacle in the relationship. It wasn't even Randall.

It was her.

Curtis' eyes searched hers. What he found must have mollified him, for he said, "Why don't we revisit this when the case is over."

She took in his warmth, his interest in her, his willingness to forgive her brusqueness the other morning. Why was she even hesitating? She should give him a chance. Especially since he was willing to give her another one. She certainly didn't feel she deserved it.

She smiled. "I can live with that."

His dimple flashed. "Do you want to talk about a settlement now? Or over dinner?"

46

Tuesday, 8:12 p.m.

It was a sign. The front door of Kate's house was wide open.

Randall shook his head. He was being ridiculous. He never believed in signs or omens. Or luck or lotteries. He made his own luck.

He climbed the faded wooden stairs to the porch, pulling his collar up around his neck. Kate had seen the marks already. But he didn't want her sympathy.

What did he want?

The sound of her belting away off key to a Taylor Swift song saved him from dwelling on the question. Her voice cracked on the final, quivering note. He smiled. His swollen cheek pressed up into his eye, protesting at the unfamiliar motion.

Jesus, he looked a mess.

He brushed a hand through his hair. It was still damp. He'd taken a quick shower at his hotel, then gone to his favorite wine boutique and bought a chilled bottle of pinot grigio. He needed a drink. And he longed to have someone to talk to.

Kate seemed like the logical choice. She had been involved in this from the beginning. He wouldn't have to give her all the background.

Be honest, Barrett. This isn't a fucking legal briefing. You just want to see Kate.

Kate's dog rushed to the door. The husky eyed him with suspicion, pacing back and forth.

"Finn, is that you?" Kate called.

Finn.

Who the hell was Finn?

"It's Randall." His voice was still hoarse. He doubted Kate could hear him over her dog.

She appeared in the hallway, an anxious expression in her eyes, brandishing a paint roller. Her arm lowered when she saw him. "Oh."

"May I come in?" No welcoming smile from her, he noted. Had she heard about the partners' meeting? He hadn't thought she would care. Maybe he was wrong. He stifled his disappointment and held out the bottle of wine. "I wanted to thank you."

Her brows lifted. And then he remembered she'd used a bottle—the same label, in fact—to hit Nick's head.

His face burned.

"That's not necessary." Her gaze held sympathy in it. But he sensed something else. Something that was holding her apart from him.

"I saw Charlie today," he said. "She's doing all right." Not great. But not getting worse, either. The lick of her tongue on his hand had almost been his undoing. This

animal had risked her life for him. And now she was
paying for it.

Would Kate end up paying for helping him, too? Nina
Woods wouldn't put up with anyone she sensed threatening her territory. And Kate, although her junior, could
be perceived that way.

He knew he should just leave. Why was he dragging
Kate into this mess? Hadn't she had enough disasters
in her own life? He should walk away. He'd given her
the wine. He'd said thank you.

He should just go.

Kate watched him, holding the doorjamb. He had an
overwhelming urge to pull her against him. He wanted
to bury his face in her hair and just feel. Not think. Just
feel. He wanted to feel every bone, every curve, every
breath until it was imprinted deep inside him.

"I'm glad to hear Charlie is holding her own." Her
smile seemed forced.

Go. Go now. "May I come in?" he asked. "I'd like
to talk to you."

She stepped back. "Of course. I'm sorry, Randall."
He didn't know if she was apologizing for not inviting
him in or if she was sorry for the fact his son had tried
to kill him. Or if she was sorry his firm had literally
thrown him out on his ass. Or if she was sorry his bad
blood with Ethan was being relived with salacious glee
on the front page of her friend's newspaper.

He followed her into the kitchen. The smell of fresh
paint thickened the air. Drop sheets and newspapers lay
scattered over the floor. Kate turned down the volume
of the radio.

"Looks nice." He gazed at the walls. He'd never been

in Kate's house before. She'd only bought it six months ago, he remembered. It still had an unlived-in air to it, as if the house hadn't completely come to terms with its new inhabitant. She was wise to paint it, to make it her own, to claim her place.

Kate smiled, this time genuinely. "Yes, it's amazing how a new coat of paint can really brighten up a place."

"This is quite an old house, isn't it?"

She nodded, digging out a corkscrew from a drawer jumbled with those awkward cooking implements that never fit anywhere: whisks, wooden spoons, chopsticks, ice cream scoop. "At least one hundred years old."

She turned her back to him, reaching for the wine-glasses lined up on a tall shelf. His eyes drank in her toned thighs, the taut curve of her buttocks under her paint-spattered shorts. He noticed a trail of paint zig-zagging down her calf muscle. He'd never seen Kate in shorts. He knew she had good legs, but he'd never guessed how good. He wanted to sweep his hand up the back of her leg and feel her skin, satiny and warm against his palm. He tore his gaze from her body. "So a house this old must have some secrets…"

She placed the glasses with great care on the counter. "Why do you say that?"

"Architecture is a passion of mine." Admitting his deepest pleasure to Kate made him feel strangely vulnerable. He added, "I've nosed around a lot of old houses. They usually have a secret cellar or staircase, sometimes a ghost in the attic…" This was cocktail-party chatter, something he pulled out when his hosts lived in historic homes, usually to their delight. Not Kate. Her gaze darted over to the closet on the other side of the kitchen.

She turned abruptly, digging the corkscrew into the bottle's cork, and leveraged it upward. He walked over to the closet. "These pantries often held secondary staircases. You know, for servants, et cetera."

"You guessed it." Her voice was flat. He couldn't see her face, but the tension in her body was unmistakable. "There's a staircase in there." She poured the wine and brought him a glass. Pleasure softened her mouth as she tasted it. "Mmm. That's good." She took another sip.

"It's one of my favorites."

His gaze fell on the newspaper spread on the floor. Bad Blood Begins to Boil, it blared. Her eyes followed his. A picture of Ethan, frowning in concentration outside Dr. Feldman's house, was juxtaposed with a photo of Randall, tight-lipped, as he left the court the day his old friend's appeal of his murder conviction was denied. "I guess it's inevitable that they brought up the Clarkson file again," she said. "I'm sorry, though. I know Nat Pitts."

He shrugged. "Oddly enough, it doesn't bother me." It was true. He could have cared less. Although he wondered how Ethan Drake felt about it. "Maybe because it's insignificant compared to what's happened."

Kate's eyes met his. "I'm sorry about your son."

His chest tightened. He stared out her kitchen window. Her yard was a typical city property: shrubs lining the boundaries, a garden with an assortment of perennials in the back. "He hates me, Kate." He turned to look at her. "And I don't know why."

She exhaled. "He's confused, Randall. He thinks he saw something that night."

Randall's fingers tightened around the stem of his glass. He tipped it to his mouth so quickly that he drank more than he intended. The liquid stung the bruised flesh of his throat, but when it reached his belly, it was worth the discomfort. Warmth filled the hollowness.

"My son thinks I killed his mother." He drained his glass. "Lucy is wondering now, too. She won't go near me."

"I'm sorry." She leaned back against the counter. Away from him.

"And now my partners think I did it." He poured himself another glass. Wine splashed over the rim. "They don't even have any bloody evidence."

What he couldn't say was that now he was wondering himself.

Kate stared at him. At this man who both attracted her and repelled her. A magnetic charge of desire and distrust. Ever since she set foot in McGrath Barrett eight months ago, he'd pulled her in. Then pushed her away. Right now, the pull was so intense, she put down her wineglass and gripped the edge of the counter with both hands.

Had Elise Vanderzell felt like this when Randall came to Toronto in June? Had she stood in the kitchen and hoped the counter would keep her from making a terrible mistake?

It hadn't.

Kate didn't want to be next. Because what came after terrified her.

She cleared her throat. "I'm not sure what the police have said to you, but they have reason to suspect you."

His lip curled. "Let me guess. Your ex-fiancé has been on the case." He drained his wineglass and reached for the bottle behind Kate.

She put her hand on his arm. "I think you should slow down."

Putting her hand on his arm had been reflexive, an attempt to defuse his temper. *Wrong move.* The contact of her fingers on his bare forearm had been like a physical shock.

He lifted her hand. But he didn't relinquish it. Instead, he turned it over to inspect the palm. "How's the cut?"

She tugged her hand. But he wouldn't let go. "It's all healed now."

His finger skimmed the red line of the jagged scar on her palm. She studied his bent head. Had she ever stood so close to him before? Probably, but not like this. Not when he studied her flesh as if it were the one thing, the only thing, that could save him right now.

Her breath caught in her throat.

He heard that telltale breath and turned his gaze up to her face. His eyes, ringed with bruised tissue, bloodshot from trauma and sleeplessness, searched hers.

Need. Desire. Fear.

She read it all.

With that one look, he had jumped over the barbed-wire fence of their distrust and she had no other protection from him.

"Please let go, Randall," she whispered. She tugged her hand.

But he wasn't ready to admit defeat. "What's wrong?"

She looked away. "I know about Elise."

His face paled. "What do you mean?"

"I know about her abortion."

His fingers released her hand, reaching for the wine bottle. He poured another glass.

"How did you find out about it?"

"Ethan."

"And you believed him?"

"The abortion clinic records don't lie, Randall." She crossed her arms. "Were you the father?"

He exhaled heavily.

"Oh, God."

47

"It's not what you think." As soon as Randall uttered the words, he was disgusted with himself. He would not make excuses.

Kate crossed her arms. "I don't know what to think."

He ran his hand through his hair. "I found out in June that Nick had stolen money out of my bank account. I was furious. I went to Toronto to deal with him."

"Why would he do that?"

He had wondered the same thing. "He was acting out. We had a rocky relationship."

"Why?" Her eyes probed his.

"Jesus, Kate, I don't know! I tried! After Elise and I got divorced, Nick actually lived with me. But he had all these learning disabilities. It was too much for me. I couldn't handle my work and get him to all his appointments and spend hours every night doing his homework…" He pressed his lips together. At first he'd tried reasoning with Nick. Then pleading. Then his frustration turned to anger. And that was the part Randall regret-ted. When he'd realized what he was doing, he'd tried to make amends. But it was too late. The damage was done.

"Nick went back to live with Elise. But it hurt our relationship. Then I moved to Halifax. Things got worse for Nick. He really struggled in school. But he was good at sports. Especially hockey." Nick had been like a dif-ferent kid on the ice. Confident. Successful. *Happy.* "But school got worse for him. After the third time he was caught cheating on a test, they kicked him off the team." What a stupid punishment. To take away the only thing that made Nick tick. "It was the worst thing for him. He became moody. Then he stole money from my bank account at the end of May. Just when TransTissue blew up. And I was furious. More with Elise than Nick. I went to Toronto as soon as I found out…" He stared at the wall. "Elise and I had a terrible fight. I went to the hotel bar. Got drunk. I went back to the house to finish our argument. But the kids had gone out. She was drunk, too."

Elise had taunted him, lashing out at him because he'd been angry with her. He knew her patterns, and he'd learned to leave. But that day in June, she'd devi-ated from her usual behavior. "She hit me. But I tried walking away."

He stared into his empty glass. "She hit me again. She grabbed my arm and wouldn't let me leave until I apologized to her. And that was not something I was prepared to do." If he'd apologized, would any of this have happened? Would Elise still be alive? "She started to get hysterical. She pounded my chest with her fists. I grabbed her wrists to stop her." After all those years of fighting, he'd still been unprepared for her next move. "And she kissed me."

Her kiss had been familiar and yet strange. Hungry, angry, laced with desperation. He should have pushed her away. He should have stopped her right there.

But he didn't.

He'd never intended to have sex with Elise. He didn't love her, didn't want her. But when she kissed him, he'd found himself kissing her back, wanting to prove to her that he was in control. Wanting to prove to himself that Kate Lange did not have a hold over him.

He'd sworn he'd never get involved with a lawyer in his firm, not after what Elise had put him through. Especially when his own position at McGrath Barrett was tenuous.

His worst impulses had driven that frantic coupling in Elise's kitchen. He'd pulled up her skirt, running his hands over the legs that had once been a site of worship, pushing his ex-wife against a wall as her hands grasped his buttocks with feverish need. He'd closed his eyes, unable to look at her face when she came.

As soon as it was over, he withdrew. She yanked down her skirt, her gaze mute with appeal.

Horror crept through his heart. *She still loved him.*

And he knew, at that moment, what a terrible thing he had done.

He left.

His hangover the next day had nothing on the sick feeling of dread that had been born that night.

And now, here he was, standing in another kitchen and confessing his most grievous sin to the woman from whom he could not distance himself no matter the lengths he'd gone. "It wasn't something I intended to do. I was overwhelmed." *By you.*

Kate refused to meet his gaze. "Elise became pregnant."

"I didn't know. She never told me. She had an abortion. The first I heard of it was when she arrived on Friday."

The shock had been terrible. And yet, he had not been surprised. One did not cross a boundary like that without consequences. Fate had passed judgment on him.

He ran a hand through his hair. "I didn't love her, Kate."

"Which makes it even worse."

"I know." The thought of Elise discovering she was pregnant, feeling she could not tell him, and then having a termination on her own made him feel like the worst kind of bastard. "I made a terrible mistake. And I will always regret it."

Silence greeted his words. He glanced at Kate. Her eyes were shadowed. Was she reflecting on her own past? Or was she judging his?

"The police think you killed Elise because of this."

"I know."

Could he have?

"Did Nick know about it?"

"I don't know."

"Do you think Nick really saw someone kill Elise?"

God, he hoped not. To think of an intruder bludgeoning Elise and throwing her over a balcony made him feel physically sick. She'd been so vulnerable that day. So wounded.

And if that intruder had been him... Was he capable of that? Had the stresses of the past few months caused him to do something he'd never believe possible?

His guilt, which the wine had held at bay, now broke free of the alcohol's dead weight. "I don't know."

"Do you think Nick did it?"

"God, no! He isn't like that. He's a gentle kid—" He felt Kate's eyes on the bruises mottling his neck. "Kate, he would never kill his mother. Never."

"But you said yourself, he'd become moody—"

"I know my son!"

The words rang in the kitchen, echoing off the empty walls.

They were a hollow pronouncement. Kate wasn't convinced that Randall knew his son, nor was she convinced that Nick hadn't killed Elise. In fact, he was the prime suspect in her mind. But she was willing to play along with Randall. "So if Nick really did see someone that night, who was it?"

Randall stared at her.

She could read fear in his eyes.

"I don't know."

His eyes pleaded with her to not ask the obvious question. For to put it into words would give the question a tangibility that neither of them were ready to confront.

They needed to rule out all the other possibilities before considering the unthinkable. "Could it have been a random intruder?"

Randall rubbed his neck, wincing when his hand

pressed on the bruising. "If it was a random intruder, he was very smart. He surprised her. There was no sign of struggle."

"You said she took a sleeping pill, right? Could she have been so drowsy that she wouldn't have woken up?" Kate thought of her own sleeping-pill-induced sleep. She'd always felt that she could be roused if necessary. But now she wondered. Maybe Elise had been so deeply asleep she didn't hear the intruder. Could the same thing happen to her? What if someone crept up her stairwell and she didn't hear them because of the pill?

The same theory was even more compelling if Nick—or Randall—was the intruder. Elise would have trusted them and would have been even less alarmed— and thus less likely to shake off the effects of the sleeping pill—if they appeared in her bedroom.

Kate studied Randall.

"I don't know if she could have woken up," Randall said. "I do know that the pill gave Elise strange side effects. Sleepwalking was one of them."

Kate's chest tightened. The thought of Elise sleepwalking in the dead of night to her death was horrible. "Do the police know this?"

Randall's lips twisted. "They think I coaxed her into taking a pill be—"

"Because you called her that night."

"No. She called me."

Kate looked away. A slight flush had crept up her face.

"I hung up on her, Kate," he said in a low voice. He would regret that, too, until the day he died. "She wanted me to come over." He closed his eyes. "After what happened in June, I didn't dare." He was scared his guilt would overwhelm him and he'd succumb to the pain in her eyes. "I told her not to call me again." She was crying when he disconnected the phone. He threw the receiver on his bed, drained the double scotch he'd been brooding over and headed downtown, the summer evening spurring his restlessness. He ended up drinking three too many double scotches. After that he lost count. "I'm not sure I can forgive myself."

He hoped that was the only thing he couldn't forgive himself for.

She rubbed her arms. Her gaze was frank. "It's hard."

"Everyone thinks I killed her, Kate."

Do you? he wanted to ask. But he didn't dare. Because he didn't think he could stand it. If she thought he did, he'd truly wonder if he'd done the unthinkable.

"The police have made this an official homicide investigation." She looked at him over the rim of her wineglass. "I have a friend who is a reporter. It will be in the paper tomorrow. You should get a lawyer."

"I already did. I hired Bill Anthony."

"He's supposed to be the best."

"I fired him."

"Why?"

"Because his defense strategy was to implicate my son and ridicule my wife." At that slip of the tongue, he darted a quick glance at Kate. The flush had crept higher in her face. "I don't know why I keep calling her my wife…" It was as if the stress had stripped away the varnish of indifference and revealed the rawness of his fractured family to him. He'd meant his vows when he married Elise. She'd broken them. And even though he eventually left her and they had a thousand miles between them, it would seem that part of him had not accepted that his life with her was legally—and now irrevocably—over.

He cleared his throat. "I couldn't let Bill Anthony destroy whatever dignity she had left."

She gave him a look he could not read. "So who are you going to hire to defend you?"

He'd been mulling that over since he'd walked out on Bill Anthony. He'd been thinking about Tony Maybourne. Tony dabbled in criminal law. But after that partners' meeting, he knew he would not hire any one of those lawyers who had closed ranks on him. Perhaps justifiably, from a perception point of view. But what about loyalty? Friendship? Integrity?

"Eddie Bent," he said softly.

Kate jerked back. "Eddie Bent? Isn't he suspended?"

"I don't know."

"Randall, he's a drunk. Everyone knows it. You need someone you can rely on. Someone you can trust. This could affect the rest of your life." His lips twisted at her euphemism. What she meant was that if he was charged and convicted of murdering Elise, he'd end up in jail for twenty-five years.

"I trust Eddie. We've been friends since law school." Eddie Bent had been a "mature" student when he was accepted into the law program. Like many of his peers, he had followed in his father's footsteps. Unlike his peers, his father had been a plumber. Eddie had dutifully worked with his father until his restless intelligence and his father's alcoholism drove him out of the family business and into law school. He'd delighted in telling his professors the family slogan: *No Pipe Is Too Bent For Us.*

When he graduated, he quickly built a reputation as a top-notch criminal defense lawyer, and joked no criminal was too bent for him, either. He began to attract high-profile cases. But with success came pressure. With pressure came booze. Eventually, the drinking corroded his liver, his marriage and his legal practice.

He'd crashed and burned, a zero-to-sixty fall from grace. He'd declared bankruptcy, ended up on the streets with the very people he defended, then cleaned himself up two years ago and put his shingle out again.

"I trust Eddie. He's dried himself out."

Night had fallen as they spoke. The drop cloths absorbed the remaining light, cloaking the kitchen in shadows. Kate switched on the overhead light.

It broke the confessional mood. Deliberately, Randall suspected. He put down his long-emptied wineglass. "I'd better get going."

Kate walked him to the door. "If I can do anything, let me know."

"Anything?" He gave her a wry smile.

She smiled in return, but stepped back a cautious inch. "You know what I mean."

"Thank you."

"I'm serious, Randall. I have your back."

So. She knew about the partners' meeting. He nodded. "I always knew I could trust you."

She flushed. "Nothing's changed."

Not yet, at least. As bad as things were, they were about to get exponentially worse.

He slipped through the door, his heart heavy but no longer raging.

He had a phone call to make.

He just hoped Eddie Bent was sober enough to take it.

48

Wednesday, 10:01 a.m.

Maybe he should just hop on a plane to Toronto and meet Elise's therapist face-to-face, Ethan thought. He might get more information out of him. Dr. Gainsford was his only chance right now. If Elise's therapist didn't give him something to work with, he could kiss his case against Randall Barrett goodbye.

But, he reminded himself, Dr. Gainsford had told him to call if he suspected Elise had been a victim of domestic abuse. After conducting a background check on the psychologist, Ethan understood why. He appeared to have a professional interest in domestic abuse. Throughout his relocations—he emigrated from South Africa, then worked in British Columbia and Nova Scotia before moving to Toronto—he maintained a steadfast interest in domestic abuse situations, volunteering for committees and board positions.

Ethan dialed Dr. Gainsford's number, scanning Elise's phone records. She'd spoken to the therapist regularly, at least two or three times a week. Sometimes every day. Dr. Gainsford was a gold mine of information. If he wanted to share it.

Dr. Gainsford answered on the second ring. "Hello."

"This is Detective Ethan Drake. I'm calling about the Elise Vanderzell investigation."

"Yes? Have you determined her cause of death?"

"We believe she was murdered."

Silence. Ethan had said those words too many times in his life, and in his experience the reactions boiled down to denial, grief, anger or shock. In Dr. Gainsford's case, it was shock. He was silent for a moment, then said, "Have you found her killer?"

"Not yet. That's why I'm calling." Ethan added quickly, "We believe it's a case of domestic homicide."

"Her ex-husband?"

"Yes." Ethan hesitated. "Possibly her son, Nick Barrett."

"Her son?" Dr. Gainsford sounded startled.

"Possibly. Did Elise Vanderzell ever indicate she was scared of Nick Barrett?"

"No."

"Do you think her son was capable of killing her?"

"I never met her son. It would be a conflict for me to treat both the mother and the son. Based on what Ms. Vanderzell told me about Nick, his behavior was becoming more wanton and reckless. But no, I do not think he killed her."

"Why not?"

"Because she told me she had a good relationship with her son. I fail to see a motive."

Ethan leaned back in his chair. The doctor was

warming up, giving more information than he probably realized. Even better, Dr. Gainsford's professional assessment of Elise Vanderzell's son confirmed Ethan's gut instinct. Nick did not kill his mother. "How about her ex-husband?" Ethan asked. "Randall Barrett."

A few pages rustled on Dr. Gainsford's end of the line. "You understand, Detective, that I've never met Randall Barrett." The careful tone of the doctor's voice and his cautionary preamble made Ethan straighten. These were the words witnesses used when they knew what they were about to say would land a suspect in hot water. "I'm just checking my notes…"

Ethan heard paper flipping, then a deep inhale of breath.

What had Dr. Gainsford just read that caused his reaction? Ethan needed those notes. He needed to see what words were used, the sequence of events, the chronicle of Elise's relationship with her ex-husband through his own eyes, not through the eyes of a therapist.

"You realize that these are Elise's perceptions, Detective," Dr. Gainsford began in the same cautionary tone.

"Yes, I understand. What did she say? Was she scared of him? Had he ever threatened her?"

Dr. Gainsford sighed. "I'm afraid so. In fact, looking at my notes, I can see an escalation of anxiety about her ex-husband, and a few indications of fear."

"Recently?"

"Yes. In fact, her concerns escalated after her—" Dr. Gainsford stopped himself.

"Abortion? We know about it, Doctor. From the autopsy."

"Oh, yes. Of course."

"Did she express any concerns the night she died?" Ethan glanced down at his notes. "When we spoke on Sunday, you told me she'd called you after she fought with her ex-husband. Did he threaten her?"

"Not in words. But he was very angry. She told me she'd never seen him so angry before."

"Did you give her any advice?"

"I suggested she take a sleeping pill. She'd slept poorly since her procedure and I felt she'd be able to handle things better if she had a good night's sleep."

So far, everything Dr. Gainsford told him lined up neatly with their findings. Just one last question.

"Can you think of anyone else who might have had a reason to kill Elise Vanderzell?" Ethan asked.

"No. I cannot."

Neither could Ethan. But what Dr. Gainsford told him wasn't any use without the documentary proof. Ethan needed the therapy notes.

"Dr. Gainsford, we need evidence to substantiate our suspicions about Randall Barrett. Your notes would help establish Randall Barrett as a key suspect, and could go a long way to ensuring that men like Barrett who are abusers do not remain above the law. Now, we could get a warrant for your notes, or…"

"Are my notes that critical to your case?"

Ethan closed his eyes. He wished he had a different answer, but he didn't. "Yes."

"I see." Dr. Gainsford exhaled. "I've seen too many women whose husbands get away with hurting them," he murmured. "Fine. Take the notes. But make sure you bring Randall Barrett to justice. I'll send them by courier tonight. If you need me to clarify anything, you can reach me on my cell phone."

Ethan laid his head back against his chair. "Thank you, Doctor. I'm sure Elise Vanderzell would be glad to know that her killer will be brought to justice."

As soon as the detective hung up, Jamie Gainsford pulled out the file folder containing the session notes for Elise Vanderzell. He read through them carefully. Then read them again.

They were in order.

He placed the notes in an envelope for overnight delivery, addressing it to the attention of Detective Ethan Drake. Then he called the courier.

His heart pounded.

He couldn't believe how everything was falling into place.

His fingers inched toward his laptop before he even realized it. He glanced at his watch. His next client wasn't due for another eight minutes.

He had just enough time—

No. He needed to calm down before the session.

Goddamn it, what difference did it make now if he hadn't prepared for his client's session? He would never see this client—or any of them—again.

The envelope had changed all that. As soon as Detective Drake received the notes, the next phase of his plan would be put into motion.

There was no going back now.

Excitement, pain, desire flashed through him.

His fingers trembled as he struck the touch pad on his laptop. The beach-and-tropical-ocean screen saver melted away to reveal the *Halifax Post*'s photo of the anguished face of a girl. A girl who had haunted his dreams for the past four months.

Lucy Barrett.

Soon he would see her in the flesh.

49

Until Randall stepped foot in Bent and Associates, he had never seen a legal practice like it. If his firm interacted with lawyers from small firms, those lawyers always came to the big office buildings that oozed space and endless gourmet coffee for meetings.

His first impression was that the historic building housing Eddie's practice was quite nice, with exposed wooden beams and unfinished brick walls. Simple IKEA-style tables and chairs dotted the main lobby area. But there was no receptionist. That was his first clue that Eddie Bent ran a shoestring practice.

His second clue came from the chalkboard on the side wall. AUGUST was written in block letters along the top, with office numbers listed beneath, and their occupants written in chalk.

Chalk?

Then he got it. Bent and Associates, Office Number 3, Randall's last—and only—bastion for legal representation, rented its office space on a month-to-month basis in an office commune.

His spirits sinking, he walked slowly to Eddie's office. He wondered, for the third time in the past hour, if he should have called first. But every time he tried to imagine that phone call, he knew he couldn't make it. He needed to see his old friend face-to-face.

He knocked on the door. Eddie's gravelly voice called, "Come in."

They hadn't seen each other for several years. Not since Bent bottomed out. Now they surveyed each other's battered faces: Randall's, by his son; Eddie's, by his booze. Neither of them commented on the changes their lives had wrought.

Nor did Eddie express any surprise or delight at Randall's appearance on his doorstep. "Have they charged you yet?" He settled himself behind his desk. The old building had real windows, and the large window behind Eddie's desk was open about six inches. A breeze stirred the ashes in the ashtray on the windowsill, sifting a fine layer of ash onto Eddie's thick black hair.

Randall relaxed into the chair opposite his old school friend. Eddie looked older than his years, his face sagging, his gut bigger than it used to be. The puffy pouches of skin under his eyes were new. But his eyes remained the same: shrewd and nonjudgmental.

That's why he trusted Eddie; there was no bullshitting with him. He knew that Eddie, like the rest of Halifax's residents, could not have missed the media reports about Elise's death and the police's suspicions about Randall's involvement.

"No. But I think it's imminent." He told Eddie about Nick.

"Jesus. But they haven't found the weapon?"

"I don't think so."

Eddie tapped a cigarette out of a crumpled pack in his drawer. He rose to his feet and leaned his bulky frame against the windowsill, cupping his hand protectively around the cigarette as he lit it. He stared at the building opposite him, inhaling deeply, then slowly blew the smoke through the open window.

"Randall, I want to help you, but…"

Not you, too, Eddie. Randall's fingers clenched. He'd really thought Eddie was different from his partners.

"But I can't. I'm sorry."

"Why not? I'll pay you up front."

"It's not the money, although God knows I need it. The problem is that the bar society is suspending me. Again." He flicked the ash off his cigarette. "Nonpayment of fees. I couldn't afford the insurance."

"How can you rent office space, then?"

"My sister-in-law owns the building. Said I could borrow the space and pay her back later."

"Why bother to come to the office if you can't practice?"

Eddie gave him a wry smile. "Beats sitting at home fighting my demons."

"How much money do you need?"

"At least five grand."

"I'll lend it to you."

"But they won't reinstate me right away, Randall. This is the second time I've done this. The suspension is part of the knuckle rap. I have to pay and repent."

"Shit."

Randall closed his eyes. He wanted Eddie to represent him. No. He *needed* Eddie. Eddie was the best criminal defense lawyer east of Montreal until he drank his career away. Now he was sober. And he had Randall's back.

The only other person who had his back was Kate.

Eddie blew a smoke ring out the window.

Randall watched it dissipate into the air. Kate had said to ask if he needed help.

Well, he needed help. He leaned forward. "What if you worked with one of my associates? You could do the behind-the-scenes stuff. She could front you in court."

Eddie shot him a look. Randall couldn't read it. "She'd have to be absolutely trustworthy, Randall. I won't work with some junior who is trying to make a name for herself."

"She's trustworthy."

"Does she work for you?"

"Yes." A slight flush burned his face. He hoped his bruises hid them from Eddie's assessing gaze.

"From what I hear, your firm wants you out, Randall. Are you sure she isn't on their side?"

"She's not."

"But they'll make life difficult for her if she takes you on as a client. They're trying to maintain a distance from you."

Damn. Eddie was right. Randall slumped back in the chair.

"What's her name, anyway?" Eddie tapped his cigarette against the edge of the windowsill, an automatic gesture. Randall wondered if some unsuspecting pedestrian was about to get showered in ash.

"Kate Lange."

Eddie's gaze narrowed. Randall expected him to make some comment about TransTissue or about Kate killing the serial killer. Instead, he asked, "Is she the daughter of Dick Lange?"

And then Randall remembered. "You defended him, didn't you?"

Eddie nodded. He dragged on his cigarette ruminatively. "Yes." He blew the smoke into the room, forgetting to exhale out the window. He waved a hand hurriedly. "Shit."

Then he peered through the haze at Randall. "Do you think she'll help you?"

"Yes."

"Why?"

"Because she's been through too much not to."

Eddie raised a brow. "Even if it means putting her career at stake?"

"Yes." Randall stood. "But that's precisely why I won't ask her."

Eddie shrugged. "If Nina Woods gets her way, you're not going to be Ms. Lange's boss for much longer." Randall wondered how on earth Eddie, sitting at his empty desk in his one-room legal practice, could know about Nina's machinations several blocks away in MB's glass-and-steel tower. "I think you should let Ms. Lange decide for herself."

50

"We've got him." Ethan waved the file folder as he strode into the war room. "We've got Randall Barrett."

Deb stood at the front of the room, marking off sections of the map of Point Pleasant Park. Lamond and Warren were on the phones. "What exactly do you have?" she asked.

He passed the folder to her. Adrenaline pumped through him, washing away the bitterness he'd felt when he read the *Post*'s front-page story. Neither he nor Barrett came out of it looking good. That Nat Pitts was a dangerous lady. She, out of any reporter, had honed in on the nuances of the dynamic between him and Barrett.

The story had made everyone on the team uneasy. More than once, he'd caught one of the investigators eyeing him speculatively. But now he had Dr. Gainsford's notes. The timing couldn't have been more propitious. What he was holding in his hand was incontrovertible. He couldn't be accused of being influenced by the old grudges of the Clarkson case after the team read this file. "These are the notes from therapy sessions that Elise Vanderzell had with Dr. Jamie Gainsford. She clearly states that she is afraid her ex-husband will hurt her."

Deb flicked open the envelope and pulled out the folder. She began flipping through the notes. "Recently?"

"Yeah. I marked all the instances with a tab." There were at least five references. "She said that she was scared he'd hurt her if he found out she was pregnant. That he wouldn't want to pay more support."

Deb's mouth tightened. "Figures. So is that why she got an abortion?"

"According to the notes."

She frowned. "The last note is from early July. Did she have any more sessions with Dr. Gainsford after her abortion?"

Ethan shook his head. "No. There are no more notes. Her PDA doesn't have any records of appointments, either." He shrugged. "Dr. Gainsford said she was re-cuperating. She had booked off sick time."

"Strange, though, don't you think? An abortion can be pretty traumatic. You'd think she'd want to talk to her therapist."

He shrugged. "Maybe she was feeling too sick to talk."

Deb handed the file back to him and strode over to the whiteboard. "What do we have on Barrett right now?"

"The notes," Ethan said, unable to stop grinning.

"Eyewitness testimony," Lamond said.

"Just from one witness?" Deb asked over her shoulder.

"Yeah. The canvass hasn't turned up anything more."

"And the search of the park hasn't turned up the weapon, either," Deb added. "The M.E.'s report didn't give us any trace. FIS found fingerprints and some hair that match Barrett's at the scene, but he could argue that he left them there earlier. FIS hasn't come up with any blood besides the victim's." She looked at Ethan. "We haven't found a thing to incriminate Barrett at his house or on his yacht. Right now, all we have is an eyewitness report and some therapy notes."

"But we have a rock-solid motive, Deb." Ethan wasn't going to let Barrett slide away from this. "He had an argument with Vanderzell just hours before she died. And his own son says he saw his father do it!"

She underlined "eyewitness." "True. But that could go either way for us, Ethan. Nick Barrett hates his father."

"Barrett has no alibi, either," Ethan pointed out.

Lamond gave a slight nod.

"So what we've got on Barrett is his son's version of events, the therapist's notes, a public argument before she died, possible fingerprints from the scene and no alibi during the time she was killed." Deb exhaled. "Not sure what the Crown will make of this."

"We need to lay charges, Deb," Ethan said in a low voice. "We can't let Barrett get away with this."

She threw him a sharp look. "You mean we can't let the killer get away with this."

"Who else would it be? Whoever killed her planned

this out. They left no evidence. Who did she know in Halifax who would want her dead?"

"Barrett," Lamond said softly.

Ethan flashed him a smile. "Exactly. There is no one else."

"A case isn't made by ruling out possibilities. A case is made by proving the possibility you believe is actually true."

"There's enough there, Deb!"

Deb studied the list she'd made. "Barely. We're going out on a limb if we charge him now."

"Look, I know most of the evidence is circumstantial. But we also know he spoke to Elise on the phone several hours before she died. And like I said, we have no other suspects. There was no one else with both motive and opportunity. Dr. Gainsford's notes confirm Vanderzell was afraid of Barrett. And his own son not only placed him at the scene but saw him commit the act." Ethan ran his hand through his hair. "You know there's no point in doing a sting. He's too smart for that. We'll never get anything on tape. If we don't charge him now, he'll just walk away."

"How about his kids, Ethan? Did they think their mom was scared of him?"

"Neither of them has come out and said it. By all accounts, Elise was a protective mother. Her therapist said that she didn't tell her children a lot about what went on between her and her ex-husband. She didn't want to traumatize them."

Deb whistled through her teeth. "What do you think, Warren?"

Warren seesawed his hand. "I'm fifty-fifty. I can't

think who else would have done this. The scene is clean, Deb. Everything we turned up—as skimpy as it seems—points to Barrett."

She turned to Lamond. "What about you?"

Lamond studied the list Deb had written on the whiteboard, pulling at his lower lip. "I think Barrett is smart enough to cover his tracks. If we didn't have the doctor's notes, I'd say no way. But…" He slapped his palm on the table. "I think we should charge him."

Deb studied the whiteboard one more time. "Fine. We'll lay the charges. Do the paperwork, Ethan. This is your show."

Relief spilled through Ethan at her words. Deb was on board. But when she turned to look at him, he saw the warning in her eyes.

If this explodes, you will be wearing it.

Because they both knew that in this case, there could be only one winner. If Randall was convicted of murder, the media would crown Ethan a hero for bringing the heinous, überpowerful ex-husband to justice. But if the Crown was unable to secure a conviction, then the media would crucify Ethan for allowing his personal grudge against a respected pillar of the legal community to color his investigation.

It was a very fine line.

He was doing his damnedest to walk it as straight as possible.

51

Randall stalked out of the elevator on MB's partner floor. He barely nodded to the new receptionist, not even trying to remember her name, and turned down the hallway to Nina Woods' office.

He flung open the door. "What the fuck are you trying to pull?"

She froze, the phone to her ear. "Can I call you back?" she said calmly before hanging up the phone. She rose to her feet. "You need to control yourself, Randall."

"You are a sneaky, conniving bitch."

Her face hardened. "I am doing exactly what you would have done. I am protecting the firm's assets."

"That's bullshit."

"Actually, it's not. We've lost three clients since Tuesday. No one wants to be associated with a man who everyone believes threw his ex-wife off a balcony."

Blood pounded in his ears. The pressure of his rage was so intense he could barely think.

But he knew that he could not lose control. Especially here.

"I have not been accused of any crime," he said.

"Not technically. But in the court of public opinion, you are the prime suspect—and guilty as hell." There was almost a look of sympathy in her eyes. She walked around her desk and leaned against it. "It doesn't matter what I believe, Randall. I take my duties as managing partner very seriously. The firm was teetering after TransTissue. We were only getting back on our feet when this happened. We have to distance ourselves from you until this matter is settled. Clients can forgive one bad apple." He knew she was referring to John Lyons. "But they can't forgive two. Not when they're both senior partners of the same firm. And when both scandals transpire within months of each other. If we don't take preemptive action now, there won't be a firm to return to when this is all over."

She was right. If he were in her shoes, he'd be compelled to do the same thing. "But you can still pay me."

"Actually, I can't."

"Why not?"

"Because your billables haven't been paid yet, Randall. Your clients aren't in a big rush to pay you, for some reason. And the compensation committee is sitting on your income share until it is clear that you have not been involved in any criminal activity."

"I'm not charged with anything, Nina. You can't invoke the criminal activities clause of the partnership agreement unless I'm charged." He ran a hand through his hair. "Why would they even do that? They're lawyers, for Chrissake. They should be able to interpret the fucking contract."

"Once bitten, twice shy, Randall. John Lyons has left everyone jumpy." She eyed him. "You know what, I agree with you. We can't have our partnership agreements not honored. I'll call a meeting of the committee tonight and we'll discuss it."

Her about-face threw off Randall. Had he misjudged her?

He couldn't tell. This could be another manipulation. He hated being in her debt. And he bet she knew it.

He hated being in debt, period. He'd reduced his income share to keep the other partners' income flowing after they lost all those clients, acknowledging his responsibility in overlooking John Lyons' fraud. Then he'd spent thousands of dollars on the new lobby. He should have financed it through the firm, but it was one more liability that the firm didn't need right now. So the partners had agreed to reimburse him at the end of the year, when they calculated their net profit.

Stress had driven him to buy the new car—the damage John Lyons had done to his old vehicle was minor, but he couldn't bear driving that car after it had been tainted by evil. He regretted it now. Combined with his larger support payments, reduced income stream, the capital costs of the home he had built when he moved to Halifax and the yacht he had purchased two years ago, he was up to his eyeballs in expenses. He had even reconsidered whether he could afford to take two weeks away from work, but had decided that Nick needed him more.

So here he was, his line of credit maxed out, his loan

payments due and no income to take the heat off. Hell, he couldn't even scrounge up the five grand for Eddie if he didn't get this check cut.

Nina shook her head. "I'm sorry, Randall—"

"Randall Barrett?"

Randall spun around. A man stood at the door, dressed in a sports jacket, dark pants and neutral tie. "Yes."

"I'm Detective Constable Lamond from the Halifax Police Department. You are under arrest for the murder of Elise Vanderzell."

Randall darted a glance at Nina Woods. Had she set him up? But her face had paled.

Ethan Drake stepped next to Detective Lamond. He held out the charge document and began to read: "Randall Barrett, you are charged with the murder of Elise Vanderzell…"

Randall stared at the two detectives. They were in plain clothes, their features impassive. But Randall thought he detected a gleam of triumph in Drake's eyes.

Why had they decided to arrest him at his firm?

The court of public opinion. People loved to see the guilty humiliated to the fullest extent.

Detective Lamond stepped forward with a pair of handcuffs. Nina's eyes widened.

"Sorry, it's police procedure." Ethan Drake did not look sorry at all.

Detective Lamond pulled Randall's hands together behind his back and snapped the cuffs on his wrists. The cool metal rubbed against his skin.

The two detectives flanked him as they left Nina's

office. Randall's jaw tightened when he saw the entourage they had assembled for his arrest. Two more plainclothes detectives led the way, telling the shocked legal staff and stupefied lawyers to "get back, get back." Behind them trailed two uniformed constables.

More lawyers came out of their offices as the procession filed down the hall. It was by the library that Randall saw Kate. She stood in the doorway, a stack of books in her arms. Her gaze darted to the tall darkhaired detective flanking him. The blood drained from her face. Drake did not acknowledge her.

Her gaze met Randall's. Then fell away.

His gut clenched. Did she think he had actually murdered Elise?

Randall didn't know if the detectives' pace was deliberately slow, but it took three times longer than usual to walk to the lobby. Finally, the elevator arrived. They stuffed themselves around Randall in the elevator, not allowing any passengers to get on as the elevator took them down to ground level.

Randall took one look outside and braced himself. News vans lined the front curb. He had the strongest urge to hide his face—his battered, bruised face—from the reporters who were gleefully taking advantage of this photo op. It had been bad enough walking through the hallways of McGrath Barrett with his hands cuffed.

But he knew that if he skulked under cover of his coat, he'd look guilty. So he stared ahead, his jaw rigid.

And remembered that he still had no funds available to lend Eddie Bent for his bar fees.

52

Thursday, 4:34 p.m.

"The police just arrested Randall Barrett, Kate," Nat announced over the phone. "Were you there?"

Kate checked her office door. It was closed. "Yes." She didn't think she'd ever forget it. To see Randall Barrett humiliated in front of his colleagues and employees made her feel sick. He didn't deserve to be treated that way.

What had the police found? What made them think Randall was guilty? "How did you know?"

"Well, no thanks to you, but I've got my sources."

"You mean someone tipped you off?"

"Your ex, to be exact. Didn't think he'd ever speak to me again, but they wanted some media coverage."

"How kind of you to provide it." Kate knew she wasn't being fair. This was Nat's job. But how could she live with herself when she paraded a man's humiliation on the front page?

Probably the same way you live with yourself after

*your client retains a biased medical expert to under-
mine a man's suffering.*

"Listen, I know this is upsetting," Nat said. "But
I'm covering the story." There was a note of pride
in her voice. "Do you want to give me the insider's
perspective?"

"Of course not."

"Come on, Kate. Better you than someone else. At
least you can give one side of the story."

"Who are you going to call for the other side?"

There was a hesitation. "Nina Woods."

"Shit, Nat. She'll skewer him!"

"Kate, I have no choice. This is my job. It's called
journalism."

"Not when it becomes a kangaroo court."

"You're the one who is always talking about how
the justice system ensures that the innocent aren't convicted. If Randall Barrett didn't kill his wife, he should
be okay."

"But he'll already have been pilloried by the
media."

"We're no worse than lawyers who argue in front of
a judge, Kate."

"Yeah, well, judges have laws to uphold."

"But they can only apply the laws based on what facts
they're given, right? That's the same with journalists.
That's why I need your statement, Kate."

The way Nat had turned the argument around
almost made Kate smile. "You should have gone to law
school."

"No, thanks. Couldn't stand the company, with

the exception of yours truly. So when do I get your statement?"

"Come over after supper."

The gravelly, smoke-stained voice was not one Kate recognized. "Kate Lange?"

"Yes."

"It's Eddie Bent. Randall Barrett's lawyer."

Kate straightened. "Hello, Mr. Bent. What can I do for you?"

"I take it Randall didn't speak to you before his arrest."

She froze. She didn't think he was referring to that wine-laden confession in her house the other night. Surely Randall wouldn't have told Eddie Bent about that? "No."

"Your boss needs your help."

"I thought he had hired you."

Eddie Bent cleared his throat. "He wants me to represent him, but there's a technical difficulty."

Kate closed her eyes. "You're still suspended from the bar, aren't you?"

"Yes. For nonpayment of fees. Randall was hoping that you could handle the court appearances. I would help you prepare."

"Shit."

He laughed. "Not what I was hoping you'd say, but I understand your sentiments."

"No, I mean, I don't do criminal defense work, Mr. Bent. I've never done any. I can't appear in court for him. He's facing a murder charge!"

"Listen, I won't beat around the bush. I wouldn't

normally agree to this. But your boss is desperate. I've known him since law school and I don't think I've ever seen him like this, not even when his wife screwed around on him." His voice lowered to a deep grumble in her ear. "He assures me that you are capable. And trustworthy. Those are the only things he needs." He paused. "Besides me."

"What if I screw up? He could end up in jail for the rest of his life."

"Ms. Lange, I don't know you personally. But I know what you've been through. If you can single-handedly kill a depraved killer—and believe me, I've met a few— you can do this."

She stared at her office door. Outside, the firm had resumed its usual efficient rhythms. The earlier events were a grotesquerie that everyone had taken great pains to smooth over.

"We need you, Ms. Lange."

She felt like banging her head on her desk. There was not a single cell in her body that wanted to do this. But how could she say no? Randall was currently up the creek of the criminal justice system with no defense lawyer to paddle him out.

She sighed. "Fine. I'll do it. But we can't meet here."

"My offices close at 5:00 p.m. Could we meet at your house?"

She wondered why they couldn't meet at his place, but decided she probably didn't want to know. The guy had hit rock bottom. Maybe his dwelling reflected that. She gave him her address.

"See you at seven."

It was only after he hung up the phone that she remembered she was supposed to meet Nat. She dialed her number.

"Nat, there's been a change of plans."

"I can come earlier," she said promptly.

Tenacity was her middle name, Nat liked to say.

"I can't give you the statement."

"You can't bag on me now." She hesitated. "I promise I'll print you verbatim."

"It's not that…" Kate shook her head. At herself, not Nat. She could not believe she was doing this. "I'm representing Randall Barrett."

"Shut the fuck up." It wasn't too often Kate could surprise Nat. She wished she could see her face. "Why didn't you tell me earlier?"

"He just hired me." She'd have to be very careful with Nat. She did not want to reveal Eddie's role in this legal triangle.

"First TransTissue, now this? How do you get these files?"

How, indeed? "Just lucky, I guess."

Nat laughed. "You always see the glass half-full, don't you, sweetie?" With those encouraging words, her friend hung up.

Kate headed into the library. She needed to get her hands on a copy of the Criminal Code. She found the thick black book and stuck it under her jacket, then hurried to the elevator.

She knew nothing about criminal law beyond her first-year courses in law school. No matter how hard she tried, she inevitably dozed off during her criminal procedure class. Now she cursed her professor. If he'd been a little livelier, she wouldn't have slept through his lecture on Murder 101.

53

Dr. Jamie Gainsford slid open the file drawer on the side of his desk. He flipped through the folder tabs until he reached the very last one.

Unmarked, the slim, plain folder could be mistaken by a casual observer as being empty.

But it held, for Jamie, one of his most treasured possessions. He opened the cover. A small, blurry Polaroid lay crookedly inside, lost in the folder's depths. Rather like his old self, blurred and lost in the depths of what he'd become.

He picked up the photo. For the first time in his life, the sorrow at his loss was replaced by a different emotion. It was, he realized, a sense of calm. Completion.

He studied the smiling girl with the light blond ponytail. Beth. His cousin. The child he had spent summer vacations with on his family's citrus farm in South Africa.

The girl he had ached for when he was fourteen years old.

His desire for her twelve-year-old body had both disgusted and aroused him, his disgust feeding his excitement at the illicit nature of what he wanted to do to her. Her body consumed his thoughts, his heart, his soul. Finally, he couldn't take it any longer. He cornered her in the shed and pulled off her panties, managing to push his hand between her legs before she ran away.

He never saw his cousin again. He was sent to boarding school. He'd been ashamed but unrepentant. His need, at that age, had been underlined with defiance.

Eight months later, Beth fell off the back of a pickup truck at her family farm. She struck her head and died of massive internal hemorrhaging.

His grief was intense. He often wondered what would have happened if he'd been able to consummate the act with her. Would it have doused his unnatural lust? Could he have gone on to a normal life?

Or would one taste of her prepubescent body have sent him over the edge at the tender age of fourteen? So blinded was he by lust, he'd most likely have ended up in prison.

He attempted to understand his compulsion by studying psychology. Initially, he'd harbored the naive hope that he could eradicate his compulsion. It didn't take him long to realize that it was something that would never leave him. So he taught himself methods of controlling it.

His victims were few, and he was proud of that fact. He could have let the beast overwhelm him years ago—he could have taken advantage of many more clients than he had.

But he hadn't.

But exercising control came at a cost. Every time the compulsion stirred, it was stronger, more powerful, forcing him to do things he had never thought possible—had never thought he'd take pleasure in—when he was a fourteen-year-old boy lusting after Beth.

And every time he allowed the compulsion to take over, it was so much harder to return to his normal life. After the Becky episode, he fled to Toronto, partly to cover his tracks, partly to regain control of whatever was left of him.

He'd managed pretty well for three years, even beginning a relationship with Elise. He toyed with the idea he might be in love with her.

And then Elise brought a vacation photo to one of their sessions.

When he saw the photo of Lucy, legs akimbo on a beach in Florida, her hair streaked by the sun, holding out a seashell, he'd fought to hide his reaction from her mother. Shock, desire, longing, lust, hurt, love—a flash flood that burst through the defenses he'd erected. Leaving him exposed and vulnerable to the beast. And unable to control his compulsion any longer. It refused to be exiled; it refused to be released on demand the way it had with Becky Murphy. It was tired of being held captive to his will; it consumed him, breathing when he breathed, but never sleeping.

It had just been waiting. Waiting for a girl like Beth to return to his life and allow him to complete a journey that had begun three decades before.

It was a one-way trip.

For both him and Lucy.

* * *

He dialed Lucy's cell phone.

She answered, her voice muted.

"Hi, Lucy," Jamie said softly. "Is this an okay time to talk? Just you and me?"

"Yes. I'm up in my room."

He settled back in his chair. Her face, caught in a moment of intense grief, stared at him from his laptop screen. "What's been going on the past few days?" He held his breath. What had the police done with his notes?

"My dad's been arrested." Lucy's voice trembled.

Jamie closed his eyes. It had worked. His plan had worked.

"They think he killed my mother."

"What do you think?" he asked, forcing himself not to smile because he knew Lucy would hear the excitement in his voice if he did.

"I don't think he did it." Then she whispered, "I don't know."

His heart pounded. Her state of mind was what he'd hoped for.

"If he's guilty," she said finally, "what happens to him?"

"He'll be sent to prison, Lucy."

"For the rest of his life?"

"For a long time."

He heard a sob. "What will happen to me, Dr. Gainsford?"

He hoped she could feel his comfort over the phone. "Don't worry, my dear. You'll be taken care of."

After a few minutes, Jamie ended the conversation.

He needed to put into action the next phase of his plan. The cat would be locked outside. He knew his neighbors often fed it. Eventually, when Jamie failed to return, he was sure Herbert would migrate over to their house. Cats were adaptable. It was all about survival.

He took out the garbage, drew the curtains and fluffed the pillows. When the police eventually broke into the house, he wanted it to reflect his state of mind: calm, controlled, at ease with the world.

He made a fresh pot of coffee and warmed his thermos for the overnight drive back to Nova Scotia. He would leave Toronto in a few hours, when it was dark. Once he was in Nova Scotia, he'd hide in his cabin and wait until the moment presented itself to snatch Lucy.

From then on, it would be simple. The plan that had begun with the plotting of Elise's death was now at its fruition. He'd managed to kill his lover, fool the police and leave Lucy emotionally vulnerable and unprotected. He couldn't quite believe it had fallen into place as neatly as it had.

All he needed to do was get her back to his cabin. He'd be finished with her in less than an hour. He knew that he wouldn't be able to avoid police scrutiny a second time around—and he didn't care.

This wasn't about trying to get away with a crime.

This was about committing it.

After that, whatever happened, happened.

Lucy would be worth it.

54

Thursday, 7:09 p.m.

The cab pulled up outside Kate's house. Eddie Bent was nine minutes late. She stood by the door, watching him heave himself out and toss a cigarette butt onto the sidewalk. *Nice.*

He walked at a surprisingly brisk pace for a man his size, Kate thought. She upgraded her impression of him from sloth to rhinoceros.

"Come in." She ushered Randall's last hope into her living room. Alaska followed. "Please forgive the mess. I'm in the middle of painting my house."

Eddie Bent plopped himself into an armchair and let Alaska sniff him. "Have you ever done an arraignment before, Kate?"

She placed two mugs of tea on the table next to some shortbread cookies that Enid had baked. "No."

He added three spoons of sugar to his tea and sipped it, his face relaxing with appreciation. "McGrath Barrett doesn't like to muddy its hands, does it?"

She thought of Dr. Mercer, Great Life's expert

witness. He had shown there were more subtle ways to get dirty. She smiled wanly. "My specialty is civil litigation."

He put his mug on the coffee table. "I've spoken to Randall. He's being held at the police station for twenty-four hours. His arraignment is tomorrow morning at Provincial Court. All you have to do is listen to the Crown's charges against him, and then ask the court to provide a date to appear in the Supreme Court ASAP. Then when you appear in Supreme Court, you ask for a date for the bail hearing."

The way Eddie spoke about it all, it sounded like a walk in the park. It would be for a pro like him. Nerves flared in Kate's stomach. She'd only appeared once in Provincial Court, in front of now Supreme Court justice Hope Carson. "Then what happens?"

"We ask the judge to set a date for a bail hearing. Because it's a murder charge, the onus will be on us to prove Randall is not a threat to the public."

Kate's heart sank. "So he has to stay in prison until the bail hearing?"

"Yes. And if we can't get bail, he'll be held in custody until his trial." He bit into one of Enid's cookies. "Which would be months away."

Kate couldn't imagine Randall sitting in a jail cell for months. It was like cooping up a tiger. All that restless energy concentrated in one small square.

The enormity of her task hit her. Randall could be jailed for years if she did not succeed in her defense of him. How the hell could she do this?

"When will your license be reinstated?"

Eddie brushed the crumbs off his fingers onto her rug. "Thirty days after I pay them."

"When was that?"

"I haven't paid them yet. Randall didn't have the money."

Two bombshells in two seconds. "I thought you were going to pay them."

"I don't have the funds, Kate." He slipped his hand in his shirt pocket, reaching for his cigarettes, then realized where he was. His hand fell back to his lap. "My wife moved to Montreal with my daughter. She sold the house and took what equity we had to start over. I'm living in an apartment."

"That doesn't seem fair."

He shook his head. "I put them through hell, Kate. They deserved to start over." He sipped his tea. "Just like you did."

Kate had just bitten into a cookie. She threw him a startled look and mumbled, "What do you mean?"

"I knew your father, Kate," Eddie said. "I defended him at his fraud trial."

"Jesus." The shortbread stuck in her throat. She gulped some tea. "How could you ask me to work with you, when you defended that bastard?"

Eddie settled back into his chair.

"You tricked me into working with you."

"That's not true," he said mildly.

"You defended my father, Eddie! You defended someone who defrauded thousands of dollars and bankrupted his family. He humiliated us. And left us without a single goddamn thing—" She stopped, afraid she would start to cry in front of the lawyer who'd tried to get the man who ruined her life off the hook. If her father hadn't destroyed their family life, then her sister might not have resorted to drugs, and Kate might not have made that fatal mistake fifteen years ago…

Her fingers clenched so tightly around the mug that the heat seared her skin.

"Look, Kate," Eddie said quietly. "I don't judge whether someone is guilty or innocent. That's the role of the courts. My job is to defend the rights of an accused. We have to presume they are innocent until the courts decide. That's the role of a defense lawyer."

"But how can you defend things like that?"

"I'm not defending their crimes. Just the person." He sipped his tea, then added, "I don't make moral judgments."

"My father was found guilty." Her legally trained mind acknowledged the rationality of Eddie's argument, but it did nothing to eradicate her anger. She still felt betrayed.

"The courts found his actions unlawful," Eddie agreed. "He repaid his debt to society by going to jail, Kate. That's the way the system works."

But what about the debt he owed me? she wanted to argue. It wasn't a monetary debt; it was an emotional one. To deprive her of the protection and care she needed in her childhood; to expose her to humiliation; to drive her sister toward addiction; to force her mother to hold down two jobs and eventually die of overwork and grief.

She cupped her mug and looked away. She did not want Eddie Bent to see the tears pricking her eyes. His hazel gaze had remained unravaged by his alcoholism.

He surveyed her with a keenness she perversely wished had been dulled by his addiction.

"I know your father felt remorseful about what he did to your family, Kate," Eddie said.

"Don't speak to me about him. I don't want to know." Her mother had shielded her from her father's incarceration. She hadn't let her daughters, on the verge of adolescence, visit the penitentiary housing her father. Ten years later, after her father had started a new life out west, Kate did not inform him of her mother's funeral. He had been excised from their lives like a tumor. Or so she had thought. In reality, the initial sickness was gone, but the seeds had been left behind to spread their toxicity.

Eddie stood. "I've got to go. I've got a meeting at 8:00 p.m. If you have any questions, don't hesitate to call me tonight. I don't need much sleep."

His words crashed her thoughts back to their current dilemma. "Did you say that Randall was going to pay for your fees but he didn't have the money?"

Eddie stopped at her front door. "Apparently, Nina Woods has put a stop payment on his income stream."

Man, oh, man. Kate's insides shriveled at Nina Woods' machinations. She hadn't realized the degree to which Nina was set against Randall.

Randall's arraignment would be all over the news tomorrow; so would the name of the junior lawyer in his firm who was representing him. Nina would be hauling Kate into her office by the afternoon, she guessed.

And the media would be drooling to see the killer of the Body Butcher defending the managing partner of the scandal-riddled McGrath Barrett on the charge of murdering his wife.

When she thought about it like that, she couldn't believe she'd said yes. But it wasn't the circus that surrounded the case that bothered her. She could handle that. She'd become quite good at deflecting the media.

No, it was the case itself. When the facts of Elise's death had come trickling in, she had been convinced Nick Barrett was the culprit.

But Nick's accusation, coupled with the knowledge that Randall had impregnated his ex-wife and then had a bitter argument just hours before she was killed, were difficult pieces of evidence to dismiss.

Why would he want Elise dead, though?

Why do most men kill their spouses? It was a control issue. And for Elise to have an abortion without Randall's knowledge, and then throw it in his face, might have been enough to tip him over the edge when his son had refused to take a vacation with him, and his law firm was rebelling against him.

But Randall wasn't like that. She closed her eyes. He'd stroked her hair off her forehead when she was lying injured in the hospital, reassuring her when she'd whimpered in fear that John Lyons was in her hospital room.

He'd also stolen her notes out of her file to protect Hope Carson. A misplaced act of chivalry, perhaps. But a breach of ethics. He had put her in a difficult position, a humiliating position with her ex-fiancé.

Was Randall putting her in another one? Was he relying on her celebrity status as vanquisher of corporate wrongdoing and slayer of serial killers to gild his own actions?

Had he killed his ex-wife?

It was awfully convenient for him to have suffered a blackout that night.

And yet, the fact that he couldn't remember his actions seemed to torment him.

She watched Eddie stop outside her house and fish in his pocket for a cigarette.

I'm not defending their crimes, Eddie had said. *Just the person.*

Her underdog instincts rose to the surface. She had agreed to act as Randall's defense lawyer. It was her job to put forth the best defense possible, to lay out the facts, repudiate unsubstantiated allegations and leave it to the judge to make a decision.

That was all she could do.

She could no longer allow her emotions to guide her judgment. She'd made a promise, and it was one she intended to keep.

After this case was complete, she and Randall would have their own judgment day.

But for now, her role would be his legal counsel. And nothing else.

Tomorrow would be hellish. If she was dreading it, she could imagine how her client felt. At least she could sleep in her own bed tonight.

Outside on the sidewalk, Eddie took several deep drags on his cigarette. Fueled with tobacco, he hurried away.

A whiff of smoke drifted by Kate, acrid and bitter.

55

Friday, 1:15 a.m.

Jamie Gainsford settled back in the seat of his Lexus. He'd been driving for an hour and a half. His thermos sat untouched in the console. Anticipation hammered his veins.

He was at the beginning of a long drive to Nova Scotia—but near the end of a much longer, more convoluted journey. One that began in South Africa on the coast of the Indian Ocean and would end in the heavy woods of Nova Scotia. Some might view where he left as more desirable than where he was going: from an open, warm coast to a dark, forested cabin. For him, though, his destination represented freedom. Completion.

For the past thirty-four years, he'd fought himself. He'd followed the road defined by the norms of society but secretly crept down a path only few dared to venture. Each time he strayed, his need escalated. Until now the dark, secret path was the only road for him.

From one end of the world to another. From respected mental health professional to soon-to-be-reviled pedophile and killer.

These were all labels. He'd used many in his professional capacity, compartmentalizing the various disorders he treated. They were designed to make sense of a world that he now realized he could never make sense of.

Why else would he be the way he was?

Why had he developed an obsession about his cousin?

Why was he able to commit these acts and not feel remorse?

Why was his need for Lucy Barrett consuming him?

He had no answers to this.

Perhaps that was the reason he could accept his fate with equanimity, that he could accept the labels society would give him after he was gone.

He could no longer attempt to understand. He could only be.

It was dark, the highway stripped down to travelers who were on urgent business. He always liked highways, especially at this time of night. Long, endless lines that avoided the mess caused by humanity.

He'd spent his life trying to help others free themselves of their baggage. Now he was going to allow himself to be free.

Just him and Lucy.

His body broke out in chills.

He stepped on the accelerator.

56

Randall stared at the peeling walls of the holding cell in the bowels of the provincial courthouse. He leaned his head back against the wall. The cold concrete seeped dampness into his hair.

The air was dank. It smelled of the various crimes of its previous inhabitants: urine from a pissed-off gang member, vomit from an alcoholic who'd mixed his regular poison with an unexpected gift of hashish, sweat from a rowdy university student who realized he'd really done it this time.

He glanced at his watch: 9:24 a.m. His stomach grumbled. He craved a cup of coffee. A good cup of coffee. The past eighteen hours had been the stuff of nightmares, although he knew he hadn't yet experienced the Technicolor version. That was awaiting him after his arraignment, when they'd send him to the correctional center.

Last night he'd spent at the police station, slumped in a hard chair in the interview room. Sleep had come at around three in the morning and had been sketchy at best. Every hour a constable would open the door and check on him.

He'd been grilled off and on since his arrest by Ethan Drake and his cohorts. They'd given him water and power bars. Nothing more. Nothing less.

Drake's barely suppressed anger fueled Randall's resolve to say nothing. Randall had been advised of his right to remain silent by Eddie over the telephone, but his real reason for keeping quiet was that he was worried he'd inadvertently inculpate his son by exculpating himself.

He couldn't even tell Ethan to go catch the real killer—because he was scared they'd haul in Nick. And Nick, despite his bravado, would never survive the criminal justice system. It didn't matter that the courts assumed you were innocent until proven guilty. The rest of the system operated on the opposite principle, and it was up to the accused to fight the bias of guilt. And Nick, who could barely get through school and couldn't even cheat on a simple math test without getting caught, would never succeed in fighting that bias.

A sheriff stopped at each of the cells, checking its occupants. Randall watched him through the bars. This man had woken up next to his wife, shaved, eaten breakfast while catching up on the baseball scores, settled a squabble between his kids, promised to catch his daughter's swimming lesson later in the day, left his three-bedroom one-and-a-half-bath split-level suburban home and then grumbled about rush hour traffic while worrying about paying for the new transmission in his wife's car. This man had a life that Randall desperately envied.

This man had the power to use the Taser that was tucked in a side holster. On him.

The sheriff nodded to him through the bars. "You're up in another hour, Barrett," he said cheerfully.

If it hadn't been for the fact that she was directly involved in the criminal matter that had brought all the media in the Maritimes to Spring Garden Road, Kate might have enjoyed the carnival atmosphere. Reporters, photographers and police officers crowded the lawn in front of the old provincial courthouse. A jazz trio busking on the corner added a festive note.

Out of the corner of her eye, she spotted Nat taking a photo of her. *You'd better get my good side,* she thought. She hurried into the building, coffee in one hand, briefcase in the other. A long line of spectators and media personnel waited to go through the security check. Lawyers did not need to go through the screening, so she skirted around the queue, and flashed her bar society membership to the sheriff. "Do you know which courtroom has arraignments?" she asked.

He smiled and pointed down the hall to number four. "But you can't take your coffee in there." She gulped it down, then walked into the courtroom, her coffee-induced bravado fading quickly. Like the rest of the building, the courtroom was designed in an earlier era, with a gravitas befitting its function. Olive-brown paneling met cream-colored walls that stretched to a vaulted ceiling arching overhead. On a dais at the front of the courtroom sat a massive desk where the judge would preside. Below the dais, the court clerk provided an effective barrier between judge and counsel. Facing the judge's desk was the counsel's table, shaped like an L. Green velvet drapes gave the room an air of dignified formality.

Fortunately, Kate was the first lawyer in the courtroom. She strode over to the L-shaped table, conscious of the eyes of the spectators in the wooden benches at the back. Eddie had told her to take a seat by the corner of the L so she could see both the judge, the Crown counsel and the accused.

Just as she sat down at the table, trying to appear as if she did this regularly, the Crown prosecutor bustled into the room, carrying a massive document box crammed with files. She dumped it on the table, yanked out a group of folders and began scribbling notes while lowering her neatly suited bottom into the chair. *Most Crowns have to shoot from the hip,* Eddie told her this morning. *They don't have the luxury of time to prepare.*

Kate tried to catch the woman's eye, but the Crown prosecutor didn't look up. She scanned the files methodically, her eyes darting behind her glasses, making notations, flipping pages, checking facts. Kate opened her own file and pretended to look busy.

At 9:28 a.m., three more lawyers rushed into the room. One of them sat next to the Crown, murmuring a greeting as he opened his briefcase. The other two walked to the end of Kate's table that faced the accused and claimed their seats. She glanced over. And wished the floor could swallow her.

Curtis Carey sat next to a frizzy-haired lawyer from Legal Aid. *What are you doing slumming in the criminal courts?* his expression said. She mustered a smile, although the last thing she wanted was to have a lawyer she knew—intimately—witness her inexperience. She mouthed, "Barrett."

His eyebrows rose. He reached over and scribbled on her notepad: "Welcome to the dark side." She glanced at him. But he had turned his attention to his files. Was his message a joke about practicing criminal defense law? Or was it a reference to her defending a man accused of domestic homicide?

"All rise," the court clerk intoned. The door reserved for the judges swung open, and Judge Norbert Miller strode in. A small man with a large nose and balding head, he perched behind his desk like a weary eagle.

Randall's case was near the bottom of a long list of accused. Kate watched the Crown present the charges for an assortment of garden-variety criminals, listened to her describe the facts, including reading for the court record the obscenity-laced threats of one drunk. Kate's admiration for the Crown prosecutors of the world rose a notch even as her apprehension grew. The criminal court was its own little planet, the procedure alien, the culture insular, the language coded.

The court bailiff escorted Randall up the narrow, low-ceilinged concrete stairwell that looked like it had been imported from a prison in Siberia.

When they entered the main level of the old courthouse, the high gracious ceilings, dark wood trims and bustling people jarred him. He rubbed his hand over his eyes. No sleep and little food were catching up to him.

He swayed. The bailiff took his elbow and propelled

him toward courtroom number four. Where justice and mercy battled it out amidst the punks, drug dealers, skinheads, drunks, mentally ill, and the drug addicted

"Regina versus Barrett," the court clerk announced. The entire spectators' gallery swiveled on the hard wooden benches to watch the bailiff escort Randall Barrett into the courtroom.

He looked terrible. His eyes were bloodshot, his face unshaven, his bruises a ghastly combination of purple and yellow. Exhaustion dragged at his face. But he walked in with his back straight, his gaze level.

Kate willed him to look at her. *I'm here,* she wanted to say. *I'm here.* She quelled the pang she felt at the sight of him.

When he saw her, his shoulders relaxed a fraction. The Crown prosecutor stood, peering down through her glasses to read the charge against him. Her voice rang in the courtroom, the earlier midmorning slump chased away by the excitement of a murder charge.

Then the Crown began reading the facts and Kate listened carefully, but she could not dispute what was being said. When the Crown described how Elise was thrown over the balcony, the row of benches in the back—which had had its share of fidgeters during the course of the morning—exploded with whispers and exclamations. A fine sheen of sweat glistened on Randall's forehead. Judge Miller barked a sharp "Order! Order!," glaring at the reporters. He turned to Kate. She rose to her feet.

"Your Honor, my client is seeking bail. To that end, I

would like to request a date to appear in Supreme Court. As soon as possible," she added.

"Very well." Judge Miller turned to the court clerk. "Set a date to appear at the Supreme Court. Preferably Monday."

The clerk peered at her calendar. "Monday, 9:30 a.m.," she announced.

"And Your Honour," Kate said. "I have received nothing from the Crown. If they are going to charge a man with murder, I need more than a charge sheet."

The Crown glared at her. Kate ignored her. The police had something that triggered Randall's arrest. She just didn't know what.

Judge Miller exhaled. "Counsel, the Crown is not required to disclose until the bail hearing has been set."

And that was it. Randall was led out of the courtroom. He didn't, as Kate expected, look back. She watched him go. He would be sent by wagon to the correctional center. There, as part of the prison population, he would await his bail hearing.

She became aware of a set of eyes watching her. Curtis Carey quickly looked away, his expression inscrutable.

There was nothing left for her to do. She packed her briefcase, bowed to the court and slipped out of the room through the same door Randall had come in.

A sheriff intercepted her in the hallway. "There's a mob of reporters waiting for you out front, Ms. Lange."

Kate stiffened.

"Let me show you out the back."

The sun was bright, warming her skin as she strode

to her car. Seeing Randall being escorted by the bailiff had been disorienting. A man who had always been a leader, who was always one step ahead, no longer in control.

Of anything.

57

"What the hell is going on?"

Kate glanced up from her work to see Nina Woods standing in front of her desk.

"Just working on the settlement for the Naugler case."

"Don't bullshit me, Kate. I know who you're representing."

Kate raised a brow, knowing Nina would correctly interpret the minuscule movement: she was throwing down the gauntlet to her boss.

Nina's eyes were hard. "You cannot do this. I will not permit it."

"Why not?"

"He'll drag the whole firm down. McGrath Barrett can't afford another scandal!"

"Randall Barrett has not been convicted of anything, Nina." And that was the crux of the matter for Kate.

"You and I both know that even the perception of wrongdoing will seriously impact our firm."

"Have we lost any clients yet?"

Nina's mouth tightened. "Yes. And we cannot afford to lose any more. We'll have to start laying off associates if things continue like this. If they haven't already fled for greener pastures."

"We can't just abandon him, Nina. He needs us to stand by him."

Nina's lips twisted. "There won't be anything left if we do that, Kate. The firm is on shaky ground. He's dragging us all down. Including you." Her tone softened. "You have your whole career ahead of you. You don't want to get dragged down by a man like Randall. He'll just take what he wants and then move on."

Kate prayed that Nina did not see the stab of fear that shot through her at her words.

"He asked me to be his defense lawyer, Nina. I can't say no."

Nina crossed her arms. "I forbid you to act as his counsel."

Nina Woods had just said the wrong thing to her. Kate was not going to be bullied by this power-hungry woman who believed she was entitled to take what she wanted. Kate had gone through too much and been forced to confront her worst fears. What had Nina Woods accomplished in her life in comparison?

Kate raised a brow. "Or else?"

"Or else you're fired."

"I see." Kate tapped a finger against her chin. "Are you sure you really want to do that, Nina? You might get away with choking Randall out of the partnership, but I don't think you can get rid of me, too. After all,

I'm the one who caught the bad guy and saved McGrath Barrett's ass. Not you."

Nina Woods' nostrils flared.

Too much Botox? Kate couldn't tell, but the woman sure as hell looked as if her face were carved of marble.

"And," Kate added, "I think 'perception' might swing the other way if people find out the partnership choked off Randall's income so now he can't afford to hire a defense lawyer—and then fired your own associate for trying to help him out." Kate's voice softened. "Just think how you could spin this—managing partner Nina Woods assigns Kate Lange to handle partner Randall Barrett's defense pro bono. Sounds pretty good, don't you think?"

"You think you're very clever, don't you?"

Kate shook her head. "On the contrary. But it doesn't take a rocket scientist to deduce this whole thing stinks."

Nina's white-blue eyes flickered over Kate. The coldness of the partner's gaze was almost palpable on Kate's skin. "Fine. You can represent Barrett pro bono."

Kate tried not to allow her triumph to show.

"Although I think you are jumping off a very steep cliff. Have you ever done criminal defense work, Kate?"

Kate kept her gaze steady, but inside she was thinking, *Nice one, Nina.* She knew how women like Nina operated. They got to where they were through hard work and sacrifice, ramming through the old boys' club until they'd proven their worth. They wore their sacrifices as a badge of honor and they weren't about to let anyone—especially another woman—get off easy.

"Didn't think so." Nina smiled. "Well, Barrett will get what he deserves."

"What he deserves is to be paid for the legal work he's done."

Nina shook her head. "Don't blame the partners. It was his clients who wouldn't pay him. Anyway, what happens between the partners is our business, so don't push me, Kate. You get to represent him, although I seriously question both your judgment and Barrett's. I will not be calling another vote on the issue of Barrett's income. He's got plenty of assets." With that, Nina Woods pivoted on her heel and strode out of the room.

Kate exhaled and lowered herself to her chair. She closed the Naugler file folder and pulled out Randall's.

All she had hoped for was that she could stay on Randall's case. She hadn't expected that she could convince Nina to let her bill her time as pro bono.

Score one for Kate Lange.

But she wouldn't gloat. Nina had exposed Kate's weakness to the light of day and given her a glimpse of what she was in for.

She supposed she should thank Nina for that.

But she couldn't bring herself to.

58

Saturday, 4:42 a.m.

Dawn lightened the highway to a pale black, studded with a darker patchwork of the potholes for which Nova Scotia highways were famous. Jamie Gainsford slowed his car to look for the track to his cabin. It had been three years since he'd been here. He was glad for a little daylight to help his search.

There. The gate was almost obscured by shrubs, but the No Trespassing sign could still be seen.

He turned off the highway. He'd made good time. In fact, the timing was perfect. He had enough light to find the track yet was early enough that there were few cars on the highway to note his arrival.

He stopped in front of the gate and slipped out of his car. The air was fresh, soft. His breath eased out of his chest. He was finally here. He was closer to Lucy. Not that his cabin was very close to Prospect; it was two hours away from Halifax. But at least he was in the same province.

During the drive from Toronto, he'd figured out the

final leg of his plan. He could see no flaws. That was the beauty of a simple plan. Less chance of it getting screwed up.

He'd grab Lucy during Randall Barrett's bail hearing, which he guessed would be in four or five days. He'd call Penelope Barrett on Monday and caution her that Lucy should not be permitted to attend because she wasn't emotionally stable. Lucy had told him that she liked to take Penelope Barrett's dog for long walks, and he'd suggest to her grandmother that Lucy be encouraged to do so. It would be easier for him to abduct Lucy if she wasn't in the house.

He unlocked the gate barring the track. The headlights of his car caught the tall, weedy bushes and small saplings that had sprouted in his three-year absence. The gate swung closed with a rusty squeak that made his teeth clench.

After five minutes of spine-jarring bumping, and a near miss with a stump that Jamie barely remembered in time to spare his muffler, he pulled into the small yard in front of his cabin. A few trees had been cleared to allow sunlight.

Compared to Jamie's luxuriously appointed house in Toronto, the cabin was primitive. But Jamie had done his best to fix it up after he bought it from the nephew of the old hermit who had built it with his own two hands—staining the shingles a deep caramel, caulking the windows to keep out the winter chill and overhauling the cellar. Over the years, he added more homey touches: a zebra-skin rug, a rocking chair, bookshelves, several games. But no mirrors.

It was just the way Jamie wanted it.

He parked the car in front of the shed, leaving the headlights on. He unlocked the small outbuilding, sweeping his flashlight around the interior, squatting to illuminate the underbelly of the truck that he had left untended. Selling it had been out of the question; he suspected too much evidence lay embedded in its seats. He ran the light around the truck's interior, along the bed and under the tailgate, making sure that the truck hadn't become home to a creature that might take it into its head to attack him.

No, the shed had withstood the attempts by the woods to overtake it.

He hurried back outside and hoisted a battery out of the trunk of the rental car. It took only a few minutes to replace the truck's dead battery. He turned over the engine. It came to life with nary a complaint. He shut off the engine and returned to his car. Lifting a suitcase out of the trunk, he walked over to the cabin.

His heart began to pound.

He unlocked the front door, the key slipping from his fingers when the unmistakable foulness of rotting flesh met his nostrils.

No. It wasn't possible.

A body could not still stink three years later.

He dropped his suitcase, skimming his flashlight over the main room of the cabin.

There, by a broken window, lay a dead raccoon. It had feasted on the poison Jamie had left for any pests that infiltrated the cabin.

He found a shovel in the shed and carried the rotting corpse out to the back, flinging it as far as he could into the woods.

The next corpse would require a little more effort.

He'd buried Becky Murphy in the basement.

And even though her corpse no longer smelled, he didn't want any reminders of her in the cabin.

Not while he waited for Lucy.

59

Eddie Bent settled himself in a chair in McGrath Barrett's boardroom. "Nice view." Halifax Harbour lay below them, silver shimmering on blue.

Kate grinned. "It's overkill to book the boardroom for just this box of files, but I decided to make a point with Nina."

It was time to take a stand with McGrath Barrett. The firm needed to understand that, as of now, Randall Barrett was a client. No more backstabbing.

And she'd forced herself to treat him like a client, and not visit him at the correctional center over the weekend. She could not afford to have the lines blurred. Not until the case was over. She'd seen him briefly this morning, at the Supreme Court. He'd looked like crap.

"The police must have been working all weekend to put this together," Eddie commented. The box in question had been given to Kate by the Crown this morning. It contained evidence against Randall that the Crown was required by law to disclose, such as the interviews of witnesses, including Randall and his family, the medical examiner's preliminary findings, the FIS notes, a blood/alcohol report and whatever else the police had dug up.

"I'll take the interviews," Eddie said, flipping the top off the box and pulling out a binder with a DVD held in place by an elastic band. "You take the rest." He popped the DVD into Kate's laptop, plugged in her earbuds and fixed his attention on her laptop screen.

Kate began with the M.E.'s preliminary findings. She did her best to maintain a professional objectivity as she read the descriptions of Elise's injuries. But to know that the "unidentified patterned injury" had been caused, according to Nick, by someone striking her with a blackjack while she slept made Kate feel sick. She visualized how Elise smashed her head against the concrete stairwell after falling over the balcony, resulting in a "depressed skull fracture in upper occipital region." Kate wondered how the injuries she had inflicted on Craig Peters were described by Dr. Guthro.

Eddie hummed lightly under his breath as he listened to the statements, flipping to the transcribed notes in the binder every so often and shaking his head. "What kind of question is that?" he muttered more than once.

Kate finally finished her assessment of the M.E.'s report and dug into the evidence box for the next file folder. Therapy Notes from Dr. Jamie Gainsford, Clinical Psychologist was written in black marker on the tab.

"Did you know the police had gotten hold of Elise's therapist's notes?"

Eddie paused the DVD. "Interesting. That's unusual.

Although from what I've seen, they don't have much to go on. They probably were desperate."

Kate poured herself another cup of coffee. Dr. Gainsford had kept scrupulous notes—the dates coincided with the appointment times recorded in Elise's PDA. But they were handwritten.

"These aren't transcribed, Eddie." She waved the first page at him.

Eddie glanced over the page. "Doesn't matter. He's just required to keep a record. A lot of therapists don't have secretaries or even receptionists. They run things themselves. I'd only be concerned if the records were spotty."

"No. The dates all match up." Kate settled back in her seat with the file. Eddie turned the interviews back on. She was glad he was occupied with the video because she felt slightly clandestine reading the therapist's notes. Maybe because she was curious to see what made Randall's ex-wife tick. She wanted to know what kind of woman Randall had chosen to be his mate, what kind of woman could screw around on a man like him.

It didn't take long for her curiosity to change into discomfort. Dr. Gainsford's notes were terse and to the point, providing a telescopic view of Elise's innermost fears and anxieties. Those should have died with her. But now they would be shared with all kinds of people who would dissect the notes—and subsequently dissect *her*. It didn't seem fair that this woman was a victim of a horrible crime and was now subject to the most intimate scrutiny in an effort to make the perpetrator pay. First her body had been taken apart. Now her mind was fair game to everyone who had a point to prove.

And her heart was, too. Her pain over her relationship with her ex-husband and her son were discussed at every session. It was uncomfortable to read. Did Randall know how much anguish he had caused? Kate wondered. She hoped not. She didn't think he was that heartless.

June 8. Client distressed. Ex-husband forced her to have sexual relations. Emphatic that it was nonconsensual. Refer to rape-counseling center?

Kate's fingers trembled. She reread Dr. Gainsford's note. She had not misread it.

Oh, God.

She dug her fingertips into her temples. *Think, Kate.* He admitted to having had sex with her. But rape? Was it true? Or was Elise exacting some kind of revenge on him? But telling her therapist would achieve nothing; the notes were confidential.

Had Randall raped his ex-wife?

"Eddie," she said, trying to keep her voice steady despite the pounding of her heart, "have you come across any witness statements that suggest Randall sexually assaulted Elise?"

Eddie paused the video and gazed at her over his reading glasses, which appeared ludicrously small on his fleshy nose. "No. Is that what she told her therapist?"

"Yes."

"Jesus." He reached into his jacket, then withdrew his hand. There were no windows he could open in this high-tech office tower to let cigarette smoke escape. "You need to talk to Randall about this."

Kate shook her head. "You do it."

He lowered his pen. "Why me?"

She looked away. "I can't."

His eyes sharpened. "Why not?"

"I don't want to know the answer."

"Kate, I've known Randall for a long time. I've defended rapists before. He isn't one of them."

"How can you be sure?"

"It's a dead woman's rantings to her therapist, Kate."

"You mean confidential records where the victim would have no reason to lie."

Eddie took off his glasses. "Maybe she had a reason to lie to her therapist, Kate. Sometimes it's difficult for people to admit they've made a mistake. Even to themselves."

Kate stared at him. "Or maybe Randall was under so much stress between all the stuff happening in the firm, and then his son stealing his money, that he just lost it. He told me he'd been drunk when it happened. And he was drunk the night Elise was murdered. He doesn't remember a thing."

Eddie arched a shaggy brow. "A blackout, huh?"

"Yes."

"That adds a twist. Has he been able to piece together any of his activities?"

Kate shook her head. "No. He was alone that night. He has no one to corroborate where he was until the harbor patrol found him."

Eddie gave a slow whistle. "I don't think he's capable of murder, Kate."

"But he's doubting himself, Eddie." Kate had seen it in his eyes. "And with these notes…" She shook the file folder. "Elise was afraid of him."

"Listen, let me tell you something. This debate we're

having shows exactly why our job is so important. We are surrounded by evidence—" He gestured toward the papers and reports that were spread all over the table, a white two-dimensional bridge that connected his chair to Kate's. "And it's all written in black and white. Some of the facts are indisputable—Elise Vanderzell took sleeping pills, has an unexplained skin-pattern injury, was killed by brain hemorrhage due to cracking her skull from a fall."

He held up his glass of water. "See how clear this is? It's transparent. And yet, if you stick this piece of paper behind the glass, like this—" he took the page of Dr. Gainsford's notes from Kate's hand and placed it behind the water "—it's not so clear, is it?" Kate stared through Eddie's glass of water. The words undulated on the page. Some were illegible, others magnified. "And that is because when we believe a fact is indisputable, it is, in actuality, distorted by the perception of those who interpret it." He passed Dr. Gainsford's notes back to Kate with a flourish. "Nothing is as it seems."

"That's a wonderfully existential perspective, but we need a theory of the case, Eddie."

"You are quite right." He gazed at her like a fond father whose child had just surprised him with her per-cipience. "You tell me yours and I'll tell you mine."

"Fine." Kate blew a strand of hair off her forehead. "I think either Randall did it or his son did. But if Randall suffered a blackout because he was so drunk, how could he have committed the crime the way Nick described it? And leave no trace evidence for the police to find?"

"Kate—" Eddie stuck one arm of his reading glasses between his teeth "—you obviously don't know many drunks. Let me tell you from personal experience that you can have a blackout and act in a nonintoxicated manner."

"So Randall could have committed the murder?"

"In theory. Yes." Eddie put his glasses back on.

"Damn." Kate exhaled. Then straightened. "But since we're defending Randall—and he hasn't admitted any guilt—we need to build a case around Nick."

Eddie leaned back in his chair. "Go on."

"He is obviously capable of violence. His attack on his father was premeditated. Then he accused his father of murder. I think Nick was trying to deflect suspicion from himself."

"It's very possible. But what about an unknown party? Do you think there could have been an intruder that has not yet been identified?"

Kate shook her head. "The only eyewitness is Nick, and he claims the intruder was his father. There aren't any other suspects. Except Nick, of course."

"The underachieving son of overachieving parents. Who each have a big life insurance policy."

"Exactly."

Eddie tapped his fingers on the table. "But Randall has emphatically stated that he does not want our defense to point any fingers at his son."

"So we're back to where we began," Kate said, her voice glum. She stared at the therapist's file. Eddie was right—if they couldn't pin this on Nick, they would have to thoroughly discredit the evidence the Crown provided, starting with Dr. Gainsford's notes. Surely there was some gray to be found in the spaces between those damning black-and-white words.

Eddie pushed back his chair. "Now, if you will excuse me, I need to obscure my thoughts in a tobacco-induced haze."

Kate nodded. "I'll finish up here. Then I'll take this evidence over to Randall. He needs to know what will be said about him tomorrow."

He'd been blindsided by his son, his firm, and now, it would appear, his ex-wife. Kate didn't know whom she believed anymore, but she would not allow Randall to be blindsided on her watch.

That being said, he'd better not have lied to her.

Jamie put his cell phone down on the table in his cabin and rubbed his hands. His nerves tingled with excitement. This was the feeling he had at the end of a long stakeout in the South African bush, when he knew the wait was about to end, that the prey was about to cross into his sights.

Ralph Moore, the Crown prosecutor who had taken over Randall Barrett's bail hearing, had just called him. He'd been reviewing Jamie's notes and had a few questions.

Barrett's hearing, he informed Jamie, was scheduled for tomorrow afternoon. Jamie had tried to cover his surprise—he hadn't thought it would be so soon. If Randall got bail, he would want to be with his family.

And that meant Jamie's opportunity to snatch Lucy would be significantly reduced.

He needed to act quickly.

The waiting was over.

60

Monday, 7:12 p.m.

Randall Barrett stared at the document box in his cell. He had thought he'd hit rock bottom on Friday when he'd been strip-searched, had all his personal belongings taken away and been assigned a prison ID number. The final indignity had been when he had to sign out a razor. Never again would he take for granted his possessions.

The first night had been grim. The correctional center was located on the outskirts of an industrial park. They'd put him in a cell by himself—for his own protection, they told him. He'd spent the night awake, lying on his narrow bed, listening to the strange noises, the yelling, the catcalls, everything hollow and metallic with nothing on the walls or the ground to dampen the sound. He thought of his massive, comfortable bed, the cool serenity of his garden, the crickets he'd hear at night. The low, throaty call of the mourning dove in the early morning. Charlie snoring at his feet. He remembered he had tickets to the symphony benefit at the end of the month. He'd tell his mother to use them.

His thoughts skittered randomly, skipping from one stepping stone to another, trying to avoid toppling into the river of worry that rushed through him: Lucy, Nick, his mother. They were his family. They needed him to steer them through this disastrous turn in their lives.

And he couldn't.

He'd failed the ones he loved the most.

What kind of man was he?

How had he ended up in this place?

The box with the Crown's evidence had provided a set of answers. They repelled him. Was it because they were the ugly truth?

Every time he thought he'd hit rock bottom, he was in reality descending to another level of misery whose depths had not been plumbed. There was no rock bottom. Just thin ledges on the sides of the abyss. And they kept crumbling out from under him.

Like this morning. When Kate had arrived. He'd stared at her, drinking in her trim figure, her gleaming hair, her calm assurance. He was consumed with a need to be with her. She was his only connection to his old life, to his old firm, to the world that had rejected him. His heart leaped, foolishly, with hope.

She hadn't been able to meet his eyes.

He knew she needed to maintain objectivity. He kept telling himself that was why she was so disconcertingly cool. Why she hadn't visited him over the weekend. She needed to keep her distance because she was too emotionally involved with him, he'd thought.

Instead, he discovered she kept her distance because she no longer trusted him.

And thus, he discovered, another ledge had given away. But he did not anticipate the depths to which he'd fall until he opened the evidence box.

How many times had he lugged the identical bland brown boxes to hearings, or stacked them in the corners of his office and asked clerks to review their contents? They were a professional appendage, a practical necessity. Not a Pandora's box that would reveal the pain he had wreaked on a woman he'd once sworn to cherish and protect.

He'd sifted through the papers, slowly, carefully. The police had only allowed him certain information prior to his arrest. Now he was given the full accounting of the horror of Elise's murder through Nick's damning statements, the M.E.'s clinical findings and Lucy's traumatized recounting of her mother's final hours.

But it was Dr. Gainsford's notes that sent him free falling into the abyss.

At first, the notes had simply magnified his guilt about leaving Toronto. Elise had told her therapist she felt tremendous stress parenting her two children without Randall being in the same city to share the load. That she believed many of Nick's behavioral issues were related to Randall's absence.

Of course, he knew all this. She'd yelled most of these accusations at him at some time or another. But seeing them written in Dr. Gainsford's scrawl gave his ex-wife's perspective an unnerving weight.

He'd always felt justified in moving to Halifax; after all, it was Elise who'd made him a laughingstock of the

Toronto bar. As he read the chronological summary of
Elise's visits to Dr. Gainsford, he could see how this
distance had contributed to many of the crises that Elise
had either precipitated or had to manage.

He'd hoped that time and distance would ease her
hurt, but according to Dr. Gainsford's notes, it magnified her feelings of abandonment and neglect.

He'd had no idea how fragile her emotional state
had been when he confronted her over Nick's theft in
June. And he was sure he'd made it worse. He crossed
a boundary with her, opening doors long barricaded.
Then retreated from her to the point where she did not
confide in him about her pregnancy. Or her abortion.
He fervently hoped that her therapist provided her with
some good support. He flipped the pages until he found
June's entries.

*…her ex-husband forced her to have sexual rela-
tions.*

He froze. Reread the notation. Subsequent entries
were equally damning: *patient fears for her safety…
ex-husband is emotionally abusive…threatening.*

Jesus. He came across as a textbook wife abuser.

No wonder Kate had looked at him like that.

The abyss yawned below him. The air around him
was black with remorse. Thick with shame.

He sprang to his feet, pacing his cell. His blood
pounded a rhythm of denial. Why did she lie to her
therapist? He'd never threatened her.

A thought stopped him. Did she believe this was true?
Did she think he would hurt her?

He was sure he hadn't forced her. He'd never forced
a woman in his life. The thought disgusted him.

But did Elise *think* he forced her?

He'd closed his eyes while they had intercourse. He couldn't bear to look at her face.

Jesus. Maybe he *had* forced her.

No. She moaned when she came.

He exhaled a deep breath. She had an orgasm. He hadn't forced her.

But why did she tell her therapist that he had?

Calm down, Barrett. Notes weren't always foolproof; maybe Dr. Gainsford misheard her. But the rest of his notes for the month of June were consistent with the claim that Elise was fearful of her ex-husband.

Randall knew he hadn't raped Elise; he truly believed it was a consensual act. But the rest of what she'd told Dr. Gainsford…

Had she really been scared of him?

And if she believed him capable of violence…

Had he really killed her?

"I hate to ask this of you, but I'm in a bind," Randall's mother said. Somehow Penelope Barrett had gotten hold of Kate's cell phone number.

Kate slowed down to a walk. It was early evening. She'd taken Alaska out for a run, craving the endorphins that would calm her nerves. Tomorrow afternoon was Randall's bail hearing and she needed to unwind. Either that or she'd end up joining Eddie on the sidewalk, smoking her nerves into submission.

"Of course," Kate responded, wondering what Randall's mother could want with her.

"Charlie is supposed to be picked up from the veterinary hospital tonight. But she still needs to be monitored regularly. And the vet wants to check her on a daily basis for another week. She's worried about infection." Penelope Barrett cleared her throat. "The problem is that Animal Cruelty won't release Charlie to my care because Nick is staying with me. They want her to go to a foster family."

There was an expectant silence. "You want me to foster her, Mrs. Barrett?" Kate asked. How in the world could she look after a sick dog? She was working flat out on Randall's file, along with the other cases that were now backed up and demanding her attention.

"Animal Cruelty said they'd be willing to give her to you."

Kate crossed the road, Alaska at her heels. They were five minutes from her house. "I'm not sure I could do it."

"Please, Ms. Lange. Lucy would be devastated if the dog were taken away from us. She's lost so much already…"

Kate's gaze fell on her own dog. On his softly plumed tail, his confident, wolflike sleekness that belied his gentle affection. She knew what it was like to be twelve years old and have your world change for the worse. Lucy had lost more than Kate had at that age.

"Fine," Kate said, trying to figure out how the heck she could make this work. "I'll go to the vet hospital and pick her up."

"I hate to ask more of you than I have already, Ms. Lange… I hope you understand that in normal circumstances I would never presume to impose on you in such a manner, but these are not normal circumstances." Penelope Barrett's voice thickened. She cleared her throat again. "I don't think the children should attend their father's bail hearing. Nick is very unpredictable right now. And Lucy is too fragile. I don't think she could bear it if bail was denied. And, if at all possible, I'd like her to avoid seeing her father in a jumpsuit."

Kate had been the same age when her father was convicted of fraud. She had seen him in cuffs and a jumpsuit. It had devastated her. And shamed her.

Until Randall was convicted of the charges against him, Kate agreed with Lucy's grandmother: his daughter should not see him like that. She would never look at him the same way again. "I understand," Kate said softly.

"I thought you might." There was something in Penelope Barrett's voice that made Kate wonder how much she knew of Kate's family history. "The problem is that I don't want to leave Lucy alone with Nick tomorrow. I'd much rather her be in town, closer to me. She'd dearly love to be with Charlie, she told me..."

"Would you like her to stay at my house?" Kate asked, resigned to the answer. "I could ask my neighbors to watch her. They are quite lovely. I'm sure they wouldn't mind." Enid and Muriel would love to have a girl to fuss over.

"Could she?" Penelope asked. "I had a friend lined up, but she wasn't able to take Charlie in her apartment. Your suggestion would make things so much easier."

"Why don't you bring her at 8:30 a.m. I have to leave after that, but I can get her settled in. You could stay with her until you need to leave for the hearing. I'll get my dog walker to check in, too."

"Thank you, Ms. Lange. You don't know how much I appreciate this."

Oh, yes. I do. "I'll see you tomorrow, Mrs. Barrett."

61

Tuesday, 9:30 a.m.

Did anyone ever get used to this place? Kate wondered as she was buzzed through the security gates at the correctional center. She hoped not, for Randall's sake. Everything was cold and unyielding. The walls, fences, floors, guards, inmates. She could not imagine Randall becoming deadened to prison life like some inmates. It wasn't in his nature. He'd probably kill himself first, Kate thought. A chill ran through her. He probably would.

She entered the same room she'd been in the last time. Randall was at the same table. Routine, routine, routine. It was mind-numbing, which was good for maintaining order, Kate supposed.

The only thing that wasn't the same was the way he looked at her. His expression was guarded. But she was glad to see that his bruises looked better. She wanted him to look as much like his old self as possible—not like a thug who belonged in that jumpsuit.

She sat down and leaned toward the glass barrier. "Charlie came home last night. She's doing well."

"She's at your house?"

"Yes. It was difficult for your mother to take her while she was caring for Nick and Lucy." Kate didn't have the heart to tell him about Animal Cruelty. He didn't need to worry about that yet.

"Thank you."

"Did you read the files in the box?"

"Yes." His eyes did not waver.

A good liar? Or an innocent man? Kate could not tell. And it was killing her. "Here's our strategy for today. We are going to request bail by establishing your credentials and the fact you are not a threat to society—"

"Bloody hell," he whispered. "Has it come to this? A threat to society?"

"I'm sorry, Randall." And she was. He had been a pillar of the community just five days ago.

He shook his head. "Fine. But whatever you do, don't drag Nick into this."

"Randall, I understand how you feel—"

"No, you don't. Until you have a child yourself you couldn't possibly, Kate."

Kate dropped her eyes so he wouldn't see how deeply those words had wounded her. He'd effectively shut her out and made her feel as if she was a heartless bitch.

She straightened. That was her role right now. Heartless bitch defense lawyer. "It would really help your case. He is the only eyewitness. We need to discredit his statement—"

"No!"

A guard looked over, his expression alert.

Kate saw how Randall forced his body language to relax. Become nonthreatening. "That's why I fired Bill Anthony, Kate. You can't screw over my son."

"Randall, he lied to the police once already."

"Look. I read his statements. I believe him. I think he lied about seeing Elise commit suicide because he thought I killed her. And that I would get away with it." His laugh was bitter. "He's an idealist, my son."

"Aren't we all."

"Kate…" The notes had shaken him, she could see that. They had ratcheted up his own doubt. His eyes searched hers, asking her: Do you think I did it?

"Randall, there is nothing to connect you to the crime. Except Nick's evidence. That's why we want to discredit him."

"I believe he saw something that night, Kate. I believe his statement."

Conviction burned deep in his bloodshot eyes. It kindled her own doubt. Maybe she'd gotten the theory of the case backward. Maybe Nick hadn't made up his story. But if—as she desperately wanted to believe—Randall hadn't killed Elise, then who did Nick see commit the murder?

"Do you think Nick saw a man that night who physically resembles you?"

Randall shrugged. "I wondered that myself. The man's back was to Nick and he had a stocking over his head. I think Nick mistook him for me because I'd been over earlier and I'd fought with Elise." He rubbed a hand over his face. "God knows what Nick really saw."

Kate hated to say this, but it was her job. "The

problem is that the therapist's notes indicate you threatened Elise. So if we let Nick's story stand, then the notes corroborate Nick's belief it was you he saw."

"I know." He stared down at his hands. "Those notes killed me, Kate." In his face, Kate saw pain. Remorse. Shame. "I didn't force her. I swear it."

Kate's heart climbed a notch out of its mire of distrust. "I believe you didn't think you forced her." She paused. "Could Elise have believed otherwise in the circumstances?" How was that for pussyfooting around the real question?

"No." He glanced down at his hands again. "She had an orgasm, Kate…"

Too much information, Kate thought. *I don't want to know this.* "I see," she managed to say. "Well, given that occurrence, unless she was into S&M it's hard to argue that the sex was nonconsensual. Do you think Elise lied?"

"I don't know. She was very upset after I left. But why would she lie to her therapist? What advantage would it give her?"

"Maybe she couldn't deal with the ramifications of what happened."

"Maybe. The whole situation was pretty horrible."

She could tell he was thinking about Elise's pregnancy. But time was running out. His hearing was this afternoon. If she didn't get him out on bail he'd have plenty of time to think about things while he paced his medium-security jail cell. She glanced at her watch. "Okay," she said briskly. "You don't want us to test Nick's credibility. That means we have to make sure the therapist's notes are discredited."

"I don't want Elise to be portrayed as hysterical or unstable, Kate," Randall said. "Everything she said up to the month of June was a fair recounting of the situation, just with her own emotions attached."

"So it's the notes from June that you disagree with?"

"Yes. I never threatened her. I never abused her. In fact, I went to great pains to avoid speaking to her."

"Why do you think the therapist wrote those things?"

"I have no idea."

The timing nagged Kate. Everything happened in June: Elise's pregnancy, the misrepresentations in the notes. "Do you think Elise could have gotten pregnant by someone else? And the therapist covered up for her?"

"But why would he do that?"

They stared at each other. "Because it was the therapist who got her pregnant," Kate said softly.

"Jesus." Randall looked at her. His eyes gleamed, giving Kate a glimpse of the old Randall. "You know, that could make sense."

And if that made sense… "Then Nick's evidence could make sense, too. He really could have seen a man kill Elise." A thought struck her. "Do you know what Dr. Gainsford looks like?"

Randall shook his head. "I never met him."

Kate stood. "I think it's time we did some digging around."

Hope gave Randall's eyes the first light they'd seen in days.

* * *

"Nat, I've got a new angle for you to work," Kate said into her headset, hunched over her steering wheel. She was driving as fast as she dared from the correctional center—which was just ten kilometers over the limit because who knew when you'd drive by a police car along here—and heading downtown for a last-minute session with Eddie. She needed to brief him on the change in strategy that Randall wanted.

"What've you got?"

"Before I tell you, I need you to promise that you won't print this until I give you the go-ahead. Okay?"

Kate sensed Nat's hesitation over the line. And it bothered her. Why did Nat always feel so driven to get her scoop over everyone else's needs? She almost ended the conversation then and there. But she needed Nat. She needed information—quickly—and she didn't have time to find it. Nat was better at it than she was, anyway.

"Okay," Nat said finally. "But it better be good. Is it about the Clarkson case?"

"No. Put that baby to bed, Nat." Before Nat could protest, Kate said, "It's about the Vanderzell murder. I need you to do some background checking for me."

"Oh?" Nat's voice sounded casual, but it seemed to Kate that the wireless waves were writhing in excitement.

"Elise Vanderzell was seeing a therapist. His notes are part of the evidence against Barrett…"

"Ooh, tell me more, tell me more." Nat was likely rubbing her hands together on the other end of the phone, Kate thought.

"We think he's lying, Nat. The thing is, we don't know why. Can you do some digging around?"

"Absolutely. When do you need it by?"

"In an hour."

"Geez. It's that critical?"

"Yes." Kate turned into the parkade of her office building. "His name is Dr. Jamie Gainsford. He's based in Toronto. And one more thing…"

"Uh-huh?"

"Could you dig up a photo of him?"

"Your wish is my command."

Right on cue, the headset cut out.

It was getting chilly on Kate's deck. It had been a lot warmer when Lucy and Finn walked the dogs an hour ago. Lucy grabbed her book and went back inside. Charlie opened her eyes when Lucy walked in, thumping her tail lightly. Alaska pushed himself to his feet, lazy after his morning walk with Finn, and greeted her with a warm nuzzle to her hand.

A child squealed with delight. Then another. Lucy had glimpsed the little kids through the leafy trees of Kate's backyard. They raced through a sprinkler, back and forth, shrieking when the cool water hit their skin.

It was the sound of the kids that had jarred Lucy. All she'd heard for days was the drumming of the ocean, the muted jangle of music coming from Nick's room, the seabirds cawing overhead while she roamed the rocks.

"Would you like some lemonade, Lucy?" Enid asked.

"Yes, please." Lucy studied the elderly woman who reminded her a lot of Grandma Penny. They were both quick, full of energy, although she guessed Enid was a lot older. Muriel wasn't at all like her sister, Enid, although it was probably because of her Alzheimer's disease. Lucy had never met anyone with it before, and it was funny how Muriel could seem so normal and then do something kind of random.

Enid and Muriel had arrived promptly at eight forty-five this morning, loaded with books, a dog-eared game of Scrabble, a puzzle of a butterfly garden and a deck of cards with a picture of two cats on the back.

Lucy had watched them bustle into the house with a mixture of trepidation and relief. She had no desire to play games or do a puzzle, but the pair did not look the type to order her around. Still, she wished her grandmother had found someone younger to be with her. She hoped the Richardson sisters would just leave her alone.

Kate conducted a series of hurried introductions and then rushed out the door. Muriel told Lucy that she better eat her breakfast or she'd be late for school.

Then they made tea. Lucy drifted over to Charlie's crate and stroked her ears while Grandma Penny and the Richardson sisters spoke in low voices over their teacups. She knew they were talking about her, but she didn't care. All she could think about was what would happen this afternoon.

Would her father get bail? She hadn't seen him for three days. She couldn't imagine him being in a large concrete prison surrounded by security gates. She blocked the image from her mind and read the directions for Charlie's medications.

Alaska got to his feet and stood by the door. A low whine in his throat announced the arrival of his dog walker, Finn. He was really cute. Lucy hunched back against the wall, watching him stride into the kitchen. He grinned at her, then joked around with Enid, devouring one of her scones in two bites. Kate had obviously told him about her, because then he turned to where she sat by Charlie and invited her to go on Alaska's walk.

Lucy hesitated.

"Go on, Lucy. You'll enjoy all the dogs," her grandmother had said. So she agreed, turning her face to the breeze from the open window of his pickup, relaxing with his easy banter. They drove to the Dingle park, one he didn't take the dogs to very often, he told her. It was a big treat. But she knew he'd gone to a different place because he didn't want to drive by Cathy's house. He didn't want to upset her.

He let her hold some of the dogs' leashes and showed her how to make Alaska sit. On their way out of the park, he pulled the truck into Pinky's and convinced her to buy an ice cream cone. At first she said no because food kept choking her when she ate, but he bought her one anyway. And when she tried it, it slid down her throat, cool and sweet.

The morning had gone by quickly. "Thank you, Finn," her grandmother had said, gratitude in her eyes. Lucy knew she was worried about the hearing this afternoon.

The thought of her father being in a prison cell terrified them both. What terrified Lucy even more was the knowledge he could be in there until she was thirty-seven. She'd read the newspaper; she knew that, if convicted, her father faced a jail term of twenty-five years. Her grandmother would probably be dead before he came out.

What will happen to you, Daddy? What will happen to me?

And Nick?

62

Tuesday, 9:38 a.m.

"Dr. Gainsford, this is Ralph Moore. We spoke yesterday. I'm the Crown prosecutor handling the case against Randall Barrett."

"Good morning, Mr. Moore."

"As you know, Randall Barrett's bail hearing is this afternoon. I'd like to run through your notes with you, if I may."

Jamie glanced at his watch. It was just after 9:00 a.m. It would take him at least two hours to get to Prospect from his cabin. And he still had some last-minute things to set up in the basement…

"Of course," he said. "I'd like to help in any way I can."

Jamie heard notes shuffling over the phone line.

"We'll start at the beginning…" Moore said. Jamie stifled a groan. Why didn't the Crown prosecutor do this yesterday when he called? "How did you meet Ms. Vanderzell?"

"She was my client."

"And was she referred to you?"

"No." The memories rushed back: Elise walking into his office, so beautiful, so damaged. He sank into a chair. "I'd been working in Nova Scotia. I had the opportunity to purchase the practice of a retiring psychologist located in Toronto. Elise had been one of the psychologist's clients."

"And you treated her for what conditions?"

"She was experiencing tremendous stress in her life over her relationship with her ex-husband and her son. She suffered from anxiety, and had a history of postpartum depression. Fortunately, we established a good rapport and I felt comfortable taking over that therapeutic relationship."

"I see in your notes that Lucy Barrett attended two sessions with her mother." The prosecutor paused. "Were you treating her, as well?"

Ah, nice try, Mr. Moore. Testing your expert, are you? "As you are most likely aware, Mr. Moore, it would be a breach of professional ethics to treat both the mother and the daughter."

"Yes, I am aware of that. So why was Lucy present at two of Elise Vanderzell's sessions?"

"As my notes indicate, Ms. Vanderzell was very concerned about her son's behavior. I suggested that her daughter might be able to provide additional insight from a peer/sibling perspective."

"Good," Moore said, his voice brisk.

And so the questions went on. Every single item in Jamie's notes from June was parsed to the finest detail. Jamie sensed time ticking away, the time he needed to drive to Prospect without risking speeding. The time he needed to stake out Lucy's grandmother's house. He made another attempt to rush the prosecutor through his notes, but the guy wasn't going to be rushed. He was methodical to the point of OCD. So Jamie answered his questions, his manner calm, patient, helpful, his gaze fixed on his truck parked outside his window.

As soon as the Crown prosecutor was done, Jamie rushed to his truck and sped out to the highway, his spine crunching as he took the rutted track much too fast. He forced himself to slow down. The worst thing that could happen—when he was so close to getting Lucy that he could almost taste it—would be getting stopped for speeding on his way to Prospect. Then his license plate would be recorded, and his out-of-province driver's license would be noted.

An hour into his journey, the sky clouded over. He switched on the radio. Maybe he'd get a weather forecast. Rain would be a good thing. It would eradicate tire tracks, eliminate his scent and make a search for Lucy slower.

On the other hand, rain might keep Lucy from taking Scrubby for a walk. And he was counting on intercepting her while she was outside. He stepped harder on the accelerator.

He was only an hour away. His heart began to pound. All this planning, all this effort.

And he was only an hour away.

He glanced at the passenger seat. A new roll of duct tape nestled inside a coil of rope. Inside the duct tape sat a bottle of orange juice. The protective seal had been removed by him hours ago.

He doubted he would have to use rope or duct tape,

but he hadn't come this far to not make sure every possibility was covered. He couldn't predict how Lucy would
react. Would she buy his story that her grandmother had
suggested he take her for a drive?

Or would he have to threaten to kill Scrubby to convince her to get into the truck with him?

Once in the truck, he would force her to drink the
orange juice.

After that, the chloral hydrate would put her asleep
for several hours. Just enough time to get to the cabin.

Nat pounded furiously on her keyboard.

"Whatcha up to?" Manny, the *Post*'s entertainment
reporter, strolled by, coffee cup in hand, ready for a chat,
but she barely managed a grunt. She was too absorbed
in the online archive of the *Durban Times*.

"Just background," she said, angling her body so
Manny couldn't peer at the screen.

She waited until he left, then scrolled through the
articles about Dr. *William* James Gainsford. At first she
wasn't sure it was the same guy, but she'd looked up Dr.
Gainsford's Canadian license, and it indicated he'd come
from South Africa and gave the name of the university
from which he'd attained his degree. From that, she'd
looked at alumni for his graduating class and found his
full name.

When she entered his full name into the internet
search engine, she grinned. Kate was right. This was one
juicy story. She couldn't wait to write it up. The man's
wife and stepdaughter had died in a murder-suicide just
before he moved to Canada. It was a bit ironic that a
psychologist's wife should commit suicide… Couldn't

be much of a therapist. *They're all quacks,* she thought. She'd rather bare her soul to the ducks on her family farm.

But she couldn't dismiss the suicide angle. Kate might be able to use it. Nat entered Dr. Gainsford's name in the search engine and added the term "suicide." She gave a low whistle when she got a whack of hits. The more recent ones related to his personal tragedy. But there were old hits, as well. Ones that referred to the sad case of Alison Gilling, a twelve-year-old patient of Dr. Gainsford's who had killed herself by swallowing a bottle of sleeping pills.

The *Durban Times* had had a field day with photos of Dr. Gainsford and his family, showing Dr. Gainsford's grief-stricken visage after the deaths of his family, and the smiling faces of the trio taken while they were on a holiday safari. Nat printed out their photos, then searched for one of Alison Gilling. She found one of the young suicide victim in her school uniform, her blond hair pulled back by a headband, a charming sprinkle of freckles on her nose. She bore a striking resemblance to Dr. Gainsford's dead stepdaughter. Same age, too. Also dead.

She peered at the photo of Mrs. Laura Gainsford. She, too, was blonde. She, too, was dead.

She thought of Elise Vanderzell. Another blonde. Now dead.

All of these girls and woman had one common connection: Dr. Jamie Gainsford. And all were initially believed to have committed suicide—except for Maggie Gainsford, who'd been killed by a suicidal mother.

Nat's pulse hammered. A coincidence?

I think not.

She printed all the photos and articles, stuffed them in an envelope and sprang out of the newsroom.

She tracked down Kate and Eddie on the helipad by Kate's office building. Eddie was having a pre-bail hearing smoke while Kate crouched on a bench, running through her notes.

"Look." Nat shoved the pictures under Kate's nose.

Kate tried to focus on the grainy photos. Nat shook them. "Look! Dr. Gainsford left a string of suicides in South Africa."

"How many?" Eddie asked.

"First one was a patient. She was the same age as his stepdaughter. She OD'd on sleeping pills. Two years later, his wife became suicidal, gave her daughter sleeping pills and drove them off a bridge."

"So one woman and two twelve-year-old girls." Kate took the pictures and studied them carefully. "The girls resemble each other."

"Why did they kill themselves?" Eddie asked.

"The patient didn't leave a note. But Dr. Gainsford's wife just said she was depressed and couldn't bear to die without her daughter by her side."

"Was it ever investigated?"

"The authorities ruled it murder-suicide."

"And sleeping pills were involved in each of the cases," Kate added, flipping through the articles.

"Including Elise Vanderzell's."

"What did Dr. Gainsford do after that?" Eddie asked.

"He came to Canada," Nat said. "Once he got licensed here, he practiced in several small towns out

West, before moving to Nova Scotia. I couldn't find any more dead patients." She sounded disappointed.

"Oh, my God," Kate whispered. She held the vacation photo of Dr. Gainsford and his family. "Look at Jamie Gainsford."

"Yeah, he's cute," Nat said. "He's got that whole outdoorsy thing working for him."

The Gainsfords were on a beach. Jamie Gainsford stood with his arms around his wife and stepdaughter, bare chested and buff. They all looked happy, Jamie in particular. He gazed at the camera, the wind ruffling his blond hair, his skin tanned, slightly sun-damaged and freckled. A light stubble shadowed his jaw.

Every hair on Kate's body quivered. "From the back, Eddie, do you think he could look like Randall?" She passed the picture to Eddie and held her breath for his response.

Eddie's eyes narrowed. "I think we just found our man."

Kate dug around in her purse for her cell phone. "I've got to call Ethan."

Eddie placed a hand on her arm. "We need to show these to Detective Drake. In this case, a picture speaks a thousand words."

Kate dialed Ethan's number. She hadn't called him on that line for months. When he answered, she cleared her throat. It didn't matter things had officially ended eight months ago, she'd thought she would be spending her life with this man. It was hard to forget that.

"Ethan, it's Kate."

"I know." His voice was terse.

"Look, I've got something you need to see ASAP."

"Can't it wait until after the bail hearing?"

"Please, Ethan." She gripped the phone tightly against her cheek. She was aware of Eddie's eyes covertly watching her through a plume of cigarette smoke; of Nat's frank interest.

"Fine," Ethan said grudgingly. "I'll meet you in the barristers' lounge of the courthouse. I can be there in ten minutes."

"Perfect."

63

Tuesday, 12:01 p.m.

Even though Barrett's bail hearing wasn't due to begin for over an hour, the media thronged the foyer and the upstairs hallway outside the courtroom.

Ethan jogged up the stairwell, hoping he wouldn't encounter a keener journalist on his way. *No. The coast was clear.* He stepped onto the seventh floor. It didn't have the traditional air of the Provincial Court, ironically, given that the Supreme Court was its superior, but the building had an air of quiet authority.

The door to the barristers' lounge was dark brown laminate. Ethan knocked lightly, then entered. Kate stood by one of the vinyl sofas. Ethan's brows rose at the sight of Eddie Bent. *Jeesh. Randall Barrett must have been really desperate to hire that old drunk.*

"So whaddya got?" Ethan asked, trying to appear casual despite the effect Kate had on him.

Would it ever go away?

Kate passed him a printout from the *Durban Times'* website. It was an article about Dr. Jamie Gainsford, with a vacation photo showing a grinning man with his arms draped around the shoulders of a woman and young girl at the beach.

"Ethan, have you met Dr. Gainsford?"

"No. He's in Toronto. I only spoke to him on the phone." He studied the picture. Without his shirt on, Dr. Gainsford was impressively built. Well-developed shoulders, trim but strong waist. He could hold his own, Ethan thought.

"Does anything strike you about the photo?"

His gaze shot to Kate's face. "This isn't Twenty Questions, Kate. What's so important about this picture?"

"Don't you think Jamie Gainsford resembles my client?"

He stiffened at Kate's reference to Barrett as her client. He hoped that was all there was to the relationship, but he didn't believe it.

"He's blond and broad-shouldered." He passed the photo back to Kate. "Like a number of men in South Africa."

"He also had a twelve-year-old patient who died from an overdose of sleeping pills."

"That happens, Kate. He's a psychologist. He deals with depressed people."

"His wife also killed herself, Ethan. And she killed her daughter, too. She drugged her with sleeping pills. And guess how old her daughter was?" Kate didn't wait for him to answer. "Twelve."

Ethan took the photo from her.

Jesus. He hadn't done much background on Jamie Gainsford beyond checking his credentials and license in Canada.

"Do you know where he was the night Elise Vander-zell was killed?" Kate demanded.

Ethan shook his head. "No," he said, feeling as if he'd been punched in the stomach. "But I'm about to find out."

"Why don't you check his office for a blackjack, while you're at it," Eddie drawled.

Ethan ignored him and walked over to the window, trying to create a small barrier. He couldn't go out in the hallway for fear of running into the media, and there wasn't enough time for him to run down to his car.

His fingers were not as sure as he wanted them to be when he dialed Dr. Gainsford's cell phone number. The phone rang three times. Ethan was just about to hang up and try Dr. Gainsford's office when the doctor answered. His voice was oddly breathless.

"Dr. Gainsford, it's Detective Drake."

"Ah, yes, Detective. I spoke with your Crown prose-cutor this morning. I believe I provided him with enough information to proceed."

"Yes, you were very helpful." Ethan watched a pigeon land on the windowsill. It fluffed its feathers. "Look, Dr. Gainsford, we are just crossing our t's and dotting our i's prior to the preliminary hearing. I need to find out where you were the night Ms. Vanderzell was killed."

He smiled to himself. "I can tell you exactly where I was."

He'd been sitting in the dank basement of Dr. Cathy Feldman's house since four o'clock in the morning. Getting into the house had been a cinch. Elise had told him

*that the house minder had put the key in the mailbox
for the housecleaner the day before.*

*Every forty minutes or so he'd stand, flexing his mus-
cles, stamping his feet, ridding himself of any cramps.
On three occasions he'd crept upstairs and used the
small powder room under the stairs in the back of the
kitchen. Each of those times, he'd clad his shoes in
Tyvek shoe covers, gloved his hands and wiped the surfaces afterward with disinfectant wipes. He put those
in a Ziploc bag and stuffed the bag into a pocket of his
black cargo pants. He hadn't eaten or drunk anything
since he'd left his car—could not risk leaving a crumb
in this house with his DNA on it—so his bladder and
bowels no longer bothered him.*

"I was at my cottage, Detective Drake. I had been on
vacation since Monday. Still am on vacation, as a matter
of fact."

"And you were there when Elise Vanderzell phoned
you at 8:25 p.m. that night?"

*"Jamie," she said, her voice tremulous. His fingers
holding the phone spasmed. How strange that she would
call him when he was staring into the deepening shadows of Dr. Feldman's basement, visualizing how he
would creep up the stairs while she slept. And then kill
her. If he believed in the paranormal, he would have
seen this as an omen.*

Calm down, *he told himself.* It's not an omen but an
opportunity. You need to detach. Right now.

*Something he'd told himself on the occasions when a
client got under his skin. He was, after all, only human.
Sometimes a client would challenge him, provoke him or
just plain irritate him. And he'd force himself to detach.*

He'd force himself to do the job he was paid to do, maintain his professional detachment and try to help the exasperating son of a bitch.

This case was no different.

Elise was his client.

The least he could do for Elise, who was weeping silently on the phone, was let her die with her mind calmed.

"Let's talk," he said, and settled his back against the damp concrete wall two stories beneath her.

A song played over the cell phone. Sounded as if it came from a car stereo. Ethan counted at least three bars before Dr. Gainsford answered, "Sorry, just took a wrong turn here. Can I answer these questions later? I'm driving."

"Perhaps you could pull over," Ethan said, alarm churning his gut. "I'm sorry, but this will only take a minute. Were you with anyone that night?"

The fluorescent dial of Jamie's watch glowed 1:15 a.m.

The house was silent.

Deadly silent.

He eased himself out of the damp corner behind the rancid armchair, knowing his wait was about to end.

Exhilaration and a fierce excitement shot through him. Just like when he was fifteen and he'd been big game hunting on a reserve. He and his father had waited in a blind, rifles in position for hours. His arm had gone numb. Dead. He knew better than to complain. His father would have knocked the crap out of him if he'd scared the game away. So he'd lain there. Not sure if lying in the bush, with flies buzzing around his sweating face and dust blowing into his nostrils, would be worth the wait.

The gazelle had been wary. Not an easy kill by any means. Just like Elise. Not an easy lay by any means. He'd had to take it very slowly.

When the gazelle finally dared to return to its grazing ground, the wait had been worth it. The adrenaline was so intense that his muscles jumped to life. He waited, breath in his throat, until the gazelle wandered into range.

Then he killed it.

He had crept up the stairs of Cathy Feldman's house, sliding the thong of the blackjack around his wrist.

In less than a minute, he stood a foot inside the doorway of Elise's room.

Her soft breathing met his ears.

He walked on the balls of his feet, his rubber-soled shoes making no sound. He stopped by the nightstand and looked at her.

Her blond hair spread out around her head. The strap of her nightgown had slid off one shoulder. Her chest rose with each light breath.

He'd never seen her asleep. They'd always made love during her therapy sessions. He admired her beauty in a detached, clinical way. Then he raised his arm and smashed the blackjack against her temple.

A low moan escaped from her mouth. He quickly pressed a gloved hand over her lips, scooped his other arm under her shoulders and pulled her from the bed.

Damn. She was still breathing. *He half carried her*

over his shoulder, her hair brushing his jaw. He could feel her breath hot and rapid against his shoulder blade.

Should he strike her again?

She convulsed, her body jerking so violently he almost dropped her. He yanked her back against him, his own actions jerky. He pulled open the patio door, his muscles so overwhelmed with adrenaline that he almost pulled the door off its runners. It bounced loudly on the track.

He stepped out onto the deck.

Dr. Gainsford cleared his throat. "No, Detective. After listening to clients all week, I craved solitude. It was just me, my canoe and my fishing rod."

"Did you see anyone that night who can verify this?"

Elise convulsed again. The blackjack had done some significant damage, but he would hit her one more time before throwing her over.

Then he'd know for sure she'd be dead.

He raised his arm.

"Mum?"

The hairs on the back of Jamie's neck rose at the sound of Elise's fifteen-year-old son's panicked voice.

"If you call an otter a reliable witness." There was a forced note to Dr. Gainsford's jocularity that had all of Ethan's nerves on edge.

"I'm afraid an otter will not cut it, Dr. Gainsford. We'd like to set up an interview at a station in Toronto and discuss this in more detail." Ethan did a mental run-through of his contacts and prayed that he could get a Toronto detective to pinch-hit for him on short notice. "Could you come for five?"

"That's not possible, I'm sorry, Detective. I'm in the middle of a plumbing project at my cottage. How does tomorrow work?"

"Just fine," Ethan said. They'd keep an eye on the airports in Ontario to make sure Dr. Gainsford didn't decide to catch an early flight. "How about first thing? I'll call later to confirm the details."

"Fine."

Dr. Gainsford would be a no-show, Ethan could tell. He called Lamond. "You need to do a background check on Dr. Jamie Gainsford."

"He goes by William James Gainsford in South Africa," Kate called from the other side of the room.

Ethan hunched his shoulders and lowered his voice. "William James Gainsford. Find out what the hell went on in South Africa. We need grounds for a warrant for his arrest. And get Detective Iqbal from Toronto Homicide Squad on the phone."

64

Tuesday, 12:10 p.m.

The call from Detective Drake had rattled him. The police could pretend all they wanted that they were just filling in the paperwork, but he knew that was bull. This was just the tip of the iceberg. Now that Jamie was a suspect in Elise's murder, they'd leave no stone unturned in his background check. Deaths in South Africa that were tenuously linked to him but had been chalked up to bad luck would now be revisited.

The police would search his house, his car, and eventually discover his cabin in the woods.

It wouldn't take them long to find the grave.

The game was up. For Lucy and for him.

He forced himself to be calm. Why was he unnerved by Detective Drake's phone call? He knew he wouldn't get away with Elise's murder. All he'd wanted was to remove the roadblock to Lucy.

He had done so.

Now all he wanted—all he needed—was a chance to be alone with her. Just him and her.

Just him and Beth.

Just him and the beast that had taunted him.

Everything he had done over the past thirty-four years had led him to this rutted track outside Penelope Barrett's house.

All he needed was enough time to ride the beast unfettered, and then—

It was game over.

This is it.

You've arrived.

The final stop on your journey.

Do it, Jamie.

You have nothing left to lose.

That realization propelled him out of the truck. His thoughts chased one another, escalating his heart rate until the blood pounded in his ears. *I can't wait for her to go for a walk. It could be an hour before she comes out.*

If I don't get her now, I never will.

His legs covered the distance to Penelope's front door without him being aware of it. He paused on the doorstep, staring at the seashell knocker on the door.

Calm down. Lucy will sense your desperation. You only have one shot at this.

He would need to use every ounce of professional persuasion to convince Lucy to leave her grandmother and come with him. If it came down to it, he would even offer to call Penelope Barrett to ask her permission and reassure Lucy. It was a gamble, but he doubted she knew what suspicions were brewing with Detective Drake.

He breathed deeply several times until his heart rate slowed, tucked in his shirt and rang the doorbell.

The chime echoed. A dog barked. Come on, *come on*.

The door swung open.

Nick Barrett scowled at him.

Christ, the kid looked a mess. He'd shaved his head. Looked as if he'd done it himself, judging by the bald nicks. Body odor, rank and musty, radiated off his skin. His eyes were dull.

"Nick, I'm Dr. Jamie Gainsford." He glanced over the boy's shoulder. "Is your grandmother here?"

"No."

"How about your sister?"

The boy's eyes narrowed. "No." Nick shifted onto his other foot. "Who are you, again?"

"I'm your sister's therapist," he said smoothly, but he felt a sudden twinge of alarm. Nick Barrett was staring at him. Hard. Had the police already called here? He forced his voice to remain casual. "Just thought I'd check in. Do you know where I can find them?"

"My grandmother is at my father's bail hearing."

Jamie tried not to show his surprise. He'd assumed that Penelope would stay with the grandchildren. Not leave them alone. Especially with Nick's unpredictable behavior.

Fear buzzed in his head. Had Lucy gone to the bail hearing with her grandmother? "What about your sister?" he managed to say.

Nick scowled. "She's at my father's lawyer's house."

"Thank you." Jamie gave him a warm smile, turned on his heel and walked to his truck.

He cursed his complacency. Why hadn't he called one final time to check Penelope Barrett's plans?

He had wanted to keep a little distance, not be too closely involved with the family when Lucy disappeared.

But he hadn't anticipated the police would suspect him already.

He swung the gate closed behind him.

All the while, he felt Nick Barrett's eyes on his back.

Lucy dropped *The Lion, the Witch and the Wardrobe* onto Kate's sofa and jumped to her feet. Although she was too old for the book, she'd always felt a special kinship with the Lucy in the story, but not today. The Lucy in the book didn't have a father in jail, a murdered mother and a brother who could possibly be a homicidal maniac.

She glanced at her watch. Her father's bail hearing would begin in forty-five minutes. Her throat tightened. Her mother had given the watch to her for her twelfth birthday. She remembered the look of anticipation on her mother's face when Lucy unwrapped the gift. Would she like it? Lucy had given her mum a big hug. She had never dreamed that she would be using it to gauge the length of time until her father could be granted bail.

Could Kate Lange really rescue her family from all this? Lucy wondered for the thousandth time. It seemed impossible that one woman could change the minds of all these people who thought her father was guilty. If she could, then Lucy knew what she wanted to be when she was older: a lawyer. If one person could change so many lives then that was something worth doing.

Had her mother affected people's lives like that? She

didn't know. Her mother had been a tax lawyer. Didn't sound as if it could have a big impact, but Lucy had never asked.

And now she never could.

Grief slammed into her again. The ice cream she'd had with Finn slithered in her stomach.

Enid walked into the living room, Alaska on her heels. "Would you like some lunch?" Her gaze took in the book thrown haphazardly on the sofa, Lucy's hunched stance on the area rug.

"Uh, no, thanks. I'm not hungry." Lucy gave her a weak smile. She felt like an intruder, an outsider, awkward and unable to settle in anywhere. Here she was, at her father's lawyer's house—a woman she didn't know—with her father's lawyer's neighbors babysitting—more women she didn't know—in a city she only visited a few weeks every year.

She wished she were back in Toronto with her friends at their local swimming pool. She squashed the thought immediately, guiltily. Her mother had just died. She couldn't go hang out at the pool. And besides, who knew where she would end up living?

"Did Kate show you the staircase?" Enid asked.

Lucy shot Enid a startled look. The question was so random she wondered if maybe Enid had the same disease Muriel had. But the elderly lady's eyes were bright and inquisitive, like a robin's.

"Um…no."

"Come on, I'll show you," Enid said, striding from the room before Lucy could protest. Alaska threw her a look over his shoulder before trotting after her.

With a sigh, Lucy followed the jingle of Alaska's tags

into Kate's kitchen. The dog sat by a closet door at the far end of the room.

"I'm in here with Muriel!" Enid called from the closet. "Come on in!"

Lucy walked into the closet and her eyes widened. In front of her was an open half-door painted lime green, reminding Lucy eerily of a modern take on the wardrobe Lucy Pevensie had discovered.

Enid grinned. "It's a secret stairway." She lowered herself to her knees and crawled through the small door. Muriel followed, her rubber-boot-clad feet sticking out behind her like a duck's. Lucy swallowed a giggle and followed them, her heart hammering. She knew she wouldn't be transported into a mythical land—she was too old for make-believe—but she wondered if she might find an old trunk, fur coats and assorted memorabilia from times past.

No. It was just a narrow staircase. Dingy and dusty. Lucy wasn't sure why Enid and Muriel were both gazing around it with a look of wonder, until Enid said, "I haven't been in here since I was a child." Her voice sounded a little hoarse. "We used to play in here, isn't that so, Mil?"

Muriel said nothing. She stared down at the scuffed, worn treads. Then she walked up the stairs to the top and pushed the door, but it didn't open. "I want to go to the turret," she said.

"The turret is locked right now, Mil," Enid said.

"Does she think this is a castle?" Lucy asked.

Enid nodded. "Yes, we played make-believe in here. The turret was at the top of the stairs. I used to be the princess because I had long hair, and she would rescue me…" Her voice trailed off. "We should have brought in the flashlight. Could you get it, Lucy? There's one just by the door."

Lucy nodded, eager to get out of the staircase. All she wanted right now was to go back to her grandmother's house.

She crawled backward through the half-door, spying the flashlight in the corner. She stood—

A hand grasped her wrist.

She gasped and spun around.

A man blocked the light from the kitchen. She couldn't see his features.

"Lucy?"

When she heard his voice, she relaxed, although she wondered why Dr. Jamie held her arm. She tried to shake it free. His grip tightened. "You need to come with me," he said in a low voice.

"Lucy?" Enid called. "Could you find the flashlight?"

Before Lucy could answer, Dr. Jamie kicked the half-door closed with his foot and shoved the shiny new bolt in the lock.

From the look in his eyes, this was no joke he was playing on the old ladies. Lucy's instincts kicked in. She grabbed his hand and tried pulling it off her wrist, but he yanked her backward, dragging her out of the closet.

The kitchen was silent.

Too silent.

"Where's Charlie? And Alaska?" Lucy cried, her eyes darting around the kitchen.

"They're sleeping," Dr. Jamie said. "In the other room."

He pulled a small bottle of juice out of his pocket. "I need you to drink this, Lucy."

She knew without asking that he had drugged it. "No."

He twisted her arm up against her back. Pain shot through her shoulders. "If you don't drink it, I'll kill your dogs." He spoke in a conversational manner. And that was scarier than if he'd shouted at her. "Do it." He put the bottle against her lips. "Drink."

"Lucy?" Enid's muffled voice came from inside the stairwell. "You locked us in, dear."

Lucy closed her eyes, her heart racing, almost gagging as the orange juice was poured down her throat.

"Swallow it, Lucy."

Tears streamed down her cheeks, but she managed not to choke on the juice.

"Good girl."

"Lucy!" Enid called again, panic in her voice. Lucy heard her pounding on the door. "Lucy! This isn't a joke. Muriel needs to get out. Open the door, please."

"Don't say anything," Dr. Jamie said. "Or I'll have to hurt them, too."

Lucy nodded.

"You are a good girl, aren't you, Lucy?" he said, leading her out of the kitchen. She desperately wanted to make sure Charlie and Alaska were okay, but she knew he wouldn't let her. "You don't want anyone to get hurt, do you?"

She shook her head.

"You need to go in the truck quietly, okay?"

They reached the driveway. The yards next to Kate's

house were quiet. No one was around. Tears filled Lucy's eyes.

Jamie shoved her in the truck.

"Lie down on the floor, Lucy," he said. His voice was calm. Just like at his office. If she closed her eyes, she could imagine herself in his study, curled up in an armchair, with Herbert on her lap. "Otherwise I will have to tie you up and knock you out. I think you are far too sensible for that."

Maybe if she pretended to go along with him, she could escape while he was driving. Whatever was in the orange juice hadn't affected her. Maybe it wouldn't. Maybe if she just tried really hard to stay awake she could escape before the drug kicked in.

She slid down to the floor by the passenger seat and crouched there.

Please let the dogs be alive. Please let them be okay.

She stared up at Dr. Jamie as he started the engine. At his tanned jaw, his open-collared shirt. He looked so normal. Nice. Not a monster. But she knew he was going to hurt her.

She started to feel sick.

Dr. Jamie backed the truck out of the driveway and drove down Kate's street. Where was he taking her?

It was very hot down on the floor, the truck engine vibrating against her back.

Dr. Jamie tossed something at her. She flinched. But it was only a hair elastic.

"Put your hair in a ponytail."

"Why?" she dared.

"Because if you don't, I'll have to do it for you."

She did not want him touching her again. Ever. She scooped back her hair and gathered the elastic around it.

Dr. Jamie glanced down at her. Satisfaction—and something else—gleamed in his eyes. He hummed softly under his breath. "This is a song I used to sing to my Maggie," he told her with a fond smile.

It was a lullaby.

Her head felt like cotton balls. She remembered that feeling. She'd felt the same way when she'd had oral surgery a year ago. Panic surged through the muzziness— *Oh, God, no, don't let the drugs—*

65

Tuesday, 12:52 p.m.

Nick threw open the front door of his grandmother's house and began to run up the path to the cliffs. The house, that fucking house, was suffocating him. He couldn't stand it anymore. His sister's sobbing across the hall, his grandmother's tentative footsteps, the hushed conversations, the worried glances.

Heather crunched under his feet. He had the sensation he was treading on tiny coils of energy. He had not left his room since his father had been arrested.

What was the point? He could no longer do anything. The justice system would give out whatever form of punishment they thought killing his mother deserved.

He'd shaved his head in protest.

The wind was cool on his scalp, fresh and invigorating. He'd forgotten what the air smelled like. Salty. Tangy. It filled his nose, then his chest, waking up the numb flesh that had slouched on his bed for the past three days.

Now, as he ran, his thoughts flew over the rocks,

bouncing against the granite surfaces, rebounding into his brain, slamming him with the truth he'd buried in his heart.

He wanted his old life back. He was weary of this existence, of the hate that fueled his rage, of the rage itself. He wanted to be able to play hockey and hang with his friends and get his fucking beginner's license.

It could never happen now. Everyone knew he'd tried to kill his father. That he'd tried to *murder* someone. The line had been crossed. He was no longer a kid. He could no longer go back to goofing around with his friends at the skateboard park and try a double wheelie to impress Steph.

He'd tried to kill his own father.

He'd grown up in the worst possible way, a below-average kid who'd mutated into a vengeful killer.

It hadn't been his fault. Any of it. He'd wanted to *save* his mother.

There was nothing left for him anymore. His father had taken his mother from him. His sister believed he was a monster.

So would everyone else.

He neared the edge of the cliff. Below him, massive rocks spread out, ready to receive him.

Glaciers had wrought these rocks. The ice had been powerful enough to break granite.

And the granite, in turn, was powerful enough to break bone.

He was no poet, but he saw the truth in dying the same way his mother had.

Nick began to run. Harder, faster, gathering speed.

He would soar off the cliff.

He would experience the same sensations his mother had in her last moments on earth.

The wind rushed around his head. It filled his ears. It promised peace.

66

Tuesday, 1:05 p.m.

Nick's feet barely slowed in time.

He'd backed up just before the cliff gave way to air, his arms cartwheeling, his legs frantically braking, digging into the heather.

He bent over and gasped for breath.

He had to get to a phone. Right away.

The picture in his head refused to go away. His mother, in the arms of the man who killed her. The man dropping her, his broad shoulders flexing, then spinning on his heel and running into his mother's bedroom.

Now a new scene superimposed itself. Dr. Jamie Gainsford spinning on his heel when Nick told him where to find Lucy. Dr. Jamie Gainsford striding down the path, his hips moving in a gait that Nick had believed was his father's—until he saw Jamie Gainsford hurry to his truck.

Not only that, but Dr. Gainsford had had this weird expression on his face when Nick opened the door.

He looked hyper. When he left, he could barely keep himself from running down the path.

As Nick watched him go, he knew the first stirrings of unease.

But his own misery was too great for him to dwell on it until he forced himself to remember his mother's last moments. And Jamie Gainsford took the form of the man who held his dying mother in his arms.

Had Nick made a mistake that night?

Could the killer have been Jamie Gainsford? The guy hadn't been on anyone's radar. But he was beeping furiously on Nick's radar now.

Nick slammed his feet into the heather.

Dr. Gainsford was looking for Lucy.

And Nick had told him where to find her.

67

Grandma Penny's cell phone was turned off. *Oh, God.*

Nick paced the small house and forced himself to think. He needed to warn Lucy. He dialed directory assistance and got Kate Lange's phone number.

But Kate Lange's phone rang. And rang.

Panic choked his breath. He punched 911.

"Put me through to Detective Drake!" he yelled into the phone. "It's an emergency."

Within minutes, Detective Drake answered.

"It's Nick Barrett. I think the man who killed my mother is Dr. Gainsford!"

Detective Drake's voice was low, intense. "Are you sure?"

"No. I mean yes. He came to my grandmother's house looking for Lucy. I didn't know. I told him she was at Kate Lange's house. I didn't know."

"I thought he was in Toronto." The detective drew in

a breath. "Okay, Nick, listen to me. If he comes back, do not let him into the house, do you hear me?"

"Yes."

"You did the right thing. Hang tight. We'll find your sister."

Twelve-year-old patient committed suicide. Twelve-year-old stepdaughter killed by his wife. Twelve-year-old girl now missing.

Ethan's heart raced as he called Deb. "Get an APB out on Dr. Jamie Gainsford. And get the hell over to Kate Lange's house. Nick Barrett just called. He thinks Gainsford might have killed his mother. Gainsford showed up at his grandmother's looking for his sister, Lucy. Nick told him that she was at Kate Lange's."

"Shit!" Deb said. "I can't believe we missed this connection."

Dread pulled at Ethan's insides. He'd had blinders on the whole fucking time.

"You talk to the Crown," Deb said. "Get them to drop the charges. And tell Barrett what's going on. If Lucy's been grabbed, tell him we're going to shut down the province to find her. Do you know when Gainsford went over to Kate Lange's house?"

"Not too long ago."

They both knew that in child abduction cases, the window of time to find the child alive was just hours.

The clock was ticking.

She'd better be alive, Ethan thought. *Or I'm not sure I'll be able to live with this one.*

He raced down the stairwell, plowing into Nat Pitts, who was opening the door to the second floor.

"Detective Drake, has anyone told you—"

He brushed by her. "No comment."

Yanking open the heavy door to the courtroom, Ethan covered the distance to the counsel's table in seconds. Ralph Moore had his back to Ethan, unloading his files. Kate sat to his left, reviewing her notes. The photos of the Gainsford family sat conspicuously at the front of the table.

"Ralph." Ethan took him by the elbow and led him to the court clerk's area, away from the spectators who filled the benches. "We need to talk."

The Crown was a seasoned prosecutor. Kate had just shown him the pictures, he told Ethan. It didn't take much explanation from Ethan for him to agree to drop the charges. "It was an iffy case to begin with," he added, giving Ethan a warning look. "You're going to have to do better next time, Detective."

Ethan didn't respond.

"We need to instruct Barrett's counsel." Moore gestured to Kate. She hurried over, her eyes a mixture of resolve and hope. "We're going to withdraw the charges—" Moore began.

"I want them dismissed. They shouldn't have been laid in the first place." Kate gave Ethan a dirty look.

"Can't do that, Ms. Lange, because Mr. Barrett never entered a plea—"

Impatience surged in Ethan with all this legal bullshitting. "Kate, Gainsford was looking for Lucy. Nick told him where she was."

"Gainsford? He's here in Halifax?" The blood drained from Kate's face. "Did he find her?"

"We don't know. We're sending patrol over to your house right now."

She looked at Moore. "You need to let him go and find his kids. You have to drop the charges. They're bogus. We all know it."

"Like I said—"

"Randall Barrett has been deprived of his liberty for the past three days. His ex-wife was murdered, his son tried to kill him and now his daughter could be in the hands of a killer. I smell a big fat lawsuit and it's going to have your name with 'miscarriage of justice' stamped on top if you don't do the right thing." Kate glared at Moore, then Ethan, the blood pounding in her head. "I'm going to inform my client that his ex-wife's killer may have kidnapped his daughter." She pivoted on her heel and half ran through the door.

Ralph Moore's face was tight. "I will recommend that the charges be withdrawn in light of the evidence uncovered by the accused." He bit out the word *accused*. "And save ourselves the pleasure of being flayed alive by Justice Carson."

68

Lucy had not made a peep in the truck. Jamie glanced down at her slumped form in the foot well of the passenger seat, calculating yet again the correct dosage of chloral hydrate for a girl Lucy's age. Had he given her too much?

He turned into the village of Prospect.

All he needed was an hour or less, alone with Lucy. He estimated that he could buy himself that much time if he stole a boat and hid in a cove until it was over.

Nick jogged into the village. He could not wait in his grandmother's house. He had to get to Halifax. Tell his grandmother he was sorry. See if he could help.

Please let Lucy be okay.

Please don't take her from me.

Maybe old Pete would be out working in his shed down the road. He'd give Nick a drive.

Nick turned the corner. Ahead, a truck took the narrow bridge too fast. Nick was about to chase after it, to see if the driver would take him to Halifax, when he realized he *knew* that truck.

It was Jamie Gainsford's truck. It swerved right, bouncing down a narrow lane.

It headed straight onto the old wharf.

Nick began to run.

"We've pinged Gainsford's cell phone," Deb told Ethan over her cell phone. "He's in Prospect."

"Why would he go there?" Ethan rubbed his hair. "You don't think he's going to take Nick, too?"

"I don't know. There's no answer at the grand-mother's."

"Shit." Fear clenched his stomach.

"We're five minutes away, Ethan. Tell Barrett to hang tight."

The sheriff let Kate into a small room with a table and two chairs. A corrections officer stood inside by the door, facing Randall, who sat at the table, his hands loosely clasped.

As usual, his gaze did not leave Kate's face as she hurried over to the table.

"What's wrong?" He hadn't missed the anxiety tight-ening her face. "Does Gainsford have an alibi?"

She took a deep breath. "Gainsford has Lucy."

His face drained of color. "How do you know?"

"Nick called us. Gainsford showed up at your moth-er's, looking for Lucy. He told him she was at my house. It was only later that he realized it might have been Gainsford he saw that night." A flicker in Randall's eyes was the only acknowledgment of the fact that his son had admitted he had been wrong about him.

"They are going to withdraw the charges," Kate added.

He pushed his chair away and headed to the door. "What are the police doing?"

"They're looking for him, Randall. He can't have gotten far…"

He turned to her. "Is your dog an attack dog?"

"No."

"So Lucy was alone, totally defenseless."

"No, she wasn't. We left her with my neighbors." Kate's voice caught. What had happened to Enid and Muriel?

Randall had the same question in his eyes, but he asked, "How long has Lucy been missing?"

"We're not sure."

"I'm going after her." He lunged toward the door.

The correctional officer barred his way. "I'm sorry, Mr. Barrett. But you can't leave."

"For the love of God, it's my daughter! She's with the man who killed my wife!"

Compassion flashed in the guard's eyes, but he put his hand on his Taser. "Sit down, please, Mr. Barrett, and let me make a call…"

"There's no time." Randall's whole body was tensed to run.

The bailiff knocked on the door. "Time to go up," he called. "You're next."

Kate put a hand on Randall's arm. "This should be over in a few minutes. The Crown agreed to drop the charges. All they need is for Justice Carson to rubber-stamp it. You'll be free to go."

How long had he waited to hear those words? Kate wondered. They had held the promise of vindication, of freedom, of a life restored.

Now the life he sought to reclaim was not his own.

But his daughter's.

69

The wind was at Nick's back, pushing him forward. His feet were moving so fast, he couldn't feel the wharf under them. Which was probably a good thing. *Just go so fast that you skim over the holes.*

A rickety structure that had been an eyesore ever since Nick could remember, the wharf had been built years ago and left to rot. And rot it had. Some of the planks were gone. The water gaped at him through the holes, a seething froth of tide and current beneath him. Despite its dilapidated condition, the wharf was still in use by a local, as evidenced by the fishing boat tied to one side.

Nick's gaze was fixed on the truck that bumped ahead of him over the wharf's rough planks, the driver barely keeping the truck from veering off the narrow edges. The wharf wasn't built to hold a car. It shuddered under him as he pumped his arms, head down. He was so close. So close.

The truck kept going. Why wasn't it slowing down?

Stop, please stop. Don't drive over the end with Lucy inside.

He could barely breathe, but he forced his body to move even faster. Brake lights glared angry red eyes at him.

Nick was so close. He was going to reach him. He was going to get there in time.

Then the reverse lights flashed on.

The truck backed straight at him with a roar. There was no room on the sides of the wharf for him. He could either turn around and run for his life.

Or jump.

Veering sharply to the right, Nick hurtled himself off the edge of the wharf.

Cold water slapped his skin, shocking the breath out of his lungs. He pulled himself up to the surface. Then dived under the wharf when he saw Gainsford jump out of the truck and peer into the water.

An eel swam by him. Nick swallowed his fear, peering upward through the underside of the wharf. The odor of rank seaweed filled his nose. He gasped for breath. He saw no sign of movement on top of the wharf. What was Gainsford doing?

A deep throbbing stirred the air, vibrating the water around Nick.

Gainsford had hotwired the boat. Nick knew the boat; it had been part of the landscape ever since he was a kid visiting Grandma Penny. A retired fishing boat turned pleasure craft, it was as rickety as the wharf to which it was tied. The name *Glory Anne* splashed in garish white and red on its stern did little to improve its appearance. The recent addition of a shiny chrome ladder on the stern merely served as stark contrast to its poorly maintained exterior.

Nick lunged toward the *Glory Anne*, kicking his feet furiously as he swam between the posts of the wharf. Above his head, the fishing boat's lines dangled, no longer attached to the deck. The boat had been cast off.

No!

Nick dived under the water, using his dolphin kick to propel him toward the boat's hull. Water churned, furious and white, repelling him as the engine shoved into full throttle. Caught between two opposing forces—the tide pulling the boat one way, the engine propelling it in the opposite direction—the boat lurched to a stop in the water. Nick knew it would last only a few seconds and then the boat would plow forward. With one final desperate kick, he grabbed a bright orange fender that hung over the boat's side. He clasped the small buoy to his chest, his heart hammering.

Gainsford hit the throttle into high gear and the boat leaped across the water.

Randall's entrance in the courtroom caused a stir amongst the spectators, who all straightened and stared. Kate hurried over to the counsel's table.

"All rise," the court clerk intoned.

Justice Hope Carson strode into the courtroom. Randall hadn't seen her since she was appointed to the bench. With her erect bearing, sleek silver-threaded black bob and formal robes, she looked every inch a Supreme Court justice.

Her tawny gaze skimmed the courtroom, resting on

Kate, then flicked away as if she was not worth her attention. She glanced at Randall, her face inscrutable, and sat down behind the broad desk.

The Crown stood. "My lady, the Crown has considered all the evidence and we are withdrawing the charge against Mr. Barrett."

The spectators began to murmur, but quieted when Justice Carson began to speak. "The Crown is requesting to withdraw the charge of murder against Mr. Randall Barrett," she said, her tone formal. "The charge is withdrawn."

She rested a stern glance on the Crown, sparing Ethan—the detective who had tried to find her daughter's killer—her censure, Kate noted. "Bailiff, please release Mr. Barrett. Now."

The bailiff hesitated, clearly taken aback by this turn of events. Accused were released down in the cells, not in the courtroom.

"Time is of the essence. Mr. Barrett, you are free to go," she said to Randall. Her eyes met her long-ago lover's. They burned into him, a tiger urging him to protect his own. "If I believed in God, I'd wish you Godspeed. As I do not, all I can hope is that your daughter does not experience the same fate as mine."

The water raged against Nick, the wake sucking him under the side of the boat. He clung to the fender, the bright orange plastic smooth and slick. His grip slipped a notch. Then another. His hands were dangerously close to the bottom of the buoy. He slid his hand upward and grasped the rough rope that attached the fender to a cleat bolted in the deck. He just prayed that whoever tied the fender onto the cleat knew his knots.

He also prayed that Gainsford would stay in the small glass-fronted cabin that housed the wheel. If he did, he wouldn't be able to spot Nick hanging on to the side.

Nick couldn't see where the boat was heading. Water streamed into his face, up his nostrils, down his throat, into his eyes. But he sensed they were crossing the mouth of the bay where it met the ocean. The water was choppier, the swell lifting the boat. The engine vibrated through the side of the hull, a rhythmic drumming that jolted his bones.

His grip slipped, the rough rope abrading his palms. He clung to it with a strength he never knew he possessed. But then in the next second his fingers became more numb, more cramped. More fatigued.

Hold on, Nick. You can't fall off now.

He couldn't feel his fingers.

He pressed his chest into the fender, trying to pin it against his body. But the rope ripped through his hands. He felt his legs splay out against the side of the boat.

I'm sorry, Lucy. I'm so so sorry.

He could not hang on.

I'm sorry, Dad.

Three things could happen to him now: he would lose his handhold completely and get left in the water, too far from shore to make it back. Or he would get sucked under the boat and be chewed apart by the propeller blades.

Or, if he was fast enough, he could grab the ladder that hung off the stern of the *Glory Anne.*

It was a split second of win or lose.

His hands grasped at air as the fender sprang out of his grip.

Oh, God. He fell down into the water, bumping against the hull. Ocean pounded into his face. Panic seized him. In a second the stern would move past him. And be gone in even less time.

A flash of silver—

Now! Now!

He lunged upward, scrabbling for the bottom rung of the ladder. His face smashed against the stern as the boat thrust upward into a wave. But it worked to his advantage. With the bow up and the stern down, he was able to grab the middle of the ladder and pull himself partly out of the water before he got dragged down into the wake of the boat.

He hunched on the bottom rung of the ladder. His heart hammered. He began to shiver.

To one side lay the rocky coastline. To the other, the ocean. Fog moved closer to shore, chill and damp. And thick. Soon it would envelop him in cold moisture. He needed to act before he was too cold to move.

He rested his cheek against his hands, gripping the ladder, his teeth chattering. How the hell was he going to overpower Jamie Gainsford, a man with fifty pounds more muscle?

You need a plan, Nick. You can't just hope this will work out. He's smarter than you. He's stronger than you.

He's playing chicken with the Coast Guard by sticking close to the shore.

The whole coastline from Peggy's Cove to beyond Prospect was made of granite. Massive cliffs looming overhead and deadly shoals guarding the shoreline. The coast was jagged and barren, with long fingers of rocky peninsulas separated by bays. Upper Prospect, home of Prospect village, and Nick's grandmother's house, sat on one of those rocky peninsulas that overlooked Prospect Bay. The bay separated Upper Prospect from the next finger, which was broader, and split midpoint into two separate tips with multiple islands clustering around it.

These jagged stretches of rocky coastline provided numerous coves to dart into. And hide.

Despair gripped Nick. With his smaller boat, Jamie Gainsford could easily play cat and mouse with the much larger Coast Guard vessel.

And then what? What was he planning to do with Lucy? He shivered. The fog was getting thicker.

The *Glory Anne* swerved around a navigational buoy. Nick prayed that Gainsford knew how to follow the color coding. Red meant pass the buoy on its port side; green meant pass the buoy on its starboard side. If Jamie Gainsford went around the buoy on the wrong side, he'd run straight onto rock.

Last summer Nick's father had taken him along this coast on his yacht, pointing out the shoals. Nick had zoned out. It was only when his father started talking about smugglers and rum-running that Nick paid attention. "There's a secret passage," Randall had told Nick, his eyes gleaming. "It's called Rogue's Roost."

He pointed at an island. It looked like many of the islands around Prospect: boulder-shaped cliffs of granite, dotted with sturdy spruce trees. "That's Roost Island." A few cormorants dried themselves in the sun.

Didn't look very exciting. "Is that where we're going?"

Randall shook his head. "No. The anchorage is behind it. But I'm going to need your help. If we don't follow the chart exactly, we'll hit rock."

It was one of the most exciting experiences Nick had shared with his father in a long time. To get to the famed anchorage of Rogue's Roost—where it was rumored that smugglers used to hide—the boat had to navigate a very narrow channel between the rocky islands. Yet Rogue's Roost was a popular spot—partly for the thrill of triumphing over the shoals sitting just feet away from the hull, partly for the illicit history the roost was famous for and partly for the sheltered anchorage it provided from the winds that beat the coast.

Jamie Gainsford didn't know it, but he was heading the boat to Rogue's Roost.

And that's when Nick had the idea. He'd knock Gainsford overboard, steer the boat into Rogue's Roost and hopefully find some other yachts that could radio for help. Even if there were no boats there, he and Lucy could wait out the fog and swells in relative safety.

All he had to do was get Gainsford off the boat.

70

Kate saw the truck with the muddied license plate on the end of the wharf and her heart shriveled.

As soon as Randall's cuffs had been removed by the bailiff, Ethan had intercepted them both. He'd apologized to Randall, but Randall had no time for it.

"Where are they?" Randall demanded.

"We've pinged his cell phone. He's gone to Prospect. Presumably to your mother's place."

Randall ran a shaking hand through his hair. "And Nick?" he asked, his voice hoarse. "Did Gainsford take Nick, too?"

"We don't know. The house is empty. We're assuming he's with them."

"What about the Richardson sisters?" Kate interjected. "They were looking after Lucy—"

"Don't worry." Ethan gave her a look she hadn't seen in a long time: tender and compassionate, although his voice was urgent. "They're okay. Just a bit shaken. Come on, I've got a car waiting. I can get you there faster. I'll fill you in on the way." His gaze urged her to get Randall to accept his offer.

Kate looked at Randall. His jaw was tight. She knew that if he'd had his car available he never would accept an offer of help from the man who'd accused him of a terrible crime and let the real killer abduct his children.

But, as he'd experienced in spades since his arrest on Friday, he had no choice.

And so Ethan drove them to Prospect like a man crazed—with remorse, Kate guessed. There'd been no sign of struggle at Penelope Barrett's house, he'd told Randall en route. Penelope, who sat in the backseat with Kate, closed her eyes with relief. Kate could just imagine how hard it must be to know that the home she'd left her grandson in was not the safe haven she believed it to be.

Ethan's cell rang as they were driving. After a brief conversation, Ethan relayed the news that one of the village residents had seen Nick on the road, shortly before a fishing boat was spotted heading out to sea.

Gainsford had obviously abandoned his truck, and Nick had disappeared around the same time. Had he confronted Gainsford on the wharf?

Had he been knocked into the water and drowned?

Or had Gainsford incapacitated Nick and taken him with him?

But why would Gainsford take Nick? He was a threat.

"Just in case, I'm going up to my house," Penelope

said. "I'm going to check the rocks, see if there's any sign of him." She hurried up the road toward her home.

Kate and Ethan strode toward the police team at the end of the wharf. They stood by Gainsford's truck. One door hung open. A detective peered inside, while another detective kneeled over the edge of the wharf and scanned the water, looking for Nick.

"Gainsford stole a boat," the heavy-boned detective with a brown ponytail said, pointing to the ropes dangling from the edge of the wharf.

"Was Lucy with him?" Randall asked, his eyes skimming the passenger seat, under the truck, the side of the wharf.

No signs of blood, thank God, Kate thought.

"We believe so," the female detective said.

"What about Nick? Has anyone found him?"

The female detective exchanged glances with her partner. "No."

"Why are you standing here? Why aren't you going after him?" Randall demanded. "What is wrong with you fucking people?"

"The Coast Guard is tracking the boat, Mr. Barrett."

"So fucking what?" He spun around and jabbed his finger in Ethan's chest. "Those are my kids. We can't wait for the fucking Coast Guard."

"We have no boat."

"What about that one?" Randall shot back, jerking his head toward a small boat moored just beyond the wharf.

"That's just a—"

Randall ran past the homicide team and dived into the water.

Kate and Ethan ran to the edge and watched Randall's head break the surface.

Thank God he hadn't slammed headfirst into a rock.

He swam toward the dory, his head sleek as a seal's.

Don't go without me.

Thought and action were simultaneous as Kate kicked off her high heels, stepped onto the edge of the wharf and jumped.

"Kate—" she heard Ethan cry just as she hit the water.

She pushed up to the surface, gasping for air, the water so black, so cold her body ached with pain. Her dream of Craig Peters, pulling her under the ice, flashed behind her eyes. But it was Randall she saw ahead, Randall who plowed the water with a determined front crawl over to the boat that bobbed placidly at a mooring.

Her suit skirt glued to her legs as she marshaled a front crawl that had been last tested when she was ten years old. The water had been pretty cold in that outdoor pool, she'd complained bitterly to her parents, but not like this. This was the Atlantic Ocean. It could turn your toe blue in less than a second on a hot July day, depending which shore you were on.

Whatever shore this was, it was friggin' cold. All of Kate's muscles rebelled against moving, her body wanting to curl up against the cold invading every orifice.

But she remembered that dream. She remembered the urgency to fight.

Right now, she was fighting to save not herself, but two kids whose nightmare had just been cranked up to a whole new level.

Randall heaved himself over the side of the small boat they were about to steal, then turned around and reached his hand out for her. "Hurry!"

She kicked even harder, feeling the seam in her skirt split. She forced her arms to slice through the water. One arm, then the next, no slacking, no time to waste. Her recently healed arm trembled, flopping awkwardly over her head as she pushed her front crawl to its limits. A minute later, her fingers touched the side of the boat.

Randall's hand grasped her wrist and yanked her upward. Kate threw herself over the gunwale, rolling into the bottom of the boat. It was just a small dory, only eight feet long with an outboard engine, designed to tootle around the islands of Prospect Bay. Not a boat to take out into open ocean.

Randall jerked the cord of the engine. It sputtered. "Come on," he muttered. He jerked it again, viciously. It roared to life.

"Untie the mooring!" he yelled at Kate. She crawled to the bow, still gasping for breath, and unhooked the rope from the small cleat on the gunwale.

Randall pushed the engine tiller hard over. The bow tipped up, throwing Kate backward into the wooden plank that was the middle seat. Her spine hit the edge. Biting her tongue, she inched her butt up to the seat and hunched over, clasping her torn skirt around her for warmth, holding on to the gunwales, as Randall opened the throttle.

The ocean, vast and empty, was carrying away his kids.

There was no time to lose.

71

Lucy lay on the deck, protected by the overhang of the open-ended cabin. She was still deeply asleep…or unconscious. One hand curled by her cheek. The breeze lifted several strands of her hair, and they tangled playfully around her head.

Jamie's eyes skimmed the ocean stretching out to his right. He longed to take the boat out there, where he could avoid the shoals, but he'd be a sitting duck. He'd have to follow the coastline until he could find a private cove and end things the way he wanted to.

It seemed to be his path in life, to take the treacherous route. No matter how hard he had tried, he could never rid himself of his desire to bury himself in a body that was not quite woman but not entirely child, that was still so innocent, so tight. It excited him to be the one to defile that transcendent purity. To bring it down to its most primitive existence.

He glanced at the girl lying at his feet.

He had nothing to lose. He would die with this young girl by his side. Complete at last.

He opened his soul and, for the first time in his life, let it free.

72

Tuesday, 2:07 p.m.

Nick's strength inched back into his muscles, spurred by excitement. He had a plan—an audacious plan. But if it worked, he and Lucy would be safe.

If it didn't…

He only had one chance. And so far, his record of success with only one chance was pathetic. He pushed Charlie out of his mind.

Not this time. Not when Lucy's life was at stake.

You can do it, Nick.

Just throw yourself at him and knock him overboard. He won't know what hit him. Then guide the boat into Rogue's Roost. He hoped he remembered where that big rock was.

He grabbed the ladder rung above his head and pulled himself up. Wind buffeted him, fog unraveling threads of mist around his head. The threads were becoming denser by the minute.

Soon the fog would envelop them all. He needed to get rid of Jamie Gainsford before the fog made it impossible for him to navigate the boat. Because once he threw Gainsford overboard, he didn't want to stick around.

Nick pulled himself up the ladder and crouched on the lip of the stern.

Ten feet away, Gainsford stood at the wheel, his back to Nick, his feet planted on the deck. Lucy lay by his feet.

Nick's heart pounded. She wasn't tied up. So why was she just lying there?

Please don't let her be dead.

Not her.

Not his little sister.

It was the sight of her lying at the feet of this sicko like some human sacrificial offering that pushed Nick's body into overdrive. He jumped onto the deck. The boat hit a swell and he stumbled.

Gainsford spun around.

Shit!

Do a running tackle. Hard. Now!

He hurtled himself against Gainsford. "You *fucker!*"

The boat hit another swell. Gainsford slammed backward into the edge of the cabin.

Nick lowered his head to tackle Gainsford again.

But Gainsford bounced to his feet like a blow-up punching doll. He slammed his fist into Nick's nose.

Nick keeled backward, pain and blood blinding him. He never saw Gainsford throw the next punch into his kidney. His back exploded into his abdomen. His legs lost all strength. He fell so hard and so fast that he couldn't put out his hand to break his fall. Hot knives of pain paralyzed him. It hurt to breathe. He lay on the deck, gasping short animal grunts that he didn't even recognize.

Focus, Nick. Focus.

He'd never felt pain like this before.

Lucy needs you.

He needed the pain to lessen, just enough so he could get back on his feet. And quickly. Before Gainsford threw him overboard.

He'd really screwed this up.

He closed his eyes, willing his muscles to obey him, his cheek pressed against the deck. The water was getting choppy. Every time the boat slammed against a swell, he clenched his teeth from a fresh hit of pain.

The deck is hard. The deck is wet. The deck is cold. He focused on the wood under his bare cheek, anything to distract him from the pain that radiated in fiery waves through his back.

The deck is—

He heard it before Jamie Gainsford.

The whisper of a glacier-carved rock scraping the keel of the boat. His breath stopped in his throat. They were going over a shoal.

By his calculations, it was a shoal off Roost Island.

He'd failed dismally at plan A.

But now he knew he had one more chance.

One more.

Don't fuck it up, Nick.

Don't.

He used his legs to inch forward, not daring to lift his face from the wood for fear Gainsford would see him move. A splinter slid into his cheek, hot pain jammed the muscles of his back.

But Gainsford hadn't noticed him.

He reached out with both hands and grabbed Gainsford's ankle.

Gainsford glanced down, a look of surprise on his face, and shook his leg angrily, viciously. But Nick held on, dragging himself up to his knees, his teeth clenched with pain. He needed leverage for what he was going to do.

Gainsford spat, "Get the fuck off, you little bast—"

With only that one whisper of warning in Nick's ear, the *Glory Anne* crashed at full speed onto the shoal. As the fishing boat impaled itself with an almost human screech of protest, Nick heaved his shoulder into Gainsford's legs, screaming, "You FUCKER!"

The combined forces sent Gainsford flying over the side of the boat.

Nick crashed backward onto the deck.

Water rushed over him, filling the cabin and the bilges below. Nick gasped for breath. The sea rolled directly under him. The boat had lost a chunk of its hull.

With another shudder, the *Glory Anne* listed heavily starboard and Nick slid straight toward the breaking water. His fingers scrabbled over the deck. Something hard and angular jabbed his back. A cleat. He twisted around, grabbing the metal fitting.

Where was Lucy? The cabin was still above water, the bow pointing upward as the ocean sucked down the stern.

He saw her lying by the inside edge of the cabin wall.

"Lucy! Wake up!"

He scrambled toward her.

The water, stinging and cold, washed over her face.

The boat listed.

And Lucy, still unconscious, toppled into the waves.

73

The little dory wasn't the most maneuverable of boats, but Randall put it through its paces, with the result that it thudded over the water, pounding awkwardly into swells.

Kate pointed out the navigational buoys, unsure of what they even meant, but Randall didn't hesitate.

"There're shoals everywhere," he yelled over the engine noise, pointing to a cluster of black, irregular rocks to their left. White foam from crashing waves flew in the air around the rocks. A seagull cruised overhead. "Keep watch."

The fog gusted closer. How it could move so fast, Kate didn't know. One minute there was an open stretch of ocean between them and the fog bank, the next minute just ten feet.

Kate shivered. She was freezing. She was terrified. How would they ever find Jamie Gainsford? They didn't even know which direction he'd gone. Their swim to the motorboat had ruined their cell phones, so Kate couldn't call Ethan to see if there was any word from the Coast Guard. It was just her and Randall, going full throttle between shoals with only hope at its most blind guiding them.

Nick hurtled himself across the deck and jumped into the water.

He sensed the lack of water beneath him just as he smashed into one of the shoal's rocks lurking under the water. Pain exploded in his leg. He gasped, inhaling the ocean.

He was drowning.

He thrashed his arms, thrusting off from the submerged shoal with his uninjured leg. A wave caught him as he broke the surface and he knew he was going to be thrown against the rocks again.

Oh, God. He was going to die. And so was his sister. I'm sorry, Lucy—

He crashed against ten-thousand-year-old rock. His breath slammed out of his chest.

But that was all.

He gasped for air, not quite believing he wasn't dead. Somehow, the wave had buffeted him. Just enough so he hadn't cracked his head. He wrapped his arms around the edge of one of the rocks, digging his fingers into a crevice and wedging his good leg between another rock.

But the other leg…that was useless. It was worse than useless. Every time a wave pulled at it, he almost blacked out form the pain. His initial euphoria of surviving was chased away by the realization that Lucy was somewhere close by. Unconscious.

And probably being thrown against the shoal right now.

"Lucy!" he called.

But he couldn't even hear his voice over the waves.

Blackness swam at the edge of his vision. Not the blackness of the sea.

It was the blackness of unconsciousness.

The sea was getting rougher. The dory slammed against the swells, water slapping Randall's arms, his cheeks, his chest.

"Put on the life jacket, Kate!" Her thin blouse was soaking wet—as was the rest of her—and the silky fabric clung to her shoulders, her breasts, her spine. "It will keep you warmer."

That wasn't the only reason he suggested it. He wouldn't admit it to her, but he wasn't sure the small boat could handle this sea. If it tipped over, she'd have some protection.

He didn't have to say it twice. She pulled the life vest out from under the seat and zipped it up, then resumed her perch in the bow. The next minute she yelped in surprise. "Turn right, turn right," she screamed, frantically pointing off the starboard side at two o'clock.

"Do you see something?" Randall craned his head in the direction she pointed, but he could see nothing.

"I think I see a boat!" Kate's arm trembled as she pointed.

Randall peered through the fog. Was that the hulking outline of Roost Island? He couldn't tell. The veil of gray obscured everything. It was disorienting, the fog. *Just you, the boat, the water below you. Nothing ahead, nothing behind.*

Somewhere off to their left, a buoy warned of danger, its discordant clanging the only indication of existence beyond their little dory.

There was a shoal by Roost Island. And they were very close. He slowed the engine, listening. What side of the buoy were they on? The ocean side? Or the shoal side?

He couldn't tell. Without a visual reference, the clanging could be coming from anywhere.

"Do you see that?" Kate called. She pointed. A shape surged against the waves. "I think it's a boat!"

His heart lifted, sank, pounded crazily. If it was a boat, it must be on the shoal. But if it was a boat, it was probably the one that carried his children. If Nick and Lucy were in the water, they'd be freezing.

If they were alive.

He forced the thought out of his head.

"Look for them in the water!" he called to Kate. But she was already scanning the waves.

"It's hard to see anything with the fog," she yelled. He could hear her frustration, sense her fear. "Go slower. You might run over them."

She was right. He adjusted the throttle, wanting to go even faster and yet knowing he daren't.

But what if one of his kids was drowning thirty feet away and he was going too slowly to reach them in time?

All they could hear was the low, heavy rumble of their engine. The wind, in their ears. The bell of the buoy clanging. For the rest of his life, Randall's stomach would clench when he heard a buoy.

"Nick!" he shouted. "Lucy!"

Kate joined in. "Nick! Lucy! We're over here!"

Their eyes strained toward the shape and it slowly revealed its jagged angles. It was the *Glory Anne*. Not much was left of it. Just its bow, the port side of its cabin and a section of the port deck.

The rest was submerged or had already sunk. This area was known for its high-energy shipwrecks, and the *Glory Anne* had now added itself to that number.

Waves thrashed against the wreck, flinging against the rocks, spume flying into fog.

Where were his ki—

Light against dark. He saw something.

"Nick!" he screamed. "Nick!"

His son huddled on the shoal, clutching a rock, his shaved head in stark contrast to the black rocks.

Randall stared in amazement. How the hell was Nick holding on? His heart raced as he eased the dory toward the shoal. Nick looked as if he could barely grasp the rocks, and the waves were breaking around him—

"Randall, I see them!" Kate yelled.

She pointed behind the dory and off to the right. Two blond heads bobbed in the water.

"It's Lucy!" Kate shouted. "She's with Gainsford!"

And from what they could see, Gainsford had a very tight hold on her. Would he drown her if he saw their boat?

Fear gripped Randall's gut.

If Nick could hold on just a few minutes more… He looked back at his son.

And his heart froze. Nick was slipping down into the water.

Kate leaped to her feet. The boat rocked wildly. "Get Nick!" she cried as she jumped overboard.

She heard Randall cry her name.

Cold hit her. Her flesh numbed almost instantly. The life jacket prevented her from going too deep and she fought to keep her face above the waves.

"Kate!" Randall looked back at her over the stern of the dory. He'd already begun moving toward the shoal. His eyes shouted, *Be careful. Don't let him hurt her.*

She waved once. *Go.* Then she began to swim toward the two heads that bobbed thirty feet away.

After ten seconds, she realized she could not swim forward with the life jacket on. She wrapped the belt around one hand, then unzipped the jacket, her fingers numb, her gaze fixed on the two heads that appeared and disappeared as the fog blew over the water.

Surely Gainsford must have seen them. Or at least heard them. Yet he didn't move.

She gripped the life jacket in both hands, using it as a flutter board, and kicked furiously toward them.

Twenty feet away now.

She could see them both.

The back of Lucy's head leaned against Jamie Gainsford's shoulder.

He was holding her in the classic lifesaving position, her back on his chest, his arm around her torso. He must have seen Kate by now. Why didn't he try to escape with her?

Was he playing possum? He was incredibly devious. Was he waiting for Kate to approach and then planning to kill Lucy in front of her eyes?

She kicked harder, face down in the water to gain speed. When she came up for air she was ten feet away.

She whipped her head back, blinking the water out of her eyes.

Was Gainsford sinking?

Adrenaline chased away the numbness and she plowed through the water. Eight feet, seven feet, six feet.

She could almost touch them with the life jacket. She wanted to throw it to them. Gainsford was struggling to stay afloat.

But it was too risky. Gainsford could snatch the jacket—and leave them to drown.

She hugged it to her chest and swam closer.

He still had his arm wrapped around Lucy.

She was limp.

Oh, God. Was she dead?

Was Gainsford luring Kate to his side with Lucy's body as bait?

Fear hit her hard in the stomach.

And then Jamie Gainsford went under.

With Lucy in his arms.

Kate let go of the life jacket and dived under the water. She forced her eyes open. The water was black. Dense. Vast. She couldn't see anything.

Anyone.

Panic seized her. Where was Lucy?

Dear God, was she already too far gone that Kate couldn't reach her?

Kate propelled herself deeper into the water, her eyes searching through the black for the whiteness of flesh.

Blond hair, swirling upward.

Lucy's ponytail.

Kate reached for it, kicking and straining, water stinging her eyes, her lungs burning.

The ends of Lucy's hair brushed Kate's fingers. And something else.

It was Jamie Gainsford's cheek.

He turned his head toward her as her fingers scrabbled for Lucy's ponytail.

His hand reached out—

A hand clamped on her shoulder. Craig Peters pulled her down into the icy black depths of the lake.

Kate's breath choked in her throat. Her lungs begged for air. She frantically wrapped Lucy's ponytail around her hand, trying to yank Lucy out of Jamie's grasp.

His eyes met hers.

Then he pushed Lucy toward her, wincing from the movement. His other arm hung by his side.

Dear God. He wasn't trying to kill Lucy. He was drowning.

He looked at her and she knew he could tell she was deciding whether to save him.

Or not.

He kicked away from her.

Her lungs couldn't take another minute without oxygen.

She spun around as a flurry of bubbles shot out from Jamie Gainsford's mouth.

He sank away. She kicked upward. Lucy was a dead weight. It had only taken seconds, those moments under the ocean, but were they too many? Had Lucy drowned?

She broke through the surface, gasping for air, dragging Lucy's head above the water. She pressed her ear to the girl's nose.

"Kate!"

Randall steered the boat toward her with one hand, while leaning an oar over the side. "Grab the oar!"

Relief shone from his eyes. "I saw the life jacket…"

She grabbed the handle, and gasped, "Quick. Take Lucy! She's not breathing."

Randall's face paled. He shoved the engine into Neutral and pulled Lucy into the dory. Kate hung on to the side of the boat, her head resting on her arm, her ears straining.

After what seemed like an eternity, she heard Randall exclaim, "Thank God!" followed with Lucy sputtering water out of her lungs.

Then Randall grasped Kate's arms and hoisted her into the dory. She lay on her stomach, draped over the seat, while Randall steered the boat.

Nick? Where was Nick?

She raised her head. Nick huddled in the bow, his leg extended awkwardly. Lucy lay by his thigh. They both shivered.

The wind skimmed ice along her numb flesh. Her hands were blue. So were her legs. Which, she discovered, were bare. Her skirt had been lost somewhere in the water.

There was no room for Kate on the floor of the boat, so she hunkered down on the seat, hunching her shoulders against the wind, and hugged her arms.

A hand pulled on her shoulder.

She started, but Randall merely gave her shoulder a squeeze. "Come on. You're freezing."

They huddled together on the small seat by the engine. Kate's thigh, bare and goose-bumped, was jammed against Randall's. He rubbed her legs briskly, then wrapped an arm around her shoulders, holding her tightly against him. They were both wet and freezing. But sitting together helped block the wind.

"Thank you."

The words were husky. Kate could hear the tears in his voice. She kept her eyes fixed on the water and said, "You don't need to thank me."

"You saved her life."

She swallowed. "I let Jamie Gainsford die, Randall."

His body tensed.

"How? Did he try to hurt you?"

She shook her head. "He was injured. I think…" She hesitated. She didn't want to portray Jamie Gainsford as a savior. She wasn't ready to redeem him. She wasn't sure if she'd ever be. But the truth needed to be told. Judgment of it could come later. "I think he tried to keep Lucy from drowning."

"But why?"

"I don't know."

And she had a feeling she probably never would. Had

Jamie Gainsford regretted his actions? Was he trying to atone for the evil he had done?

But could he ever atone? Was saving Lucy's life atonement enough?

She couldn't think about it right now.

She was too exhausted.

After a few minutes, Kate realized that Randall was steering the boat in a small circle. "I can't see through the fog," he said. "We haven't hit any rocks in this radius, so I'm going to keep doing it until the Coast Guard arrives."

"If we run out of gas before they come..." Kate tried to joke but neither of them could smile. When would the Coast Guard come?

Ten minutes later, they heard the engine.

Twenty minutes later, they were wrapped in survival blankets, cupping mugs of hot tea, slumped in the heated cabin of the Coast Guard vessel.

74

Kate hadn't known Alaska had been a victim of Jamie Gainsford's until she and Randall returned to shore with Lucy and Nick.

They had been numb: with cold, with shock, with everything life had dealt them in the past few days. When they staggered off the boat they were whisked into ambulances and taken to the hospital, where they spent the next few hours recovering from hypothermia. Randall and Kate were released, but Lucy and Nick were admitted. They wanted to observe Lucy's brain function. Nick had multiple fractures in his leg, cracked ribs, a broken nose, and was suffering from hypothermia.

As soon as Randall was told he could leave, he hurried to the children's hospital to be with his kids. Kate rushed to the vet hospital and picked up both Alaska and Charlie. "Fortunately, they weren't given too much chloral hydrate," the vet told her. "It could have killed them."

When Kate arrived home, Finn was waiting with

a hot cup of tea and a plate of spaghetti for her, and a small plate of spaghetti for Alaska. When he saw Charlie, he scraped the pot, scrounging up a second serving. "I think they earned it," Finn said. Kate nodded, tears pricking her eyes. Then she saw the closet. Finn had nailed shut the half-door leading to the staircase. "Enid asked me to," he said. "I didn't think you'd object."

After fussing over her and doing the dishes, Finn offered to come back later and spend the night on the sofa in the living room. Kate was tempted, oh, she was tempted, but in the end she refused. If she said yes, she'd want him in her house every night. It wasn't fair to Finn. He wasn't her babysitter.

He left, promising to come back and check on the dogs the next day. Kate ran a hot bath and lay in it, eyes closed, luxuriating in the warm water on her skin. Her arm ached. Every muscle in her body felt as if it had been stretched to the limit. She let her body go limp and her mind go blank. There'd be time enough to piece all the day's events into one complete picture; right now she just needed to get her head back on straight.

When she dried herself after her bath, she hesitated. Would Randall come by tonight to pick up Charlie? If so, she should get dressed. But she longed to put on her jammies. She glanced at the clock. Randall still had not called. It was late. They were both exhausted. He was probably sleeping at the hospital.

She slipped on a tank top and a pair of silky pajama bottoms, then wrapped herself up in her fleecy bathrobe. Although it was summer, fog chilled the air. Besides, she wasn't sure she'd ever feel warm again. She heated up a mug of hot chocolate, then curled up on the sofa, the phone by her side.

She was being silly. Randall was with his children.

But she longed to have someone to talk to, someone who'd been there, who understood what she'd just been through.

And that was him.

But he didn't call her.

Instead, he showed up on her doorstep. Wordlessly, she let him in. They stared at each other in the dim hallway.

"I came to get Charlie."

Then he opened his arms and she stepped into them.

He held her against his chest. One hand stroked her hair. She pressed her cheek against his shoulder. It was warm, solid, unyielding. Charlie limped toward him, nuzzling his leg.

"Kate, I'm sorry," he murmured. "You could have died out there."

She felt a sob build in her chest. She pulled away from him, managing a wry smile. "I've dealt with worse situations." She pushed a strand of hair off her face. "How are the kids?"

"Lucy is coming around. I think she'll be okay." Her eyes searched his. He knew what she wanted to ask. He added softly, "She says that Jamie Gainsford didn't hurt her."

He looked away, his gaze bleak. Kate knew it would take a long time for Randall to get over the fact he failed to protect his daughter.

"How about Nick?"

"He's doing okay," Randall said. "Gainsford gave him a beating, but Nick took him down." There was no mistaking the pride in Randall's voice. "You know, he looks a mess, but he seems less…tangled." Randall rubbed a hand through his hair. "I don't know how to explain it. But he just seems to be at peace with himself."

Kate knew exactly what he meant. She'd felt the same way after surviving Craig Peters' attack.

She wasn't sure how she felt about what happened with Jamie Gainsford. She'd been stricken with guilt when she realized he'd been injured. That he couldn't save himself.

But maybe he hadn't wanted to save himself.

There had been something in his eyes. She'd been expecting to see Craig Peters reflected back at her.

Instead, she'd seen resignation. Acceptance.

Peace.

Part of her was relieved. But there was a part of her that felt Gainsford didn't deserve the peace he'd claimed just before his death. And she wasn't sure if she should feel ashamed or self-righteous.

She wanted to tell Randall about it. But this wasn't the right time. Exhaustion carved grooves between his brows.

He looked at her, a question in his eyes. A question she didn't know how to answer.

"Kate." He stepped closer. "I want to thank you. You saved my daughter's life."

She pulled her bathrobe more tightly around her.

She knew she should just smile and accept Randall's gratitude, but she didn't want him indebted to her. Their relationship seemed to swing from one extreme to another. She knew firsthand how devastating it could be when the pendulum stopped and there was no real weight to balance it.

"You already thanked me," she said, then regretted it. What a lame response. *What are you supposed to say when someone thanks you for saving their child's life?*

His eyes burned into hers. "You don't know how much it meant to me that you stuck by me."

She shrugged. "I had to."

"Why?"

"Because I've been there."

He rubbed a hand over his neck, hesitating. His eyes searched hers. Finally, he said, "I need to mourn Elise."

"Agreed." Elise Vanderzell deserved no less. But she knew it was more than Elise he was mourning. He was mourning the place he and his ex-wife had gone, the place where they both became less of what they were.

Charlie whined deep in her throat. Randall knelt down and rubbed her head. Then he pulled her leash from his pocket and clipped it on her collar. He glanced up at Kate. "I'll call you tomorrow and let you know how the kids are doing."

"Thank you."

He opened the door. "Kate." He turned to face her. "I didn't just come here to say thank you."

A slow flush rose in her chest.

"You know I care about you." His eyes searched hers.

She reached over and kissed him on the cheek. His skin under the stubble was smooth, warm. Tasted of salt.

"I know. Now go to bed. You look like you're about to fall over."

He captured her hand and pressed it against his chest. His heart beat hard against her palm. She didn't want him to let go.

"We will continue this discussion when the time is right. For both of us." His eyes searched hers.

Kate's heart caught. He was right—this wasn't the time to start a relationship. But she also knew that sometimes the timing never worked out.

Unwilling to defeat the hope that had finally rekindled in Randall's eyes, she nodded.

He stepped into the fog-bound night, Charlie at his heels.

She locked the front door and found Alaska dozing on the sofa in the living room. She plumped up the pillow, unfolded the throw and curled up to his warm, solid body.

75

Ten days later

Ethan studied the photo in the file from Cold Case. Becky Murphy stared at him, her face on the defensive.

He felt sick. Becky Murphy's remains had been found in a shallow grave a hundred yards behind Jamie Gainsford's cabin. Her parents were notified, closure was finally achieved, but was justice done?

No. Jamie Gainsford had manipulated them all, manipulated the justice system with his devious use of "expert witness" notes, manipulated Ethan by pretending to reluctantly dribble out confidential information that Ethan was only too eager to eat up and use against Randall Barrett.

Jamie Gainsford had left a trail of victims, some alive, some dead. And no one had ever suspected him. He'd used his professional persona to such effect that no one questioned him.

And now the bastard was dead.

"Can you come to my office?" Deb asked, stopping by his desk.

Here it comes, he thought. He grabbed his notepad and followed her. She closed the door behind him.

His stomach sank.

"Ethan, what the hell happened?" Deb said. They both knew exactly what she was talking about.

His eyes dropped to the Murphy folder. "I screwed up."

"Don't be too hard on yourself. You weren't the only one to be fooled." She stared at him, her jaw working. "But here's the problem. I'm getting some flak on this one. First Clarkson—" Ethan tried not to wince at her reference to the file that made Randall Barrett his bête noire "—and now this. Both cases have the same common denominator—Randall Barrett."

"I know."

"We'll be lucky if he doesn't sue our asses off."

"Look, Deb, I did the best I could. He was the prime suspect after Nick gave his eyewitness testimony."

She exhaled. "I agree. Based on what you investigated, he was the prime suspect. We all know that. But the public doesn't. The deputy chief called me and gave me the 'public is losing confidence in the police' line."

Becky Murphy stared at him.

"Hindsight is twenty-twenty, Deb. We get this all the time. But you know what it's like in the heat of an investigation. You have to go with your gut."

Deb picked up a pencil and rolled it between her fingers. "Ethan, everything you say is valid. But the fact remains that if the public doesn't have confidence in the police, then we can't be effective."

He caught Deb's eye. "Do you have confidence in me?"

She studied the point of the pencil. It was perfectly sharpened. "Yes."

She let him absorb this, then put the pencil down and opened up a folder. "But we think you need a break from Homicide, Ethan."

Oh, shit. Sweat pricked under his arms.

"We don't want to waste your skills. Cold Case needs someone with your expertise. You can report to Sergeant Salter on Monday."

His fingers tightened around the file folder. They were taking him off the hot seat. He couldn't blame them.

And part of him, a small part of him, was grateful.

His brain was so screwed up right now he doubted his abilities, as well.

Deb stood. "I hope you don't view this as a demotion. It's not."

He gave a brusque nod. "It could be worse, I suppose. You could have put me back on patrol. And since it's Cold Case, all the bodies are decomposed, right? I won't have to go to any more autopsies. At least fresh ones."

"Always looking on the bright side, aren't you, Ethan," Deb said, a smile tugging her mouth. "Now get out of here."

"What do you do in the winter?" Kate asked Eddie, watching him light a post–celebratory dinner cigarette as they sat at an outdoor patio on Halifax's waterfront. Only a few restaurants allowed smoking nowadays, and strictly on the patio. When the weather got cold, the patios were closed.

He grinned. "I just put on my long underwear and huddle outside with the hoi polloi. You'd be amazed how many clients I get."

"So the bar society took pity on you and reinstated your license?"

Eddie took a deep drag, then coughed. "Yes…" He sputtered, and sipped his water.

"How did you get the money, if I may be so indelicate?"

He grinned. "Our client paid me. As soon as the charge was dropped, McGrath Barrett couriered a check to Randall. I'm officially back in the black with the law society. And they decided they'd been overly onerous. So they've given me my license. And—" he waved his cigarette, almost hitting the edge of the umbrella tilted over their table "—thanks to all the publicity on this case, I'm getting quite a few new clients." He tapped his ash into his coffee saucer. "You wouldn't be interested in joining me, would you, Kate? We could go fifty-fifty. Bent Lange." He took another drag on his cigarette and squinted at her through the smoke.

Kate smiled, regret in her eyes. "Thank you, Eddie. But I have to refuse."

He shrugged. "Just thought I'd ask. You're good at this. Your first criminal matter and not only do you get the charges dropped against your client, but you also figured out who the real killer was. Bravo." He saluted her with his cigarette. Ash, still glowing, flicked onto the table.

She grinned. "Not bad for a civil litigation lawyer."

His expression turned serious. "Have you thought about switching to criminal defense work? You know, you could probably convince the partnership. They'd have a hard time saying no to their golden girl."

Kate shrugged. She was aware her reputation was larger than life, fueled by her slaying of a serial killer, her whistle-blowing of a tissue-brokering scandal and her successful defense of her managing partner's murder charge. She'd asked Randall not to mention her role in saving Lucy from drowning. It was too personal, struck too deep a chord. "You know I almost quit McGrath Barrett."

He raised his brows. "This should be good."

"I was involved in a case where the expert hired by my corporate client was clearly biased and bullied the plaintiff. I didn't like representing clients who threw around their money and wore down the plaintiffs. It seemed a perversion of the law. The scales of justice were too heavily weighted in favor of the corporate interest."

"It's the way business is done, Kate."

"I know. So then I got to thinking about it." Her gut told her that leaving was the wrong thing to do. She'd only been hired permanently in June. It made her feel like a quitter, as if the minute something happened that she didn't like, she couldn't stick it out. So she thought long and hard about how she could make a career work at McGrath Barrett without selling her soul. "And I realized that instead of going to a small firm with little resources, I should leverage the resources of a big firm like McGrath Barrett for clients who have nothing."

Eddie eyed her speculatively through the haze of smoke streaming from his mouth.

"I spoke to the partners about letting me do more pro bono work." Even if it meant her total billables were less than other lawyers', she knew they could not refuse to put their star associate on charity cases. It made the firm positively glow with community goodwill. "They agreed. Of course, I also have to work on regular files, but I told them no more insurance clients." She gave Eddie an arch look. "I thought maybe you and I could work on some pro bono cases together."

He nodded slowly. "I'd be delighted to."

The breeze shifted and tobacco smoke drifted in her face. She coughed. "But I didn't survive a serial killer to die of secondhand smoke."

He laughed so hard he choked. He ground out the butt in his napkin. Kate was relieved to see this one wasn't cloth. "That's the most compelling argument for quitting I've heard so far. But despite your success in the courtroom, it won't change anything." He sipped his now cold coffee. "Kate, do you know why I smoke?"

His eyes were sad. Kate regretted making a joke about it.

"Because it keeps me busy. Ever since my wife and daughter left, I've had nothing but time to reflect on the mess I've made of my life. For an alcoholic, that's an invitation to disaster." He played with the handle of his coffee cup. "I hit rock bottom two years ago. I didn't want to end my life there. So I dried myself out even as my wife decided she'd taken enough crap from me.

I attend AA meetings five days a week. I also have a sponsor who checks in with me. And right now, even though I shouldn't be indulging in addictive habits, I smoke until I can get to the next stage of my recovery." He gave her a small smile.

The waitress arrived with the check. Eddie insisted on treating Kate. "To our first case together." He signed the credit card slip with a flourish. His hand tremored just a little.

Kate didn't look away fast enough. Eddie gave a wry smile. "Just a little reminder to keep me on the straight and narrow. I hope my recovery will come sooner rather than later. But until then, bear with me."

Kate smiled at him. The guy had grown on her. A lot. "With pleasure," she said.

They walked along the waterfront. Neither was quite ready to end the evening. The temperature was perfect, a slight breeze lifting Kate's hair. She looked at the harbor.

It was calm. Smooth. Benign.

She thought of diving beneath the cold water of Prospect Bay. Of searching for Lucy in the vast blackness.

Of knowing that if she failed to find her, she'd be haunted for the rest of her life.

But she had found her.

She had saved her.

That was something.

Actually, it was everything.

* * * * *

Acknowledgments

I wholeheartedly thank those who took time from their busy schedules to share their expertise with me.

Detective Sergeant Mark MacDonald, of the Halifax Regional Police Department, who was instrumental in helping me understand the police procedure for the murder investigation in this book. I enjoy our "what if" sessions!

Detective Constable Curtis Pyke, Forensic Identification Unit, of the Halifax Regional Police Department, who explained the forensic identification process for the murder investigation, and demonstrated—to my great delight—some methods in the bowels of the police station.

Dr. Martin Bullock, MD, FRCP, who has helped me yet again with the forensic pathology aspects of the case.

Paul Carver, LLB, and Shauna MacDonald, LLB, who guided me through the legal procedure and took my last-minute phone calls with grace and patience!

Any mistakes in this book are mine alone and I apologize to my experts in advance.

I would also like to thank my editor, the fabulous Valerie Gray. She is a joy to work with and it is my privilege to be one of her authors.

In addition, there are so many people at MIRA Books to whom I am indebted for their work on this series, including: editor Miranda Indrigo; the incredibly talented designer of my covers, Sean Kapitain; Alana Burke and MIRA's marketing team, who have put tremendous effort into getting my series out there; the sales team for sharing their enthusiasm to great effect; the digital marketing team for creating a terrific trailer; my publicist, Michelle Renaud, who has graciously answered my many novice questions.

I also want to thank my agent, Emily Sylvan Kim, of Prospect Agency. She is always there to help me.

I've been blessed with friends old and new. The support I've received from them has touched me deeply. Thank you.

And as always, my deepest thanks go to my family. You are my joy.

MEGAN HART

Gilly Soloman has been reduced to a mothering machine,
taking care of everyone except herself. But the machine
has broken down. Burnt out and exhausted, Gilly doesn't
immediately consider the consequences when she's carjacked—
her first thought is that she'll finally get some rest.
Someone can save *her* for a change.

But salvation isn't so forthcoming. Stranded in a remote cabin
with this stranger, time passes and forms a fragile bond between
them. Yet even as their connection begins to foster trust,
Gilly knows she must never forget he's still a man teetering
on the edge. One who just might take her with him.

precious

and

fragile

things

Available wherever books are sold.

Antoinette van Heugten

Max Parkman—autistic and whip-smart,
emotionally fragile and aggressive—is
perfect in his mother's eyes, even though
attorney Danielle Parkman knows her
teenage son's behavior has been getting
worse. But she can't accept the psychiatric
facility's diagnosis that her son is deeply
disturbed. Dangerous.

Until she finds Max, unconscious
and bloodied, beside a patient who
has been brutally stabbed to death.

Trapped in a world of doubt and
fear, Danielle clings to the belief
that her son is innocent. She'll
do whatever it takes to find the
killer and to save her son from
being destroyed by a system
eager to convict him.

saving *max*

*Available wherever
books are sold.*

MIRA®

NEW YORK TIMES
AND *USA TODAY*
BESTSELLING AUTHOR

CARLA NEGGERS

The small town of Black Falls, Vermont, finally feels safe again—until search-and-rescue expert Rose Cameron discovers a body, burned almost beyond recognition. Rose is certain that she knows the victim's identity...and that his death was no accident.

Nick Martini also suspects an arsonist's deliberate hand. Now the rugged smoke jumper is determined to follow the killer's trail...even if it leads straight to Rose. Nick and Rose haven't seen each other since their single night of passion, but they can't let unhealed wounds get in the way of their common goal—stopping a merciless killer from taking aim straight at the heart of Black Falls.

COLD DAWN

Available wherever books are sold.

MIRA®

REQUEST YOUR FREE BOOKS!

2 FREE NOVELS
FROM THE SUSPENSE COLLECTION
PLUS 2 FREE GIFTS!